THE DEVIL'S CANDLE

Memoirs of a Lady with a Little Dog

For Niall, Thom and Nick with thanks for their technical assistance and
for Jill and Flora, with love.

'A woman can only become a man's friend in three stages; first she is an agreeable acquaintance, then a mistress and only after that a friend.'

Doctor Astrov, 'Uncle Vanya' by Anton Pavlovich Chekhov (1860-1904)

'What breadth, what beauty and power of human nature and development there must be in a woman to surmount all the palisades, all the fences within which she is held captive.'

'My Past and Thoughts' by Alexander Herzen (1812-1870)

PROLOGUE

Moscow. March 15th 1954.

Snow falling steadily through the night muffled the footsteps of passersby on the street below my apartment, though it did little to silence the agonized squeal of metal as the early morning trams jolted their way along the frost damaged rails on Komsomolskaya ulitsa.

Awakened as usual by this untimely morning call I was enjoying the luxury of a few extra minutes after my late duty at Moscow City Library the previous evening when I heard the sound of footsteps on the stairwell leading to my apartment, should one be generous enough to give a single room of nine square metres with shared kitchen facilities for sixteen families in a kommunalka such a grandiose title.

The cautious citizens of our capital city only one year after Stalin's death are still only too aware of what this intrusion on their privacy might entail. As we say, my soul went down to my heels as I thought back to my recent minor indiscretions at the library, namely contradicting the Archives Head of Department and missing yet another Agitprop meeting without a satisfactory excuse. Surely neither of these transgressions would warrant an official visitation, I tried to reassure myself, as there came an insistent knocking on my door. Pulling on my dressing gown I fumbled my way towards the door, opening it with the security chain firmly in place.

Standing there was no greater threat to my existence than our postman, who handed me a buff coloured envelope. This in itself was unusual as mail to our kommunalka is always delivered to a shared mailbox and later distributed to residents by our all-knowing concierge. Seeing the evident alarm on my face he apologized, explaining that a signature was needed for the receipt of the letter he was delivering, addressed to me personally, Anna Pavlovna Platonova. I signed and settled back in bed to read what I knew in my heart was likely to be unpleasant news. As I opened the envelope I recognized the official insignia of the Soviet Writers' Union, of which my grandmother had been a member.

The letter was from Comrade Chairman of the Moscow Branch of the Soviet Writers' Union. In it he expressed his Committee's deep condolences on the recent death of my grandmother Anna Ivanovna Platonova and paid tribute to her contribution to the Soviet literary scene over so many years.

Unfortunately her apartment now had to be returned to the authorities. I must understand, he wrote, how critical the housing situation in Moscow was and the Committee would be grateful, if I as the only remaining member of her family, could arrange for her effects and furniture to be removed within the week.

However the Committee had unanimously agreed that the modest dacha in the Peredelkino Writers' Colony, which my grandmother had been given in recognition of her contribution over many years in the field of Soviet literary criticism, should be bequeathed in perpetuity to the surviving members of her family. Would I therefore, as the sole surviving relative, please write and confirm whether I wished to accept this generous offer?

There was a possibility, the Chairman continued, that some unpublished work of hers might still be in the apartment, a fact that my grandmother had apparently alluded to at times in the last weeks of her life when she was still conscious. Would I therefore make a thorough search of the apartment as it was being cleared of her belongings and inform the Committee if I found anything which might be of literary interest?

The work roster for the next few days saw me back in the Archive Department of the library, once again on evening duties. I had therefore ample time during the day to start clearing my grandmother's belongings. There was precious little furniture to dispose of. Single people in Moscow are fortunate to have even one room to call their own and I soon managed to sell cheaply or give away to neighbours her bed, cupboard, tables and chairs and assorted paraphernalia.

I took more seriously a search for any literary work that she might have hidden away. I had a vague memory of her telling me on one occasion when I was much younger of her infatuation for a man she had once met on holiday before she married grandfather. Grandmother had a well earned reputation for mischief and instead of acceding to my request that she tell me more about this incident in her life, she had hinted with a gleam in her eye that all would be revealed when I was older. At that tender age I had no idea what she was alluding to by this cryptic remark.

The removal men cleared the apartment of furniture and when all that was left were a few cardboard boxes into which I had stuffed any papers that looked of a personal nature, I returned with them to my apartment to examine them in more detail.

It was then that my grandmother's mischievous remark, made all those years before, became clear. Hidden amongst a pile of old letters I discovered a diary covering the years 1898/1899/1900, its leather cover stained but with most of the manuscript entries still just legible. Tied to it were a number of pages, again in manuscript and bound together with string. The title on the first page was almost unreadable, the words ' memoir' and 'little dog' being just decipherable.

Completing the package was another sheaf of loose leafed sheets, nineteen in total and obviously typed on an old fashioned typewriter. The title on the first page read: *The Lady with a Little Dog. A short story by Anton Chekhov. December 1899.*

Alone in my little room where in that wretched winter of 1954 the heating in our communal block was as always pitifully insufficient, I huddled by the radiator, fully dressed and draped in a blanket, trying to put these pages into some sort of order.

An added complication was my discovery that two of the pages were in a different hand. Starting to read, I quickly realized that they must have been written by the gentleman with whom grandmother had become acquainted on her first visit to Yalta. What I found so fascinating was the intimate description of my grandmother by a male admirer, a description that in the genre of memoirs would otherwise not have been made available to the reader. I decided to place these pages, even if not chronologically accurate, at the beginning of her story.

Then over the space of one long evening and one even longer night I read slowly through what my grandmother had penned in all the innocence of her youth. How poignant an experience it was for me, given that the vicissitudes of Russian history, the Great Fatherland War, the Revolution and the purges of the thirties had later in her life robbed her of all family save me. Husband, son and daughter in law all had perished, leaving me as the sole surviving member of the family. Oh grandmother, if only we could have travelled back together to a more gracious age and met again in Yalta. How we would have enjoyed ourselves on that famous Promenade!

Yalta, Crimea. September 28th 1898.

Here you are, my darling. This is what you begged of me that evening when first I came to you. Do you remember my unfastening your hair from its golden pin and kissing you so tenderly, and how we lay together at our summer's end, my beautiful Anushka? And how later that night you loosened your arms from my embrace to take up pen to write in your diary the wildness of the happenings of the day? I confided to you then how jealous I had been of the minutes your writing had stolen from me. And through your tears, you begged me to reassure you of the love I had professed when you gave yourself to me. You must excuse this scribbled reply to your request for being so poorly written, but please trust only in its sincerity….

***

A sunny late summer's morning between the hours of ten and eleven. I am standing on the corner of the Promenade, where it meets Ekaterinskaya Street, and gaze with a languid eye at the fishing boats sailing into the harbour. Their progress is slow, there being little but a light breeze to bring them to the quayside, where the Yalta housewives wait impatiently to haggle over the catch.

At last the full heat of summer has passed and as I start to stroll along the esplanade past the Opera House I can feel on my face the fresh breeze from the sea and to my ears there comes the lighthearted chatter of passersby. And in the distance the music of the municipal band playing a medley of Russian and Ukrainian melodies beckons me to my accustomed deck chair in the shade of the ornate cast iron band stand.

To exchange the claustrophobic atmosphere of the darkened rooms in the hotel where I am lodging, with its shutters closed against the daytime insistence of the sun, for this glittering spectacle of society taking the air is something to be enjoyed. A pleasure I might even deem to constitute the highlight of my day.

As I proceed along the esplanade I exchange polite greetings with the other promenaders. The women in fashionable apparel and in the colourful panoply of their parasols, their men folk in military uniforms or well cut suits, little boys in their sailor suits, all this demonstrates that Yalta is a fashionable place to be seen in and that Yalta is well aware of itself and its position.

Two distinguishing features of the Yalta smart set have already caught my attention; the older women dress like young girls and behave accordingly and there is a ridiculous number of generals. The music stops and I realize that I am too late for the concert. Never mind, I will find instead a seat at Vernet's bar and sit in the shade of the palm trees lining the sea front, grateful to rest my legs and while away the idle minutes before luncheon, which is yet an hour away.

I indolently watch the world pass by, becoming quickly aware that I am in good company with the other gentlemen here who are occupied in similar fashion. I have evidently stumbled across a favourite place for those of a certain disposition to observe the ladies as they parade past. Though the generals' wives, portly and plain and behaving, as I have already observed, like so many younger ladies, do not arrest our attention for very long. Real young ladies are unfortunately few and far between on our Promenade.

And then I see approaching in the distance a young lady who stands out from the crowd for two very different reasons. She is on her own, though I cannot truthfully describe her as being alone as she is accompanied by a small dog. As she approaches closer I notice her dark brown hair in a chignon, a strand of which has mischievously escaped to slip downwards to her shoulder. In one quick glance I have time to admire her superbly cut muslin blouse edged with lace and set off by the dark red stone at her throat, and her long grey skirt, whose tight belt accentuates the slimness of her waist. From her slightly diffident manner I conjecture that she has only recently arrived in Yalta. She is strikingly, admirably beautiful.

I turn my attention to her dog. I like dogs and know their penchant for sniffing around tree trunks and lampposts. So I am not surprised to see that this little fellow has added table legs to his repertoire as he pauses momentarily in front of me. "Come away, Tuzik," I hear a gentle command and I raise my hat to its owner to show that there is nothing to excuse in her dog's behaviour. As she looks at me demurely and I sense with a certain embarrassment, I can see that her eyes are beautiful in their unusualness, a light grey colour, which the grey of her skirt by chance or by design matches exactly.

Having finished my cognac and my cigarette I leave some coins on the table, and having nothing better to do, follow this disconcertingly beautiful young lady at a distance. Her little dog knows where it is going. It pulls on its leash till they arrive at the entrance to the Botanical Gardens. I observe how she lets it free, settles down on a park bench and starts to write in what from a distance appears to be a diary. From time to time she looks up to check on her dog, who is either busy sniffing out the newly discovered delights of Ukraine or else scuffing up the leaves that have fallen from the avenue of acacia trees which line the park and warn us, as Shakespeare puts it, that summer's lease has not long to run.

Or is she simply pausing to seek inspiration for what she is writing? I would not wish for her to recognize me as the man who had attracted her attention outside Vernet's Bar just a few minutes previously. So I steal away unobserved to take a luncheon of sea bass with a sauce vierge and a glass or two of a dry Crimean white wine at Morskoy sea fish restaurant overlooking the harbour.

I spend the afternoon idly wondering whether perhaps our paths may cross again. And indeed they do, as fate has conspired for us to meet that same evening. And as our lives have become so entwined since then, I feel I can do no more than to let this young lady, my Anya, take over from me to continue our story. And of course I have no need to introduce myself to the reader. I will leave my Anushka to do that herself, since she is so much more gifted in putting pen to paper than I....

{1}

Yalta. 22nd September 1898.

My name is Anna Ivanovna von Melk. Both my husband's family and mine, however, are pure Russian, my husband's side of the family moving, for reasons unknown, to St. Petersburg in the eighteenth century from an austere Austrian monastery on the banks of the river Danube, and mine traceable back to the time of Peter the Great and the earliest days of his city on the Gulf of Finland.

You will also discover, that I am known by two other names, one of which is an alias. The necessity for my taking an alias, which you will admit must be unusual for a young lady of my status, as well as my assuming a second change of name in the short period of two years, will become apparent should you have the patience and continued interest to read further through these memoirs.

And before I forget, I have a little dog, a white Pomeranian by the name of Tuzik, who plays an important part in my story. You may well be relieved to learn that he does not change his name throughout these memoirs!

I will not dwell at any length on my childhood. I do not intend to mix fact, fiction and emotion in my writing in order to render the moods and thoughts of its narrator. If you wish for such a literary masterpiece then you must turn to the writings of our Lev Tolstoy and his description of childhood and youth. As for my modest scribbles I believe that the facts speak for themselves and there is quite enough emotion in my writing to dispense with any need for fiction.

As to my childhood, suffice it to say that I was born in St. Petersburg in the year 1874 and grew up in that city as a single child of solid middle class parents. My mother took little notice of me, being absorbed in her work for the church and her various charitable institutions which took up much of her time.

To compensate for a lack of love from my mother I developed a close relationship with my father, a teacher of Russian language and literature at our Gymnasium. I can recall my favourite activity, snuggling up on my father's lap in his book lined study, carefully taking off his spectacles and pulling the ends of his straggling moustache down towards his chin. I would giggle and call him 'Papa Walrus.'

My mother called me a mischievous child, which I can well believe, as that trait even in my adult life still shows itself when the mood takes me and is one that I can rarely resist.

I can all too clearly remember the day at the age of seven when my father called me into his study. He seated me on his lap and told me the terrible news of the assassination of our Tsar Alexander. At that age I did not fully comprehend the seriousness of this event, but I do remember reaching for his pocket handkerchief to wipe away his tears.

Why ever would anyone, he wondered aloud, want to murder a Tsar who had liberated the serfs and was about to institute a form of democratic government in the form of a Duma? These words were beyond the comprehension of a seven year old, but as I grew older I realized that my father had been a true Westerniser and believed like Alexander Herzen that democratic progress in Russia could only be made by following the examples of the governments of Western Europe, where such democratic institutions already existed.

At meal times we would talk about books and my father guided me in my reading with suggested titles. But it was inevitable that in that day and age politics would always intrude into our conversation. I was told by my father that the regime instituted by the new Tsar Alexander the Third was becoming ever more reactionary. Civil liberties, such as those that had existed under the previous Tsar, had become a thing of the past. For example, universities losing their autonomy had closed their doors to women, a sad development which particularly affected my father who had instilled in me a love of Russian literature and had hoped that upon graduating from my Lycée I would pass into the Arts Faculty of St. Petersburg University. His health began to deteriorate, he took early retirement and died, I believe of a broken heart, witnessing the sad events that were happening to his beloved Russia.

Since there was now no chance of my entering university and there were few career opportunities in autocratic Russia for a girl with little else to offer than a graduating distinction in Russian Literature from her Lycée, my mother turned her attention to finding me a suitable husband.

I was just eighteen years of age, by all accounts a pretty girl with chestnut brown hair, a good figure and unusual grey eyes. Being an only child I was often lonely. I took solace in reading. I discovered the novels of Jane Austen which I devoured in translation as well as those of Ivan Turgenev. I sympathized with their heroes and heroines in their requited and so often unrequited loves, which both these authors expressed in such a genteel manner. I was Pushkin's Tatyana.

"Now with what eager concentration
She reads delicious novels through.
With what enlivened fascination
She drinks deception's honeydew.
In fantasy she visualizes
The characters that she most prizes."

I read novels, therefore I was in love! I was quite content to prolong this virginal state of mine, but had not reckoned on my mother. I had reached the age of eighteen without falling in love with a real man of flesh and blood and this state of affairs was not allowed to continue for long. My mother had endured enough of my fantasies and was determined to succeed in marrying me off.

I had already been made aware of the fact that men found me attractive and I would often be teased by them on the subject of possible suitors. Such a suitable young man was eventually produced by my mother and somehow, almost by accident it seemed, I found myself engaged to a certain Viktor Aleksandrovich von Melk, a junior civil servant in local government with a promising career ahead of him.

We were married within the year after a courtship and consummation of marriage that in hindsight can only in the most generous of terms be described as tepid. From the start it proved to be a loveless marriage, but only now, two years later, do I find to my chagrin that I am beginning to dislike my Viktor more and more, both as a man and as a husband.

In this case absence here in the south will certainly not make my heart grow fonder. And out of sight I will perhaps find myself able to forget my husband for a few weeks.

***

But to return to the present. The year is 1898, the season late summer and I find myself in Yalta on the Crimean peninsula of Ukraine. I wake up to another hot, sunny day. I can see that the sun is shining without my needing to get out of bed to open the window. A crack in the shutter etches a strip of sunlight across the ceiling towards a dark spot in the plaster. By the time it reaches as far as this I know that the hour is approaching eight of the clock.

The noise of the cicadas in the pine trees in the garden of the villa, where I am staying, reminds me of how far I have come from home in northern Russia, where autumn will already be imprinting its delicate mark on the silver birches lining our street. I rise, splash my face with cold water from the wash basin and open the shutters. The promised sunlight streams into the room together with a fresh breeze laden with the smell of oleanders. I lift my eyes to the mountains and the unbelievably blue sky and feel my spirits lift. The anxieties that I have experienced since my arrival here begin to fade.

Varvara Ivanovna, my landlady in the 'White Eagle' pension, where I am staying in Yalta, has suggested that I take breakfast on her terrace in order to take advantage of the early freshness of the day. Yesterday evening I observed a couple of youngish men on the terrace enjoying the sunset over the sea, their experience noisily enhanced, it would appear, by a bottle of Ukrainian champagne. I have had enough of Ukrainian young men for the time being, so it is a pleasure to sit here by myself without them and to plan my day.

I am four days into my stay in Yalta or 'rest cure' as my doctor called it back home, and so far each day has followed the same pattern, which since nothing of note has happened to me I can only describe as monotonous. After breakfast I take Tuzik for a walk down Pushkinskaya Street to the sea front or to the Nikitsky gardens.

I feel that the women I pass look at me critically, a young woman to whom their husbands doff their hats whilst looking at me rather too attentively. No doubt they recognize me as a socially respectable married woman in Yalta probably for the first time, alone and bored. I could well do without their attention. A coffee on the Promenade listening to the brass band playing a selection of Ukrainian and Russian airs passes the time.

Then about twelve at noon I take Tuzik for a short walk to his favourite spot, the Botanical Gardens, before returning to the Pension. I have lunch, a light salad and some fruit, a siesta in my bedroom in the heat of the afternoon, an evening walk with Tuzik, and finally dinner at a restaurant on the Promenade that has become my favourite.

The waiters there are already familiar with me and accommodate my needs. I have my own corner table, eminently suitable for a single lady, where I will not encounter the gaze of men of a dubious nature, of whom there appear to be an abundance in Yalta. And of course they are kind enough to allow me to bring Tuzik with me into the restaurant to sit quietly in our corner.

Varvara Ivanova, whom I have already marked down as something of a gossip, related to me this morning, as she cleared away the breakfast things, a little anecdote which made me laugh. She told me that yesterday as she passed Vernet's bar on the Promenade on the way to the fish market she had overheard a group of middle aged men discussing the new arrivals in Yalta. One thing I have already found out is that Vernet's enjoys something of a reputation here as a rendezvous for gentlemen on their own, who enjoy imbibing a drink at any hour of the day, or to be more precise at all hours of the day.

They spend their time assessing and commenting on the passersby, particularly if they happen to be young single ladies who are easier on the eye than those generals' stout wives at whom they usually have to gaze.

As far as I am aware, there are not many of us of the younger set around, so I believe that I have already been assessed and commented on. And so it proved to be. Varvara Ivanovna overheard them referring to me, not knowing my name but seeing me with Tuzik, as 'the lady with a little dog.' Fortunately she did not stop to impart any further information on the identity of one of her guests.

To avoid the possibility of meeting the above mentioned gentlemen at Vernet's, I today proceeded by a different route to the Promenade along Gogol Boulevard. On the way I chanced upon a small bookshop "Bukva", where an elderly shopkeeper was arranging a new window display. I stopped to look at the selection of books he was hoping to promote and my gaze was taken by a diary for the current year, reduced to half its original price.

I reflected that keeping a diary would be a good way to pass the time. In it I could describe my current degree of boredom day by day and possibly record any slightly more exciting moments of my enforced stay in Yalta. Though this latter possibility seemed highly unlikely, given what I had observed so far of this fashionable Crimean resort.

The shopkeeper proved to be a charming, cultured man who, guessing that I had just arrived in Yalta, suggested that I might enjoy visiting the new house that Anton Pavlovich Chekhov was having built at Autka. Quite close to my pension, he informed me. I love literature in any genre and in fact have read a couple of Chekhov's short stories as my husband subscribes to the literary magazine *Russian Thought,* which from time to time publishes his work.

Picking up my newly purchased diary I was on the point of leaving the shop when I caught sight of a book, the title of which seemed familiar. I remembered having heard it mentioned on a previous occasion, a government office party to which my husband and I had been invited. I loathe these parties but my husband insists that I attend, so I do so against my will.

On this occasion, as always happens at these functions, all the men were gathered together at one end of the Assembly Hall, making a great deal of noise, and all the women were at the opposite end, discussing the most boring of subjects. As usual my husband had left me in the company of one or other of his rather dull office acquaintances while he, sycophant that he is, went off to catch the Governor's eye.

Having escaped with the weakest of excuses the boredom thus threatened, I made my way surreptitiously to the bar to have my glass of champagne replenished. I must be honest and admit to this being the only way I can survive these functions, which my husband inflicts on me far too frequently.

While waiting for a waiter to refill my glass I overheard a group of young men talking about a French author by the name of Gustave Flaubert and a book that had recently been translated into Russian entitled *Madame Bovary*.

On our return home after the party and before retiring to our separate bedrooms, I asked my husband why he thought their conversation had so abruptly come to an end when I was within earshot of these gentlemen. He made a vague answer to the effect that, as far as he knew, the book's subject matter was not suitable for respectable ladies. He was not to be drawn any further on the subject and after a perfunctory kiss on my cheek he retired to his room. I can remember being furious. Why in this day and age should women not be allowed to read the same books as men? I suspected that my husband had retreated to the privacy of his bedroom to read up on his official papers, leaving me in my room seething with indignation.

Now at last here in Yalta I had the opportunity to buy *Madame Bovary* and to find out at first hand the nature of a book that my husband had deemed unsuitable for the attention of a respectable lady. If nothing better I hope that it will serve as a more exciting way to pass the long siesta hours in my bedroom than the reading of yet another outdated fashion magazine from Paris, which along with a bible, I have discovered by my bedside.

{2}

Now that I have my diary here in my bedroom, I am able to fill in the events of the days leading up to my arrival in Yalta. It seems a strange way to write a diary, going backwards in time, but I have no experience in these matters and in any event this writing is most likely to be for my perusal alone. I can therefore be perfectly truthful in what I write and I have no compunction in recalling the subterfuges, which led a young girl of twenty two years of age to find herself alone in a strange town.

I must admit straight away that I have not been honest in my relationship with my husband. Since our marriage and my move from St. Petersburg, where I had lived all my life, to Shchyolkovo a boring provincial town close to Moscow, which our Nikolay Gogol might have described as 'mortally wearisome', had he ever had the misfortune to pay us a visit, I have become painfully aware that not only do I not love my husband, but that the day to day life of a respectably married wife with a husband in Government service is slowly driving me mad.

I feel that there must be more to life beyond the narrow confines of my existence here; a chance to meet more cultured people, both men and women, who might consider me for my own worth and with whom I would be able to carry on a worthwhile conversation without being perpetually overshadowed by my husband. And perhaps, who knows, they might be of a younger age and outlook than my husband's colleagues who all seem to be middle aged or older.

The few female friends that I have made in my new home town are sympathetic. They understand and excuse my moods. After all most women who had just been told by medical experts that there was little chance that they would be able to conceive would in all likelihood exhibit similar traits. Unfortunately I feel that my husband is less understanding. It is becoming ever clearer to me that he never really wanted a child and possibly not even a wife. His sole interest is his career.

There is a saying that where there is marriage without love there will be love without marriage. From my very limited experience I know that men find me attractive and have on a number of occasions made me clearly aware of their attraction. The fleeting thought that I might somewhere encounter someone with whom I could pursue a closer relationship, however vague and ill defined at this moment that might be, excites me in a way that I have not felt before.

I do not regard myself as a promiscuous woman. After all there is precious little chance of promiscuity in Shchyolkovo, but I am young and feel fully the barrenness of my present life and my more and more consuming desire to get away once and for all from this boring town.

Thus under the pretext of illness I visited a sympathetic doctor, recommended by my mother- in-law as an expert in 'women's problems', who prescribed as a cure a complete rest and recuperation in the benign climate of Crimea.

My husband quickly made enquiries of friends in his office about finding a suitable place where I could stay. He was offered advice from a close work acquaintance, who from first hand experience could recommend not only Yalta but a very suitable pension 'The White Eagle.'

This he described as being a very stylish, secluded villa with some six bedrooms, set back a short distance from the Promenade on a small hill. The building had been a large private home and guests were still made to feel that they were staying en famille.

***

And so in a matter of days it was all arranged. What I remember of the journey is sketchy. A short train journey to Moscow, arriving at the Yaroslavsky station, a night spent at the house of a distant aunt and the next day a carriage to the Kursky Station to catch the afternoon express to Simferopol. I do remember that the Kursky Station, which had only been opened a year, was magnificent, more like a cathedral than a railway station.

However I could have done without a vexing scene occasioned by the behaviour of a petty station official. The latter ordered me to put Tuzik in the guard's van rather than keep him in my compartment as I had expected to be able to do. I wanted my husband, who had come to see me off, to call for the Station Master and countermand the orders of this unpleasant railway employee. But as in my less than charitable moments I have thought of my dear husband as a petty government official himself, I was not surprised to see no positive action on his part, other than his accompanying me and Tuzik to the relevant part of the train.

By this time the second departure bell had rung and passengers were hurriedly scrambling aboard. I had hardly time to kiss Viktor goodbye before the third bell rang and the train shuddered into life, belching acrid black smoke as it set off on its long journey to the south.

My husband had booked a ladies only compartment for me, though as we set off I noticed that in addition to two other ladies already installed there, a man at the last moment had entered the compartment and sat down opposite me. He hastily assured us that he was leaving the train at Tula, well before the guard would come in to set up our seats for the night, and that his presence in the compartment had been approved by the guard himself.

Ignoring the two older ladies, to my consternation he engaged me in light conversation and made some humorous aside about bringing samovars to Tula, the first station on our journey, which in my flustered state and naïvity I did not fully understand. Worse than that, he asked if I would like to sample some gingerbread which he told me was a Tula speciality. Then he offered to escort me to the guard's van to check on the well being of Tuzik.

This offer, like the ginger bread, I declined with a certain degree of awkwardness, which to him probably bordered on impoliteness. Luckily he left the train as promised at Tula, but not before I had the experience of ascertaining at first hand that young ladies travelling alone seem to attract the unwanted attention of a certain kind of gentleman.

I can remember the train stopping at Kursk and Kharkov and my sleeping fitfully during the night and through the second day as we passed into Ukraine. It was a pleasure to wake up, raise the window blinds and see the mountains of Crimea replacing the flat lands of Russia.

The sun shone and the temperature in the train reached an uncomfortable level. My two ladies regretted the need to observe sartorial etiquette in keeping their heavy clothing in place. They did not include me in their conversation, perhaps my brief conversation with the gentleman from Tula having cast me in their eyes as an unsuitable person with whom to converse.

Our train pulled into Simferopol, its final destination, as darkness fell. By then it was too late to continue on to Yalta by carriage, so I was put up at the Station Hotel for the night. The next morning my luggage, Tuzik and I were loaded onto a very ramshackle carriage for the eighty five versts to Yalta. Luggage, I called it, rather a very heavy and unwieldy portmanteau which I soon found out was to become a nuisance to my fellow travellers. But the length of my stay in Yalta was so uncertain, its conditions so vaguely anticipated, that I had been advised, quite unnecessarily as it turned out, to take with me a vast array of clothing against changes in the weather.

For the onward journey I found myself sharing a carriage with two gentlemen, one older man, garbed all in black, who spent most of the time immersed in reading what appeared to be a bible and a young rakish type dressed in nautical gear, a blazer with brass buttons and white drill trousers completing an outfit of which he seemed inordinately proud.

There were only three of us occupying the carriage, but with my large portmanteau taking up one corner the young man had an excuse to sit directly opposite me. His close proximity made me feel a little awkward and I suggested that he would be far more comfortable in a corner seat, if he were to help me move my luggage.This offer he politely declined, rather taking the opportunity provided by his close presence to engage me in conversation. He informed me that he was travelling to Yalta to join a crew of young men who would be cruising the Black Sea in a schooner after victualling the vessel in the port.

I felt that out of politeness I should show some interest in his plans but in my naïvity I must have appeared too interested. Whereupon he said I must come aboard for a tour of the boat, as the Esmeralda was lying alongside a pontoon and could be easily identified by her beautiful teak decks and gleaming brass work. How had I been indiscreet enough to conduct a conversation with a stranger and lend myself to such an invitation? And my indiscretion was compounded by a most awkward incident which then took place.

Whilst dressing in the hotel I had foreseen how unpleasant a long journey by carriage over rough roads would be. I had therefore folded up my corset, which would have cut into my skin with every jolt, and placed it in my travelling bag.

The weather by this time of the morning had become intolerably hot, so whilst talking to the young gentleman I eased my light jacket off my shoulders to reveal a white muslin blouse which I had bought specially for my stay in the south. Unfortunately, as I was doing this the carriage gave one of its customary jolts and the light material of the blouse stretched across my upper body. My nautical companion, sitting opposite me as I said, must have observed this, just a slight hesitation in his speech suggesting that he was aware of what I had in all innocence revealed.

Fortunately this young man dismounted from the carriage at Alushta, where we stopped briefly to change horses, in order to light up a cigarette. The elderly gentleman took his absence as an opportunity to put down his book and address me as if he were speaking to a young granddaughter. He had obviously overheard the conversation regarding the Esmeralda and my apparent enthusiasm over its description.

He warned me that there was a certain laxity of morals on the coast, especially in Yalta. As a young woman travelling alone for the first time in her life in unknown surroundings I must be aware that men would follow me with their eyes and speak to me with one secret aim in mind, which even I in my naïvety could hardly fail to guess.

At this moment the young gentleman entered the carriage again, throwing his cigarette stub through the window with a careless gesture. Fortunately he did not pursue the subject of the Esmeralda any further,but rather pleasantly described the passing countryside, the pine clad mountains and the undulating fields, which he promised me, that if I were to return in spring, I would find bedecked with poppies.

I had time in the silence that ensued to reflect on how little I really knew about men. My literary heroes were no help at all. How was I to tell when men were being sincere, pleasant and helpful? Or as my bible reading travelling companion would have it, should I tar them all with the same brush? Perhaps the next few weeks would give me the confidence and experience to assess encounters with the opposite sex more astutely, should such encounters ever occur.

We arrived in Yalta at dusk, as myriads of lights were beginning to twinkle along the Promenade like a shining necklace lighting up the dark blue of the sea. Stiff with long sitting I transferred to an even more rickety cab, driven by a coachman, bald headed and with straggling whiskers, for all the world a modern day Taras Bulba.

Fortunately, just five minutes later we arrived at the 'White Eagle Pension for Respectable Married Ladies', to give it its full appellation, to be met by Varvara Ivanovna, my landlady for the next few weeks. She showed me to my room, which was simple enough, but had been decorated in good taste.

There was a vase of flowers on a shelf by a large old fashioned bed and on the walls were hung a number of prints depicting scenes from around the Crimean peninsula. A wash stand with a jug of water and a bowl decorated with Ukrainian motifs completed the decor.

Varvara Ivanovna pulled aside the long net curtains in front of the window to close the shutters and the room was plunged into darkness. Lighting the one and only candle she wished me good night. It was obviously time for bed. Overpowered with weariness I needed no further bidding.

{3}

24th September 1898.

As I have mentioned, I bought my diary with the simple aim of describing the anticipated boredom of my daily round in Yalta. But events that have so unexpectedly taken place today have left me with no clear idea of how I am to write them into my diary. I need to relate everything as logically and clearly as possible, though this will be difficult, given the incidents and strong emotions that have choked these recent hours.

Today I spend a long siesta in the heat of the afternoon lying comfortably on my bed, divested of all clothing save my chemise. I find this siesta time of the day most sensuous. There are no sounds of human activity, even the dogs find it too hot to bark. The only noises are the banging of a loose shutter in the breeze and of course the thrumming of the cicadas, punctuated now and again by the bad tempered screeching of a pair of jays in the olive trees outside my bedroom window. The net curtains stir languidly in the heat adding a sensuousness, which has been intensified by my having read a hundred pages of *Madame Bovary.*

So far I cannot understand the reputation it has enjoyed as a risqué novel, but I imagine that Emma's developing relationship with the young Leon may not continue platonically. I shall read on! What I have come to appreciate, though, is how similar Emma and I are. Both of us are respectable married women, but we have husbands whom we do not love or even respect. What is more remarkable and brings the strands of our lives even closer is the chance encounter that took place this evening.

Tuzik and I spend a pleasant hour walking in the Municipal gardens before heading for the Promenade. I plan to take my evening meal in my usual restaurant, but this time I hover on the doorstep, uncertain whether to enter. The waiters have rearranged the tables to accommodate a large group of young diners, amongst whom to my horror I recognize my nautical companion from the Esmeralda.

Luckily he does not catch sight of me before a friendly waiter bows me to my customary corner seat. Regrettably, due to the large number of diners in the restaurant, an extra table has been set very close to my own. This is occupied by a single gentleman, whose features seem vaguely familiar.

I eat my dinner as discreetly as possible, without looking up, eager to avoid making eye contact either with my erstwhile travelling companion and his friends, who are obviously the crew of the schooner, or with my fellow diner seated in rather too close proximity at my side.

Neither is Tuzik happy with the new seating arrangement, having less room to stretch out, though given his small size he seems to be unduly worried by his cramped environment. However, he is to be central to what happens next.

Out of the corner of my eye I am aware of my neighbour coaxing Tuzik over to his table, where a large lamb chop has been half eaten and left unfinished on his plate. He then wags his finger at Tuzik, who realizing that there is food around, does his trick of putting his head on one side and looking as if he has not been fed for days. When no lamb chop comes his way he gives a little growl. I am aware of what is happening, look up momentarily but lower my eyes again to my plate.

"He does not bite," I say quietly, feeling that I have already started to blush.

"May I give him a bone?" he enquires and when I nod he asks affably, "Have you been long in Yalta, Madame?

"About five days." I reply.

"And I've almost survived my second week here," he laughs.

There is a slight pause and I feel that I should make some contribution to the conversation.

"The time passes quickly, but it's still so boring." I say without raising my eyes from my plate.

"That's the done thing to say here in Yalta. It's boring," he replies. "But all these visitors have their perfectly interesting lives back in their home towns, but get them down here and they complain: "Oh, the dust, the heat, I can't survive."

I laugh, hopefully a little less awkwardly and more naturally than in previous encounters with strange gentlemen. We carry on eating in silence and Tuzik, realizing that there are no more treats coming his way, retreats into his corner.

When I finish my meal I realize that I will have to disturb my fellow diner in order to leave the table. He obligingly makes way for me, having finished his meal at the same time, and we leave the restaurant together. I am pleased to be in the company of a male companion since the crew of the Esmeralda, who have evidently dined well and drunk copiously, look up at me as I pass by their table. They are so evidently passing comments about me that I blush. Fortunately they are deterred from any further unseemly badinage by the presence of my fellow diner.

Outside, the heat of the day has cooled as evening approaches and we stop to breathe in the fresh air. For the first time I am able to take in the appearance of my new companion; tall, slim of figure and dressed with a certain careless elegance, which is defined by a kerchief around his neck in place of a traditional cravat. He introduces himself.

"Dmitry Dmitrych Serov from Moscow at your service, Madame." And I reply. "And I am Anna Ivanovna von Melk from the town of Shchyolkovo."

This introduction sounds so formal, what with our shaking hands and giving each other a mock bow, that we laugh. I feel more at ease, especially when we discover that we are in fact near neighbours, Shchyolkovo being no more than seventy versts from Moscow.

Dusk is falling and Dmitry Dmitrych suggests a gentle walk along the Promenade to admire the sunset over the sea. This immediately places me in a quandary. Do I accept his offer and enjoy a pleasant evening stroll in the company of a gentleman, who probably seeks nothing more than the opportunity to avoid yet another boring evening on his own?

Or rather, remembering the advice of my elderly, bible reading traveller on the coach, is it more diplomatic of me to decline, citing perhaps the need to take Tuzik back to my pension? However my new acquaintance makes the obvious suggestion which is to take Tuzik with us. This forestalls any further prevarication on my part.

We set off along the Promenade. The 'lady with a little dog' is this time accompanied by a male companion, a fact which must have set tongues wagging in Vernet's drinking establishment as we pass by. As we walk, we remark on the unusual light on the sea. There is a vague sheen upon its surface. The water is the soft, warm colour of lilac and a golden strip of moonlight lies across the harbour.

This inconsequential, light hearted conversation sets me at ease and for the first time in my adult life I feel less than awkward, even self confident in my responses to the questions of a stranger. He tells me that he is a graduate of Moscow university, where he read literature, but that he is now working in a bank. When younger he had trained as an actor but had given this up, though he still loves the theatre.

He is married, with a twelve year old daughter and two younger sons. No mention of his wife. Is that deliberate, I wonder?

For my part I tell him that I am married, do not like Shchyolkovo as I had been born, brought up and educated in St. Petersburg, which I still desperately miss.

Dmitry Dmitrych asks me about Shchyolkovo. I tell him that, to use Gogol's description, it is a "mortally wearisome" sort of place. His 'Dead Souls' hero Pavel Ivanovich Chichikov would not have felt out of place, had he included Shchyolkovo in his travels around provincial Russian cities. Nothing has changed in fifty years. We still have unpaved roads, with dust everywhere and mud the moment it starts to rain. No gaslighting, just one hotel and a theatre, a few municipal buildings and a prison…

Dmitry Dmitrych interrupts. He says that surely I am a bit too disparaging in my comments. After all there is a branch of his bank in the town, but on reflection he does remember a junior cashier being transferred there, who wept copiously on his departure into the unknown.

We walk on in silence for a minute or two. My companion is obviously intrigued. Here is a young married woman alone in Yalta. He asks me about my husband, but I am loathe to give him more than the scantiest of details. I feel I am so far away from Viktor at this moment that I want to be seen as a separate person and for the first time in my life not as my husband's appendage.

When he presses me about his work, I say that he is either in the rural council or the county council but I can never remember which. This makes him laugh. He hopes it is the rural council or Zemstvo, as it is called, as it would be the less boring of the two councils.

He explains that there has been an influx of newly elected landowners, who have brought a degree of informality into the dull work of government administration. I bite back the temptation to say that I doubt very much whether my husband would have added anything in the way of humour to the proceedings, but restrain myself.

Dmitry Dmitrych escorts me home to my 'Ladies' Residence', as he calls it. As the path becomes somewhat rougher he asks if I might do him the honour to accept his arm. I laugh and taking his arm for guidance tell him lightheartedly that I like a gentleman to be formal. A formal offer, he replies, but one based on necessity. Within one hour of our becoming acquainted he would not like to witness the sight of such a charming young lady twisting her ankle on a path as uneven as this.

I think he is intrigued to see where this young single lady is staying. Varvara Ivanovna has retired to her own separate annexe and there are no lights in the rooms of the other guests. At the gate he takes my hand and kisses it in what he calls 'the French style'. He wishes me goodnight, addressing me simply, and to my surprise, as Anna without the formal patronymic Ivanovna.

As I undress and climb into bed I recall how Emma had parted with Leon 'in the English style'. Will our two parallel paths continue in similar fashion, or might they converge at some unforeseen point in the future? The thought intrigues and excites me.

Though my candle has burnt down and I am laid down to bed, sleep does not come to me. I reflect on what has happened in the course of this one short day. I remember now where I had first seen Dmitry. He was the gentleman outside Vernet's who had raised his hat to me earlier in the day. But he seems so refined. Surely he is not be considered as one of the establishment's habitués? Is my behaviour in the restaurant, when I replied to a question from a perfect stranger and then continued a conversation with him, to be deemed unseemly?

I could so easily not have uttered those few fateful words, 'he does not bite,' and my silence would have indicated that I was a lady who did not enter into conversation with a strange man, who was so blatantly using Tuzik as a pretext to introduce himself. And was I not wrong to finish the evening by walking back to my pension arm in arm with a total stranger and having my hand kissed in the French style. Too late. The die had been cast and what the effect of those four fatal words 'He does not bite' would have on my life I could not at this stage have foreseen. On the other hand I was fully aware of the interlaced strands of pleasure and potential danger that were the result of this chance meeting.

The sounds of the day, the cicadas, the banging shutter at last closed and fastened and the dogs tired out after their day's barking, are now replaced with a deep silence, which eventually calms my emotions and in the small hours of the night lets me finally fall asleep.

***

25th September 1898.

No arrangement had been made for us to meet again and it is therefore a disappointment not to see Dmitry today. Thank goodness the Esmeralda set sail this morning. I certainly feel no regret for losing the opportunity to inspect her teak decks and gleaming brass work and of course to renew acquaintance with my young nautical gentleman, who had so enjoyed talking to me in such close proximity on our journey to Yalta!

According to Varvara Ivanova, whom I meet again over breakfast on the terrace, Anton Pavlovich Chekhov has definitely taken up residence with 'that actress woman from Moscow', as she describes Olga Knipper with a note of disapproval in her voice. She informs me that both of them are living quite openly together in his new villa, which is located at a short distance from the pension.

I agree with her that it would be nice to visit the house, but do not mention that I think it would be much more pleasant, were it to take place in company. If Dmitry and I meet again, and if a suitable opportunity should arise, I think I will suggest an outing there. I hope that such a suggestion would not be considered too bold for a lady to make, certainly if a love of Chekhov's work were to be subtly introduced as a reason for wishing to make the visit.

Should we be lucky enough to meet the author, I might even be able to make a comment about several of his earlier short stories, which might impress Dmitry. I have this worrying feeling that he sees me as a girl not much older than his own daughter, rather than as a woman in her own right.

I spend my siesta relaxing on my bed and reading *Madame Bovary*. The gentle novels of Jane Austen and Ivan Turgenev have not prepared me at all for the pure eroticism of Flaubert's writing. I am at the point where Emma has just met Monsieur Rodolphe Boulanger, who is determined to seduce her at the first available opportunity. I can now see why my husband considered the book so unsuitable for my consumption. But reading it in this illicit manner adds even more spice to the novel. Rodolphe is so different from my refined Dmitry. Or is he? How can I tell?

I do not see him at the restaurant this evening and I eat alone. I hope against hope that every time the door opens my dining companion will walk in and ask if he may make a formal request to join me at my table, a request that I shall demurely accept, with equal pretence of formality. But this is not to be. He does not appear. Nor, alas, is he to be seen on the Promenade as I take Tuzik for his evening walk. I tell myself that he is deliberately avoiding me and that this one brief encounter had been for him no more than a pleasant way to spend an otherwise dull evening.

***

26th September 1898.

I am to be proved pleasurably mistaken. This morning, whilst I am taking Tuzik for his walk in the Nikitsky Gardens our paths cross. This is quite a surprise, as I do not see Dmitry as someone who would go to the Gardens for exercise, there being a steep ascent from the sea which requires some physical effort.

On the other hand I do remember having told him him that most mornings I am to be found there with my dog. Perhaps, I fondly imagine, he had deliberately headed that way in the hope of meeting me. Deep in my thoughts I do not see a figure seated on a bench in a shady part of the gardens, smoking a cigarette and gazing at the few passers by who had made their way up the hill so early in the morning.

"Anna Ivanovna, what a pleasant surprise," I hear a familiar voice and there is Dmitry rising from his seat and raising his hat.

"Dmitry Dmitrych, I'm so sorry, please excuse me. I didn't see you there. I was deep in my thoughts."

"Please do not apologize. It is I who should apologize for daring to disturb those deep thoughts of yours. I had the advantage of prior warning of your approach. Your little dog evidently recognizes me as someone here in Yalta who produces bones for him to nibble. He ran up to me, so I knew you couldn't be far away." He pauses for a moment and then continues.

" I am so glad that we have met again. I need to apologize for my behaviour since we last saw each other.

Yesterday I felt a little under the weather, I could not face the heat out of doors and as I had no appetite I thought it would be pointless to go to the restaurant, where we dined on our first meeting and inflict myself on you in such a state. But after an early night and a good sleep I feel a new man. If you like, we could spend the day together, if it would not be presumptuous of me to suggest such an idea."

"No, on the contrary, that would be most pleasant," I begin my rehearsed lines. " If it isn't too bold of me to suggest it, I was thinking of visiting Chekhov's new villa at Autka. It's hardly any distance from here. I know that I would feel dissatisfied with myself, if before I left Yalta I had not made the effort to pay my respects to a writer whom I admire so much. And I would certainly appreciate your company. Men are so much more adept than women at finding the way to unknown places. I always seem to come across unpleasant dogs or beggars when I strike off on my own. But of course you may have other ideas, so please do not let me coerce you out of your formal politeness into accompanying me just because I want to visit Autka."

Dmitry replies that he can think of no more pleasant way of spending the day and we set off without further delay. What a pleasure it is to have my arm taken again by a good looking, attentive, well dressed man and to continue the light hearted conversation of the evening we first met.

Our path leads slightly uphill along a rough track bordered on both sides by rows of umbrella pines. It has become hot and we stop from time to time in their shade to recover our breath. Then we go on again, Dmitry guiding me over the potholes.

There is a slight frisson of sensual pleasure as he puts his arm round my waist on such occasions. As I lift up my skirt to avoid the rough stones and reveal an ankle and a pair of newly purchased black boots, Dmitry jokingly pretends to avert his eyes. Looking up to catch my eye he begins to quote:

The ladies gowns so well designed
I love their feet, although you'll find
That all of Russia scarcely numbers
Three pairs of shapely feet. And yet
How long it took me to forget
Two special feet. And in my dreams
They still assail a soul grown cold
And on my heart retain their hold.

It isn't difficult to recognize the source of his quotation, Pushkin's *Evgeny Onegin* in which the poet writes long, lyrical digressions about the 'little feet' which he has come across in his sexual conquests.

"Dmitry Dmitrych, if I am not mistaken, those lines come in Chapter One of *Evgeny Onegin.* But excuse me for correcting you, I think you have made a slight mistake. The line should end '*and in my slumbers.*' Otherwise you have nothing with which to rhyme '*number*s.'

"Anna, of course you're right. It has to be '*slumbers*', how stupid of me. I stand corrected! I would not presume to dispute literary matters with a graduate from a St. Petersburg lycée who has evidently been brought up on the classics of Russian literature. However, I do think that Pushkin is being totally unfair to your sex when he says that one would be unlikely to find shapely feet on Russian women."

"Is that based on your own personal experience or just your romantic notion of Russian women?" I can hardly believe that I have the temerity to ask such a question. But Dmitry seems delighted that he now has the chance to reply in similar vein.

"Oh Anna Ivanovna," he teases. " These special feet, if you only knew how long it has taken me to forget them, and in my dreams, excuse me, my slumbers, how cold my soul has grown and how my heart still retains their hold. Perhaps you can rekindle my ardour with more quotations from Onegin."

I laugh. "So, like Pushkin, I see you do have a predilection for little feet," I reply far too brazenly, and this is the first time I see him blush.

No matter, for my part I am blushing as well. Was it indelicate of me to refer to these sexual fantasies of Pushkin's in conversation with a man I hardly knew? My love for Russian literature had been nourished in my St. Petersburg lycée, and now I had been led innocently, as I believed, into a discussion of the poetry of Russia's most sensual poet. But Dmitry only looks at me a little more closely. Might I be a little less naïve than he had hitherto supposed?

We continue on our way without pursuing the topic, but a new degree of intimacy has appeared between us. We walk closer together. I am amazed and delighted at how bodies can send a promise, a careful signal, to each other through no more than the occasional contact of the clothes that one is wearing. I feel a sudden conviction that our relationship has entered a new and potentially more intimate phase.

***

We approach Chekhov's house with a certain trepidation, not knowing whether our visit would be welcome or not. As we enter the garden we are met by a cacophony of sounds. Carpenters are taking boards into the house to lay a new parquet floor and two gardeners are busy planting trees and flowers. Most intriguing of all, a cage had been constructed to house a tame crane, a present from a female admirer, it later transpires.

The foreman of the carpenters informs us that Chekhov and his lady friend have left on an excursion but are expected back at any moment. He doubts that they will be gone long owing to the oppressive heat. And indeed, as he speaks we hear the rumble of carriage wheels and Anton Chekhov and Olga Knipper come into view.

When the carriage stops we excuse our presence. We explain our curiosity in the new villa and make every effort to leave. Olga Knipper graciously excuses herself, she has a migraine due to the heat and the jolting of the carriage, but Chekhov himself seems pleased that we had come to visit.

He explains that the noise made by the carpenters has made it impossible for him to write and that anyway he has reached an impasse both in his latest play *Uncle Vanya* and, what is potentially more serious, in a short story that he is finding difficult to start.

He complains that both his theatre producer and his publisher are constantly writing to him demanding completion dates for both these works. He has written to them in Moscow saying that he is unwell and that a delay is to be expected. But that is all boring and of no interest to us, he says, and orders the samovar to be brought out in to the garden. Bliny appear from the kitchen and we comment on the homemade strawberry jam that accompanies them. Our initial conversation is interrupted by the appearance of Chekhov's tame crane, whose cage we had seen as we arrived. Chekhov tells us that the bird is a pompous old brute, totally ignoring and mistrusting everyone except his pious servant Arseniy. The latter had developed a close relationship with the bird, which now follows him faithfully around the garden. He has been trained to jump, wave his wide open wings and perform a characteristic crane dance which makes visitors laugh. Sadly on this occasion Arseniy is not to be found, so the bird does nothing more dramatic than pathetically flap one wing and croak before being shooed away in disgrace.

Dmitry, to his credit and to my admiration, seems totally at ease talking to Anton Pavlovich. I recall his telling me that he had studied to be an actor in his younger days and still enjoys visits to the theatre. Chekhov is eager to hear the latest news from Moscow, so they have a great deal to discuss.

When I am drawn into the conversation I tell him that my husband subscribes to *Russian Thought* and that I had read some of his earlier short stories. Which one did I like most, Chekhov asks, and thank goodness I have an answer. *The House with a Mezzanine*, I answer and have the temerity to question the ending. How can a man give up his love for a young girl simply because her elder sister drives her away?

He looks at me and replies. "The artist must be only an impartial witness of his characters and what they say, not their judge. You, the reader, can interpret the story as you wish. The writer is allowed to suffer with his characters, can cry and groan with them but it must be done in such a way that the reader never notices."

He looks at me ironically and smiles. "That is probably not a very satisfactory answer, but if you read any more of my stories, do look at them from this point of view."

I could most willingly have carried on this conversation. Here was a chance to talk to a famous writer about my favourite subject. But it is not to be, for at that moment Olga Knipper appears in the garden. She tells us that she is feeling better and needs some fresh air. She sits down on a bench in the shade of an acacia tree and beckons me to a swing nearby. She asks me how I am enjoying my holiday in Yalta, and I in my turn ask her about her work in the theatre in Moscow.

As she is replying to my question I have time to look across to the two men. Chekhov is deep in conversation with Dmitry. By this time I am swinging my legs gently on the swing, listening to Olga's first hand account of how Stanislavsky and Nemirovich- Danchenko, her directors in Moscow, are planning to establish a new theatre to be called the Moscow Art Theatre. *The Seagull* is to be its first production, followed by *Uncle Vanya,* the play that Chekhov is currently working on. She tells me in confidence that she has been promised a leading part in both plays.

My attention wavers for a moment. I look across the garden and catch Dmitry watching me on the swing. He glances up to my face, our eyes meet and he gives me a quick smile, as if he had read my thoughts. Has he guessed that I am falling in love with him, the simple truth, which I cannot hide from myself..

Anton Pavlovich turns to us after hearing his name mentioned. Looking at me on the swing, he declares to no one in particular. "That has to be the way to set Scene One." He stops, feeling that some explanation is due.

"I'm so sorry. I'm having so much trouble with Act One of my *Uncle Vanya.* I've been trying to group too many characters on stage at the same time, all clustered around the tea table in the garden, just as we are here. But if we introduce the idea of the swing, that will clear the stage a little. Stay on the swing, young lady, you're Elena, and you Dmitry Dmitrych play the part of Doctor Astrov and I will be Uncle Vanya, one admirer on each side of her, like this." He positions Dmitry and himself on either side of the swing.

"My Olga playing the part of Elena will be perfect there, just as you are, one beautiful lady replacing another. This way nobody can upstage our egotistic Stanislavsky, you know how paranoid he is about that sort of thing on stage.

And there will be plenty of room around the tea table for the rest of the characters. C'est impeccable."

Afternoon progresses into evening, the samovar stops bubbling, the bliny are finished and we begin to take our leave. As we do so, Chekhov asks me to repeat my name. Just as I am about to answer, Dmitry breaks in, jokingly informing Chekhov that I, Anna Ivanovna, have been referred to as 'The Lady with a Little Dog' by the drinking gentlemen of Vernet's Bar. I am a new arrival on the Promenade and they do not yet know who I am or where I come from. After a brief pause Anton Pavlovich turns to me. "My dear Anna Ivanovna, I will remain forever in your debt." I look at him perplexed.

"I told you this afternoon how much trouble I was having with the opening scene of *Uncle Vanya*. Thanks to you and your swing that is now resolved. But I have another problem with a short story that I have undertaken to write. Total failure so far, I must admit. My heart is just not in it. All I have is a young lady arriving in a strange seaside resort, but who she is and what she does is beyond me.

With your visit here I have resolved two problems. I now have the stage setting for Act One of *Uncle Vanya* as well as a perfect title for my story which in your honour I will call *The Lady with a Little Dog*. Thank you once again, my dear young lady. Please come and see me whenever you wish. My obstinate muse will move aside and I know that you would provide me with the inspiration that I need to write this wretched story."

As we leave I have one lingering hope that the heroine in his story, whoever she may be, will experience something of the happiness that I have known today. How could I have guessed at that stage how interlocked our two destinies would become, how parallel our two paths?

After dinner at what we now call 'our restaurant', I plead tiredness after our eventful day. We walk back to my pension arm in arm, finding our way with difficulty in the darkness. At the gate we stop and turn towards each other, uncertain how to part.

As his face comes up to mine and he draws me closer he calls me Anya for the first time. We will part 'in the Russian style', he says with the intention of kissing me twice on alternate cheeks. In the darkness our faces come together but it is our lips that meet accidently. I could have stepped back, curtailing the kiss before it had scarcely started. Instead I do not and he leaves his lips on mine for an instant.

"You must go now, Dmitry Dmitrych," I whisper as I push him gently away. I know that this was no chaste kiss and the consequences of continuing it would have compromised me. He does not know, how could he guess, but this kiss, together with the use of my name in its familiar form and without the patronymic, has taken our intimacy to an impossible level. I know that I am in love.

I settle down in bed but cannot put my confused thoughts aside. Sleep is far away and all I can do is pick up my book and renew my acquaintanceship with Emma Bovary. Now I turn the pages to find out how far she has succumbed to her pursuer's charms. Late at night I feel my eyes closing. I put Emma down but my head is still too full of the events of the day, my indiscreet references to Pushkin, the walk up to Chekhov's house, that shared intimate smile in the garden and of course the fleeting kiss on my lips. "Anna Ivanovna, you may not have a lover as I imagine Emma will have by now, but there is no hiding the fact that you are in love," I whisper to myself as at last sleep comes.

{4}

27th September 1898.

I wake this morning to find clouds massing on the tops of the mountains surrounding Yalta. The weather has changed. Indoors it is stifling, but it is even worse outside, where the wind sweeps the dust in swirling clouds along the streets, tearing off the hats of the few people who have ventured outside.

I had forgotten that today is a public holiday and the town is unnaturally quiet. After taking Tuzik out for the shortest walk that I can get him to accept I decide to remain indoors. Apart from the heat my main motive for doing so is to discover what has happened to Emma Bovary.

Yesterday I had quite understandably had little time for reading, so now I am able to catch up on Rodolphe's progress in his attempts to seduce Emma. Using the pretext of worrying about her health Rodolphe suggests that riding might well be beneficial and he can arrange for two horses to be made ready for a ride. I can sympathize with Emma, her situation being so close to mine, but I cannot really like her as a person. She is so materialistic that she only accepts the offer of a ride when she realizes that she will be able to order a new riding habit. Eventually she and Rodolphe ride away through the fields. Dismounting, he advances on her and after a feeble attempt to disengage herself she submits to him and they make love.

Back home again, and after her husband has gone out for the evening, she goes up to her room. Looking in the mirror she notices her reflection and starts in surprise. Never have her eyes looked so big, so dark, so deep. Her whole person has undergone some subtle transfiguration. "I have a lover, a lover" she says to herself again and again. She had suffered enough in a loveless marriage and now she has her revenge. She is in love for the first time and she savours her triumph without remorse or distress.

I pause in my reading. My mind is in a whirl as I come to realize the potential similarity of our two lives. Can I really be following Emma's actions in my relationship with Dmitry and if so where will this lead me? Where will it end?

I stop reading. Time has sped past and it is already late afternoon. The wind has dropped a little, and as Tuzik is making it clear that he would like to be let out, I put on my grey dress, remembering only afterwards that it is the one that Dmitry had first seen me wearing and on which he had complimented me. I leave my bedroom and step out into the heat. Heavy clouds hang ominously low, obscuring the mountains whence comes the first rumble of thunder.

***

Dmitry and I meet as arranged by the bandstand on the Promenade. There is a holiday feel about the place and the town brass band is playing a selection of military pieces which we listen to for a while. I know I am behaving in a fretful, childish manner, sending Dmitry off all the time for cordials and ice cream. Later on the wind drops completely and we go down to the pier to watch the arrival of the evening steamer from Sevastopol.

I tell Dmitry that my husband had half promised to join me in Yalta towards the end of my stay, and since he would be travelling through Sevastopol this would be the ferry that would bring him. Dmitry is alarmed by what I tell him. I calm his agitation by saying that my husband would have written if he were coming. I have received no letter from him to this effect. However Dmitry is not totally reassured.

Crowds of people are strolling along the landing stage. They are there to meet passengers off the boat and are holding bunches of flowers with which to welcome friends and family.

Dmitry jokingly buys me a bunch for my future meeting with my husband. I take them unwillingly.

"He won't be on the boat, Dmitry. Don't worry." I try to reassure him, though this nervousness of mine, manifested all evening in my ludicrous demands, has returned and can be doing little to calm his apprehension.

Delayed by rough seas the steamer arrives towards sunset and has difficulty in entering the harbour. As it ties up at the jetty I feel so strange, almost as if I have to peer at the boat to see whether my husband is on board, though I keep on telling Dmitry that this is quite impossible. I can remember talking a lot, asking questions and forgetting both what I had asked and the answers that came from a more and more exasperated Dmitry.

The smartly dressed crowd disperses, no more passengers disembark and of course there is no sign of Viktor. We both feel calmer, relieved, drawn closer together by the lifting of these shared moments of anxiety.

The sun has set behind stormy clouds and darkness is coming on. We stand alone on the jetty, as though waiting for some delayed passenger to alight. We are awkward together, as if we both have a premonition of what might lie ahead. I sniff my flowers, eyes downcast on the wooden boarding below my feet. I cannot meet his gaze.

"The weather's improved a bit now it's evening," Dmitry says. "So where shall we go? How about driving out somewhere?" I can remember so vividly staring at the ground and giving him no answer.

Then it all happens so quickly. He pushes my head up so that I can see him staring at me, then pulling me to him and kissing me fully on the lips. I sense the fragrance he is wearing and feel the dampness of my crushed flowers. He looks around fearful lest someone has observed us. "Let's go to your place," he whispers. We walk hand in hand, defying convention, back along the pontoon where in my agitation I nearly trip on a loose board.

At the gate of the pension we stop to find the latch in the dark. Dmitry breaks the silence, a little joke about not having to decide whether to say goodbye in the English, French or Russian style. He must have taken my laugh as my final signal of surrender.

We enter by the side door, which gives entry directly to my room. It is stuffy and smells of some perfume I bought in the Japanese shop next to my book store on Gogol Boulevard. I had forgotten to tidy my room and I notice that *Emma Bovary* still lies on my crumpled bed. I remove her discreetly and light a solitary candle on the table. It barely illuminates anything, just pushing the shadows a little further towards the walls.

Dmitry begins to kiss me, one kiss for each button on my blouse that his fingers are undoing. Then he turns me round, kissing my neck as he loosens the laces of my corset. "Anushka, my darling," he whispers. My modesty prevents him from going further. I find myself lying on the bed in my chemise and stockings.

Dmitry joins me on the bed and we make love. But although it is beautiful and tender I do not share Emma's ecstasy. No, I have a lover, it is true, but the emotions I now feel are not those of Emma's. I feel embarrassed. It is not what I should have allowed to happen.

I get up from the bed, move the candle closer to the mirror and look at myself, as Emma had done in her bedroom. But instead of Emma's radiant loveliness all I see now is the reflection of a face that appears sunken and lifeless. My long chestnut hair, my beautiful hair as Dmitry calls it, hangs sadly down on each side of my face, making me look dejected and sad.

I remember being taken to the Hermitage in St. Petersburg by my Art teacher at the Lycée. We had stood in front of the picture 'Christ with the Woman taken in Adultery' admiring the woman's expression of shameful helplessness. With a shudder I now recognize myself as the woman in that picture. Dmitry had taken his pleasure in me and I am simply an adulteress. He has not even mentioned the word love in our fumbled lovemaking.

I recall Pushkin's narrator in *Evgeny Onegin* cynically describing men's sexual conquest of women.

"The less we show our love to woman
The easier she is to win,
The easier to snare and ruin,
In seduction's net of sin."

I feel that I have become just another in a long line of Dmitry's conquests and I am dirty and defiled. I turn to him. "This is wrong", I say. "You will be the first to lose respect for me now. You don't love me."

He does not answer straight away. On the table is a watermelon. He cuts himself a slice and slowly starts eating it, arranging the pips in an intricate pattern on the plate. Time passes slowly in silence.

"May God forgive me!" I say, my eyes filling with tears. "It is terrible what we have done."

Dmitry speaks at last. "Why should I lose my respect for you? You seem to be defending yourself, but you and I have done nothing wrong."

But how could I defend myself? I am wicked, I despise myself and I will not excuse my actions. I had known full well what was going to happen between us and I had been happy to consent. Dmitry had done no more than ask if we were going to go for an excursion. When I did not answer he was quite right to think that I was ready to accept his next suggestion, my silence appearing to him to be my unspoken acquiescence.

I have deceived myself, not my husband or Dmitry. It is Emma who has led me on, not Dmitry. And I had found out too late the falseness of her intoxication. My feelings, from the time I had decided that it was impossible to stay in Shchyolkovo with my husband, to my first meeting with Dmitry, to the magical day spent with him at the White Dacha, and to be honest, the excitement of our love making, all this I now see as the actions of a vulgar, worthless woman, whom everyone had the right to despise.

I am now a fallen woman who, dissatisfied with her boring, unfulfilled life, has sought an adventure which all too quickly has turned into a sexual relationship. I had had a longing for romance, for a poetry around love and sensuality to equal what my literary heroines had experienced. And all I have achieved is to corrupt my previously innocent behaviour into something inappropriately sexual.

I can see that all this, this unexpected remorse for my actions, is very tedious for Dmitry.

"If it was not for the tears in your eyes, I would think that you were joking or at any rate play acting. I just do not understand," he says softly, taking me in his arms. "What is it you want?" I bury my face in his chest and cling to him. I could have told him to leave and to never see me again, but I am not able to go that far. Call it ambivalence or what you will, but my remorse, my disgust with myself is not strong enough for me to take that final step.

"That is enough, enough," he says softly, kissing my eyes to dry them. My tears begin to subside. His soft and gentle words gradually calm me. I had cried my grief away and incredibly, despite or perhaps because of what had happened to us both, we start laughing.

"Wash your face and brush your hair," he says "and we'll go out and take a cab to Oreanda." We steal out of the house and walk down to the Promenade to find a cab.

***

There is not a soul to be seen at this hour. The streets lined with their cypresses and olive trees seem completely dead, but the sea, still rough after the high winds of the day, roars as it breaks on the shore. A small launch with its little lamp glimmering at its mast head is tossing on the waves. Despite the lateness of the hour we find a cab driver willing to take us to Oreanda.

The night is warm with a bright moon. The carriage rolls softly along the white road following the coast and then at length through the forest, laced with black shadows. Dark rows of tall cypresses tower against the sky, the ruins of a castle glimmer in the moonlight and it is all very beautiful. In Oreanda we find a bench near the church and look down at the sea below us without saying a word. Yalta is just visible through the morning mist. White clouds lie motionless on the mountain tops. Not one leaf stirs on the trees, cicadas shrill and the monotonous hollow roar of the sea reaches us from below. All this seems to be saying to us that nature will be the same for all time, utterly indifferent to the vicissitudes of lovers' lives.

Someone comes up, probably a watchman, glances at us and goes away. We can see the steamer arriving from Feodosia, illuminated by the sunrise, its lights extinguished. I think back to the last steamer I had seen, and what since then has happened to me. "I have a lover, a lover," I repeat to myself and this time the thought thus kindled brings no tears to my eyes.

I notice there is dew on the grass, that this wondrous night is over and that a new day is beginning. Dmitry turns to me, one last lingering kiss, and we agree that it is time to return.

{5}

Our days have begun to follow a delightful routine, a sweet uniformity. We meet on the Promenade at noon every day, have lunch together, dine together and admire the sea and the sunset. Dmitry has introduced me to the local wines, grown in a vineyard recently planted by Prince Lev Golitsyn, Governor General of Crimea. We enjoy a sparkling wine before dinner and a Massandra white or red wine with our meal. I enjoy the relaxing effect of the wine, which is something new for me to add to the sensuous, heat induced languor that infects me.

When we find ourselves in the square or the municipal gardens and no one is near us, we share a passionate kiss. In a secluded corner we sit on a stone bench, warm from the sun and feel intoxicated by the glory of the day. This complete idleness, the kisses in broad daylight, when we look around fearful that someone might see us, the heat, the smell of the sea, all this lends a wonderfuly erotic ambience, in which our relationship steadily progresses.

Dmitry is impatient in his passion, constantly telling me how beautiful I am, how seductive.

I turn to him "What is beauty?" I ask. "If beauty is what you love, do not think of me. You will change your mind as soon as you catch sight of another pretty face, and then I will slip out of your memory. All I can ask of you, please stay constant for these few days we have together. I can ask no more of you."

"You see me in a very fickle light," he replies. "I deem that beauty is in the eye of the beholder and not a measurable quality. By that equation, Annushka, I will love you forever."

But these fine words are not enough, I need constant reassurance. When drugged with sleep, we wake in the half light of dawn, which creeps unwelcomely upon us, and I find him looking at me, why then do I fear that the words of the night, when he tells me time after time how beautiful I am and that he loves me, may not survive the day? Does he still love me when I ask too many questions or seem too childish for him to take me seriously?

Perhaps he does. He puts my doubts at rest with tender words and a stolen kiss. I make myself believe that I am not just one of his conquests, though maybe a little younger and certainly more naïve and unsophisticated than his previous ones.

But my doubts return. I tell him that I've heard it said that men believe love is better in the chase than caught. I admit to him that if this is the case with us, then I have nothing more to offer. The excitement of the chase for him had been so quickly over and with so little struggle on my part. He cannot possibly have any respect for me now that I am caught, that he cannot love me and that he must see me only as a vulgar woman. He denies this vehemently and we make love again. That is enough in my innocence to reassure me.

And so I am in a state of complete limbo. I am living outside of time. It is enough for me to exist as if every day is my last. I have no thoughts of tomorrow or what that day may bring. I have the luxury of the present, with no sense at all of the burdens of the future or that I might be punished for the glory of these moments. Ecstasy, as I experience it, carries within itself the delusion that it will last forever.

One morning as we walk towards the Nikitsky gardens to give Tuzik his exercise we pass a shop, where on a table at the window an elderly lady is cutting out strips of leather. She has one of these new Singer sewing machines and is evidently about to make a bag of sorts from the material she is working on.

To my surprise Dmitry tells me to wait outside while he goes in. Through the window I can see him deep in conversation with the seamstress, holding his cupped hands together to form a circle. Of course I am curious, but when he comes out Dmitry simply replies that I will have to wait till tomorrow to find out the purpose of his visit.

And so the next morning finds us back at the same shop. Dmitry goes in, hands over a few coins and comes back to me with a self satisfied look on his face. He unwraps the parcel to reveal a leather patchwork ball the size of a small orange.

"Anna, here's a little present for Tuzik to play with in the park. I'm getting a little tired with throwing sticks for him to chase. The little devil always bites them in half before he gets them back to me."

We reach the park and Tuzik is in his element chasing the ball across the grass and dropping it after some persuasion at the feet of Dmitry, who seems to be loving the game as much as Tuzik.

"There you are, Anna" he jokes, after picking the ball up to show that the game is over. " I am in love both with your little dog and with his mistress. Tell me, am I not a lucky man to have the two of you?"

Another day, as we walk down Pushkinskaya Street past the statue to the poet, Dmitry tells me the story of Pushkin's brief sojourn in Crimea. Banished from St. Petersburg for expressing anti-government sentiments, Pushkin arrives in Odessa where he is put under the jurisdiction of the Governor General, Count Mikhail Vorontsov. He immediately seduces the said Governor's wife, who gives him a gold talisman ring which he wears until he dies thirteen years later in a duel, occasioned by the behaviour of his unfaithful wife.

I jokingly point out that I too have been seduced, but unfortunately have no gold ring to give my lover. Seduction seems to be part and parcel of life in Crimea, I remark, which makes him blush and admit that there may be an element of truth in my observation.

****

Dmitry loves the prospect each evening of the walk to my pension, the clandestine entry through the side gate and the anticipated pleasures of our lovemaking. I cannot risk Varvara Ivanovna catching sight of him around the pension, as she rises early to lay the breakfast on the terrace table.

We wake in the half light of early morning and I make him leave. I put on my peignoir and open the side door onto the terrace. Checking that there is no one around we have one final embrace and then he is gone. I can just hear him cursing softly as he fumbles with the catch on the gate.

How can I have any regrets? After all, Emma never spent a whole night with Rodolphe,satisfying herself with early morning trysts in his bedroom after running through the fields to his house. Whereas I have whole days and most of the night with my lover!

3rd October 1898.

The entry in my diary tells me that today my idyll ends. This bitter day had to come, though I had no idea it would be so soon.We set off for a walk to the Uchasu waterfall, taking Tuzik with us as he has been dreadfully neglected these past few days and must be bored with the Nikitsky Gardens, where Dmitry and I spend such long hours together.

The weather is fair and everything promises another happy day. Yet for some reason my mood turns melancholic and I have a presentiment that something unpleasant is in store for us. And so it transpires.

When we return home I find a letter waiting for me. I open it over dinner. I read aloud to Dmitry. My husband writes saying that he has an eye infection and begs me to return as soon as possible.

Dmitry agrees that I should go the next day. I say that it is a good thing that I am leaving, hateful as the parting will be. It is fate. The idyll of these past few days cannot be prolonged. Dmitry does not come to me in the evening, sensitive to my grief and my wish to be alone. In my bedroom I stop my ears resolutely against the inner voice that keeps telling me of our coming separation. My duty is to my husband and I must go home.

Dmitry arranges for two places in the carriage to Simferopol and once again I find myself being jostled and bumped over the rough Crimean roads. We speak little to each other, both aware of the poignancy of the situation which becomes ever more of a reality as we draw closer to Simferopol.

At the station and when the second departure bell has rung, I tell my Dmitry that I will think of him, I will remember him.

"God bless you and take care of yourself. Do not think badly of me. This must be our final farewell since we never should have met in the first place. Goodbye Dmitry, God bless you, I will always remember you."

He reaches for his pocket handkerchief, but my eyes are dry. He pulls me to him and whispers, "My darling Anna Ivanovna, my darling Anna, my darling Anya, my darling Anushka. We have been happy together, have we not? Please do not think ill of me for what has happened. I too will always remember you, my lady with her little dog."

I shiver. Here at the station there is already a breath of autumn in the air and the evening is cool. The third bell rings, a moment's silence, broken only by the humming of the telegraph wires, one final kiss and we part, as I believe for ever. I feel the little death of departure invade my body with its impersonal coldness. I pull my shawl around my shoulders for warmth and I take my seat in the compartment. The long journey north has begun and the holiday romance is over. Surely it was never more than that, I tell myself. It could never have lasted. There was simply too much happiness for it to endure.

{6}

Shchyolkovo, 10th October 1898.

I am returned safely to my home. In the privacy of my bedroom I take my diary in my hands. Am I to continue it in its present daily format or close it at my last entry, to be cherished, read and reread as consolation for the moments of desolation that come upon me, as they do so often now? Can there be anything more to write about the story of a young girl who in the space of two short weeks grows to womanhood in the exotic setting of a seaside town?

I had thought that a final entry had surely been written that day I left Crimea. Through the quiet medium of time I realize now that the reason why I had bought it in the first place had been no more than to describe the boring details of my early days in Yalta.

Then my further entries were to record the details of my affair with Dmitry. My purpose now that I am back home is simply to evoke a maudlin sentimentality, a burning need to confide somehow, to someone, my anguish, my desolation, my unhappiness over the past weeks. Perhaps a few pathetic entries in my diary will keep my memories of past happiness alive. And so I have decided to continue writing.

My journey back to Shchyolkovo is uneventful, though both long, very long and very tedious. I spend the time finishing *Madame Bovary*, but I can no longer identify with the heroine. Our destinies have become untwined and I feel no sympathy for her despite her dreadful fate. For myself, I am numbed of all emotion through the long days and nights as the train rumbles northwards, unable to summon up to the slightest degree the excitement that I experienced on my innocent journey south.

***

I dread arriving home to find my husband really ill. As my cab from the station enters our street and once again I see our house hidden behind its grey wall topped with nails, I have a feeling that I am entering a prison. Most unfortunately I arrive in advance of my letter, in which I had informed Viktor that I was on my way. Consequently my entrance is unannounced and unexpected.

My fears for my husband's health are unfounded. He is recovering well from nothing more than an eye infection which is responding well to treatment. A full time nurse is in attendance to change his bandages and I feel rather uncharitably that he had not really needed my premature return. My presence in the house is superfluous as our servants scurry around to satisfy his every need.

And so life here resumes its monotonous pattern. Tuzik and I take walks in the local park. I play the piano without any great enthusiasm. Autumn has come and gone, the silver birches have wept their leaves from the branches, the first snows have arrived and the stoves have been lit. It is dark in the morning and the servants light the lamps for my husband's breakfast before he sets off for another day's work in his office, wherever that may be.

I remember Dmitry laughing at my ignorance in this regard and tears well involuntarily in my eyes. But I feel no desire to question Viktor further on this subject. He and his work have long been of little interest to me.

I have already packed away my blouses and skirts that I wore in Yalta and selected my winter wardrobe. There is no one here to admire or appreciate what I put on, so I am usually to be found wearing an old severely cut black dress. One of the servants, Dunyasha, asked me the other day why I always wear black. I do not need to tell her the reason why. I wear black because I am in mourning for my life.

I have no one with whom to share my sorrow. When I go out with Tuzik I put on my fur lined coat and warm gloves and tread carefully along the snow covered roads. But the ancient lime trees and birches on our streets, beautiful as they are, covered in snow and hoar frost, are not as close to my heart as the cypresses and palm trees lining the Promenade, where my memories and my heart remain.

My husband has remarked on my paleness, my listlessness and general inertia and has suggested a shopping expedition to Moscow. But I do not have any need for expensive jewellery or new outfits, the very things that brought Emma to her downfall. Nor do I want the attention of a younger man like Leon. Whenever I wake in the night and need comfort, all I want is to find myself in the arms of Dmitry and have him whisper Anushka as he makes love to me. In pitiful contrast, here all I have is a weekly visit to my bedroom from my husband, who comes to claim his conjugal rights.

I feel like slamming the door on him, but I know only too well that married women are not permitted to behave like this. The world of my bedroom is a solitary one for me. Viktor takes his pleasure from me, it is only our bodies coming together, not our souls. After he leaves me I sob into my pillow and wonder if I can ever be happy again.

***

Time goes by so slowly and I have only my diary to differentiate the days, the weeks, the months one from another. Life is a ritual of misery, the monotony of a daily, never varying routine bounded by housekeeping and my husband's demands.

I find fault with the servants. " Pelageya," I scold. "How many times must I remind you to trim the wick of the icon lamp in the hall. You know perfectly well that it's the first thing visitors to the house see when they come in. We cannot have them crossing themselves in front of a smoking icon. And I can see that the oil has not been refilled. And while you are doing that, go and check all the lamps in the house. Otherwise the wicks will need replacing and Viktor Aleksandrovich will be furious at the cost. "Yes, madam," replies Pelageya and departs, muttering something in her peasant Russian which I cannot catch.

And then the fish man arrives and I have him brought into the kitchen. I berate him for the quality of the sturgeon which we had last night. Viktor is a fussy man at the best of times and sturgeon baked with a cheese sauce is his favourite. On this occasion he left most of it on his plate. Our menu for this evening was to be carp stuffed with buckwheat and mushrooms, but I look suspiciously at the fish he has brought with him.

My mind is not on household matters. I think every moment of the waking day of Dmitry, remembering those wonderful days in Yalta. For a hundredth time I tell myself that I will never see him again and I must come to terms with the fact that for him I was just one more conquest, one more affair to while away the boredom of a solitary sojourn in the south.

For days on end the icy weather has prevented my stirring beyond the garden gate. When it becomes a little milder I take Tuzik out to play in the snow, as usual throwing Dmitry's leather ball for him to chase. But one day, after two or three throws the ball bursts as he carries it back to me. The stitching around two of the panels has broken and the rags that filled the ball unwind like the entrails of some mutilated animal. This had been Dmitry's little gift, my only tangible memory of him. The broken ball lies in the discoloured snow, a symbol of our sullied affair. Tuzik turns it over with his paw, realizes that it has no further use, discards it and finds a stick to bring to me instead.

But then something happens to break the monotony of my life. I feel that at times my husband regards me more as a daughter than a wife, and as a Christmas treat for me he has suggested a visit to our local theatre to attend the first night performance in Shchyolkovo of an operetta, *The Geisha*, which has had great success in Moscow. Naturally he is keen to go and to be seen there by his fellow Government lackeys and of course by the Governor, whom Viktor, sycophant that he is, has already found out will be attending.

I can do nothing other than accept his invitation and agree to accompany him. After all, anything is pleasanter than experiencing the tedium of another evening at home. Though to be truthful I do not particularly like opera and even less operetta. I certainly do not have any desire to meet his office colleagues again. I still retain the painful memories of the incident at the last party we attended, the occasion when I overheard those young men discussing a subject that they felt unsuitable for the ears of a young lady.

A mischievous fantasy comes to me. I would love to tell these gentlemen, should I meet them in the theatre, that this young lady was aware of the subject of their whispered conversation and hint that I too had read Madame Bovary. I could imagine their embarrassment and for the first time since leaving Yalta I found myself smiling.

But putting all these fantasies to one side, I dress for the theatre. The stalls, where we have seats in the third row, the Governor and his daughter being in the first row as my husband is quick to point out, are filling up and there is noise and excitement in the gallery. As the orchestra tunes up, the local dandies in front of the stalls, where everyone can see them, are preening themselves, arms crossed behind their backs to show off the slimness of their figures and the fineness of their attire.

I am not enjoying myself. My husband refuses to sit down, thinking it necessary to try to catch the Governor's eye, even that of his ridiculous daughter flaunting a tasteless feather boa. Eventually everyone is seated, the orchestra plays the overture atrociously and the curtain slowly rises. I settle down in my seat and wait patiently for the interval.

But how could I ever have foreseen what was to happen next? As the curtain falls at the end of the first act my husband goes out for a smoke and to chat to his colleagues, leaving me on my own. Suddenly I hear a familiar voice. "Good evening, Anna Ivanovna." I turn round and feel that I am going to faint. I look up in utter consternation to see Dmitry standing at my side. Neither of us speaks a word. In a trance I get up from my seat and make my way awkwardly towards the exit. I sense that Dmitry is following me.

In my imagination I can feel the whole theatre looking at me. I know that I have to hide somewhere where we cannot be seen together. In my panic I drop both my fan and my lorgnette, which a gentleman in uniform wearing an insignia on his chest, picks up and returns to me with a puzzled look on his face. We walk aimlessly up and down the corridors, Dmitry a few paces behind me so that we are not to be taken for a couple.

Searching for a place to be alone we go up and down staircases, people loitering there, past cloakrooms with their smell of damp fur coats on hangers, women arranging their hair in the mirrors on each side of the counter. My heart is throbbing. "Why all these people? Why can't they go back to their seats?" I ask myself. And then the bell rings to announce the start of the second act and the corridors clear as if by magic. We find a stairwell, deserted except for two schoolboys sharing an illicit cigarette. We can talk at last.

"What a fright you gave me," I gasp, my breath catching in my throat. "Why have you come? How did you find me? How did you know that I would be here?"

"Please understand me, Anna, please understand. I just had to see you again." Dmitry stands there uncertain of my reaction. He has changed, he looks older and for the first time I notice some grey in his hair. His self confidence has gone and now I see in him a new persona. My easy going, charming, seductive man about town whom I met in Yalta is now the anxious supplicant, fearing that his actions may be rebuffed. He is saying something but I am not listening.

"It has been so awful for me", I whisper. "There is not a moment in my life that I do not think of you. But why have you come?"

The two schoolboys are still smoking and looking down on us, but Dmitry is oblivious to them. He draws me to him and starts kissing my face, my cheeks, my arms.

"What are you doing? What are you doing?" I cry out in horror, pushing him away."We have both gone out of our minds. You must leave tonight before my husband finds out that you've been here. I've told him nothing about our meeting in Yalta. Even he might suspect something if we are seen together. You must go, go now! I implore you, by all that's holy, I beg you. Listen, someone is coming."

We can hear steps coming up the staircase. The two schoolboys disappear in a trice.

"You must go, Dmitry Dmitrych." I use his patronymic, hoping that this may lend more authority to my voice. "I will come and see you in Moscow. I have never been happy here. I am unhappy now, and I never will be happy unless I am with you. I swear I will come to you in Moscow. Tell me how and when, but don't ever write to me here, my mail is always checked."

Dmitry tells me to write a letter to his bank marked 'Private and Confidential', to book into the *Slavyansky Bazaar* hotel on Nikolskaya Street and to let him know when I arrive. He will then come to me. His words calm me a little but I am still terrified of our being compromised by being seen together.

"Dmitry, get your coat and go. I must join my husband, he's bound to wonder where I've been all this time. He knows that I am unwell, he'll be looking for me." I realize as I am saying all this that our relationship has changed. It is me now telling Dmitry what needs to be done.

I press his hand and go swiftly down the stairs. I keep on turning round for a last glance, tears in my eyes, and in my emotion trip on a stair and nearly fall. I stop to gather myself and adjust my shoe. Dmitry has disappeared from sight but I can still hear the sound of his footsteps echoing on the marble stairs.

I find my seat in the stalls, whisper to my husband that I am feeling unwell. We leave the theatre at once and take a cab home. Viktor is not at all pleased with me as he now has no chance to talk to the Governor in the interval after the second act. What a nuisance a wife can be, I can hear him muttering.

***

Now my life of deception has begun in earnest. I survive the monotony of the days and nights only by thinking of what awaits me in Moscow. There is thick snow all around and a freezing wind blows off the Klyazma river. My walks with Tuzik to the park have had to be curtailed, owing to the snowdrifts on the paths which have not been cleared of snow. Instead I take him to the city centre, walk once around the Cathedral of the Holy Trinity where the paths are clear, and return home.

There is no poetry in this winter. The house is warm, but the gales and blizzards outside make the stoves howl, like hobgoblins the superstitious servants say, crossing themselves as the winds blow. I have no view from any window, just the grey, nail topped fence around the garden. It is a sad house, the silence, when my husband has departed and the servants are busy in the kitchen, is as solid as darkness. My sadness has sucked everything away, every feeling except grief itself forgotten. Even the wintry sun is dull. I am as cold as a stone inside, waiting for the days to pass until I can see Dmitry again.

But how can that happen, I ask myself? I watch the snow falling endlessly on the trees outside my bedroom window and with my finger draw a heart on the frozen pane. It melts as I put my lips to it. Dmitry, I cannot survive unless I see you again.

I am a prisoner in my own house, though a prisoner who is allowed one indulgence, to read and have access to books. Some days ago I found a copy of Lev Tolstoy's *Anna Karenina* as I strayed into my husband's study. My curiosity is aroused. This must be another unsuitable book for a respectable lady to read, so in order to avoid detection I hide Anna under my clothes in my bedroom cupboard. Languishing in my prison, with my jailor visiting me only in the evening, I have plenty of time to acquaint myself with Tolstoy's heroine.

My namesake proves to be another unfortunate heroine. But as with Emma Bovary I find myself so closely identified with her. All three of us betray our husbands. But neither Emma nor Anna provide me with guidance as to my future conduct or a solution to my predicament. I am not going to commit suicide. I have not taken upon myself any terrible financial debt. Nor have I flouted society's laws by living openly with a man who is not my husband. Neither woman can tell me how to loosen the chains of my incarceration. However I have planned an escape from my prison, even if it amounts to no more than a temporary parole.

I pay another visit to the doctor who originally advised me to take the cure in Yalta. Trusting in her professional confidentiality, I tell her that I am desperate to get away to Moscow for a few days. I do not elucidate on the reason for this, but sense that she guesses that it may not be for medical reasons. She recommends a colleague in Moscow, who specializes in 'women's problems', and says that she will write to confirm an appointment.

On returning home I find my husband in an unusually charitable mood as I tell him of my need to consult another doctor in Moscow. He evidently feels that my depression is due to the effects of a recent medical diagnosis, when yet another gynaecologist hinted that there is a possibility that I may never conceive. This was not necessarily the case, the specialist assured me when we met, as Viktor had refused to submit himself to any medical examination. If we as a couple are found to be unable to produce an offspring, then in my husband's opinion of course it will have been my fault and not his.

But it seems to him to be a good enough reason for my intended visit to Moscow. He agrees quite readily to my request, arranges for me to have money for the trip and asks if he should write to the aunt we stayed with on my journey down to Yalta.

I answer his well intended question by saying that I have college friends from St. Petersburg, now married and living with their husbands in Moscow. I am anxious to catch up with their news and one of them will no doubt be pleased to put me up.

I think it was Sir Walter Scott's quotation '*What a tangled web of lies we weave, when first we practise* to *deceive*' that I first came across as a young innocent Lycée schoolgirl studying

English literature. Then the lines had meant little to me, but now the sentiment comes to me unbidden and unwelcome. Even though my husband has been kind in this instance I feel no remorse for what I am doing. Am I becoming more like Emma and Anna, I wonder, the deeper I become entangled in this web of deception?

{7}

I note in my diary that I have an appointment in Moscow for 30th January. My doctor has arranged a meeting with a medical colleague who will see me on that day. Should Viktor express any interest in my consultation and I need to continue this pretence to its logical conclusion, I plan to spend just a few minutes with this doctor who specializes in 'women's problems'. I would then have something to relate to Viktor on my return, if in the unlikeliest of instances he should show any interest in my visit.

But do I really need to continue with this subterfuge? It is almost as if I have a death wish subconsciously to be found out. It would be so easy for Viktor to check on my activities in Moscow. If he asked me for an explanation I would not be able to tell lies to his face. I would have no choice but to own up to the truth. But for the time being he does not seem to have any suspicions or even any interest in my activities. Whether misguidedly or not I do nothing further to cover my tracks.

30th January 1899.

It is snowing when I awake, but before long a pale wintry sun breaks through and makes even Shchyolkovo look beautiful. I put on my best furs, take the mid morning train to Moscow and book into the *Slavyansky Bazar.* I send a messenger to Dmitry at his bank, telling him I have arrived and am expecting him as soon as possible. A reply comes back. He has been able to absent himself from the office to meet an important client on business who has been writing to him privately and confidentially! He will be with me this afternoon. He is not the only one who deals in deception.

I do not know why Dmitry chose this hotel for our rendezvous, apart from its central position on Nikolskaya Street. Perhaps in our frenzied meeting at the theatre it was the first one that had come into his head. But it has turned out to be a happy choice. While waiting for Dmitry I take lunch in the restaurant.The walls are plastered with newspaper cuttings relating to the world of the theatre. I notice a familiar face, a photograph of Chekhov smiling out at me. I mention to the waiter that I had recently met Anton Pavlovich in Yalta.

The last diners have left, the dining room is empty, and seeing that he has a captive audience the manager asks if he might take the liberty of joining me at my table. He relates to me an extraordinary event that had taken place on these premises. Last summer on June 19th Konstantin Sergeevich Stanislavsky and Vladimir Ivanovich Nemirovich-Danchenko had met here to discuss plans to establish a new theatre in Moscow, to be called the Moscow Art Theatre. After seventeen hours of discussion the deal was done, the hotel obligingly staying open until two o'clock in the morning. The first production by the new theatre was to be *The Seagull,* followed by *Uncle Vanya* at a later date. Will I have the chance, I wonder, to see this production with Elena played by Olga Knipper reclining on my swing?

I retire to my room after lunch to prepare myself for our rendez-vous. I am filled with conflicting emotions. Excitement of course in that I will see Dmitry again, but a growing apprehension, a nervousness that our meeting may prove awkward and that we will be ill at ease when we meet. I do not know about Dmitry's experiences in such matters, but it is fair to say that for my part I am not accustomed to entertaining my lover in a hotel bedroom!

I am fearful that this clandestine encounter may appear in retrospect to have all the banality and vulgarity of a stereotyped fictional adventure. If we find that we are still in love with each other I want this love to manifest itself in a purer way.

Dmitry comes to me earlier than I expect. He taps gently at the door, enters my room shaking off the snow from his fur coat and gives me a demure kiss. He is holding a bunch of flowers.

" These are for you, Anna," he jokes. " I've counted them, there are exactly nineteen. Never give a woman an even number of flowers is part of our family folklore. Otherwise they will bring bad luck. You didn't kmow that I was so superstitious, did you?

It is no more than a weak joke, but we are each so nervous that it serves its purpose. I call for tea to be brought up. We sit facing each other, neither being certain whether our former intimacy would allow for closer contact than this. We begin to talk.

Dmitry tells me of his feelings after his return to Moscow. How he too had found life boring and how memories of our time together in Yalta had come flooding back. That first meeting with me and the lengths he had to go through that evening in the restaurant to get 'this young lady's' attention. Thank you Tuzik, without his bone it would have been impossible, he jokes. Then we recall the events on the jetty, that early misty morning in Oreanda, the steamer from Feodosiya and those first stolen kisses.

He confides that back in Moscow, in the quiet of his study in the evening, he felt that he could hear me breathing and even the gentle rustle of my dress, that I followed him everywhere, like a shadow watching him. In the street he followed women with his eyes, thinking that he had seen someone who resembled me. Then these memories turned into dreams and the past merged in his imagination with the thought of what the future could hold if he were only to take the necessary steps.

And so during the Christmas holidays he deceived his wife by saying that he was going to St. Petersburg on behalf of a certain young man he wanted to help. He took the train the short distance to Shchyolkovo, booked into the only half respectable hotel we have, and set about finding out from the porter where we lived.

This was easily accomplished, my husband being well known in town. Dmitry realized that he had made a mistake by arriving on a public holiday. But here he was in Shchyolkovo and it was too late to change his plans. He presumed my husband's office would be closed and that he would be at home. But the difficulty was that if he sent a note to the house it would most likely fall into my husband's hands.. His best course of action, he reasoned, was to trust to luck.

He found the house quite easily from the porter's directions and waited nearby. He walked past the house and took several turns in the street. There were few passers by and as time went by he felt more and more conspicuous. A beggar entered through the gates and was set upon by the servants, who after giving him bread told him to leave the premises.

Then an hour later he heard the faint, indistinct sounds of a piano. It must have been my playing, I tell him, as there is no one else in the house who plays. The front door opened and a maid came out with Tuzik. Dmitry wanted to call the dog, but realized just in time that the dog would recognize him and bark in excitement at seeing him. The door slammed shut. Dmitry was cold and irritated at his lack of success.

He became convinced that I had forgotten him and that perhaps I was already having a liaison with another man. He decided to return to his hotel, but on the way saw an advertisement for *The Geisha*, an opera that had played in Moscow before transferring to the provinces. He thought that this would relieve the boredom of an evening alone in a strange town, and only later did he realize that as this was a première, I might possibly be attending the performance with my husband. At the theatre he booked a seat in the stalls and caught sight of me entering in the company of a tall, stooping figure with short side whiskers, whom he took to be my husband Viktor. As we looked for our seats he seemed to be perpetually bowing to all and sundry. And with these movements and his sickly smile, Dmitry remarked, there seemed to be something of a flunkey's subservience about him. I felt that I should not have done so, but I could not restrain a laugh at his succinct but cruel summing up of my husband's whole essence.

It was fate that led us to meet again, he says, pausing for a moment' reflection. I had been silent up till then, but there were questions for which I wanted answers. I wanted to know more about his wife and his relationship with her. Up to now he had told me very little, just that he was married and had a daughter and two sons. In Yalta I had not had the courage to press him further, no gentle probing, none of the clumsily disguised leading questions that he must have expected from me as a woman and which, he said later, had intrigued him by their absence. But now here in Moscow I am his mistress, my naïvity is a thing of the past and I feel that he should tell me something more about the other woman in our lives.

So he confides to me that he had married at a young age whilst still at university, that his wife is much older than he is and that he no longer finds her attractive. She calls him Demetrius, when he senses that she is upset with him, and he admits that he is frightened of her. He dislikes being at home, spending his leisure time at his club or with friends. Yalta, he confessed, had been a sublime interlude in a marriage which was held together only by obligations to his wife and their children and the need to maintain their respective positions in Muscovite society.

Then we talk about our traumatic meeting at the theatre and how we had arranged to meet at this hotel. I tell him about the sadness of my life at home, mostly the sentiments that I have confided to my diary. I hide nothing, and taking his hand and looking directly into his eyes I tell him again that I love him. There is a moment's pause, a moment's silence. "My Anushka", he whispers and he takes me in his arms. "What can you make of me?" he asks. "The proverbial Don Juan who has fallen totally and utterly in love."

***

Later in the evening Dmitry confides to me that he has informed the bank that he might be taking his important 'private and confidential' client out for dinner at the *Slavyansky Bazar* and would not be at the bank till later the next day. At the same time he had told his wife, that if the dinner and business discussions went on later than expected into the evening, he would book a room at the hotel so as not to risk a cab ride home in the snow. It is only then that I realize that we can for the first time in our relationship spend the whole night together.

Does the relationship of a bank manager with a special client usually extend both to dinner and a night of pleasure in a hotel bedroom, I ask, pretending ingenuousness. He looks me in the eye and replies with feigned seriousness, that 'yes' it does happen from time to time. I react as he hoped I would!

Rousing ourselves some time later, I tell him in an intimate and risqué manner that his client is hungry and could she now have her dinner as part of the business arrangement that has been promised her? This light hearted, sensuous conversation seems quite natural now. The innocent young lady with the little dog, sent away a few weeks ago by her husband for the 'cure', has become a woman in her own right, flirting outrageously with a man who is not her husband.

In the restaurant we are served by the same waiter who attended me at lunch. He seems initially a little surprised that I had so quickly found myself a handsome gentleman with whom to share my dinner table. He is the soul of discretion.

We awake late the next morning. The bedroom floor is covered with our discarded clothing and the bed reveals a voluptuous disorder of sheets and counterpanes. We order breakfast to be brought to our room. When we finish eating, Dmitry looks out of the window at the snow that is now falling heavily.

We decide not to venture into the cold outdoors, but to spend our last few precious hours together in our sanctuary away from the problems of the world. We are silent, a silence that is companionable, each with our own thoughts. Mine are ones I could never have shared with Dmitry even though we are lovers.

Their essence is that women of our class and social position have a duty to appear indifferent to sex and to treat it as a necessary evil. Women are not expected to be sexually fulfilled and satisfied. This is how my husband regards our intercourse. My body is for his pleasure alone and never has he considered the fact that I too might have a sexual appetite. But now, through Dmitry's guidance I have discovered my own sensuality.

I am curious to know where he has learned some of the things that give me pleasure, and through gentle instruction from him, to take his pleasure from my body. Is it from nice respectable Moscovite ladies with whom I know he has had affairs, or is it from the wilder embraces of the gypsies whom he and his friends care to entertain in closed rooms at his club?

It doesn't matter, I just know that for the moment he is mine. I turn to him and find him lying on his chest. With a finger moistened in the glass of water on our bedside table I draw the letters D D S on his back and kiss the imprint of these letters. He turns over and presses his lips to my breasts. "Dmitry Dmitrych Serov, I love you," I whisper.

Later that day Dmitry returns reluctantly to his office and I equally reluctantly take the train back to Shchyolkovo. We have arranged to meet again in Moscow, as soon as I am able to persuade my husband that I need another visit to my specialist. If having my body intimately examined once again is the price to pay for such a meeting, then it is indeed a small price to pay.

February 28th 1899.

Today is the start of Maslenitsa. To pass the time I help Dunyasha in the kitchen. We make mounds of bliny using up all our supplies of butter and fat before the start of Lent. She has her own jealously guarded recipe handed down from her grandmother involving the customary wheat flour and buckwheat oats, but adding, as all peasants do, her own special ingredients such as pumpkin, apples and mashed potato. She finishes with caviar, mushrooms, jam and sour cream as a topping. We gorge ourselves on the pancakes, shaped a golden round to symbolize the return of the sun.

Later in the evening she and I escape from the house and venture down to the river where bonfires have been lit on the bank. We make an unlikely pair, mistress and servant together, but we both share a heightened sense of adventure and we enjoy each other's company. On our way we stumble across a scarecrow dressed in women's clothing, a symbol of Maslenitsa, being paraded along the river bank, and we witness its fate as it is tossed onto the flames of a bonfire.

Further along the river we come across a great Siberian bear standing high on its hind legs within the confines of a roughly made cage of birch logs. We watch transfixed as onlookers shout encouragement to a circle of men, who defying the cold are stripped to the waist. They release the muzzled beast from its cage and wrestle the creature till it is brought to its knees in the snow. At that stage we decide that it is time for us to make a strategic retreat before we are discovered.

Unfortunately Viktor is still awake when we eventually make our way home. He is not pleased with my account of the evening. He berates me firstly for going down to the river and secondly for taking Dunyasha with me. I apologize and ask him to forgive me. To make matters more poignant, the final Sunday of Maslenitsa is held by the church to be the traditional day for forgiveness. I tell him that couples are supposed to forgive each other for grievances and arguments that they have experienced together over the past year. Viktor and I have had our fair share of these, but he does not forgive me for my misdeeds.They are obviously all my fault. I retire to bed, once again chastised.

***

March 15th 1899.

Six weeks have gone by without my being able to find a way to see Dmitry. I cannot confront Viktor again with the need to visit yet another specialist in Moscow. I have therefore planned a subterfuge that will I hope bring us together. I have read in the latest edition of *Literaturnaya Gazetta* that the première of *Uncle Vanya* will be held at the Moscow Art Theatre in October this year, but that before the first performance the play will be touring the provinces.

I am excited to see that Shchyolkovo, being close to Moscow, is one of the first towns to figure in this brief tour. It is also rumoured that Chekhov himself will be attending these performances. The article in the magazine hints that even after numerous rehearsals the playwright is still not fully satisfied.. The reaction of live audiences, albeit from the provinces, will be useful to assess what needs to be changed.

I write to Dmitry another 'Private and Confidential' letter, the gist of which is that although his client cannot expect a repeat of the services of the bank that she had previously enjoyed in Moscow, perhaps her personal banker would like to visit her home town informally and attend this performance.

The matinee performance *of Uncle Vanya* has been scheduled for March 20th and in the hope that he will be able to come I book two seats in the stalls. My intrigue has worked. He writes back, confirming that he will be there on the day.

Dmitry arrives in Shchyolkovo and checks into his hotel. He has taken two days leave from the bank. Knowing full well what temptations might befall me as a consequence of a visit to his hotel room beforehand, I deliberately arrange to meet him at the theatre. It has been confirmed that Chekhov will be attending the performance. Dmitry will present his card at the box office before the performance in the hope that we will be invited backstage afterwards.

I am thrilled to see the stage setting as the curtain rises for Act One. It is just as we had planned it those months ago in the garden of the White Dacha. There is the swing that I had sat on, and the table and the bench with the samovar bubbling on its bed of charcoal. The poignancy of these memories brings me to the verge of tears.

Elena, played of course, by Olga Knipper swings languorously on 'my swing.' She is courted by Vanya and Astrov standing as Chekhov had directed, one on each side of her. Astrov is played by Stanislavsky, though I find his method of acting too intense and complicated.

The performance is reasonably well received, though I doubt whether our provincial audience fully understood the nuances of the play. To my delight Chekhov has remembered Dmitry's name from his visiting card and we are invited backstage. In his crowded dressing room he introduces us to Stanislavsky and his Director Nemirovch Danchenko.

"Dmitry Dmitrych Serov and Anna Ivanovna von Melk, the lady with a little dog," he quips with a twinkle in his eye as he introduces us. Even though the mention of this appellation, when explained to them, causes some mirth, there seems to be little warmth in their relationship with Chekhov. Both actor and director soon make excuses to leave us, pleading tiredness after the journey from Moscow.

Chekhov himself is as charming as ever and invites us to dine with him. I begin to demur. "No, no, it's the least I can do to repay you for your visit to me in Yalta," he says, taking me to one side. "After all, I am not often lucky enough to have a charming young lady visit me and provide the inspiration for my stage settings. And tonight, I'm sure you will agree, the audience caught that same frisson of sensuousness that both you and Olga displayed on your swing. What an introduction."

The conversation over dinner turns to the problems Chekhov is having with his actors and his producer, which may explain the cool atmosphere I had sensed backstage. When they had asked him how he wanted *Uncle Vanya* played he had written out a brief explanation to give to the cast.

"Above all avoid theatricality. Try to be as simple as possible. Remember that they are all ordinary people," Chekhov had written to Stanislavsky, who then deliberately went out of his way to ignore these instructions by adding an extraneous melodramatic excess to the role of Astrov. On stage he wandered round the house and garden, noting everything, examining the plants, picking off the dead heads from the flowers. Even worse, he swatted imaginary mosquitoes and as extra protection had taken to putting a handkerchief over his face.

Chekhov turns to us and says jokingly. " In my next play I'll make a stipulation. The action takes place in a country which has neither mosquitoes nor crickets nor any other insects which bite or sting and hinder conversation."

After the meal we part, thanking Anton Pavlovich for his hospitality. He invites us to visit him again after the Moscow première of *The Seagull* later in the year. If his health holds up and he can leave Yalta, he adds ominously.

Dmitry and I stand outside the theatre looking for a carriage to take us to our separate destinations. We know that there is no way that we can spend the night together in his hotel. I have already sent a messenger to warn my husband that I will be coming home late, but apart from that I can think of no reasonable excuse to stay away for the night. Our frustration is almost palpable.

Eventually Dmitry finds a driver. They seem to be in a lengthy discussion, which is cut short by Dmitry bundling me into the carriage.

"Poidi!" shouts our cabbie with a crack of his whip and the ramshackle vehicle sets off. We pull down the blinds to make ourselves inconspicuous to any passersby out on the streets at this late hour. We know that we will not be able to spend long together and give ourselves up to the most passionate of embraces.

The moon has risen and in the snow the streets, lanes and open countryside are clearly visible. At a given destination, the church of a neighbouring village, our driver halts to rest his horse and waits for a further command. The similarity with Emma Bovary and Leon in their hansom cab in Rouen comes involuntarily to mind. Fortunate Emma, I think, she has hours with her lover whereas I have only minutes.

All too soon we are back in town and stopping at the grey nail topped wall that encloses my prison. It is midnight and only one light still burns in the hall, where a maid is waiting for me, my husband presumably having retired to bed some hours earlier. I hurry indoors covering bruised lips and burning cheeks with my fur stole. It is my Dunyasha who hands me my candle. Diplomatically she does not comment on the disarrangement of my clothes as she helps me undress. I retire to bed, but cannot fall asleep till the early hours of the morning, such is the intensity of my unfulfilled passion.

{8}

March 25th 1899.

Today I find myself in something of a quandary. Over our evening meal Viktor informs me that he has been invited to attend a Government conference in St. Petersburg, a singular honour for his Department, he tells me more than once. He generously offers to take me with him for a few days. He rather sarcastically points out that I might still find there a few of my former Lycée friends who, surprisingly enough, have not yet moved to Moscow with their husbands.

My heart misses a beat, my first reaction to this remark being that Viktor is suspicious. But on reflection I persuade myself that it is no more than one of my husband's misguided attempts at humour. When I recover my senses and can think clearly again, I tell myself that he cannot be suspicious. If he were, and knowing my husband's innate curiosity, he would immediately want to have details of those friends of mine, with whom I purported to have stayed during my visits to Moscow. And the interrogation would have gone on until he had forced the truth from me.

I wish, how I wish, he would go to St. Petersburg alone, spend as long as he wanted there, find himself a nice mistress and leave me in peace. I could then spend the time in Moscow with Dmitry and on his return confront Viktor with the fact that I too had a lover.

But this is no more than a ridiculous day dream. What he will do instead is spend his free time discussing politics with his cronies rather than going out to the bars and clubs of our capital city with his more fun loving colleagues. As a woman I cannot know for sure, but I imagine that there must surely be some men, even those in Ministry circles, who would be eager to discover the charms of young ladies of an easy disposition, with whom to spend a pleasant evening after a day's discussion of Government matters.

Trying not to sound churlish I decline his offer on the grounds that another long train journey might complicate my medical problems. It is now two months since I have been to Moscow and I long to be back there. My room in the *Slavyansky Bazar* is beckoning. I tell Viktor that I will be able to amuse myself in his absence, that I may go to Moscow but that as yet I have nothing definite planned. Not yet having written to Dmitry I suppose that there is a certain modicum of truth in this statement.

But as always with these deceptions it makes me sad that I have to conceal my real intentions. My husband accepts my refusal with an irritable shrug of the shoulders. I tell him to go out in the evening and enjoy himself after a long day's work on Council matters, but I really do not think that he understands the concept of enjoyment as other men do. There must still lurk some intangible puritanical thread in his character linking him with his family's ancestral past in that austere, forbidding monastery on the Danube.

I write to Dmitry to tell him that at last I will be back in Moscow and I give him the dates that my husband will be in St. Petersburg. All I can do now is to wait, but time passes agonizingly slowly. I must find something useful to do to fill these empty hours. I attend to household matters to such an extent that Viktor praises me for my diligence. Dunyasha and I spend long hours together preparing for the spring cleaning which will start in a few day's time. We chat together as we work. She tells me about the fisherman's boy who helps his father on his rounds and takes advantage of their visits to the house to ogle her. He is perfectly presentable, but is he the right one, she wonders? She blushes as she admits to me that she has resorted to peasant superstition to find the answer.

One night she placed a couple of cockroaches under her pillow when she went to bed. That way she hopes to dream of the man she is to marry, but so far the results have not been encouraging. I do not like the thought of cockroaches escaping from under her pillow during the night, so I tell her that she should try an alternative superstition which is to take a pack of cards and place the king of diamonds where the cockroaches had been. Had I tried that myself, she asks and I have to admit that I had not. If I had, perhaps life would be different now, who knows?

Pelageya comes in from the kitchen to receive her orders for today's dinner. We are in joking mood and we tell her about cockroaches and kings of diamonds and she joins in the conversation, citing superstitions of her own. This very day she saw a blackbird land on the kitchen window, but she chased it away before it could bring bad luck.

Dunyasha and I have been laughing so much that our eyes are watering. "Madam," says Pelageya, mistaking my tears for an irritation, "If your right eye itches you are soon going to be happy, but if it is your left eye then you will be sad."

"And we all know about lips," teases Dunyasha. "Pelegaya, I do believe your lips are itching. This means that you will be kissing someone soon." Our good maid collapses in giggles, blushes to the roots of her hair and retreats to her kitchen. She has gone back, says Dunyasha, to pass all this nonsense on to her domovoi, her house spirit who lives in the kitchen.

Lying in bed that evening I reflect on our Russian society and the gulf that exists between the peasants and our cultivated middle and upper classes. We speak, read and write in two languages with almost equal ease, whereas they are illiterate and speak in a patois which is scarcely comprehensible to us. They believe in cockroaches and house spirits and all sorts of superstitions, have never travelled further than a few versts away from home, whilst we have wider horizons, St. Petersburg, Moscow and other cities. I love them all dearly, not forgetting our faithful Afanasy with his outdoor duties, carriage, sledge, horses, log cutting and so on. Where would we, our privileged, pampered class be without them?

***

April has arrived, the spring thaw setting in earlier than usual. Icicles that have hung from roofs for five months are now dropping onto pavements like lethal daggers. The local authorities have closed areas of the city where this is likely to happen, so Tuzik and I are denied our usual routine. We have to make do with walks along the river. A fretful wind blows from the water and I walk fast, urging Tuzik to keep pace with me. Along the river bank the trees shedding their winter coats of snow are the only danger now. The new walk is boring in the extreme, but I do not care. Each completed circuit brings me closer to Moscow.

At last the day finally arrives. I pack a light bag of clothes, take the afternoon train to Moscow and once again book into the *Slavyansky Bazar*. But back in the city of my dreams I learn too cruelly the frustrations of being a mistress, its passion and its heartbreak. Afternoon lengthens into evening and I wait in vain for Dmitry. I go down to the vestibule of the hotel to while away the time. On the walls hang a number of portraits by Ilya Repin, a little known artist. They are of famous Russian musicians. Amongst them two strike my eye. I recognize Pyotr Ilyich Tchaikovsky and Nikolai Andreyevich Rimsky Korsakov, both of whom Dmitry and I had seen dining at the *Slavyansky Bazar* on our previous visit.

However I am plagued by the attention of two gentlemen who quite uninvitedly engage me in conversation and give me their opinion of the pictures. I suppose a single lady waiting in the vestibule of a hotel gave them the wrong idea of her intentions! But it is annoying to say the least to be mistaken in this vulgar way. I curtly dismiss their unwanted attention by going out onto Nikolskaya Street, which has an admirable heated arcade. I've been told that it is the first of its kind in Russia and it certainly makes a pleasant place for shopping on a freezing spring evening.

I discover a wine shop in the arcade that at this hour is still open and on a whim I enter. It will be a nice surprise for Dmitry, when he does come, to have a glass of sparkling wine waiting for him. However the shop assistant is less than welcoming. I suppose I am probably the first single lady to enter his shop and he presumes that I know nothing about wine.

In the most condescending manner he starts to tell me about his wines. On the shelves I catch sight of some familiar vintages. Give me a Magarach sparkling wine and a Cabernet Sauvignon from the Massandra Imperial Estate in Yalta, vintage 1896, I interrupt his flow of words. I remember how Dmitry and I had enjoyed both of these during my initiation into wine over those leisurely dinners on the Promenade. The wretched man continues to serve me in silence!

After that rather unpleasant sortie I take the bottles back to my room, placing the red by the radiator for warmth and the sparkling wine to chill between the inner and outer panes of the window. I look around the modest room. It seems so bare and ordinary whilst I am in it by myself, but know that it will be transformed as if by magic into our love nest the moment Dmitry comes to share it. I gaze anew at the pictures on the walls depicting scenes of Moscow, the familiar inkstand in the form of a mounted horseman holding his hat in his uplifted hand and whose head has been broken off.

I move it aside to make room on the table by the window for two champagne glasses. I wait, wait patiently and then as time passes, more and more impatiently. Come soon, my darling, come now or I will die of wanting you, I plead.

But my waiting and all my well laid plans are in vain. A messenger from the bank late in the evening delivers a note to the effect that Dmitry will not be able to join me owing to some unforeseen meeting. Not with a female client he has heavily underlined! I had selected his favourite grey dress in which to greet him, but now in a fit of pique I rip it off, leaving the hateful garment discarded on the floor.

Before I settle myself for the night in my solitary bed I have an abundance of time to reflect on our lives. It seems so awful that these meetings have to be conducted under the cloak of secrecy. The need to live a double life, these assignations in a hotel bedroom, now appear to me sordid and not worthy of our love. I am jealous of everything that takes him away from me, of his wife, his daughters, his work in the bank and of every moment we cannot be together.

***

The next morning Dmitry comes to me after taking his daughter to school. The spring weather of the past weeks has disappeared. A thick wet snow is falling though it is three degrees above freezing. As he comes through the bedroom door the cold comes in with him, trapped in the folds of his clothes and clinging to his hair. I am acting like a child, having a tantrum, crying and sobbing.

Dmitry does not have time to divest himself of his coat before I rush at him, hitting him on the chest with my fists to vent all my pent up anger. I feel exhausted, having slept badly and to spite him I have deliberately not put on the grey dress, which as a rebuke to him still lies discarded on the floor. In silence he picks it up, folds it neatly and puts it carefully on the bed. Probably for the first time in our relationshipship he sees me angry, unsmiling. I brush his kisses away and pour out my heart to him between sobs.

"I've missed you so much, it's not fair, how can you make me suffer like this? If I cannot see you, I think I will die. Oh Dmitry, please promise me this cannot happen again."

He does not answer. What is there he can say? He orders tea to be brought up. These tears of mine are something new, something he cannot deal with. He turns his back to look through the window at the snow falling from a sullen, grey sky. Eventually I stop crying and find myself able to continue in a more measured manner. I tell him that I am angry with myself, that our lives are ruined, that there can never be a happy outcome, that we are trapped, meeting in secret, hiding from other people like thieves in the night, constantly deceiving those close to us.

Dmitry takes me in his arms, smoothing down my hair, which in our fighting has become dissheveled. He reassures me, says that we will find a solution,but for the time being we can put these problems to one side. What we need now is some activity to distract us.

Now that I have someone to admire my looks, I have developed a predelection for shopping. Before leaving for Moscow I told my husband that I needed some new clothes and he kindly gave me money to spend as I liked. Braving the snow Dmitry and I leave the hotel and spend some time visiting shops on Petrovka Street, where I look in vain for a new dress and some ribbons for my hats.

I tell Dmitry that there are a number of balls in Shchyolkovo, which the Ministry arranges and which I have to attend as an appendage of my husband. On the last occasion, when I encountered the young men whispering about Madame Bovary, I had worn a nondescript black dress. As a new woman with a lover on my arm to advise me about Moscow fashions on the cusp of the new century I feel that I can wear something more alluring.

Dmitry tells me that he knows an excellent French fashion shop further on at the crossroads with Kuznetsky Most. I have not the temerity to ask him how he knows of such a shop, though of course it would be naïve of me if I did not have my suspicions. We stop in front of what looks like a hideously expensive boutique displaying in the window some of the most exquisite dresses I have ever seen.

"This is the Moscow branch of De Moncy's Paris Fashion Shop", Dmitry informs me. "There's been a shop on these premises since the early part of the century. If we can't find a gown for you here, we may as well give up and keep you in your bustle!"

I hesitate outside the shop but Dmitry is not to be gainsayed. "Come on, don't be shy. A beautiful woman like you deserves nothing less than a beautiful dress to match. I know the staff here. I'll make certain that they don't intimidate you."

We enter the premises, whereupon Dmitry is greeted warmly as the regular customer that of course he is. We are seated and brought tea and cakes. There seems to be no hurry at all to start showing us the latest Parisian fashions.

Instead, Madame Blanche, the Head Couturier, recounts an amusing anecdote apropos one of the shop's first customers back in the 1820s. This was an eccentric, elderly and very rich lady by the name of Anna Annenkova, who lived on this same Petrovka Street. She bought many of her ball gowns here at De Moncy's but at night time, instead of putting on her night clothes to go to bed, she would get dressed up in her latest gown, silk stockings and elegant shoes and then retire to bed. Thus she was ready at any time of the night if a call should come inviting her to a ball.

Dmitry turns to me and jokes that here is another Anna with such an amazing social life in Shchyolkovo that she too will have to go to bed in the very ball gown, which we are bound to find here.

This stirs the staff to action and two shop assistants take .me into the fitting room. In the scant privacy that a curtain across the door of the cubicle provides they tell me that I have a remarkable figure and recommend a fashionable ball gown which will accentuate my shape.

It takes some considerable time to make certain that I have arranged the dress *comme il faut*, as the assistants insist. The reason for this becomes apparent when I look at myself in the mirror. To my embarrassment, instead of my usual modestly cut ball gowns with long sleeves and a bustle I catch sight of a woman with a décolletage and a corset that pushes up her breasts to an extent that I feel is outrageously immodest. The shop girls find a pair of long gloves which are apparently now de rigeur to cover my bare arms and an elaborate necklace to wear around my neck to complement my décolletage and my bare shoulders.

I am preparing to take off this immodest gown when Dmitry, who with a degree of impatience has been waiting outside the fitting room, puts his head round the curtain. He gazes at me admiringly.

"Anna, you look divine. Leave it on for a moment so that I can admire it properly. You will be the envy of every woman at your balls in Shchyolkovo and should there be any red blooded men in that provincial backwater of yours, they will be fighting amongst themselves to claim a dance."

My thrill over the new gown is tempered by the sad reflection, that I will never be able to have him see me dressed in all my finery. Moscow balls for him, of which there are a number each year, will be attended by him and his wife. Mistresses are not likely to be invited! After my precious dress has been packed up I choose some new ribbons for my hair to match my new wardrobe and a mother of pearl encrusted fan, which strictly speaking I do not need, but which simply takes my fancy.

It is at this stage of the proceedings that I realize I am still wearing the necklace. I turn to one of the assistants to have the clasp undone. However Madame Blanche insists without a moment's hesitation that I keep the necklace, that I should wear it to the ball and return it to the shop when I am next in Moscow. It is only then that I fully understand how important a client Dmitry must be. He is evidently seen as surety for the safe return of such a precious loan.

The temptation to accept this proposal is almost too great to resist. I look at myself in the looking glass, hesitate and then decline her offer. I remember a heart breaking story by the French writer Guy de Maupassant. I recount his story of a young lady borrowing a diamond necklace from a friend to wear to a ball, losing it and spending ten years repaying loans of 40,000 francs for a replacement necklace which she has to buy, only to be told by this friend, when they meet years later by chance, that the necklace she had borrowed was made of paste and was worth no more than 400 francs at most.

I take off the necklace as if it is burning my throat and return it to Madame Blanche. She says that she must read some stories by this Frenchman if they are all as poignant as the one I have related. As I pay for the ribbons and my fan from my own money, or to be more accurate from the amount Viktor has given me for my purchases, I realize how easy it is for me to do so. I feel a moment's sadness for poor Emma Bovary. I have my own money and in addition, Dmitry will pay for anything I want. So unlike the fate of wretched Emma whose inability to settle her debts contributes to her death.

We still have some precious hours together so we take a cab to the newly opened Tretyakov Art Gallery. I remember Chekhov telling us on our visit to Yalta that Isaac Levitan, a relatively unknown artist, was a friend of his. So we find the gallery where his paintings are on display and admire his evocation of the Russian landscape through the changing seasons of the year.

The knowledge that we will shortly have to part saddens me once again. Dmitry leaves me for a minute to buy cigars in the gallery's shop and in his absence I fall into reflecting on how, since my first meeting with him, the nature of my desire for him has been transformed. Our first love making had been inevitable, my being carried along irrationally, scarcely knowing what I was entering into. But now it is different. He has become a physical necessity. I need to smell the scent of his body, his hair and his clothes, feel the smooth skin on his body. He is something that not only do I want to possess, but a possesion to which I have a right.

For the hundredth time I wish we were a married couple, walking through the deserted galleries arm in arm without fear of being recognized, maybe simply spending the evening in our own company in our own home. But there is no going back to a home together, no meeting with mutual friends, no normal life ahead of us. Just the futility of sharing a love while not sharing a life.

We dine in our usual restaurant, served by the same sympathetic waiter, but the magic of our previous dinner there is not to be repeated. We now recognize the enormity of our dilemma. This time there is no holding hands under the table, no anticipation of physical pleasures to come, only a darkening of our mood as we count the hours before we have to separate.

During the night we make love, but almost as if we are man and wife, two very dear friends. We talk and talk. We feel that destiny has intended us for each other and it is a mystery why Dmitry should have a wife and I a husband, partners whom we do not love. Whereas the person we do truly love is unattainable except for brief moments each month. We are leading a double life of duplicity and deception.

It begins to snow again during the night. Sleepily I watch the flakes settle on the window pane, silvery against the lamplight in our little haven. We have no desire to leave the warmth of the bedroom. We take a leisurely breakfast in our room and try again to make sense of our complicated lives.

I do not want a fate similar to that of the characters in another of Chekhov's short stories, *The House with a Mezzanine.* There the possibility of happiness is destroyed through inertia and a wanton act of jealousy. We must act to save ourselves.

We discuss various possibilities. The idea of a trip to Yalta each year to meet for two to three weeks. That we discount out of hand. The memories would be too poignant and the journey too long. Or we could flout society's conventions and live openly together. Dmitry says that this is impossible. He has a wife and children and a position in the bank.

A divorce, but on what grounds? The thought of needing to provide sufficient evidence of adultery makes us both feel sick. Or we could just carry on seeing each other as we are doing now. To live for the excitement of a clandestine tryst every month, despite the deceptions involved. To make love, to go to concerts and galleries, to be entertained by Dmitry showing off his beloved Moscow, all this would be so wonderful if only we could achieve this perfection without deceiving our respective partners. But how?

***

It is time to leave. I have a train to catch and Dmitry has work to attend to in the bank. We dress and go out onto Nikolskaya Street. At last the snow has stopped, the sky has cleared and a weak wintry sun lights up the golden cupolas of the Kazan Cathedral. Moscow suddenly looks beautiful again and our mood lightens.

Life will be equally beautiful. We love each other, that is enough for the moment. No one knows us in Moscow. We can walk close together, clutching each other's arm as we cross the road avoiding puddles left by the melting snow.

In a few minutes we reach the Yaroslavsky Station, where my train back to Shchyolkovo is waiting. Standing on the platform we kiss goodbye, both knowing that if we are constant enough in our search to find it, a solution will appear. Dmitry jokes that as a last resort we could go back to Yalta, visit Chekhov in his White Dacha and ask him for the denouement of his short story *The Lady with a Little Dog.* After all, as Dmitry reminds me, I had provided Anton Pavlovich with the title for this short story. Perhaps he could help us a little more now by writing a satisfactory solution to our dilemma!

However, being fully aware of how ambiguous and inconclusive Chekhov's endings to his stories so often are, I reply that perhaps he has no more idea than we have of how to solve the dilemma, in which his hero and heroine find themselves. We kiss again as the third bell rings. The final solution to our dilemma may be far, far away, but I am certain it will be found, and then a new and beautiful life will begin for both of us.

So I believed in my innocence. But belief in this new and beautiful life seems illusory the moment I enter through the gates of my prison and take up the daily drudgery of life again in Shchyolkovo. Neither could I at this stage have foreseen the momentous events that were shortly to take place in my life and ultimately shape my destiny.

{9}

By the start of May this year spring has finally arrived. May Day itself, with a warm wind blowing off the Klyasma river, heralds the arrival of our beloved storks flying in to take up their customary residence in their nest on our chimney. I wonder where they've spent the winter, perhaps in the warmer climes of Ukraine or even in Crimea.

I feel a pang of envy, remembering being taught in school that the arrival of these birds heralds the advent of Spring and the season of fertility We were told that their lifetime mating and care for their offspring was an example to us humans. Bitter thoughts come to me. I am doomed to be childless and mated for life with a man for whom I do not care.

But now on the first of May, even here in our boring little town, there bodes an unexpected diversion. By nine o'clock my husband has taken himself off to the Ministry. Despite recognizing the traditional festivities associated with May Day, his office remains open for the likes of dear Viktor, who wishes to attend to some important matter of business. Before leaving the house he warns me that I am not to go out into the city centre. For some time he has been reading aloud to me at dinner time articles from the local Shchyolkovo newspaper. He mutters in indignation at what he reads.

The cause of his muttering is an inflammatory pamphlet which a certain Vladimir Ilyich Ulyanov has written on behalf of the Kharkov Committee of the Russian Democratic Labour Party. In it there is a call for no less than the political liberation of the Russian people. Viktor has warned me that there is likely to be a demonstration by the proletariat, a new word in our language referring to the urban working population. Rumours proliferate that there could be civil unrest even here in Shcholkyovo and I am to keep away from the city centre.

My husband is certainly not going to tell me what I can or cannot do. So deliberately disobeying his orders I make my way to the Cathedral Square to witness the happenings at first hand. I am met by a sight that causes me concern. The age old May Day traditions of people rejoicing in the return of Spring with music, roundabouts and swings, food and drink stalls, street entertainers, fortune tellers and of course the obligatory shackled dancing bears, are still in evidence. But on this occasion they are set against something new and disturbing.

A large procession of workers is making its way towards our Local Government buildings, unfurling red flags and waving placards. The demonstration, unusual though it is, seems peaceful enough. It reaches the steps of the building where its leaders ask permission to present their demands to the Governor. From what I can see scrawled on the placards their demands are for an eight hour working day together with some sort of limited political representation.

Some of the placards bear the names of the factories taking part in the demonstration. Amongst these the brick works and the tannery are the most prominent. With a shudder I imagine the working conditions in each of these. It is bad enough taking a carriage through the outskirts of Shchyolkovo where these places are situated and to smell the stench from their chimneys. Here for one sunny day these labourers are able to enjoy the fresh spring air, yet at the same time they feel a need to make public their discontent. I hope the procession will pass off peacefully and that the police, or worse still the soldiers, will not be called out.

I wonder what Viktor would be thinking if he were to peer out of the windows of his office. Arrest the whole lot, shoot the ringleaders and this will deter any more of their ridiculous demands.This would be his reply. The crowd begins to drift away peacefully after it becomes clear that no one is going to come out onto the steps and receive their petition.

Later that evening, when we are dining together, Viktor laughs at the lack of organization shown by the strikers here in Shchyolkovo. He admits that events in Kharkov and elsewhere in the country pose much more of a threat than here in our little backwater. Civil unrest will be put down with the greatest show of force, he assures me. Should there in future be another incident of this nature, soldiers will be ordered onto the streets to dispel participants, with no concern for injury or loss of life.

The new century is about to begin with a threat of violence, a stupid, heavy handed reaction to peaceful demonstrations which surely can only lead to bloodshed and class conflict. Russia is an unjust society, whether you are classed as a proletarian worker, a peasant or in my case simply a female, who does not accept her place in the social order.

***

May 2nd 1899.

My daily routine, however, has to be followed and life reverts to its usual pattern. It is a fine day and I take Tuzik for his customary exercise. I embark on a longer walk into town, knowing that the latest edition of the literary magazine *Russian Thought*, to which Viktor subscribes, will be waiting for collection at the bookshop on Central Square. As I approach the square I join a group of curious sightseers watching workmen erecting lamp posts along the four sides of the square. On my enquiry I am told that Shchyolkovo is installing gas lighting in the central areas of the town. To this end workmen are busy putting up last minute decorations for the inaugural ceremony at which the lights will be switched on. I vaguely remember Viktor telling me something along these lines since his department has been responsible for the project from start to finish. But like most of the things that Viktor tells me over dinner I must have been listening with only half an ear and had paid scant attention to his remarks.

Our daily custom is for my husband and me to meet at dinner time. These meals are not something that I could say I look forward to. To break the silence that usually accompanies our meal I ask him to tell me the latest news about this gaslighting project. He replies, that despite the opposition of many local people, the Council has decided to go ahead with the project to erect gas lights in the city centre. In that pompous, patronizing voice of his which I loathe so much he begins.

"We have spent years trying to overcome the prejudices of our townsfolk and peasants who see gas lighting as no more than 'the devil's candle', as they call it. These people are intensely suspicious. They consider it to be a diabolic mockery of the Divine, calling it a sacrilegious parody of our natural God-given light source. Not one of them has travelled the few versts from here to Moscow, where they have had street lighting since 1865. No doubt our own servants, your beloved Dunyasha included of course, will join the chorus of our peasantry calling it ' the devil's candle' and cross themselves when we switch on the gas lights. Just as they believe there are goblins howling in the stove when the wind blows from the north. It would be no exaggeration to say that they contribute to a contagion of superstition that lies across this country and hinders our progress into the twentieth century."

I interrupt. "Of course they are superstitious, Viktor, don't be so disparaging and critical. Just remember that they are not fortunate enough to have had the sort of education that you and I have been privileged to enjoy. For them hobgoblins really do howl in the chimney and when they see a gas flame the Devil really does light a candle. Thanks to the lack of any meaningful education for them here in Shchyolkovo they are all illiterate and are unable to read the holy books to know any better."

Viktor is not to be knocked off his high horse. His religious beliefs mixed with prejudice lead him on. He does not take kindly to women crossing him in argument and he is not to be interrupted.

"They don't have to read, they can listen to readings from the Bible in church. They would then learn that in Genesis the first thing the Creator did was to separate light from darkness. In our own way the Council is doing no more than that. That is why I have been so busy these past few weeks and I will not brook any opposition to our project from any quarter whatsoever. In some ways I consider it a mission given to me by God.

By the way, I need to inform you that we are arranging an opening ceremony at which the Mayor, Governor and local dignitaries will witness the illumination of the lights. Following that there will be a Grand Ball at the Assembly Rooms to celebrate the admirable achievement of being the first town in the province to have gas lighting on its streets. As I have been instrumental in setting up and masterminding the successful completion of this project, I am to be guest of honour at the reception. I will be expected to make a speech during the Ball. You will of course as my wife be attending these festivities with me. I suggest that you buy a new dress for the occasion."

I can scarcely refrain from laughing. Little does he know that I have my new dress ready for me in my wardrobe. I now have the ideal opportunity to launch myself into Shchyolkovo society in my new persona. The prospect of a ball with music, dancing and champagne, even with the most boring of councillors and their wives, will make a pleasant change to the monotony of evenings spent in our dismal house.

Dmitry's remarks about the effect that the new dress will have on those attending the ball, both male and female, ring in my ears. It makes anticipation all the more exciting. I think of the young whisperers at the last function I attended. I calculate that I must be roughly the same age as them. It would be amusing to converse with them and perhaps even to be invited on to the dance floor. Though on reflection that might not be such a good idea. No doubt they would be overawed by the fact that I was their Department Head's wife!

My diary entry for the next day is brief in the extreme. After my outburst over dinner I had written: *Teach Dunyasha to read and write.* I had been so annoyed with Viktor's disparaging remarks about our servants. Dunyasha, despite our difference in class, is my closest friend and we often discuss intimate matters together when in the evening she helps me undress. I know that each time I send her to the shops she must be embarrassed by her illiteracy. She is unable to read what I write on the shopping list and I can imagine how awkward she must feel when she has to hand over her scrap of paper for the shop keeper to read.

Yet here am I with a fine secondary education, fluent in both my native language and in French, living cheek by jowl in the same house with an equally intelligent woman, who through no fault of her own is destined to remain illiterate for the rest of her life. If I am to remain true to my professed liberal ideals I can do no better than to put them into practice here in my own household.

And so I put my suggestion to her. Dunyasha proves to be a quick learner and within a few weeks with my help she will be writing her own shopping lists and starting to read simple childrens' books. A start, however small and insignificant, has been made. One female servant out of the millions in our glorious empire is becoming literate.

***

The great and glorious gaslight inauguration is set for Saturday evening, to be followed as widely advertised by the Grand Ball at the Assembly Rooms. Viktor has been on edge all week preparing his speech and working late at his office on last minute details of the ceremony. When the great day finally arrives we all process to Central Square. The band strikes up as the Governor, Viktor in his capacity as Project Coordinator, the Mayor and assorted dignitaries in their various uniforms mount the platform which has been erected in the square.

At a given signal the band stops playing and an expectant silence falls upon the crowd. The order is given to the firelighters, each one with a ladder in position against his respective lamp post, to light the gas mantles. Many of the onlookers cross themselves and an apprehensive murmur spreads across the square.

I must say that the effect is dramatic. One moment the pavements are in semi darkness. The next moment the whole square begins to be bathed in light and we can make out the faces of spectators lining the four sides of the square. The potholes, broken paving slabs and the general rubbish which always litter our streets are also clearly visible, which rather diminishes the hoped for overall magnificence of the scene.

"Bravo," a shout rings out from one of the spectators and the crowd joins in a spontaneous round of applause. The Governor seems to be delighted with the whole ceremony and I can see him chatting to Viktor and shaking his hand. No doubt my husband will regale me later with a tedious account of their conversation. But I am spared for the moment, as it is time to take the carriage home to dress for the ball.

Viktor and I dress in our separate bedrooms. Dunyasha helps me dress, looking in amazement at the ball gown, into which I am struggling with some difficulty. She helps lace up my bodice and tighten the stays round my waist before we both ease the gown over my head. She gasps as she sees the full effect of the dress taking shape around my body The combined effect of bare shoulders and arms is something she has never seen before. She is used only to helping me into my staid black dresses and bustles. For warmth I pull my shawl around my shoulders and put on a light coat for the journey to the ball, thus hiding effectively from my husband the full effect of my dress.

It is only when we arrive at the Assembly Rooms and leave our outer clothes at the cloakroom that Viktor catches sight of my new gown. I have put matching ribbons in my hair. My dress in its full glory, my bare shoulders, long gloves up to the elbow and a dazzling necklace complete my attire.

Holding my new fan and dance card lightly in one hand and with a gracious smile I casually curtsey to my husband, as if he is inviting me for the next dance. There is nothing out of the ordinary, I wish to imply, in a young lady's ball gown chosen with care for the most important social event of the year. I give another flirtatious curtsey, open my fan and take him by the arm. I feel a moment's pity for him. Poor man, he could so easily have stumbled. His demure, utterly respectable wife, whom at previous social functions he is accustomed to seeing in her unremarkable, chaste black dress, has suddenly been transformed into a young woman wearing a ballroom gown that is the height of fashion in no less a capital city than Paris. At the entrance to the ballroom we take our place on the marble staircase amongst the other guests waiting to be received by the

Governor and his wife. Only then does Viktor have a chance to speak to me.

"Anna, where on earth did you get that dress?" he whispers.

"It's quite simple, Viktor," I whisper back. " You told me to get something new for this occasion. I found a little shop in Moscow on my last visit. I didn't realize that it was so , I pause to find the right word, so 'revealing' when I tried it on. But I was assured that the style was quite à la mode. Anyway I'm certain that it will be a great improvement on what I was wearing last time. I really believe Shchyolkovo must be the last town in Russia where women still wear the bustle and parade around in dresses that look like tents. I wanted something more fashionable, I wanted to be worthy of you, and dear Viktor, I wanted something that would enhance your reputation in the eyes of your Ministry colleagues here tonight."

This last remark produces the effect on Viktor that I knew it would. As soon as I mention the word ' reputation', the old Viktor surfaces. My lackey of a husband is clearly thinking about the enhancement of his status in Government circles, to which a wife as attractively turned out as I am, will no doubt contribute. An ordinary husband would have complimented his wife on her appearance, but Viktor is no ordinary husband and his thoughts for the time being are directed elsewhere.

At last we reach the head of the queue. A liveried footman announces our names to the Governor and his wife. He greets us.

"My dear Viktor Aleksandrovich, a pleasure to meet you again. We will talk later about your achievements in the Ministry, but tell me, why haven't you brought your charming wife to previous functions here in Shchyolkovo?

Although he is addressing my husband he is gazing at me rather too attentively. I am about to reply to the effect that

I have indeed attended such functions in the past, when Viktor breaks in. In his view a mere wife does not address a Governor. However the latter seemed to have lost interest in Viktor's reply. Regarding my gown with an appreciative eye, he raises his voice and in a bantering tone continues.

"Viktor Aleksandrovich, what a card you are. How have you managed to hide away such a beautiful and charming young lady for so long? I must claim a dance with her before her card is filled." His wife does not share his enthusiasm and turns to welcome the next guests.

Viktor is delighted with the impression that I have made on no less a person than the Governor. He even goes so far as to lead me onto the dance floor as the strains of the first waltz are heard. Since he rarely dances, this is an unusual honour for me.

Perhaps on the dance floor he wishes to show me off to as many of his circle of petty Government officials as possible. If this is true, it is a new insight into my husband's behaviour. His very ordinary wife is now exposed to the cream of local society by a proud husband and the Governor's remarks are still ringing in his ears.

To my good fortune the dance is soon over and Viktor excuses himself, saying that he needs to continue his conversation with the Governor. After that he will make up a foursome at cards. And of course I must not forget, he tells me, he has to read over his speech, which he is to deliver during the dinner interval.

Normally when left on my own in such a situation I turn to the wives of his colleagues and engage in boring small talk. On this occasion, however, I am pleasantly surprised to find a number of these wives' husbands asking if they may mark my dance card.

The evening progresses well enough, save for one dance when a portly Government official gazing down my décolletage treads repeatedly on my toes. I find him irksome to a degree. At the end of this particularly painful experience and massaging my feet I tenderly make my way towards a small anteroom, where an enticing buffet is laid out. A large part of the evening still lies ahead and I am sorely in need of sustenance. The acquisition of a further glass of champagne will help me endure any further painful experiences that I may be subjected to on the dance floor.

As I wait for my glass to be replenished I catch sight of a young gentleman, whom I recognize as one of the group of Madame Bovary whisperers, as I had named them. Perhaps seeing me temporarily on my own he approaches me and introduces himself.

"Sergey Ivanovich Platonov, at your service, Madame von Melk. I believe, however, that we are already acquainted. I am employed in your husband's office and if I remember correctly, we met at a previous Government function. If you are not already engaged for the next dance, might I have the honour of making a request ?"

I thank him, though for the life of me I cannot remember any such prior encounter where our paths might have crossed. Which is true as he does in fact have the honesty much later in the evening to reveal that he had simply used this excuse in order to engage me in conversation. However it is a pleasant surprise to find out that at least one of Viktor's subordinates is not so in awe of his Department Head's wife as to ask her for a dance.

As by chance my card shows no partner for the next dance, a quadrille, I feel that I am honour bound to accept his offer. His youthfulness, good looks and full head of black curls will make a pleasant change from my previous aged and bald headed partners. My new gentleman dances superbly well. While we are resting in the quadrille as other couples complete their set I feel relaxed for the first time this evening, confessing to myself that I am finding enjoyment in his company. After the dance my partner seems loathe to let me go. We walk together towards the table where I have left my fan, shawl and dance card. Once ensconced at our seats there is a moment's silence. Out of politeness I feel I have to continue our conversation.

"Well, Sergey Ivanovich, where did you learn to dance so well?" I ask. The bravado and the self confidence which he had shown in his dancing is now replaced by an awkwardness, an uncertainty as to how to proceed in such a novel situation. I feel for him and put my head close to his to catch his words in the noisy atmosphere of the ball room.

"I'm a graduate in engineering from the University of St. Petersburg," he replies. "As students we always attended balls held at the Faculty. It was a pleasant way to enjoy ourselves and to meet the young ladies of our capital city. A certain ability on the dance floor was de rigueur. After graduating I obtained a post here in the local Council. I'm employed in your husband's Department, which as you know is involved in our city's street lighting project. As part of the Engineering team I was invited to attend this celebratory ball. So here I am, a little bit out of my depth in this august company."

Out of the corner of my eye I can see a number of elderly gentlemen hovering around the dance hall, looking for partners as the strains of a waltz strikes up. I have an urgent need for this conversation to continue.

"Then we have a number of things in common," I reply, uttering the first mundane thing that comes into my mind. "Let me see, firstly we have a patronymic in common. You are Sergey Ivanovich and I am Anna Ivanovna, secondly we both come from St. Petersburg. I was brought up there and graduated from the Lycée for Young Ladies on the Fontanka. And thirdly we both love dancing."

Escaped temporarily from my would be partners on the dance floor I feel an irrational urge to flirt with this attractive young man. I know full well that I should not be doing so, that it is inappropriate of me to continue in this vein, yet I am unable to resist a final flirtatious remark. "And fourthly we are admirers of Gustave Flaubert, since we have both read *Madame Bovary*. He looks at me in amazement.

"How on earth do you know that?" he asks.

"You won't remember me, but at that last Government party in the spring I heard you talking about *Madame Bovary* with your young friends. I walked past you on the way to the buffet. In my innocence I thought you were discussing some French lady in the town, but then one of your group mentioned the word novel and I realized that you were talking about a book which you had all read. I couldn't understand why all of you stopped talking as I went by and looked so embarrassed."

"That may well be the case", interjects Sergey, recovering his composure a little. "Now you mention it, I do recall the situation, but that doesn't explain how you came to read *Madame Bovary*. It is hardly the sort of book you would come across in our local bookstore in Shchyolkovo."

I tell him of my stay in Yalta and how I found the novel in a local bookshop. I do not elaborate any further, just adding that I had been alone there without my husband. So you see, I confide, there was no one to stop me buying it and reading it surreptitiously. He laughs, realizing that I had done such a wicked thing without my husband's knowledge. And that thanks to this admission on my part he is now complicit in this little act of defiance, of which his superior is unaware.

I can see that our conversation and the intimacy of our sitting together has had an effect on my youthful companion. Sergey wishes to continue discussing this risqué subject. But surely, I think, it must be unseemly to be seen spending so much time with one partner, a good looking man at that. So I rise from my chair to draw the conversation to a close. Alarm spreads across his young face.

"Please, Anna Ivanovna, if I might take the liberty of calling you by your patronymic, let me get you something from the buffet. As you may have guessed, I have been drinking too much. I really should eat something. And I notice that your glass is empty."

I hesitate but in a moment of indecision I allow Sergey to guide me back to the adjoining ante room. We are filling our plates with a selection of zakuski when the music stops. Dancers return to their tables, leaving us alone.

"Oh my God" says Sergey, "It's time for the speeches. Your husband will be making his about the achievements of our local Government in bringing gas lighting to our benighted town and demonstrating his part in it."

I laugh. We now have discovered something else in common, both sharing the same opinion of the banality of our home town. We sit down at a table in the now deserted room, from where we can hear snatches of my husband's speech through the adjoining door, which has been left half open.

"Do you not want to listen to what my husband has to say?" I ask.

"No, there's no need," he laughs. "I wrote most of it myself. The technical parts were, I am afraid, and with no disrespect to your husband, a little complex. I am just an engineer with a slight gift for writing, so they put me in charge of composing the speech. They teach you sycophancy at an early age in Shchyolkovo," he jokes wryly. " I only hope that what I've written makes sense to the Governor and his friends in high places. Heaven forbid, I've mentioned them enough in the speech."

I laugh, sensing that in our mutual dislike of authority we have established a further bond between us. I feel so easy and careless, surprised to see that my glass is empty though I have no recollection of putting it to my lips. Sergey refills our glasses.

" I love champagne" he says, looking at the bubbles in our flutes. He quotes, " When a feast is laid before us and there is music for dancing and I am with a beautiful woman generous with her laughter and her smiles, then I am intoxicated."

I am amazed by his words. "Sergey Ivanovich, I must say, you have a way with the spoken word as well as, it would appear, with the written. You are quite a flatterer for your young age. There may be a feast before us as well as music, and I may have been far too generous with my laughter and my smiles, but for your part you are much too bold in telling the wife of your Department Head that she is beautiful. I should be scolding you for your indiscretion, not encouraging it by continuing this very risqué tête à tête."

Sergey senses that my scolding is not to be taken seriously and we sit close together eating the caviar, blini and smoked fish piled on our plates. I feel that we are like youngsters who have raided the kitchen store cupboard while the grown ups are absent elsewhere.

I can see that Sergey is intrigued by my having read Madame Bovary and we begin to discuss the moral question at the heart of the story.

"*...and now I would like to pay tribute to our worthy mayor......contributing so much to the successful completion of this magnificent project...*"

My husband's words come faintly through the open door. By now Sergey is defending Emma's actions. For my part I am playing the devil's advocate, defending a wife's position in society against all attempts at seduction. Even if she has fallen out of love with her husband, marriage is marriage, I tell him, and the pledges taken at the altar cannot be broken.

Sergey leans across to me so that he can whisper an answer. I notice that a piece of caviar has lodged in his moustache and I can not resist putting a finger to his mouth to wipe it away. I know that I am behaving outrageously but I cannot resist myself.

"But Anna Ivanovna, do you mean to say that if you really could not abide your husband, would you really always trust yourself to act as you say Emma should have done?"

I think of Dmitry and our relationship. I cannot lie any more.

"Perhaps not, it would depend on the circumstances," I admit lamely.

"....and finally we have to thank the Engineering Department for its expertise in making our great town the first to...."

The rest of the sentence is drowned by applause from the audience who can sense with relief that Viktor's speech may at last be coming to a welcome end. It is time to end our intimacy and rejoin the throng. But Sergey does not move. He takes my hand. "Anna Ivanovna, I told you that the girls in St. Petersburg are especially beautiful, but that was before I met you. Anna, I must see you again. I don't know how or when, but I cannot bear the thought we might never meet again."

"Look, Sergey," I reply, gently extricating my hand from his and in my confusion forgetting to include his patronymic. "You remember Emma telling Leon to get a younger mistress. You are young and very attractive, go and find a beautiful girlfriend and leave respectable married women alone."

This is far too harsh a remark. It is not at all what I meant to say, and I soften my words with a squeeze of his hand. "Sergey, you have acted injudiciously, but I am just as much to blame. I'm not excusing myself in any way. It was simply so pleasant to be with you instead of with my husband's colleagues. And of course the champagne which I should not have partaken of so freely led me astray. Should we ever meet again, I promise you that you will find me behaving like a proper civil servant's wife. Though to help me return to that status, you can do something for me. Thanks to you, I have hardly heard a word of my husband's speech. Viktor is bound to ask me on our way home for my opinion. I haven't the slightest idea what he was talking about and I don't understand any of the technical points. I see I have the final dance of the evening unmarked, so I will keep it for you. You can tell me then what I should say."

***

We rejoin the main ballroom where the official guests at the high table are preparing to leave. Viktor is amongst them, flushed with the success of the evening and his speech, on which he is being congratulated.

When he catches sight of me he takes me roughly by the arm and whispers, "Where on earth have you been? You were supposed to sit next to me up here at the top table. I couldn't leave my seat to look for you. It was all so very annoying of you to disappear like that. I might say that your presence was missed here. The Governor specifically asked where you were. Can you imagine, he wanted to mark your card for a dance and you'd simply disappeared. Anyway, we are going now, I have called for our carriage. Go and collect your coat while I say goodbye to our party and try to think of an excuse for your absence."

"Viktor, I am not going home with you. Go back by yourself if you wish. You can send the carriage back for me at the end of the ball. I have a couple of dances promised and I cannot refuse them."

Never in our marriage had I spoken to Viktor in such a contradictory manner and I am expecting an outburst from him. Fortunately there are one or two people within earshot and not wanting to risk a scene, he simply mutters something about playing another round of cards and that he will wait for me after the final dance.

The band strikes up, but by now the evening has lost its magic. I am worried that my behaviour towards Sergey has been far too immodest and that I have led on a young impulsive man too easily. I could hear Dmitry back in Moscow reprimanding me for my indiscretion. All I can do is to blame my misbehaviour on champagne and my dress, both of which are very inadequate excuses. "Not well done, Anna," Dmitry's reprimand rings in my ears.

Sergey joins me for the final dance. He looks apprehensive, as well he might, though I am equally to blame for the intimacy that has taken place. He is obviously worried that I might report his conduct to Viktor and as a consequence be transferred out of Local Government. For all he knows the reward for his indiscretion could be a posting to Siberia.

He can see that I am no longer in a flirting mood. But I want to make amends for my earlier indiscretions.

"Please do not concern yourself, Sergey Ivanovich, you have given me a most pleasurable evening. All I will tell my husband is what an accomplished dancer you are. And for your part, you promised to help me out of my predicament. Viktor's speech you wrote for him, what do I tell my husband?"

"Tell him that it was an excellent speech which went to the heart of everyone here", Sergey replies. "There was something in it for all of us. The achievement of the Council in carrying the project through on time, and of course the engineers in the Technical Department who overcame the difficulties of providing sufficient insulation for the gas pipes by laying them vertically underground to a depth of three metres to counteract the effect of permafrost. And don't forget to mention the pipes and joints especially bought in from Germany Your husband must have come across not only as an able administrator but also as someone who has a thorough grasp of the technical problems which we encountered and overcame."

The music comes to an end and we salute each other. I want to sound more like his mother giving him advice. For the first time I call him by his diminutive.

"Seryozha, I am so grateful to you. Pipes and joints and permafrost and insulation. I'll show him that I fully understand all the problems you and he had to overcome. I must say goodbye, Viktor is waiting for me and I really must go. The next time we meet, should we ever do so, I want to see a lovely young girl on your arm. No more married women, please!" Once again he blushes, takes my arm and leads me back to my husband who is waiting impatiently.

"Viktor Aleksandrovich, I have the pleasure of returning your wife to you. May I congratulate you on the success of your speech. I know that Anna Ivanovna will want to add her own words of praise to mine."

"Sergey, you little rascal!" I mutter under my breath. As we go down the staircase side by side he whispers, "Don't forget the vertical sinking of the pipes and the new joints imported from Germany." As I turn towards him, he winks and discreetly squeezes my arm. Shchyolkovo is a small place and there may well be more Ministry balls that I have to attend. I have a premonition that we will meet again, but whether or not on that occasion there will be a young mistress on his arm I cannot hazard a guess.

Viktor and I leave the Assembly Rooms and find our coachman Afanasy waiting patiently for us.

"I'm so sorry, Afanasy, to keep you out so late," I apologize. "It's all my fault. I love dancing so much that I never noticed how late it was."

Afanasy replies that he never minds waiting for me, puts my foot on the carriage step and helps me in. Viktor takes his place silently by my side. He is in a very strange mood, a mood I have not seen before and therefore have no experience of interpreting. I can see that he did not like the way I had contradicted him on the subject of returning home, nor had he liked the way I had so evidently enjoyed dancing with so many partners, particularly my last one, the young man from his office.

On the other hand he must have enjoyed seeing me as one of the more attractive ladies on the dance floor, probably finding it entertaining and flattering that so many of his colleagues had sought his wife out for a dance.

How was this husband of mine going to treat me now? For me, bruised lips, dishevelled clothing and sexual frustration had been the result of a previous journey home by carriage. But sexual passion is not a sentiment I associate with Viktor, though perhaps jealousy combined with a desire to punish me for my behaviour at the ball might be the necessary aphrodisiac.

He puts his hand in mine and turning close to me he whispers,

"Tell me, my dear, what did you think of my speech? Did it go down well with our young man in my Department?"

I cannot reveal that I know full well who had written his speech for him. I simply repeat what my young partner had told me, ticking off one by one the points he had told me and finishing by saying that the Governor must have been so impressed. Have I not gone too far, I wonder, surely Viktor will see that I have been fed my lines? But no, he swallows the deception whole and only draws me closer to him.

"That's so kind of you." he murmurs. "I do value so much your judgement as a woman. It is always so in keeping with the sentiments expressed by all my colleagues."

Something very untoward is happening. I cannot believe my ears. Never in our married life has Viktor ever asked me for my opinions, let alone my judgement on a single subject. But here he is in the carriage, leaning towards me and giving me a kiss on my cheek. I feel apprehensive. How ever will this evening finish?

When we arrive home in the small hours of the morning the house is in darkness. The servants had been told to go to bed and only Afanasy is available to light the lamps before putting the carriage away.

" What a nuisance. Dunyasha has gone to bed so she cannot help me undress. I don't want to spoil my new gown," I mutter to myself. Viktor must have overheard me.

"Anna, let me help you. I will come to your room. It will be just like old times." I cannot remember any old times when he has undressed me, but I accept his offer. After all that I have consumed during the evening, I doubt that I am in a position to manage the buttons, laces and other fastenings on my clothes. I go to my room and light a lamp. A feeling that something unusual is going to happen, something that is totally alien to my husband's usual behaviour reinforces my previous misgivings.

A few minutes later Viktor comes down the corridor from his bedroom. His usual habit is to enter my bedroom after a discreet knock on the door. He often arrives holding a book or paper, on which he wants my opinion and which serves as a pretext for his coming to see me in my boudoir. By this time my head is spinning. I am in a strange and confused world. Despite my concern I have just managed to loosen the fastenings on my dress.

"Anna," he starts to speak. I raise a finger to my lips to silence him, and as I do so, a strap falls from my shoulder. With a shrug the other strap comes loose and I hear the silken sound of my dress falling to my feet. His fingers quickly undo the straps of my bodice, my petticoat falls to the floor and I face my husband naked for the first time since our wedding night. I feel him pull me onto the bed. Is it really only Viktor in the room I wonder in my intoxicated state. Somewhere in the dim light of the lamp, in my blurred vision I can see Dmitry there looking down at me. Then Rodolphe in his riding habit, leather boots and whip fondling my breasts, and Leon caressing me gently, whispering in my ear, and Sergey gasping in wonderment as he explores my body.

And all the time an insistent thrusting which comes to a climax as these other figures dissolve and disappear. I am left alone with the image of my husband, gasping as he finishes making love to me. Instead of his returning to his bedroom, as he does after our weekly trysts, we lie side by side and fall asleep.

When I wake in the night I discover that he has gone back to his room. Is this what I have become, I wonder? A woman who flirts with older men, all but seduces an impressionable young man and incites unbridled lust in her husband? I must get back to Moscow, where I have nothing more complicated to do than simply continue my life as another man's mistress. I laugh wryly. How is this all going to end, I ask myself for the hundredth time.

{10}

Despite the events of that turbulent night my relationship with Viktor does not improve. He does not once refer to what had happened in my bedroom. Once we have resumed our normal married life we do not see a great deal of each other. Viktor spends his days at the office and the evenings at his club. I think of Dmitry and the similarity of his and Viktor's lifestyle. It comes to me that this is how men who do not share a loving relationship with their wives spend their time.

Of course our paths do cross once a day when we meet for our evening meal. Dinner time has always been an awkward experience for me, though our silences do not seem to worry Viktor. I have little news to impart. News about the day to day running of the household and gossip about the few visitors who come to call is usually my only contribution to the conversation. I have learnt that it is better to avoid controversial subjects.

However Viktor has now taken it upon himself to educate me about the true state of Russia, of course as he sees it. Between courses he tells me about the achievements of the economy under our Minister of Finance Sergey Witte, how Russia is building more railroads than any other country in the world, how we have recently surpassed France in steel production, how the oil industry has grown to match that of the United States, and so on.

On this occasion I cannot let these remarks of his go unchallenged. I argue with him to the effect that rapid industrialization is being achieved at terrible human cost. I have read in the more liberal newspapers which I can get my hands on and are not banned by the Government, that the influx of peasants into the cities to provide the new labour force has created appalling living and working conditions. Typhus, cholera and tuberculosis are rampant and my beloved Petersburg has been cited as having the highest mortality rate of any major city in Europe. Viktor gives me one of those patronizing and sanctimonious looks of his that I hate so much.

"My dear young woman," he counters my argument, "You must not believe everything in those ridiculous newspapers you get your hands on. The country is well governed by the Tsar and his humble ministers. He pauses briefly to let the significance of his remark about the government sink in. "We just need a little patience until our police round up the few dissidents that are still at large."

This is too simplistic a view for me to accept. But I have few facts and figures to argue my case any further. And besides I am more concerned with my own role as a young woman in my husband's autocratic Russia and I am not particularly interested in the economy of the country. Just the social effect that the economy has on our suffering classes.

What I need to know is what the future holds for me, should I be able to get away from the stifling confines of Shchyolkovo. I have come across the term *feministka* in the monthly magazine *The Women's Cause* which I have been able to read discreetly in the town's bookshop. Of course I have not dared to buy a copy and smuggle it home. That would be far too risky.

I am surprised to learn that there are so many women in Russia who see the twin problems of education and employment for women in the same way that I do. There must be kindred spirits out there somewhere that I could relate to, should I only be able to get away. But for the time being life in a provincial backwater has to be endured.

***

August 25th 1899.

The summer passes slowly. The warmer, sunny weather has brought no relief to the utter boredom of my life. I brood over my sorrows in gloomy dejection. I can think of no reasonable excuse to visit Moscow again. I think that any suggestion of needing another appointment with my lady doctor would not be taken seriously by Viktor and I dare not write to Dmitry and implore him to come again to me in Shchyolkovo.

However some days later something unusual happens which breaks the torpor of my life. I am taking Tuzik for his daily walk and as we approach the house on our return he suddenly begins to wag his tail and bark. In the distance he has caught sight of Anatoly, our old postman, approaching towards me along the road.

These two have become firm friends. I imagine this is mainly because Anatoly always seems able to find a morsel of dried sausage in his pocket whenever they meet. This, however, is an infrequent occurrence. For security reasons my husband's official mail is usually sent directly to his office and I for my part receive few letters.

On this occasion we both arrive at the gate at the same time, and unwittingly I suggest to Anatoly that I take in the bundle of letters he is holding. He hesitates, replying that he has been instructed by my husband to deliver all mail into the hands of one of our servants, who is then to hand the correspondence over to my husband on his return from his office. I am speechless with indignation and try to explain to Anatoly that there might be a letter addressed to me and that I would take responsibility for taking it from him.

I feel so sorry for him standing there by our gate, twisting his cap in his hands in agitation. Of course he cannot be blamed for my husband's ridiculous instructions and so I have no other option than to let him accompany me up the path to the front door. There he rings the bell and hands over the mail to Dunyasha, who sees me standing by his side with a furious look on my face.

My dearly loved and faithful servant girl finds the whole situation incomprehensible. She looks from me to Anatoly and back to me again in confusion. But she knows that she can do no other than to take the letters away, as she has been instructed by her master.

This whole episode is so farcical that I am determined to demand an explanation from my husband at the first opportunity. I do not have long to wait as dinner is shortly announced. As usual we meet for the first time that day in the dining room. He is carrying a letter, which he informs me is addressed to me.

I cannot restrain my sarcasm. I am fully aware that the day's mail has arrived, I tell him. What is the point of ordering all our letters, even ones addressed to me, to be handed over to a servant? Viktor replies that the postman has been given official orders to hand over the mail, even if it is only into the hands of Dunyasha, rather than to me. I cannot believe my ears.

Does my deranged husband really not trust me and prefers the services of a maid to carry out his orders? Or is he stupid enough to suspect that I am carrying on a liaison and my lover is communicating with me by post. He makes some pathetic excuse, saying that for government security it is better to have mail delivered both by an illiterate postman and handed over to an illiterate servant. In that way there is no risk of letters being tampered with.

I am not appeased. I reply coldly that I am quite aware of the Russian Government in St. Petersburg having its own Security Department for State Affairs, but is there really the same level of security needed for official correspondence at local level here in Shchyolkovo covering matters such as drainage, road repairs and gaslighting?

I feel insulted and Viktor can see my fury simmering. The final straw which causes me to lose my temper is when I ascertain that the letter he is holding is in actual fact addressed to me. I recognize the hand writing on the envelope straight away. To my consternation I see that it is from Chekhov. In my former subservient role as the wife of an important government official, and in the very unlikely circumstance of receiving such a letter, I would have opened it there and then in front of my husband, as he would have instructed me to do so, and revealed to him its contents. However our present relationship has changed.

I wish to spite him and thus I keep it unopened by my plate during our meal. We do not talk. I can see that my husband is consumed with curiosity, desperate to find out the identity of the sender of one of the very few letters I have received in my married life. But he deliberately holds back from asking me directly. In my present mood I do not vouchsafe him an answer.

After grace has been said at the end of the meal and the servants have cleared the table I open the letter. How Anton Pavlovich had known my address is one of the questions that had been tormenting me during our silent meal. When my composure has returned a little and I am able to think more clearly, I recall that both Dmitry and I had handed in our visiting cards at the box office before the performance of *Uncle Vanya.* Afterwards, during our dinner together I had asked Anton if he would be kind enough to sign my programme. This he had done together with an inscription: 'To Anna Ivanovna, my lady with her little dog!' He must have kept my card with my address and I now have a letter in my hands from a man whom my husband knows only by reputation. Viktor waits impatiently for an explanation. Let him wait a little longer.

{11}

In some trepidation I break the seal. As I am later to learn to my cost Chekhov's handwriting is appalling and I have the utmost difficulty in deciphering his words.

Yalta, August 18th, 1899

My dear Anna Ivanovna,

It was with the greatest of pleasure that I was rewarded with the opportunity to renew my acquaintanceship with you and Dmitry Dmitrych on the occasion of 'Uncle Vanya' visiting your delightful home town.

Please forgive me for my delay in replying to your letter. As you will see from my address I am here in Yalta again, where I have been busying myself with house and garden, both of which I can report with some pride, are progressing well. I wish it were a similar situation with my writing but I will come to that in a moment.

I am so glad that you both enjoyed the performance in Shchyolkovo. In my estimation provincial audiences are less critical than those in Moscow or St. Petersburg. I am so relieved that you saw the play in your home town and that I did not give you tickets for the first night in Moscow. By all accounts Stanislavsky did not act well at the première. I had told him he needed more testosterone in playing the lecherous Dr. Astrov. And then he had the audacity to tell my Olga that she needed to be more sensual in her portrayal of Elena. It was just as well that I was down here in Yalta, otherwise I would have bounded onto the stage, if my old bones had allowed , and remonstrated with him in full view of the audience. However, by all accounts the second performance was a success. My darling sister Masha, I am reliably informed, was invited on stage to receive the audience's acclaim by proxy. What a triumph for all concerned!

Now, my dearest Anna Ivanovna, enough of the theatre! I kiss your hand in the hope of forgiveness. Why, you may well ask. Because, my dear, this will count as the most ill considered proposal you have ever received. So feel free if you so wish to reject it out of hand as the outrageous suggestion of an ill and elderly friend.

As you know, I have been working on the structure of my next play, urged on by our incorrigible Nemirovich-Danchenko. He does not seem to mind killing me by setting impossible deadlines, just so long as he can fill his beloved Moscow Art Theatre with a new play by his esteemed playwright Anton Chekhov.

However, this esteemed playwright has replied to his demands by saying that he would not even consider starting a new play until he had finished his next story, which thanks to you will be called 'The Lady with a Little Dog'. I do not wish to weary you with my financial problems, but I have a deadline to meet for the completion of this piece. If I am late in completing this onerous little story, then I stand to lose a considerable amount of money from my editor. And more importantly I cannot turn my attention to my 'Three Sisters', the title of my new play, until this story is finished. I am at an impasse.

This is where I kiss your hand, again! The story has not evolved at all and my muse is as obstinate as that damned crane of mine whom you saw on your visit to Autka. I have written a letter to Viktor Aleksandrovich Goltsev, you may be familiar with the name as he is the editor of 'Russian Thought, telling him that I have been delayed somewhat. But he replies that a contract is a contract and cannot be broken without my incurring a financial penalty.

To make matters worse and to be absolutely truthful, I have not even begun writing yet. My excuses are that our carpenters are still banging away and that the fine weather has tempted me to be out of doors more than I should be. But of course I cannot send these excuses to Goltsev. And I ask you, since what I tell you here is in confidence, not to let anyone else know that I am experiencing what I hope will be only a temporary writer's bloc.

However, even if I have not yet been able to put pen to paper, I have been reflecting a great deal about the format of the story. If you would allow, and here I must confess to being outrageously presumptuous in my proposal, I would envisage a portrayal of your relationship with our mutual friend Dmitry Dmitrych. I believe that by doing so I could produce a short story of maybe twenty pages that would interest our reading public and just as importantly satisfy the demands of my publisher.

Both you and Serov are extremely interesting characters and I would see myself placing emphasis on Dmitry's capacity for abstract thought and his ability to analyze his own actions. At the same time I would like to describe the heroine's married life in Shchyolkovo. (The town could avoid identification perhaps by simply calling it "S".) From talking to you both at my villa and later at the theatre I feel that your continued affection for each other is so unusual, so unlike the normal pattern of an affair between man and woman, that it is something to be cherished and admired. Therefore the themes of adulterous love and the tyranny of marriage, as personified in your private lives, are ones which with your permission I would envisage using. From your concern over the ambiguity of the conclusions to my stories that you expressed when we talked in the garden at Autka, I would propose leaving the denouement unfinished. Let our readers decide it for themselves.

So, my dear young lady, here is my proposal. Would it in any way be possible for you to come down to Yalta and, in your role as the lady with the little dog, help me with slightly more just the title for my story? I am certain that your presence here in Autka and your retelling of the details of your affair, should you be amenable to so do, would enable me to complete most of this story in two to three weeks. This would allow me to finish it by myself if necessary after your return home.

I do not know whether Dmitry Dmitrych would be able to excuse himself from his work in the bank to accompany you. This would be most agreeable and enjoyable, but should he not be able to, please rest assured that all proprieties would be observed. I have both my sister Masha and a house keeper living in the house, which if you were to come down, you would find a little closer to be being finished than when you were last here.

However, it is not yet what you could describe as comfortable. My study and bedroom have turned out pretty well, and guests have their own rooms, even if they are a little Spartan in the way of furniture. I believe you told me that you play the piano, and I have to report that we have just taken delivery of an upright piano. So you could relax and play to us in the evening if you felt so inclined. On the other hand you could of course stay in the pension where you previously resided, should you prefer that arrangement. And then walk the short distance over to me each day. But these are minor details.

Forgive me once again, Anna Ivanovna, for this outrageous suggestion. I am being totally selfish. I have this enchanting vision of retiring to my study with you and being excused the boring visits that I am constantly subjected to from well wishers, local tradesmen and the like. My being involved in writing again, in effect my dictating the story to you to write down, would mean that we were not disturbed. My mood and health would improve and our old cook Mariushka, you no doubt remember her, might even be persuaded to produce some half decent meals.

However, my dear, after rereading the above ramblings, I see how impossible all this nonsense is, so you must ignore this ridiculous and pathetic letter. I kiss your hand firmly again and beg forgiveness. Please give my sincerest regards to our Dmitry Dmitrych when you see him next, and if by some miracle you do decide to come, just send a telegram or letter, or better still just arrive. Thanks to the autumn storms the mailboats cannot always dock in Yalta and the telegraph service is haphazard.
Communication is therefore unreliable. Just come unannounced if you wish. You would be so welcome.

In conclusion, I beg you once again to forgive these ramblings, forgiving but not forgetting your affectionate friend,

Anton Pavlovich.

***

Viktor is waiting impatiently for me to finish reading. I have taken a long time to read through Anton's letter, the handwriting as appalling as usual, and I can see the frown on his forehead as he mentally lists the questions he is preparing to ask me. I am in no hurry to reply. Let him make the first move. I taunt him with my silence. Leaning forward and drumming the table with his fingers, a sure sign of his barely contained impatience, he begins.

" Anna, please do me the courtesy of identifying the writer of this letter. You receive very few, so this one must be important. I do not recognize the stamp on the envelope. It is not a Moscow or St. Petersburg one. Let me guess. Perhaps you have a secret admirer who has fallen in love with you and is writing to declare his love. But it cannot be that young man you spent so much time with at the ball. He would need a local stamp."

His remarks are so patronizing that I dismiss them with a sarcastic laugh.

"You sound like Mr Sherlock Holmes, the great English detective. We will have to find you a Doctor Watson to help you. Then your detection will be elementary," I joke.

But of course all literary allusions are lost on my husband. Viktor looks disconcerted, as he always does when on the rare occasion I mention matters of a literary nature. He is not acquainted with the stories of Sir Arthur Conan Doyle which have just arrived in Russia in translation and are being read with great acclaim. My ironic jibe is lost on him. He remains seated opposite me, playing with his silver napkin ring and drumming the table with his fingers.

"Anna Ivanovna," he is cross now and resorts to using my patronymic. " I am waiting for your reply to my question. Would you please have the civility to tell me from whom you have received this letter?"

I cannot delay my reply any longer. As if it is the most natural thing in the world I reply.

"As a matter of fact it happens to be from a certain Anton Chekhov. You may have heard his name being mentioned, even here in Shchyolkovo. As it happens, I went to see a performance of his *Uncle Vanya* when it was being rehearsed here. I can recall perfectly clearly that I told you that I was going to the theatre. No doubt you've forgotten, like most things I tell you."

" For God's sake Anna, can you never give me a straightforward answer to my questions? I know perfectly well who Chekhov is, without any assistance from you, my dear. You may remember that I subscribe to *Russian Thought* and I have actually read a couple of his short stories. Rather banal to my mind, and I don't imagine our audience here in Shchyolkovo appreciating his *Uncle Vanya* either. Two men lusting after the same married woman, I have been led to believe, and certainly not a suitable subject for a play which may well be seen by impressionable ladies and children. But that is by the by. Why ever would a certain Anton Pavlovich Chekhov be writing to you? What on earth would you two have in common?"

I have no desire to satisfy his curiosity. I refuse to answer, simply slipping the letter back into its envelope and rising from the table. Viktor half rises to intercept me, but he can sense the futility of any effort to restrain me from the urgency I show to leave his presence. I receive a sympathetic smile from Dunyasha as she hands me a lamp for my bedroom. Once there I fall on my bed and reread Anton's letter, my head in a whirl.

The decision that lies before me now is of course whether to stay in Shchyolkovo as a penitent wife or risk a serious row with Viktor by accepting Anton's proposal. I know that owing to pressure of work at his bank it is most unlikely that Dmitry would be able to join me, even for a few days. And strange as it may seem, I feel that I do not necessarily want him there. If I go to Yalta, it will be on my own terms. I will be a woman there in her own right, whose presence has been requested by a writer of some note. I will succeed or fail purely by my own efforts.

I think of the long winter days ahead, the daylight dying by three of the afternoon, the endless blizzards and the hours cooped up indoors with only the piano and my books for solace. And I contrast this in my imagination with the sunshine, the light, the southern autumn warmth of Crimea, and of course the exciting prospect of working with Anton Pavlovich.

I lie back on my bed and look around my dear familiar room, the warm, tiled stove, my books and ornaments, my Palekh painted boxes holding my jewels. My secure if boring life stretches out in front of me. Am I really ready to leave all this on some mad whim, an escapade more akin to the elopement in the middle of the night by one of Pushkin's heroines than the reasoned response of a mature married woman? But the scene I have just endured with Viktor and the still vivid memories of the treatment I received at his hands after the Ministry ball help me make up my mind.

I have no desire for my husband to see Anton's letter so I conceal it within the pages of *Anna Karenina*. If he were to find it, he would imagine quite wrongly that Anton Pavlovich and I had developed some sort of relationship during my stay in Yalta and that was the reason why he wanted me to help him write my story, based on the events of a turbulent few days together in Yalta.

I go down stairs and knock at the door of my husband's study. I find him uncharacteristically calm after his recent outburst. This calm however is not to last long as, taking a deep breath, I start to reveal something of the content of my letter.

"Viktor, I will not hide anything from you. In Yalta I visited Anton Pavlovich, met his fiancée Olga Knipper and enjoyed a pleasant afternoon with them. We discussed his new play *Uncle Vanya* and the problems he was having with it. I reminded you at dinner that I saw a performance of the play when it was staged here in Shchyolkovo. What I failed to tell you, and I apologize for my oversight, was that I met Chekhov again after the performance. A friend and I were invited backstage, where we were introduced to some of the cast. He then invited us to have dinner with him.

Viktor, I know what you think of the theatrical world, but you must believe me when I tell you that there was never any suggestion of impropriety on his part at any time that evening. Afterwards I wrote a letter to him simply thanking him for the evening we had spent together.

So you see, the letter I received today was a delayed reply to mine. What has come as complete surprise, Viktor, is that he has invited me down to Autka, his new house in Yalta, to help him with a new short story he is trying to write. I imagine my role in this would be something akin to revising the text, rewriting corrections. Rather like Tolstoy's wife Sofia Bers rewriting his *War and Peace*. But as it is only a short story, I imagine I would be back in time for Christmas!"

My attempt at a joke obviously misfires as a quick look at Viktor's face confirms my failure to soften the impact of my words. He replies heatedly.

"My dear Anna, I do not catch your meaning. You must be out of your mind if you give this invitation any sort of credence. I admit that I do not know a great deal about the literary world. However, I do recall the case of that wretched Fyodor Dostoevsky who inveigled a young girl into acting as his stenographer when he was writing one of his stories, *The Gambler*.

If I remember the facts correctly, within a month he had seduced her, making her work all the hours God gave her, in order for him to be able to deliver his story to the publishers on time. Do you not realize that this Chekhov of yours, however famous he may be, has the reputation of being an incorrigible philanderer. Why does he not marry that Olga Knipper woman whom he is rumoured to share with some theatrical producer? And I have just read an article in the latest issue of *Russian Thought* which suggests that the Petersburg literati are hinting that there is another actress involved with him, some Mariya Andreyevna, whoever she may be.

As your husband I am responsible for your care and well being. Your Anton Pavlovich, to my mind, has no morals whatsoever and I deem it fortunate that up to now you have been able to escape his clutches.

His idea of your joining him in Yalta is just a ploy on his part to get another young woman to join his harem. This would be a second opportunity for him to seduce you, having failed I presume at the first attempt. I expressly forbid your going."

"Viktor Aleksandrovich, you treat me like a simple young girl who has no ambition to better herself. You are quite happy to keep me here as your dutiful wife, an aid to your career, to be produced to order at Government functions as and when you like.

I cannot go on like this. I am an educated woman, I have my own opinions on a range of subjects and my platonic relationship with Chekhov is one that I cherish. And as he has asked for my help, it is my decision alone whether I go or not."

I pause for a moment but on this occasion Viktor does not interrupt and he allows me to continue.

"I would like to remind you that in a few short weeks we will be living in the twentieth century. Your nineteenth century attitude to women and our marital relationship must change. I am not going to be treated by you any longer in the way you have done so up to now.

If I decide to go, I will do so even if I do not have your blessing. I have sufficient funds of my own, and I know that Anton Pavlovich would be pleased to help financially if necessary. No doubt he would be surprised that you had been unwilling to contribute to my expenses, were I to arrive destitute on his doorstep.

I can see that this last jibe has curtailed the possibility of any further discussion. I turn on my heel, return to my room, slamming the door in a gesture of defiance and throw myself on my bed. But sleep does not come, tormented as I am by the need to make a decision as quickly as possible. Am I to remain a prisoner here in Shchyolkovo, or do I take the plunge, disobey my husband and travel down to Yalta to take up Chekhov's invitation?

{12}

August 26th 1899.

This morning I sleep late and only wake as my husband leaves for the office. It is raining and overcast and I have a sudden yearning for the warmth and brightness of the Crimean coast. My thoughts turn to Viktor. Do I really mind what he thinks of me? He cannot ban me from the house and he can always explain my absence to his colleagues as the result of yet another occurrence of my 'woman's problem', requiring rest and recuperation in Crimea. Viktor will be regarded widely as a kind and generous husband dealing affectionately with a suffering wife. He has repeated to me once, when he questioned me about my trips to Moscow, the whisperings in high office concerning a husband who had been openly deceived by his wife. The Department Head had on that occasion commented that a man who could not govern his wife could not expect to continue for long in governing his country. This hapless, cuckolded husband was not seen again in government service.

With a shiver of apprehension it comes to me that if the truth about Dmitry and me ever came to light, my marriage to Viktor would no doubt come to an abrupt end. His career would count for so much more than his marriage. This he would sacrifice without a second thought, demonstrating that by this sacrifice he could govern his wife and thereby continue in service to his country.

And so in the end my decision is an easy one. I will travel to Moscow, packing clothes that will be suitable both for the winter up here in the north as well as a wardrobe for the warmth of Crimea. But first I have to tell my husband that I need another visit to my doctor in Moscow. It is not difficult. To my chagrin I realize how adept I have become in uttering falsehoods. It is easy for me to say that all the unpleasantness of the past few days has upset me and that I need to get away to spend time with some friends of my own age in an atmosphere that is more conducive to recovery. I do not tell him, heaven forbid, that I may well continue my journey down to Yalta. He will find that out soon enough if I decide to go.

***

Two days later I find myself back at my hotel on Nikolskaya Street. I am restless and bored with being alone. A moment of pure devilment takes possession of me. I have always wanted to see Dmitry in his place of work. There could be no danger in that, I assure myself. No one knows me in Moscow. It would be so exciting to be invited into his office, to close the door and to pretend to be discussing the opening of a new bank account, fully aware that in next few hours we would be sharing the intimacy of our hotel bedroom.

To this end I send a message to Dmitry requesting an appointment with him. He enters a fictitious name in his diary and writes down an afternoon appointment with yet another important client.

Dmitry at work is a revelation. Here is my lover dressed in a superbly cut suit, seated in a sumptuous office in a prestigious bank in the heart of Moscow. He is attended by a couple of clerks who run in and out of his office to fulfill his every command. When we are finally left alone, yet knowing that we may be interrupted at any moment, we begin our charade. We discuss a fictitious business arrangement. In this new persona of successful banker as I now perceive him, Dmitry's grey hairs and serious manner seem entirely appropriate. He play acts with all the theatrical skills that he acquired as a student.

I sit demurely in front of his great desk laden with important looking documents and try to think, should we be disturbed, of suitable questions regarding deposits and rates of interest. Keeping a straight face he answers them with aplomb. But I am determined to put him off his stroke. My devilment returns. I mischievously cross my legs thereby raising the hem of my dress to reveal the same black boots I wore all that time ago as we walked to Chekhov's house. Looking at my legs he hesitates and stumbles over his reply to a question.

With that hesitation on his part I feel that I have won our little contest. I want to consolidate my advantage by asking him if he recalls our conversation about Pushkin and his fixation over little feet. Dmitry regains his composure. He replies that he remembers it only too clearly. It was the first occasion, he now intimates to me, that he had thought I might be less naïve than I had up to then appeared. He reckoned that I was a young woman who could well be worth pursuing with more than just a distant chance of success. He can see me blushing.

Back in my bedroom at the *Slavyansky Bazar* I caress his greying hair and ask him to be serious, putting to one side the images of nubile client and faithful mistress, which had tempted him a minute or so before. I tell him about Chekhov's letter and his invitation. How, with our approval, he would like to fashion his fictional story around the events of our own liaison. Dmitry foresees a difficulty.

"Anna, as I see it, here are the consequences of your helping Chekhov with his story, should you decide to accept his invitation. However much names and location are changed, Chekhov will go ahead and complete this story. After all, that is why you have been invited down to Yalta to help him.

So we take it one stage further. The story is published and your husband reads it, or perhaps is told about it by a colleague. He then discovers that you are in fact the fallen woman with your little Tuzik being instrumental in identifying you as ' the Lady with a Little Dog.' How will your Viktor react to the fact that his wife is the protagonist in a tale of adultery and continued debauchery? We can guess what the likely outcome will be. So looking at it logically,what sort of a relationship do you envisage with your husband when you are identified as the mistress of a Muscovite banker?"

I have asked myself this same question. I tell him what I have already told myself a dozen times, namely that anything that jeopardizes his position in the Government and upsets his standing with his circle of friends would be anathema to him. At best I would be severely chastised and punished for my infidelity and of course be forced to give up my lover. At worst I could envisage his demand for a divorce, grounds for which would not be difficult to establish. The management of the *Slavyansky Bazar* would no doubt respond to a financial incentive to provide evidence of our shared bedroom in their hotel.

We continue to talk. Is he not worried, I ask him, about his identity being revealed? No, he replies. I probe him further. Surely his relationship with his wife would suffer, as would his position in the bank. Dmitry argues that his wife does not read much, her circle of friends is limited and she would never be perspicacious enough to identify him as the hero of the story. As for the bank, he says, his reputation would only be enhanced amongst both management and colleagues. Many of them already have mistresses and would welcome him to their number, whilst those who do not would only be envious of his success with women.

***

We talk while we eat our dinner, but answers to these questions lie unresolved. Other guests have finished their meal and we are left alone to finish our wine.

Our waiter comes over to us, table napkin characteristically slung over his shoulder. Can he offer us a liqueur? Dmitry and he discuss some political matter involving a demonstration on Red Square. Busy with my own thoughts I have deliberately excluded myself from their conversation. Suddenly into my subconscious floats an image of another restaurant with familiar waiters. I am back in my restaurant in Yalta. One of them is showing me to my table and patting Tuzik on the head.

I tell Dmitry that I have made up my mind and am going to accept Chekov's invitation to join him in Yalta, no matter what the consequences may be when I return home.

"Being parted from you for two weeks or more tears my heart and I know that I will miss you dreadfully," I tell him. He replies that my eyes are sparkling, that there is a new colour in my cheeks and I look so beautiful that, if I am not careful, he will change his mind and counsel me not to go.

***

Dmitry arranges my journey for me and buys my tickets. This time I am to travel by mail train to Odessa and then complete the journey by taking the ferry to Yalta. He says that it will be a more comfortable way to travel, avoiding the pain of the long carriage ride from Simferopol which I endured on my first visit. Dmitry pointedly remarks that the ferry from Odessa will be the same one that we had seen arriving that fatal evening at the start of our affair. But this time, if Chekhov receives my letter in time, he may with luck be waiting at the quayside to welcome me.

However I have another letter to write, one that will be greatly more difficult to compose than the happy, confident one I have just sent to Anton confirming my acceptance of his invitation. How to impart the news to my husband that I am deliberately disobeying his orders?

"My dear and ever understanding husband, I trust you will not hold it against me if I tell you…."

No, that would be useless. I cannot explain in a letter what I have decided to do. He will tear the letter up in a fit of rage. So I content myself with simply writing, that I have decided to travel down to Yalta. I have sufficient funds with me and he is not to worry about me. I will write again to let him know the date of my return. I am certain that this letter, ripped into small pieces in rage, will finish in the wastepaper bin, but I have the satisfaction of not apologizing for or excusing my actions.

We arrange the date for my departure for the day after tomorrow. It would be most inconvenient if I arrived unannounced at Chekhov's dacha and this delay will allow time for my letter to reach him. And for purely selfish reasons I want to enjoy being alone with Dmitry in Moscow.

{13}

We have two tickets for the Saturday night performance of Mussorgsky's *Boris Godunov* at the Solodovnikov Theatre. Fyodor Chaliapin has been engaged to sing the title role in Rimsky Korsakov's version of the opera. This is a first for Moscow. Muscovites are always jealous of the cultural scene in St. Petersburg and persuading Chaliapin to join the operatic world here in Moscow is a feather in their cap.

Since the evening promises to be one of the social events of the season Dmitry insists on taking me shopping. We visit one of his favourite fashion shops, there seems to be no end of them, and he buys me an exquisite Jacquard woven silk dress and matching jacket and accessories.

The evening, to my relief, is a pleasure from start to finish. Dmitry meets a number of friends during the intervals and I am introduced as an acquaintance of his who happens to be visiting Moscow. No one questions this rather threadbare explanation of my presence on his arm. For them it seems quite natural that Dmitry should be at the opera with a woman who is so clearly not his wife.

Even though we have not been seen in public before, word has passed round that Dmitry and I are more than casual friends. I am accepted as his regular consort. I hope that I come across as a benign influence on him and that I am seen as the one woman in his life who has influenced him towards giving up his predatory approach to women. A Don Juan who has been tamed. And this tamed Don Juan meekly returns to his wife's bed that night, leaving me alone in mine.

The next day we pack my clothes and take a cab to the Kursky Station. This time no officious attendant orders Tuzik to the guard's van and I am allowed to keep him in my compartment.

The long train journey is completed without incident. This time there is even a dining car where I can take my meals, which is greatly preferable to jumping out at stations in search of a buffet stall on the platform, as happened on my first journey. I arrive in Odessa in time to catch the evening ferry.

I am booked into a single cabin and I spend the night in comfort together with Tuzik at my feet. He growls from time to time to the rhythm of the engines. Perhaps he is dreaming of a return to Yalta and the prospect of more lamb chops.

With some apprehension I remember the state of some of the passengers arriving in Yalta, when Dmitry and I had watched the ferry docking with difficulty in the rough seas. I have never been on a ferry before, but the weather is kind to us and we arrive next afternoon to a warm breeze and sunshine.

I go up on deck to watch us enter the harbour. I scan the crowd waiting for the arrival of the boat. I hope against hope that Anton will be there to meet me. And indeed he is. I catch sight of the familiar figure dressed as usual in morning coat and brightly coloured waistcoat, holding up his lorgnette to inspect the passengers waving from the rail. I wave and catch his attention.

Suddenly I am gripped by a mad panic. Here am I, a very ordinary young woman with no literary pretensions whatsoever, presuming to be able to help a famous writer in the writing of a short story. All I have given him so far is the title for the story. Here now is his 'lady with her little dog' arriving to deliver chapter and verse against a deadline of two to three weeks.

But it is too late to turn back and within minutes Tuzik and I find ourselves on the quayside being greeted by Anton with a bunch of flowers, a kiss for me and a pat on the head for the dog. He instructs a porter to take my luggage to Autka. I sense a certain formality in our meeting. After all we hardly know each other and the ensuing small talk does little to settle my nerves.

" Tell me, how was your journey, Anna Ivanovna? Are you well? You look a trifle pale. Perhaps the sea was a little rough. And tell me, how is Dmitry Dmitrych. It is such a shame that he could not join us here." I answer his questions.

"I'm fine, thank you Anton Pavlovich. No, the journey was excellent. Much better taking the train to Odessa and then the ferry. I would not want to do that overland trip again. And Dmitry is well. He sends his regards and apologizes for not being able to accompany me. He has little leave from his bank, and what he has will be spent helping his mother move to another apartment in Moscow. He is a very conscientious son."

I can see that something is bothering him. " Anna Ivanovna, perhaps as we will be working so closely together for the next week or so, we could dispense with the formality of using patronymics. Anton and Anna, just two simple Russian names, if I am not being too bold to make such a suggestion."

"Anton Pav.." I stop and laughingly correct myself. Anton, I would be delighted. Thank you. I imagine here in Crimea life is much less formal than in Moscow."

"Yes, I don't think that anyone will take our informality amiss, even here in Yalta, the hotbed of rumour and counter rumour," he laughs. " And as regards your pallor, I am sure that a few days of sunshine and sea breezes will restore the colour to your cheeks."

There are so many emotions fighting for a place in my head that I am hardly aware of his words The jetty where I am standing now is where Dmitry had first embraced me and I had committed myself to an adulterous liaison. I recognize the broken plank, where following him in a daze,

I had nearly tripped. And this time it is Anton Pavlovich by my side instead of Dmitry. He is being greeted every few yards by people who obviously know him. While all the time I am being looked at quizzically.

It comes to me that there is nothing strange in Chekhov being seen with a young lady on his arm. I am to learn soon enough that the young ladies patrolling the Promenade and whose paths so fortuitously cross that of Anton's, are called 'Antonovkas' after our famous apple.

I can see that certain older ladies are looking at me with a degree of veiled hostility. Who is this new woman on the arm of our famous writer, they will be asking themselves. It is certainly not his fiancée Olga Knipper, she's still in Moscow and acting in that *Uncle Vanya* play of his. But there was mention of another actress in his life, was there not. But surely this one does not look like an actress, attractive as she may be.

And the older set, the residents of Yalta, recall that the little dog seems vaguely familiar. Was there not talk last year of a lady with a little dog? Vernet's drinkers coined the title if we remember rightly. No doubt we will find out soon enough, there are precious few secrets here in Yalta that are not revealed one way or another!

Yalta in the late autumn sunshine looks so enticing after the grey skies of Moscow. Anton suggests a walk along the Promenade so that I can stretch my legs after the voyage and enjoy the fresh air. Everything seems exotic, as if summer had never passed. The cypresses stand just as tall as I remember, tapering gracefully as they reach upwards to touch the sky, the olive trees and pines are as fine as ever. Even a few hardy oleanders are still in flower, making little pools of yellow and pink on the pavement as the breeze plucks the last of their petals. And people are strolling along in light clothes, sitting out of doors, drinking coffee, for all the world as if it is still high summer.

As we pass the restaurant where Dmitry and I had eaten so often, a familiar waiter comes out to collect some plates. He throws his napkin over his shoulder in that gesture I remember so well. He stops in amazement when he sees me and Tuzik. " It is a pleasure, Madame, to see you back here in Yalta. And you sir, I do hope we will shortly have the pleasure of your dining here."

Chekhov replies jokingly that this is a real possibility. His very old and venerable maid Mariushka has been given the extra duties of cooking for the household. Unfortunately all she has in her repertoire is fish and soup, the monotony of which is not well received. He promises that a visit to the restaurant to sample its Crimean specialities will make a welcome change.

We continue along the Promenade and come in sight of Vernet's Bar. If last summer I had been walking with Dmitry we would have continued past this establishment without stopping for a drink or even passing the time of day with these same gentlemen, who glass in hand spend their life gazing at the passers-by. However things are very different this time. As soon as Anton Pavlovich and I are sighted, invitations are extended to us to sit down and take a drink. It is unusually hot for this time of year and we are both in need of something to quench our thirst. Anton needs no second bidding. We take our seats at a table facing the sea.

I am flattered to see that I too with Tuzik have been remembered. This time instead of being simply 'the lady with a little dog' I am introduced by Anton as Anna Ivanovna von Melk from Moscow, Shchyolkovo being so insignificant that no one would have heard of it. Several gentlemen tell me that they recognize me and the little dog from my stay the year before. "Be careful, Anton Pavlovich," jokes one of the habitués. "If my memory serves me correctly, I remember her being escorted around our town last summer by a very distinguished gentleman!"

"Thank you, Vasily Vasileevich for your advice, but I have invited Anna Ivanovna down here purely to help me with a short story that I am writing. She will be spending two to three weeks with me on this assignment before returning to Moscow."

Whether this explanation of my presence on Anton's arm satisfies their curiosity or not I do not know. What I do know, however, is that my arrival, that of a potential Antonovka, God forbid, will now be common knowledge throughout the town.

Anton turns to me as we leave Vernet's to look for a cab, it being too hot to continue on foot.

"Anna, I'm afraid that I may have made a slight mistake." My heart stops for a moment as I envisage the worst.

"No, please don't worry yourself, it's just that I don't think you should be put up in my house. I know I told you in my letter that my sister Masha would be here to act as chaperone. However her plans have changed a little and she's decided to stay in Moscow for a while longer. I had arranged for her to take up a teaching position in a local school here but it's not yet been confirmed. So she's spending a few more weeks working for us in Moscow. She and Olya get on so well and it will be nice for her to spend longer in her company.

And of course two women together in Moscow can write and tell me much more forcefully what I should be doing here. Keep off that cheap Crimean wine, eat proper meals at the right time. Concentrate on your writing and don't waste time working in the garden. And of course keep yourself well away from the Antonovkas!

As regards your sleeping arrangements I think you would be more comfortable at your Pension. As you will realize when you see the new house, not everything has quite been finished. The bedroom doors were only put in last week and already they seem to have warped and don't close properly. There is dust everywhere and not a great deal of furniture. But at least my bedroom and study have turned out pretty well so I can assure you that we can work together in some comfort. And of course as I mentioned in my letter we now have an upright piano, so you can have some relaxation. But as far as sleeping is concerned, I think it would be wiser for you to return to your 'White Eagle' in the evening.

If you agree with this suggestion, I will send a messenger round with your luggage and tell your landlady Varvara Ivanovna that she can expect you later today. At this time of the year she's bound to have rooms available. I suggest that you sleep there, have breakfast and then walk over to me here in the morning. We'll have the day together, relax in the garden for a while if the weather's fine, have some dinner at the house or in town and then I'll accompany you home at the end of the day."

He hesitates for a moment. "I hope that meets with your approval. I apologize for going ahead with this change of plans without consulting you. But I think that only having Mariushka in the house over night as the sole female might start tongues wagging. You saw the sort of reception we had at Vernet's. We need to be as discreet as possible. Otherwise our relationship may be seen to be more than just a working one, and we would not wish for that, would we."

I nod my agreement, secretly relieved that I will have some time to myself at the 'White Eagle' where I can indulge myself in the most pleasurable of nostalgic memories. And of course I do not want to earn the sobriquet of being yet another Antonovka on my first day back in Yalta.

My luggage is taken care of and after a quick tour of Anton's new house and garden I return to my Pension to meet Varvara Ivanovna. When I see the familiar building I have to stop and gather myself before going in. I have such vivid memories of the house.

There is the gate with the latch that Dmitry found so difficult to open. There is the side door leading directly to my room on the ground floor. There is the terrace where I took breakfast and reflected on the possibility that I might become an adulterous woman. And most poignant of all, there is my old room with all its associated memories. My bed where I consumed whole chapters of *Madame Bovary* before being seduced by my lover. The mirror on the wall that reflected my image of the woman taken in adultery and the remorse that I had felt afterwards. So different, I reflect, from that blissful room in the *Slavyansky Bazar,* where all my inhibitions disappeared and Dmitry and I experienced the physical fullness of our love for each other. I attempt a reply to Varvara Ivanovna but my words choke in my throat.

She gives me my key and tells me that she will prepare breakfast in the dining room, since at this time of the year the terrace would be too cold to sit out on. Having unpacked, I am left alone to decide on my plans for the evening. Tuzik is in need of a walk, so we set off towards the Botanical Gardens in the last of the day light. I have not eaten much all day. I feel tired after all the emotions and stress of the day and a less than full night's sleep on the steamer. So after a short walk Tuzik and I make our way to my favourite restaurant.

It is so enjoyable to be back there and to be welcomed by all the waiters. My usual table is prepared for me and Tuzik takes up his customary position in the corner. All that is missing is the presence of a handsome fellow diner at a neighbouring table asking if he may be allowed to feed my dog.

{14}

To my surprise I sleep well and after a late breakfast, during which I have diplomatically to answer Varvara Ivanovna's delicately posed queries as to what exactly I will be doing at Monsieur Chekhov's house, I leave the pension and start up the hill. My first literary engagement awaits me, but I cannot concentrate. Memories of my first visit to the White Dacha come back at each step.

Here are the potholes in the lane where Dmitry took my arm, here is the rough spot where I lifted up my skirt to reveal my boot and stocking and initiate our conversation about Pushkin and his fantasies. I recall how I had bitten my lip in embarrassment and how we had walked on in silence till we reached Chekhov's house.

As I enter the grounds I catch sight of a familiar figure. Arseniy the gardener is busy digging holes to plant the lemon trees, oleanders and camellias which Anton Pavlovich confessed to me he bought too frequently. At the same time I can hear him reciting to himself a passage from an eleventh century religious chronicle, the *Lives of Boris and Gleb,* describing the death of two Russian saints who had been assassinated by their elder brother, the thrice accursed Sviatopolk.

Catching sight of me he throws down his spade, snatches his woollen hat from his head and greets me with a low bow. Anton has told him that I am to be expected. I apologize for having interrupted his recitation and to make amends suggest that after my day's work with Anton Pavlovich he take me on a tour of the estate, whre he can relate the whole story of his beloved saints' martyrdom and at the same time show me all the improvements that have been made during my absence.

"By the way, how is your pet crane?" I ask. " My colleague Dmitry Serov and I had such fun with him the last time we came to visit. We tried to get him to dance, but it was a very hot day and I don't think he was in the mood to entertain us."

"He's fine, thank you Missy, all the more so now that he's got a lady friend for company. We thought he was lonely, so one of my master's friends gave him a present for his birthday, last January it was, and freezing cold. We didn't think the poor thing would survive the winter, but she did. Now I'm trying to teach her the same tricks that her boyfriend can do. But she's a bit on the stubborn side and so far she won't do more than just flap her wings."

The problem of what to do with Tuzik all day is quickly solved. Arseniy tells me that Anton had taken in a stray puppy a few days ago and if the two of them get on together they will be company for each other. The puppy proves to be the same size as my fully grown Tuzik, but they seem happy enough playing around the garden, where Arseniy keeps a watchful eye on them.

I had so delayed my entry into the house that Chekhov, on hearing our voices, comes out to greet me and give his gardener instructions.

"Arseniy, I would be greatly indebted to you if you could stay working in the front garden here in sight of the gate. Keep an eye open for any visitors who may try to come round to see me. I'm afraid that the whole of the local Famine Relief Committee may well come by today. They are a curious lot and they may have had news of a new assistant working here. Simply tell them that I am unfortunately meeting with a literary agent from Moscow and cannot be disturbed." Anton turns to me and with the usual twinkle in his eye invites his agent into his study for the start of our assignment.

The study is far more comfortable than I had been led to believe. The door actually closes, the wood stove gives out a welcoming crackle, the room is warm and the furniture includes a sizeable desk for Anton to sit at and an armchair for me to make notes.

I look at him anxiously. I am conscious that the time for pleasantries is finally over. We are alone and my inadequacies will be revealed. But I do not need to worry. Anton has planned our first meeting meticulously.

"You will remember what I told you in my letter," he begins as we settle down. "The situation is still the same. To put it in the simplest of terms, we have a deadline of the end of the month to produce a manuscript of a short story and deliver it to my publisher in Moscow. This gives us a scant two weeks to work something out.

So what I propose, with your consent of course, is to start by asking you to describe in more detail your relationship with Dmitry Dmitrych and how this evolved from the time you first met. This depiction of your relationship will be the first theme of the story. Following that I will ask you to give me details of your respective marriages,which will allow me to complete my second theme, namely the tyranny of marriage, which justifies the act of adultery when such marriages, existing in name alone, ultimately break down.

I can see that there may be a hostile reaction from many readers, the church for example. And of course our dear friend Leo Tolstoy is likely to become apoplectic, should he ever come across our little story.

On the other hand it may strike a chord with the general reading public. At best they will think that old Anton Pavlovich, despite the rumours of his moribund state, does have something new and original to write about! At worst it will pay a few bills.

I quite understand that what I have asked from you will sound as an unwarranted prying into the intimacies of your private life, which in normal circumstances I would never dream of doing."

The fire has burnt down and Anton stops for a moment to add logs to the stove.

"May I continue in this vein," he asks, " Or do you feel that all this is too personal. Believe me, I will not be offended or surprised if you do."

"No, Anton," I reply. "I knew perfectly well from what you wrote in your letter that I would need to reveal a great deal about myself. Please go on, I have nothing to hide."

Anton is relieved. "You have told me enough about your initial attraction to Dmitry, your longing for some fulfillment in your life, your need to prove yourself as a woman. All that I can understand. But it is Dmitry's changed relationship to you that intrigues me. If I may be bold and frank enough to say this to you, I imagine that Dmitry saw you to begin with as just another holiday romance. You are a very beautiful young lady and he imagined that it would be pleasurable to add you to his list of conquests. After all, as far as he could judge, you were unhappily married, on your own for the first time in your life and that you needed some distraction.

What makes him such an interesting study as the protagonist of my story is how his feelings for you changed so dramatically when he returns to Moscow. Quite simply, here is a Don Juan who falls in love. As far as I can see, he must occupy something of a unique position in the field of Russian literature. I really think that any potential readers, if there are any of course, would be interested in learning about the course of events which changed what was nothing more than a simple liaison into something so much more substantial and lasting."

All this time I have been sitting quietly, nodding in assent as I listen in fascination, witness to how a writer's mind works. Now for the first time I realize that here is the essence of a successful story. It will contain the sensual aspects of a holiday liaison, but will be far more than that.

A psychological analysis of the motives of hero and heroine will add substance to the simple plot.

"Let us start from the beginning then," he says. " Sit back and tell me about your first meeting with Dmitry."

Anton sounds like one of those new psychotherapists who I read are taking Vienna by storm. I dispel a momentary image of Dr. Sigmund Freud and his consulting couch from my mind and begin to relate the account of my first days in Yalta. Chekhov nods and says that this is exactly what he needs.

"I suggest we stop there for a moment and I'll ask you to write down what I dictate. If that sounds acceptable to both of us I see no reason why we shouldn't continue in this vein till we finish the story. The title I already have, thanks to your visit last year."

I balance my note pad on my lap, dip my pen nervously into an inkwell, spill ink on my fingers, find a better pen and begin to write as Anton dictates.

"People said that there was a new arrival on the Promenade: a lady with a little dog. Dmitry Dmitrych Serov, who had already spent a fortnight in Yalta and who was by now used to the life there, had also begun to take an interest in the new arrivals. As he sat on the terrace of Vernet's restaurant he saw a young, fair-haired woman walking along the Promenade, not very tall and wearing a beret. A white Pomeranian trotted after her…."

Anton turns to me. He is satisfied with the opening paragraph. It is time for lunch. I feel that the first paragraph is more than satisfactory. In a few words it has presented us with the two protagonists and set the scene for the story. I tell Anton this and he shrugs modestly.

"Let's hope the rest works out as easily. By the way, I have disguised you as being fair-haired, I hope you don't mind, and I have invented a beret for you to wear for your walk along the Promenade."

"As a matter of fact I did have a beret," I reply. "But I found it was not at all fashionable in Yalta and it was far too hot to wear. It was more suited to the climate in Shchyolkovo. I must have misguidedly bought the silly thing, thinking that I might join the ladies of Shchyolkovo in wearing this latest fashion from Paris. That is how out of touch we are in the provinces. Worse still, Dmitry found it in my bedroom. He laughed when I tried it on for him. He said that it didn't suit me and I should give it to my landlady. So I did and she was delighted with it. "

I have a vision of an intimate bedroom scene when Dmitry was looking through the clothes in my wardrobe and telling me try on what caught his fancy. He did not just undress me, to put it indelicately, he took my wardrobe in hand and dressed me as a young lady with a degree of elegance. But there is no need for Anton to know any of this. The beret can stay.

Lunch is not a great success. Slipping somehow unnoticed through Arseniy's cordon, a visitor by the name of Olga Vasilieva has arrived. She wants to discuss matters of some concern with Anton. Having embarked on the translation of Chekhov's works into English she asks him which English journals he thinks might print her translations. Anton replies acerbically that he is of so little interest to the English public that he doesn't care in the least. I can see that he is tired and annoyed with her questions.

To make matters worse, the fish soup which Mariushka has prepared for us has too much salt in it. Anton makes a joke of it by quoting the proverb that a cook who puts too much salt in her cooking must be in love. When she comes back into the dining room to take the tureen away he confronts her with this. Is it Arseniy she is in love with, or one of the carpenters to whom she has been seen offering tea and biscuits in an intimate corner of her kitchen?

Mariushka makes a tut tutting reply. "Anton Pavlovich, I do declare that you are becoming worse and worse by the day. The next thing you will be doing is writing me into one of those plays of yours."

Anton jokes. " And what makes you think I have not done that already? Not just a play, Mariushka, you will find yourself in some of my stories as well. I really must teach you to read when we have some quiet evenings."

The mood around the table lightens as Olga Vasilieva collects her papers and departs for town. I suggest to Anton that he take a rest before we carry on. He can sense that I am concerned for his well being.

"Anna, I feel that you are going to be far more to me than just someone relating her life story. I can see you as a nurse fussing over a sick old man like me. Just with your presence here you are able to calm me down and soften my bad temper. The way you dealt with that dreadful old battleaxe Olga Vasilieva was wonderful. I would love to see you in action with the League for Famine Relief if they get past Arseniy's barricade.

Anton takes himself off to his bedroom for a siesta and I wander out into the garden to play with Tuzik and his puppy companion. Arseniy takes me for a walk around the estate and shows me his newly planted camellias.

"We had ten degrees of frost here last February and the camellias were still in bloom. Master Chekhov was so proud, said he was a better gardener than he was writer. I don't know about that. I have had people, the educated sort you know, read one or two of his stories to me, but I can't make head nor tale of them. Too many people sitting around and drinking tea from the samovar for my liking. Why can they not be upstanding and doing something useful, like gardening, I'd like to know." I slip away before he has time to continue with the story of Saints Boris and

Gleb and their untimely and unfortunate end at the hands of Sviatopolk the thrice accursed.

Anton is waiting for me in his study. This time he does not dictate but takes notes on how Dmitry's and my relationship developed over the first few days of my stay in Yalta. Of course he remembers our visit to the dacha when we discussed the setting for Act One of Uncle Vanya. At that stage Dmitry and I were not yet lovers, and I find it difficult to describe every detail of the events leading up to my seduction.

By six o'clock we are getting tired. The nights are drawing in and daylight is fading as we finish work. Mariushka has lit the lamps in what passes for the sitting room, but the odd collection of chairs and a deal trestle table, which constitute the only furniture apart from the upright piano in the corner of the room, hardly make it an appealing place in which to spend the evening. In addition the wood stove is smoking badly. Otherwise I would have suggested that I spend a few minutes trying out the piano. I have noticed some sheet music inside the piano stool, nocturnes and preludes by Chopin, which I could have practised if the smoky atmosphere had been more conducive for playing.

Anton is embarrassed by the dismal effect of the room. He says that the least he can do to make amends for the lunchtime fiasco is to suggest we dine in town. Down on the Promenade at my restaurant, as he calls it. Our waiter will be pleased to see us so soon and our table will be waiting.

I am hungry and look forward to tasting again some of the specialities that Dmitry and I tried last summer. Anton calls out to Mariushka, telling her that we are dining in town and that she is free to take the evening off. Time enough, he adds with a gleam in his eye, to feed Arseniy or her male friend on her speciality of over salted fish in the romantic setting of her kitchen. The jibe is met by further tut tutting from the kitchen.

As I had discovered to my dismay, the washing facilities in the dacha had not been a priority for Anton. So we stop off at my Pension on the way into town. I change into a dress more suitable for the evening, put on some perfume that Dmitry bought me for our last evening together in Moscow and dab ineffectively at my inky fingers. I overhear Anton chatting to Varvara Ivanovna while I am so engaged, both of them laughing over some remark he has made. He can be so charming when he wants to be. No wonder his Antonovkas follow him around Yalta in droves. As I check my hair in the mirror I tell my reflection that tonight I am his alone. What a privilege!

The Promenade is well lit and we make a conspicuous couple as we saunter the length of it to our restaurant. The fresh air revives me and Anton, galant as always, tells me that I have an enchanting flush on my cheeks. Hats are raised to us by the officers who still seem to dominate Yalta society. It is pleasant to see that I am also included in this gesture, but I can see that their wives are regarding me, if that is possible, with even more suspicion than before.

Do I really look like a femme fatale, I wonder? I would like to tell them that my relationship with Anton is a purely platonic one and explain the kind of work I have been engaged on for most of the day. Though even that I doubt would stop their speculation.

Over dinner Chekhov tells me about some of his visitors to Autka. One of them is Isaac Levitan,a close friend of his. Anton is gratified that Dmitry and I had admired his landscape paintings in the Tretyakov Gallery.

I feel that I know Anton well enough by now to enquire about Olga Knipper. How is she getting on playing Elena to packed audiences in Moscow? She is fine, he answers briefly, though she is tired and wants to come down to Yalta.

I can see that he does not want to elaborate. Anton's sister Masha has kept him informed about the continuing relationship between Olga and her theatrical director Vladimir Nemirovich Danchenko. What I as a simple provincial girl had not gathered is that in Moscow a leading lady in the theatre tends by tradition to be the director's mistress. Though Chekhov is aware of this state of affairs he remains faithful to his fiancée despite the attentions of the local ladies. For the first time I wonder whether his comments on my appearance and references to the enchanting flush on my cheeks might constitute more than the simple expression of one of a number of lighthearted compliments which come so easily to him. But I quickly brush aside such an unworthy thought. After all my relationship with Anton has already been elevated to that of unofficial nurse, confidante, copyist and emanuensis. Whether my flushed cheeks are enchanting or not, I cannot foresee my duties being required to cover any further eventualities.

{15}

27th October 1899.

It is another sunny day. My faithful sun beam is etched across the ceiling, telling me yet again that it is time to rise. But I need no such urging. There is so much to be done. It is warm enough to breakfast on the terrace and exchange a few words with Varvara Ivanovna, who is wielding a pair of shears prior to pruning her oleanders.

I walk up the hill to Autka, delighting in the freshness of the autumnal morning. As I arrive I spot Arseniy working as usual in the garden. But this time he is not reciting the Lives of the Saints, today being the feast day of his beloved Nestor the Chronicler. When he sees me, he drops everything and hurries over. He is evidently excited.

"Missy, please to come round the garden with me later when you've finished with Master Chekhov. I want to relate to you the life of our sacred Chronicler." How can I refuse? I promise a rendezvous for later in the day.

Anton is waiting impatiently for me in his study and begins dictating to me as soon as I am seated. He asks me to tell him about the events leading up to the moment when Dmitry and I become lovers. I feel very awkward disclosing my feelings before and after our first night together. This, I know perfectly well, is an integral part of the story and I am required to reveal both my and Dmitry's most intimate feelings as our relationship developed.

Chekhov is such an accomplished observer of the human heart that he has exactly captured the essence of Dmitry's ambivalent feelings towards me. Mine in comparison are so simple. I tell him that I had become attracted to Dmitry from the first moment I saw him in the restaurant, and knew that I had fallen in love with him that afternoon at Autka. So conventional, yet so true.

Dmitry's feelings, however, are so much more complex. Anton dictates and I copy his words, realizing as I write that he has fully caught the essence of this ambivalence. Here is my lover, standing on the platform in Simferopol, waiting for the train to depart and take me away from him for ever. Dmitry muses:

"So, this was just another adventure or event in his life, he reflected, and that too was over now, leaving only the memory. He was deeply moved and sad, and he felt a slight twinge of regret: that young woman, whom he would never see again, had not been happy with him, had she? He had been kind and affectionate, yet in his attitude, his tone and caresses, there had been a hint of casual mockery, of the rather coarse arrogance of a victorious male who, besides anything else, was twice her age. The whole time she had called him kind, exceptional, high-minded: obviously she had not seen him in his true colours, therefore he must have been unintentionally deceiving her…."

I finish writing down words which bring me close to tears. This is exactly as Dmitry and I explained our feelings to each other that first time we met in the *Slavyansky Bazar*. How could Anton have sensed this and composed the lines that he had just dictated? I feel that before long he will be privy to every last detail of our adulterous liaison.

***

Anton's words wake me from my reverie. The moment before I had been on the platform kissing the man I had fallen in love with and whom at that stage I thought I was never to see again.

"Anna, rather than going back to our restaurant this evening I have a suggestion to make. We have been invited to dinner by the Headmistress of our local Girls Lycée. It would be churlish of me to refuse her invitation, and I think you would enjoy her company. Varvara Kharkeevich is a remarkable woman and has become a real friend. Bless her, she took me under her wing, her very ample wing as you will see when you meet her, when I first arrived in Yalta. I did not know a soul here, so she introduced me to the great and good in the town, not all of whom I wanted to become acquainted with, but of course she did this with the best of intentions.

To extend a favour to her in return, I volunteered to accept the position of Governor at her school. As a quid pro quo I was able to obtain a teaching position in the Lycée for my sister Masha. She will be the new Geography teacher when the present one leaves, but there is a delay as to when she can start, as I explained to you.

I told Varvara Kharkeevich that you were in Yalta for a few days, so she was kind enough to include you in her invitation. She is very good company, something of a free thinker with very determined views on a number of issues, as you will find out. I can promise you an entertaining evening in her company. If you would like to accept the invitation, we would need to leave quite soon. The boarders eat early as they are set two hour's homework after dinner."

I do not demur. My last experience of a Girls' Lycée was my leaving graduation and prize ceremony at my own school in St. Petersburg some four years ago. Then as a shy, tongue tied young girl I would have been terrified at the thought of attending such a dinner as this.

However, it turns out to be a pleasant evening. The school is housed in a magnificent building in the classical style of the last century, set amongst manicured gardens that would have brought tears of admiration, or perhaps envy, to Arseniy's eyes. We sit down somewhat formally at the dinner table where we are served by some of the senior girls. Their uniform of long blue skirts and matching blouses edged with white lace collars and cuffs, I note with amusement, is exactly the same as the one I had worn as a school girl in St. Petersburg.

After grace has been said conversation flows easily. Dining with us are a couple of elderly teachers, bachelors who prefer to take their meals in the school rather than risk the sometimes suspect offerings in local restaurants.

Varvara Kharkeevich makes a point of including me in the small talk that accompanies the meal. "If I remember correctly," she says, " Anton Pavlovich told me that you were brought up in St. Petersburg, but that you are now living somewhere near Moscow in a town whose name I cannot recall. But never mind, how fortunate for a young girl to receive her education in such a cultured city. And may I say, how lucky your teachers were compared with my own staff, who, given half a chance, I know would escape to Peter's city tomorrow."

I laugh and reply with a little anecdote to the effect that our teachers, lucky as they may well have been, were not always properly prepared for their lessons and on such occasions we were marched off in file to the Hermitage, where we were told to compose a project on some arcane exhibit in one of the many galleries. The Winter Palace was a place where I had spent many happy hours, escaping unsupervised to devour the Western European Art galleries.

Continuing our conversation Varvara Kharkeevich asks me what I intend to do when I return home. I feel for the first time that I can in this sympathetic company explain the very real frustrations of life in Russia for a young woman. I tell her that I had left my Lycée with good grades and a love of literature, not just Russian but all of European literature that was available in translation. I did not include Flaubert!

I mention the fact that as far back as 1859 women in Russia had been allowed to enroll in university courses, but that this privilege had been retracted a few years later. Thus any higher education is effectively denied me.

I realize to my consternation that the table has fallen silent, and what I had intended as a short reply to her question is being listened to by all the table. But since I have their attention I carry on.

Here we are, I argue, on the cusp of the twentieth century and women enjoy fewer rights than anywhere else in the developed world. We are all familiar with the character of the superfluous man in Russian literature. If I had any ability to write I could easily pen a portrait of his counterpart, a superfluous woman in present day Russia. There is no higher education available to us, no suitable careers for us in government or elsewhere, no opportunity for us to aim to be our men folk's equals intellectually. What are we supposed to do?

Other countries have given women the right to vote, at least in local elections. For instance New Zealand apparently gave universal suffrage to women in 1893. In many countries women have control over their earnings and their property, and universities have opened their doors to women. For example in England women at the University of London have achieved graduate status. When will we be accorded these rights in Russia?"

I pause for breath. I notice that I still have the table's attention, so I continue. "Victor Hugo wrote that the 18 th century proclaimed the rights of man and that the 19 th century would proclaim the rights of women. There are precious few days left in this century here in Russia for these rights to be officially proclaimed. So, in answer to your question,Varvara Kharkeevich, what can I do other than return home and remain a virtuous but bored married woman?"

My outburst is met with a moment's silence as my fellow diners digest what I have said. One of the bachelors at the far end of the table breaks in. He had been introduced as the senior history teacher at the Lycée and is obviously eager to continue the conversation.

"As a social historian I do sympathize with you, my dear, and I do take your point. If we look at the problem from a purely philosophical point of view, we must all agree that to some extent social change is taking place here in Russia, but that the change is too slow. Alexander Herzen expressed it so well in his *From the Other Shore.* He argues that the death of our contemporary form of social order ought to gladden rather than trouble our hearts. Yet what is frightening for him is that the departing world leaves behind it not an heir but a pregnant widow. Between the death of the one and the birth of the other he foresees a long night of chaos and desolation. This, I fear, is where we now find ourselves."

I had not expected the conversation to take such a serious direction, but I am fascinated to hear his words which seem to echo so closely my own sentiments. He continues.

"We abolished serfdom some forty years ago but the peasants are still tied economically to their masters. There is widespread famine in the countryside, unrest spreading through the land and there is in St. Petersburg an unsympathetic government which is totally out of touch with the realities of the situation. Anti Government factions are forming abroad and there is a strong possibility that the Menshiviks or Bolsheviks, or whatever they call themselves, will arrive in Russia and ferment discontent even more. Herzen's long night of chaos and desolation may be darker and nearer than we think.

Look at our Czar Nicholas, a harmless family man but one who is determined to hold onto autocracy despite his inadequacies. The Russian Orthodox Church supports the status quo, the Government is adamantly opposed to any attempt at democratization and the formation of political parties is forbidden, though that does not prevent them from emerging as illegal organizations.

My dear young lady, social change, perhaps even political change, is coming, it is true, but so slowly that I cannot foresee for the time being a way out of your predicament, namely your search for a worthwhile goal in life."

Varvara Kharkeevich breaks in. "Of course, Anna Ivanovna, if it is of any consolation, the same situation faces my own girls on graduation.They too have limited career opportunities. However, for what it's worth, my secretary told me yesterday about a new career for young girls as stenographers and typists, for which the introduction of this new invention, the typewriting machine, is responsible.

A representative from some American company, Underwood I think it was called, installed two of his writing machines in my secretary's office and left her a short pamphlet. I have not read it myself, as I need to ask one of our English teachers for a translation. Apparently it explains how this invention has acted as a catalyst for social change in the United States.

Instead of men occupying office jobs as clerks, the introduction of the typewriter has made employment in these same offices available to women. And they have proved far more adept at mastering the necessary skills than the men, with whom they are competing and whom they are now replacing in ever growing numbers. So maybe one day we will see our girls doing the same.

Well, enough of politics, Anna Ivanovna. Let us change the subject. I suggest you discuss literature with Anton Pavlovich here, he always enjoys talking to pretty ladies and discussing his latest stories with them. It is a lot safer in this country than talking politics."

Anton Pavlovich, who had remained silent up to now, joins in the conversation. He tells Varvara Kharkeevich that he has engaged me as his copyist for his latest short story.

In a small way he has provided a modicum of employment for a young lady.

The Headmistress is obviously intrigued by my role as Anton's assistant, but is too polite to enquire directly as to why Anton should suddenly need one. He for his part is loathe to explain the need for this collaboration, when he has up to now been able to write perfectly well without outside assistance. He has no time to answer as Varvara Kharkeevich catches sight of my ink stained fingers, on one of which a callous is forming. I explain that my job requires a certain amount of writing.

"Anton, my dearest man, why on earth don't you buy her one of these new typing machines? Our Underwood man said that they have an agency here in Yalta. My secretary swears that it is a wonderful invention. It has a special Cyrillic keyboard and she tells me proudly that she can even make copies using some sort of special carbon paper."

Chekhov listens attentively. "Yes, I have heard of typewriters and I quite agree, they have their place, maybe in an office. But the noise of all those clicking keys would drive me to distraction. Whereas my lovely Anna sits in my studio, quiet as a church mouse, and transcribes what I dictate. I am utterly selfish, as in so many other things, and I don't think I could change my working habits. On the other hand, if what you tell me about making copies is true, I could have my prejudices overturned. In the world of the theatre one always needs more than just the single manuscript."

Turning to me he gives me one of those smiles that would make any woman his Antonovka. "Anna my dearest, when you get back to Moscow and I know how much you love being there, you could use one of these newfangled machines in the Art Theatre office and type up everything I send you, complete with all those copies. What do think to that idea?" Before I have time to answer, Varvara Kharkeevich interposes.

"Anton Pavlovich, you are impossible, just like a man, so impractical. You cannot just expect Anna, clever as she may be, to learn this typewriting business overnight. My secretary says that it takes a great deal of practice and training to..." She pauses for a moment. "What's the word I want… to touch type I think they call it in the new jargon. On the other hand she could quickly learn to type with two fingers as apparently beginners are taught to do. She would be most welcome to visit us again before she goes home to see how our secretary operates the machine."

The evening draws to a close. The senior girls clear the table and depart to do their homework, while Anton and I bid our hostess goodbye. We find a cab without any difficulty, but instead of returning directly to my pension we decide it would be more pleasant to take a stroll along the Promenade.

Anton pays off the cabbie and we make our way by the sea, both of us absorbed in our own thoughts. Thanks to Anton's vague suggestion, in my imagination I am working at the Moscow Art Theatre. I have told Viktor that I am fully employed during the daytime. On what I get up to outside office hours he can only speculate. Such stuff are dreams made of!

We pass Vernet's Bar, which at this late time of the evening is deserted. We sit at one of the tables looking out over the sea. Anton is the first to break the silence.

"Anna, I know that I did not make a great contribution to the discussion at the dinner table, but I do agree that our privileged aristocratic and middle class lives will one day have to change. Once I have *Three Sisters* out of the way I have a mind to write another play based on this subject. Perhaps a noble family fallen on hard times through their own inadequacies. You are so good at it, you can give me the title before I start writing," he jokes.

I think for a moment, trying to remember something Dmitry had told me. "You can call it *The Cherry Orchard,"* I reply.

Anton looks at me quizzically. "That sounds like a very good title, but why a cherry orchard?"

"As I remember it," I reply, " there was a case in which Dmitry's bank was involved. I think the family was forced to auction their famous orchard to pay the mortgage on their estate. The irony of it was that the son of one of their former serfs bought it. He decided to cut down their beloved cherry orchard and build dachas for the affluent middle classes, who had grown rich with the growth of industry around Moscow. There in a nutshell you have the title and plot for your next play, the social and economic forces in play in our Russia, as symbolized in the destruction of a cherry orchard."

Chekhov takes hold of his monocle and starts cleaning the lens with his pocket handkerchief. It is a mannerism which I have observed before when he has been dictating to me. I have learnt to remain silent and wait to be made party to his thoughts. But this time I am impatient.

"Anton, I'll give you five kopecks for your thoughts."

"I'm so sorry, my dear. You know me well enough to guess in what direction these thoughts were heading. As soon as my *Three Sisters* is finished, you and I will start work on this *Cherry Orchard* of yours. He thinks for a moment.

"I can see the final act now. The family leaving their ancestral home, furniture covered in dust sheets and as the curtain falls on an empty stage, the distant sounds of an axe cutting down their precious cherry orchard, which as you say is a symbol for the passing of their privileged way of life. The ending of a play is always the hardest part to write and there we have it completed already.

But wait a minute. In theatrical terms the sound of an axe off stage needs to be complemented with a visual image on stage. I don't think that a director, even our esteemed Nemirovich Danchenko, would know when to drop the curtain on an empty stage. Perhaps we could have someone, perhaps the family's aged retainer, make a slow painful entry. He tries the handle of the door. "Locked. They have forgotten about me, it does not matter. I will sit here a moment." He lies down on one of the dustcovered sofas. Silence, as the audience gradually becomes aware that he has died, a silence once more broken by the sound of a far off axe chopping down a tree in the cherry orchard. An elegy for a lost world, a lost estate and a lost class. I could even write some humour into it, call it a vaudeville in four acts. That would be a challenge for our director."

He leans toward me and gives me a kiss on my cheek. I look around in some concern, but the evening has turned chill and at that late hour there is nobody on the Promenade to see us. A fit of coughing takes hold of him.

"Anna", he says, "You see how the cold here in Yalta affects me. Pack your bags. You and I will work on this *Cherry Orchard* on the French Riviera as soon as I am done with my *Three Sisters.* I know a fine hotel in Nice, the Pension Russe. I was there last year and the climate is much kinder to my lungs. France is very civilized. The chambermaids smile like duchesses and even the beggars are addressed as Monsieur or Madame. I even saw the English Queen Victoria drive by in her carriage. France is very much to my liking."

I reply with a coquetry that I know Anton loves. "And I believe that there is a boardwalk along the seaside called the Promenade des Anglais. I'll bring Tuzik with me and when we finish writing each scene we will take the air arm in arm. The English passersby will recognize Monsieur Chekhov, the well known Russian playwright, and will raise their hats to you. They will look at me and not knowing my name they will refer to me as " the lady with a little dog."

Anton rises from his seat. As if rehearsing this scene he draws my arm within his and we start to walk along the Promenade.

"Priceless, my dearest Anna, do not tempt me any further. What you propose is so seductive I cannot wait to finish *Three Sisters.* I may have to introduce a murder or a duel in Act Four to hurry things along."

After a few steps Anton finds it difficult to continue our walk. His breathing is laboured and I suggest that we sit at the next bench along our path to rest a little. He takes to polishing his monocle till his breath comes back. I wait patiently till he recovers sufficiently to continue.

"What I have to say, ma chérie, is serious. As a doctor I know the gravity of my illness. I cannot expect to live very much longer. I certainly will not be writing anything after this *Cherry Orchard* of yours. If, God willing, I'm given time to do even that.

Here is a suggestion, a mad one as you must expect coming from me. Come to Nice with me and transcribe my play, line by line and scene by scene, as you are doing with our short story. And look after me, if you will. Make certain that I take my pills and go to bed at the right time." He waits for my reply.

"Anton, I'm speechless. I don't know what to say. Help you with your play? Yes I would love that. But how long would I have to be away?"

"Of course, your selfish old Anton Pavlovich would ideally love to keep you in Nice till he had finished the whole play. But you wouldn't have to wait till I write "*Sound of axe off stage. Curtain falls,*" at the end of Act Four. You could go back to Moscow before then of course if you wanted to. I would simply send you the manuscript Act by Act as I am going to do with my *Three Sisters.*

Don't give me an answer now. Just let me live the short time left for me with the hope that one day we may be walking together along the Promenade des Anglais, a scene which you, *ma chérie*, described so enchantingly."

There is not a soul to be seen on our Promenade. I turn in my seat to face him. "Oh Anna, my dearest Anna, if only you and I had met...," he begins as a violent fit of coughing takes hold of him. He cannot complete his words. But it does not matter, I know without them being spoken exactly what he would have said.

{16}

30 October 1899

We work well together over the next few days and the story progresses most harmoniously. Anton now has enough information on his protagonists' feelings for each other that he tells me it is time to concentrate on the second part of his enquiry, namely the tyranny of marriage. He asks me to describe my married life.

This is not difficult. I start with my mad agreement to marry Viktor when I was only twenty. I tell him that it was a terrible mistake, one that I realized within a few weeks of married life. Instead of my finding a new role as a married woman and a chance to discover a more exciting life, I found myself a virtual prisoner in my own home. It became so apparent that Viktor and I had nothing in common. We exchanged small talk when we were together and slept in separate bedrooms once our honeymoon was over.

I mention the incident with the post when I was not allowed to receive my own mail and how this had laid bare my husband's patriarchal views on marriage. I briefly describe my experiences at the Gaslighting Ball and even more briefly the manner in which that evening finished. How only the thought of Dmitry kept me sane during those loveless days and nights.

Anton makes notes and then asks about Dmitry and his relationship with his wife. I tell him what Dmitry had told me that night, when for the first time I had the courage to ask him about her. How he too was locked in a loveless marriage. Married off when he was only a second year student at university to a woman who seemed to be half as old again as he was, of whom he was afraid and whom he thought of as narrow minded, not very intelligent and rather unrefined. He disliked spending time at home and so spent most of his free time at his club. He had begun being unfaithful and had found that it was easy to carry on affairs with a number of women who found him attractive.

"So there you are, Anton," I say as I finish my narrative of conjugal despair. "Two lovers caught in the tyranny of marriage as you so aptly describe it."

Over the days spent together in such proximity we have developed a close and intimate, though platonic relationship, if that is not a contradiction in terms. He calls me his platonic Antonovka. Though is it possible, I wonder, as I describe most intimately the details of my adulterous affair that I may be able to discern within this unguarded remark a note of wistfulness?

***

The next day Anton suggests that as we are making such good progress it might be time for me to write to my husband and give him an indication of when I am likely to return to him: a little piece of Chekhovian irony, I detect! There is also the matter of booking tickets for the ferry to Odessa and the train to Moscow and these mundane activities bring me to my senses and clear my mind.

No longer a dream existence in Yalta, where I have been working for a man whom I admire so much and who tells me that my work in writing this story is invaluable to him. My dreams are about to end but before they do so completely, there is one reprieve. In the day's mail there is an invitation to Anton Pavlovich Chekhov and the partner of his choice to attend a Charity Ball organized by the Crimean Committee for Famine Relief. Anton says that he is obliged to attend this function as his public status as a Committee member demands his presence. He will hate every minute of it, he confides to me.

I remember with amusement his instructions to Arseniy to keep the Famine Relief ladies at bay, should they try to visit Autka. Anton says in his beguiling way that the evening will only be bearable if I consent to be the partner of his choice.

"It is one of the social events of the year in Yalta," he tells me. "You will have a chance to meet the cream of Yalta society, for what it's worth, and I will have a chance to show my public that with a beautiful woman on my arm, there is still some life in this moribund old hack. As regards a dress for the occasion I believe that Masha has left some things in a cupboard, though I think you are a bit slimmer than she is. But that could be solved by Mariushka if necessary...."

I interrupt him. I had packed my one and only ball gown, the one I had worn to the Gaslighting Ball in Shchyolkovo, in order to show it off to Dmitry in Moscow. In my hurry to pack for the Crimea I had neglected to take it out of my valise and leave it with the rest of my clothes that were not wanted for Yalta. I had found the gown when I unpacked my things in my pension, and hung it up in the cupboard, never thinking that there would be an opportunity to wear such a beautiful dress here in Yalta.

I ask Anton what sort of gowns the local ladies will be wearing. He jokes that the Yalta belles, of whom there will be many at the Ball, consider that the Crimean fashions they wear here are well ahead of anything available in Parisian fashion shops. I mention that I have a gown of my own, which Dmitry had chosen for me in Moscow and which my husband had considered a little risqué when I wore it to a ball in Shchyolkovo.

Anton says that the Antonovkas will doubtless be quite put out by a woman from Moscow upstaging them both in beauty and haute couture. But it will be beneficial both for his image and for them to see him arrive with a new woman on his arm. These young ladies, supposing that their Anton

Pavlovich has a new conquest to show off in public, might take to sulking and leave him alone for the evening.

He confesses that he is not a great dancer and that in any event he will have to spend most of the evening engaged in polite conversation with local dignitaries. On the other hand there will be a number of pleasant young people of my own age, to whom he will introduce me.

The next morning reveals low-lying clouds resting on the mountain tops around the town and a damp mist forms over the sea, turning my face and hair damp as I make my way to Autka. However instead of finding Anton waiting patiently for me in his study, I learn from Arseniy that he has been called out to attend a sick child in a village close by. He is in fact having to attend many more patients than expected as the effects of the famine on the peasants' health take their toll. His visit consumes most of the morning and he returns tired, cold and wet through. His doctors in Moscow would be aghast.

After a change of clothes he orders lunch to be served. Having consumed a glass of wine, followed by a second, he recovers his spirits. He jokes about the obligations of being both a doctor and a writer. On a previous visit to a farm where he had been called to visit a sick patient, the farmer's wife had run out as he approached, saying that it was far more important for Anton to check on a cow, which was having trouble delivering her calf. Her husband, whose illness was the reason he had been called out, could wait till the calf was born.

"Never mind, I'm lucky to be in demand both as a doctor and as a scribbler. I suppose medicine is my lawful wife and literature is my mistress. When I've had enough of the one, I can go and spend the night with the other," he laughs. "Well, I've had my morning with my wife, now let's see what demands my mistress has on me."

We climb up to his study to consult his mistress. On his note pad I can see a number of questions. He needs to probe further into my feelings after I returned to Shchyolkovo. A young girl who has entered ino a relationship with an older man whom she is never going to see again. Once again I have to bare my soul!

I tell him about the journey home after parting with Dmitry, my firm belief that I am never going to see again the man with whom I had fallen in love. I feel annoyed that Viktor's supposed eye problem is not serious after all and that he had just wanted me to cut short my stay in Yalta and hurry home. His remarks, that having spent a considerable amount of money on my cure, he can see no visible improvement in my appearance or my general health also annoys me. An eye infection, my foot, he must be blind, I think uncharitably. I know full well that I look and feel better than for a long time. After all, as proof I have a lover who has told me this repeatedly.

Then I describe the events that took place at the theatre when Dmitry suddenly appeared. Anton stops writing in amazement. "This needs more of an explanation from you," he exclaims. "How did a serial philanderer, I'm sorry Anna, but that is how he has come across to me so far, how did this man suddenly realize that your relationship was different from that which he had enjoyed before with a number of other women?"

"I don't really know, Anton. You would have to ask Dmitry himself," I reply. I cast my mind back to that night in the *Slavyansky Bazar* when we had talked for hours. He had told me then how he had found it impossible to put me out of his mind, how he had come to realize that he had to see me again and confess that he had fallen in love with me, in absentia as it were. I tell all this to Anton.

"A Don Juan who falls in love." he interrupts. "What a marvellous story this will make. Go on, Anna, this is fascinating." So I reveal to him our secret trysts in Moscow and our meeting at the rehearsal for *Uncle Vanya* in Shchyolkovo.

Then I tell him about the incident with the post when I, for the first time, realize that I despise my husband and feel no remorse for deceiving him. I amuse him by telling him about my flirting with a young man at the Gaslighting Ball. And finally a brief mention about the few occasions when Dmitry and I can be together in Moscow. How our happiness has been marred by the need constantly to deceive our partners.

"Don't go any further, Anna, I have enough material here to finish the story. Why don't you take Tuzik out, have a chat with Arseniy and Mariushka. No better still, why don't you go up to the Lycée and see if you can practise on one of their Underwood machines? I don't need you back here to transcribe my scribbles for at least a day. Come round tomorrow afternoon and we will see how far I have progressed. But what we have done today is good, very good, have no doubt about it. Off you go and enjoy your free time."

I go down stairs, pick up the mail and return with it on tiptoe to his study. Anton is making notes,writing furiously, oblivious to my presence as I put his letters by his side. At this rate, I realize in despair, I could be booking my ticket home within a couple of days. But I take comfort in the fact that Anton has obviously not forgotten the suggestion which he had mooted at Varvara Kharkeevich's dinner party. That I should type up his manuscript when I get back to Moscow. Possibly even the manuscript for *Three Sisters*. But as usual my thoughts are racing ahead too fast. Anton has not even mentioned that possibility again. All that farfetched talk about a cherry orchard must have pushed it out of his mind.

I had almost forgotten one important factor in my daydream. I still have a husband! Where Viktor comes into all this is unclear, but I do know that he is becoming more and more irrelevant as the days pass. He can be dealt with if and when *Russian Thought*'s winter edition appears.

Such are my musings as Tuzik and I walk through the imposing gates to the Lycée and cross the lawn to the front door. My first lesson in typewriting is about to start.

{17}

31st October 1899

This morning I arrive at Autka in good time, to find Anton again waiting for me in his study. Yesterday's mist has cleared with the weather turning colder. But the room is cosy and warm with the stove crackling away. However, our noisy carpenters disturb our start. Heavy footsteps ring out on the stairs as they bring up offcuts from their sawn timber to replenish the log basket.

Finally all is quiet again. Anton asks about yesterday's typing lesson. I tell him that the secretary at the Lycée had told me how difficult it was to learn to " touch type," as she calls it. But with a little practice I had found it quite easy, cheating by using two fingers and looking at the keys. The fact that I would be able to make copies by using a kind of carbon paper impresses Anton. If I am to type his manuscript in Moscow, there would be a copy for me to take to the publishers and another to send down to Anton here in Yalta.

It is a revelation to see how much Anton has written in note form from the sketchy information I provided him with in our previous session. I write as he dictates. The story of Dmitry's journey to find me in Shchyolkovo and our encounter at the theatre comes to life so vividly.

The moments of happiness, frustration and sadness that Dmitry and I experience in that little love nest of a bedroom in the *Slavyansky Bazar* are portrayed with such delicacy and sensitivity that I all but feel Anton's physical presence in these scenes. He suggests that we leave the story with an ambiguous and inconclusive ending, with both protagonists parting in Moscow. As far as he is concerned, the story is complete in itself.

I write from his dictation. " *And it seemed-given a little more time- a solution would be found and then a new and beautiful life would begin. And both of them clearly realized that the end was far,*

far away and that the most complicated and difficult part was only just beginning."

I put down my pen and look at Chekhov questioningly. "*Et voilà*! That's it, finished," he says. "We don't need to add another word." Yes, he is happy with the way the story has evolved. Yes, he is relieved that his precious manuscript will shortly be typed and given to his publisher. And yes, he is delighted that together we will meet this stringent deadline, which has been constantly at the back of our minds over the last days.

He goes down to the cold cellar and brings up a bottle of champagne. We drink to our success. But I see that something is worrying him.

"Anna, do you not realize that unless we disguise Dmitry's and your identity, give you different names and perhaps even change the title, our reading public will in all likelihood identify you as the lady with the little dog and Dmitry as your lover. I could say that you come from the town of S, not Shchyolkovo, for example, and even call the story 'The Lady with the Large Dog', anything you care to think of. Though on reflection I don't think 'large dog' has quite the cachet of the original title."

"If my husband reads our story and thinks he has identified me as the heroine, then let it be," I reply. " His position in Government service will mean that he thinks he is required to take strong, decisive action against an adulterous wife. That can only mean a divorce. Dmitry and I have already discussed this possibility. As far as I'm concerned, it would be a welcome relief from what I have inflicted on me now in this farce of a marriage.

So to be realistic, if Dmitry and I are identified as the real life characters, then the story will have acted as the catalyst for a better future. So please, Anton, don't feel guilty. What you have written is no more than the truth and neither Dmitry nor I are ashamed of what we have done.

I realize that I will be branded as an immoral woman and that for your part you will be seen as condoning adultery. But times are changing and people's attitudes to these issues are now more sympathetic and understanding. Women are asserting themselves more and more. They will not stand for men telling them what to do with their lives and their bodies. They will not accept the subservient role they have foisted on them in marriage.

For every male fulminating against my actions in the story and against your sympathetic treatment of adultery, which threatens their pathetic view of male supremacy, there will many more women lining up to support us. So I'm quite happy with what we've written."

Anton thinks for a moment. "Alright then, Anna. You are now Anna Sergeyevna von Diederitz and your lover is Dmitry Dmitrych Gurov. If you don't change your mind in the next day or two, and trust me, you are at perfect liberty to do so, then go back to Moscow, type up the manuscript with your changed identities and hand it over to Goltsev. I will write and warn him to expect you. One thing, though, I beg of you. Whatever you do, do not lose the manuscript."

Anton takes down a calendar from the wall above his desk. " I hate to mention this, but it really is time we looked into booking your ferry ticket. You're probably not aware that sailings are not so regular in the autumn and because of that cabins get booked up early. Then after booking the ferry there is the train ticket to think about. I'll ask one of the young men at the ball tomorrow to help you with the tickets. He works for the Shipping Line here. I know he will be delighted to help you. He's a nephew of our Headmistress and knows about you already, so there will not be a problem.

But let's put all that aside for the moment. Our great Charity Ball takes place tomorrow evening and my invitation tells me that our attendance is required at eight of the evening. I'll come and pick you up from your Pension some time in advance of that and we'll arrive in style at the Assembly Rooms, courtesy of a municipal carriage, which those formidable women on the Famine Relief Committee have deemed necessary to convey me in my ill state of health the short distance to the ballroom. I must say I look forward to hearing their comments when they set their eyes on my partner. Anton Chekhov, the old dog, still has enough life in him to appreciate beautiful young women!"

Despite this gallantry I can see that Anton is tired after such a long day. We part at the door and Tuzik and I walk back to the Pension. There I am met by Varvara Ivanovna, who is evidently in the mood for a little conversation. This is a little ominous! Not only does she not have any other guests staying, but she has up to now not been able to obtain the information she really wants from me. What exactly is my work with Anton Pavlovich, she asks.

In answer to her questions I tell her that I will be leaving for Moscow in the next few days, but before I go I am invited to attend the Famine Relief Ball. When it comes time to dress, it would be most beneficial if she could help me with my costume.

Her surprise that I am leaving Yalta and not staying on as one of Chekhov's Antonovkas is so clearly visible on her face that I can hardly restrain myself from laughing. I show her my calloused, ink stained fingers and tell her that I have been employed to do little more than transcribe his story, the story of *The Lady with a Little Dog*. This task has now been completed and there is no reason for me to stay longer in Yalta. I need to get home to see my husband, a statement that has no more than an economy of truth about it.

I spend the rest of the evening in my room trying to compose a letter to Viktor. I certainly do not intend to compose an explanation for my actions to date, nor to attempt an apology for them. Eventually I settle on brevity. I simply inform him that I will be home within the week. A week will give me time to get to Moscow, spend a night or two with Dmitry discussing our future together and the most dreadful of thoughts, to catch the local train back to Schyolkovo.

{18}

1st November 1899

I have the indulgence of having the day to myself, sleeping late into the morning. I attend to my toilette and by late afternoon go in search of Varvara Ivanovna. We lay out my dress on the bed, select the bodice that best goes with it and check that my silk stockings and gloves are *comme il faut.* Varvara Ivanovna lends me an inexpensive necklace. When I finish dressing, my ball gown produces the same effect on my landlady as it had on my darling Dunyasha, whom I miss so much. I am exercised as to how it will be received.

I know that the evenings in Yalta at this time of the year are cool, so out of modesty as well as expediency I wrap a shawl around my bare shoulders. Anton arrives on time, compliments me on my appearance, as of course I knew he would, and we set off for the Assembly Rooms. Yalta looks especially beautiful. The cooler weather makes the sky seem clearer. The stars shine brightly above the dark semicircle of mountains encompassing the town and for good measure a full moon reflects in the dark waters of the harbour. I want Dmitry by my side to enjoy this romantic scene. But I will have to leave such thoughts behind. My duty this evening is towards Anton.

To my pleasurable surprise the evening turns out to be most enjoyable. I am introduced to the great and good of Yalta society, who prove to be less starchy than I had anticipated. The Committee ladies jokingly compliment me on my choosing Mr Chekhov to accompany me to the Ball. They ask how long I will be staying in Yalta, but their attention is on Anton, who after a discreet pause they wrench from my arm and take off to discuss details of their Famine Relief activities.

Fortunately I am not left alone for very long. Varvara Kharkeevich's nephew Andrey introduces himself and politely insists on my joining his party of friends during the interval, during which refreshments will be served.

I call to mind another Ball when a young man had sought me out to share the zakuski in the interval. Seryozha, I wonder,what young ladies have you been dancing with since I was your partner on the dance floor? I must admit that I had hardly given a thought to young Sergey Ivanovich Platonov since then. Yet irrationally I now felt a certain jealousy when I imagine him with those very ladies whom I had encouraged him to seek out.

I am invited to dance. This time to my relief I find that I am not being besieged by a file of lecherous old men eager to present themselves as partners. The sophistication of the proceedings here in this stylish Crimean city stand out in marked contrast to the boorish behaviour I am accustomed to back home. Though my dress is remarked on favourably I am relieved to see that it is no more décolleté than a number of other gowns being worn. Perhaps people are more accustomed to seeing bare flesh here in the warmth of the south than in the "frozen north", as they refer to my home town near Moscow.

During the course of the evening I am introduced to the rest of Andrey's party, all young people of my own age. I find this a pleasant change, having spent so much time recently in the company of older men, my husband, Dmitry, Anton and others. Now I have a chance to talk to young men and women of my own age. And to add to this pleasure I am engaged to dance with several of them.

Andrey tells me that his friends are planning an excursion tomorrow to the Livadia Palace. The idea is to explore the grounds and then have a picnic on the beach. They would be delighted for me to be included in their number.

Andrey has evidently been told by his aunt to concern himself with procuring my ferry ticket. He suggests that we meet at the ticket office at the port and start our promenade from there.

However I have one more duty to perform. I leave my new friends and take my place at the top table. It is a surprise to see Anton looking nervous. I have been parted from him for no more than an hour, but he looks so thankful and relieved when I join him. I think how sad it is that he has to content himself with me, when the obvious person to be by his side is Olga Knipper. Anton's written work in itself is so full of ironies, yet here is the most poignant of ironies. His illness confines him to Yalta while Olga's acting keeps her in Moscow.

The evening finishes with a number of speeches from the platform. We fall silent as speaker after speaker conveys the same message. The famine that had started earlier in 1898 due to a disastrous crop failure is still continuing and accounting for hundreds of thousands of deaths. Peasants are pulling thatch from the roofs of their houses to feed their livestock as there is no hay left. Cattle are being slaughtered rather than being left to die of starvation. The Russian Government has provided only 900,000 roubles to fund a famine relief programme, whilst at the same time continuing to build battleships, each one costing ten times the amount set aside for feeding the peasants.

At least two million roubles are needed to offer any hope of averting imminent disaster. All present at the Charity Ball are asked to dig deep in their pockets to help fund this appeal. Anton makes a little speech in which he promises a financial contribution when his next literary work is published. Other dignitaries promise to make similar donations to the Appeal.

On this rather sombre note the evening draws to a close. I just have time to confirm with Andrey that we will meet at the Ferry Office at 1 p.m before Anton hands me into the carriage that has been laid on for us. He is obviously exhausted, says he does not feel well and just wants to be left alone. On parting at my Pension he kisses me, holds my hand and thanks me again for the support I have provided. I tell him that I have done so little, but he assures me that is not true. "My darling Anya, your presence by my side was more than enough to make the evening bearable."

{19}

2nd November 1899

The day has been delightful. I wake and am up before my faithful sunbeam etches itself across the ceiling. It promises a sunny day for our picnic. This Crimean autumn of 1899, according to Varvara Ivanovna, has been one of almost endless sunshine and today bodes to be almost as hot as at mid summer.

Tuzik has been invited. We can't have the Lady with the Little Dog without her dog, Andrey had quipped as we parted the night before. I make my way to the port after a leisurely breakfast. The matter of buying ferry and train tickets is completed competently by Andrey in a matter of minutes. Holding these tickets in my hand makes me realize once again that this is my last full day in Yalta and that my short retreat from the realities of the world is nearly over.

But to compensate, I must admit that this precious day could not have been spent in better company. Andrey counts me as his partner and introduces me to the other four couples making up our group. We are a merry bunch of picnickers as we set off along the coastal path towards the Livadia Palace. The men carry our picnic hampers between them while we girls hang behind, chatting and laughing as young girls do.

We must have looked a pretty sight; the men, jacketless in their coloured waistcoats and light trousers, boaters jauntily on the back of their heads and the girls in their light cotton dresses and crocheted lace blouses, parasols shading their faces from the strong midday sun. After a few versts the path leaves the sea and winds up through a pine forest to the grounds of the Palace. Here Stiva, who I had noticed the night before as being the most extrovert of the party, takes up the role of tour guide.

"Please note," he begins, imitating the intonation of an official guide, "Here we have before us the complex of buildings that constitute the Livadia estate. Please pay attention at the back there, I do not wish to have to repeat myself! The Palace is built of white Crimean marble in the Neo - Renaissance style of architecture. It was completed in the 1860s as the official summer residence of the Russian Imperial Family. The Palace has been frequented by both our emperors Alexander the Second and Alexander the Third."

By now our tour guide is losing the attention of our group. It is hot and we are hungry and tired after our walk. But Stiva is not yet ready to give up his self appointed role.

"Please take care as you walk down towards the beach. The pine needles are slippery and some of the steps are in a poor condition. Thank you for your attention. If you have found my tour of interest a small financial contribution would be most appreciated."

He puts out his boater more in hope than expectation and is rewarded with a selection of sweets and chocolates, most of which look as if they have melted in the heat.

We make our way down to a small cove with a secluded sandy beach. Here the men drop their picnic baskets in the shade of the pine trees, take off their boots and socks, roll up their trouser legs, and start climbing over the rocks at the far end of the cove. Just like overgrown school boys, we young sophisticated ladies agree. These sophisticated ladies settle down on the beach and naughtily divest themselves of their shoes.

"Anna," one of the girls turns to me. "Please excuse our curiosity, but we would love to know a little more about you. Last night at the Ball you told us about St. Petersburg and your home town. But we did not know you then and our conversation was somewhat formal. We rarely meet anyone from the north and someone told us that you were here in Yalta last year. If we are not being too inquisitive, could you tell us something about yourself?"

"You're quite right, I was here last September. I came down for what should have been a month, but in fact was less than two weeks. My husband sent for me after a false alarm over a suspected problem with his eyes and I had to return home earlier than I had wanted to."

The girls digest this sketchy account of my stay in Yalta but it obviously does not satisfy them. Another girl asks, "Anna, how did you spend your time here? If I may say so, you're so beautiful that it must have been hard to keep our menfolk away. Yalta has a reputation for its laxity of morals and men quite freely strike up conversations with members of the opposite sex, even with ones to whom they have not been properly introduced. Did this happen to you?" The other girls edged closer to hear my reply.

"If you promise me to keep a secret," I reply. " I did actually meet one man I really liked. That's ridiculous, I didn't just like him, I fell in love with him. But my lips are sealed as to what really happened between us."

To their dismay I hurry to change the subject. "You know Anton Pavlovich and I have been busy this last week working on a story together."

"Of course we believe you when you say that yours is just a professional relationship. But as you know half of the young ladies in Yalta are in love with Anton Pavlovich and these Antonovkas, as we call them, are spreading the wildest rumours about you and Anton."

" Let them, if that is what they want to spend their time doing. I am sorry to disappoint you, but I can only repeat that I am here at Anton Pavlovich's request. I can say no more than that. However, as to last summer, that is a different matter. To satisfy your curiosity, all I can say is that what happened to me then will appear as the short story that Anton and I have been writing.

I suggest you go to that nice bookseller in the 'Bukva' bookshop, you know the one on Pushkinskaya, towards the end of December and ask for the winter number of *Russian Thought*. If all goes well our story should be published by then."

It is strange to think that back in my bedroom in the pension and hidden under the mattress of my bed is the manuscript for this very story that we are talking about. And here am I, quite blasé in telling myself and others that by December I will have typed up the manuscript, passed it over to the editor of *Russian Thought* and that it will be published.

My young friend will not let me go that easily. "Anyway you could at least tell us the title of the story," she urges me.

"Well, alright. I don't think Chekhov would mind a little indiscretion. It is called, as you would expect, *The Lady with a Little Dog*. That will be no surprise to you. But I am warning you, once you have read the story, you will probably change your opinion of me." And on that note of mystery the girls can see that I will not be drawn further.

By this time the men have finished clambering over the rocks. In merry mood they now roll up their trousers even further and wade into the water. Judging by their shouts the sea must be cold, but it does not deter them from splashing through the waves.

The girls decide that they too can do with more entertainment. Simply sitting chatting is not at all enough, particularly now that the most interesting subject of conversation for them has come to an unsatisfactory conclusion. We make certain that we still have the beach to ourselves. With a giggle we roll down our stockings. How wonderful to emulate the boys in the water. Holding up our skirts and petticoats all five of us approach the sea. I have never before felt anything so delicious as the complete novelty of sand and sea on bare flesh.

The men return as we, slightly embarrassed, are standing at the sea's edge. Andrey, who seems able to quote the whole of Pushkin's *'Evgeny Onegin'* by heart, addresses this audience of bare footed nymphs.

'On the sea shore, with storm impending
How envious was I of the waves
Each in tumultuous turn descending
To lie down at her feet like slaves
I longed like every breaker hissing
To smother her dear feet with kissing.'

I find myself thinking of Dmitry. How he would have relished this scene of naked feet and ankles. Andrey is not to be deterred. He declaims. " I long to smother your dear feet with kisses. In return for my verses I request you girls to present your feet for my caress."

I personally would willingly have presented my feet for his kisses. After all, had not Dmitry initiated me into such delights? However, the rest of the female company demur and reluctantly decline his offer.

We stand at the water's edge, urged on by our menfolk. We wade gingerly in up to our knees. The water is indeed cold and before long, holding up our petticoats and skirts in front of us, we head back towards the beach.

I am the first to leave the water. I turn round to see a line of young girls, for all the world a chorus line of cancan dancers at the Folies Bergères in Paris.

"We just need the music to start dancing the cancan," I shout to them as we come out of the water and cross the beach holding our skirts and petticoats way above our knees. Our men are there to receive us. Never have they seen such a spectacle as the one we reveal to them. Our modesty has quite deserted us.

My reference to the cancan is lost on the girls, but Andrey who has been to Paris on his travels with the Ferry Company explains rather too explicitly for my taste exactly what the dance entails. And what are the Folies Bergères?" the girls ask.

I explain."You know the paintings by the French Impressionist artists. Perhaps you've seen illustrations in our coloured magazines. There's one by Manet called "At the Bar of the Folies Bergères." And then there are all those paintings by Toulouse Lautrec of cancan dancers in the music halls in Paris. There was an exhibition of Impressionist paintings at the Pushkin Museum in Moscow a few years ago which my mother was not keen to let me go to. She thought that the subject matter was totally unsuitable for her daughter's eyes, which naturally made me determined to disobey her. And of course I did.

"It's alright for you," one of my new friends replies sadly. "You live near Moscow, you can visit all the art galleries there, and when you were younger you had the Hermitage in St. Petersburg to visit whenever you wanted. Here in Yalta we have nothing like that, we are just plain provincial folk," she complains.

"I studied French at school," says one of the girls. Bergère is the French for shepherdess, isn't it? What has a French music hall got to do with shepherdesses?

I know the answer to this. I had asked Dmitry the same question. I pause, feeling that the subject matter has become a little risqué. However I can see that Andrey is keen for me to give an explanation. He urges me on.

We sit in a circle on the sand and I begin, reciting what Dmitry had told me. "Well, in the early part of the century a great number of girls were needed as so called dancers to perform on the stages of French Music Halls. Being France of course this would require a minimum of clothing on the dancers! The public did not want to see young girls who had had their beauty spoilt by small pox performing for their delight. There was no vaccination at that time for smallpox which in France had reached epidemic proportions.

However, by a strange coincidence it was noticed that shepherdesses did not contract smallpox, having already contracted a mild form of the disease from their sheep. This, for reasons unknown at the time, did not harm their looks. These girls were brought to Paris where they were taught to dance and take their clothes off on stage to the delight of the audience, who of course were mostly men.

As to the music, the most popular tune for them to perform was a tune from Offenbach's opera 'Orpheus in the Underworld.' It's commonly known as *The Cancan* and the girls are expected to raise their dresses above the knee and kick their legs out as they dance. So now you understand why I said we looked like *Cancan* dancers."

I can see that by this time I have become even more of an enigma to my new friends. A married woman of their own age, possibly with a gentleman friend in Moscow who buys her expensive clothes, a husband she hardly mentions, and an experience of all the racier topics in life about which normally only men discuss. And of course this special relationship with Chekhov. But they reluctantly put aside their questions as our men folk mundanely declare themselves both hungry and thirsty.

After our picnic of chicken, salad and a local wine we move out of the shade of the pines. The sun has lost its midday strength and we stretch out on the sand. Our conversation begins to falter a little after the effects of food and wine. The boys start complaining that our company has become excessively lethargic. What shall we do to rouse ourselves?

Boris, who some of the group had teased about his position as a junior councillor in the Yalta Local

Government Office, suggests that we play a game. Each of us is to relate something exceedingly interesting or exceedingly boring, not more than five minutes in length. When we have all finished, we will vote on which one has bored or interested us most. He says that as Andrey and I have already entertained the party with our description of the cancan and the Folies Bergères in Paris, not forgetting the fairness of the shepherdesses's skin, we are excused the contest. He obviously has a story that he is dying to tell, so we let him start.

"This is a true story that by chance continues the theme of our bathing activities this morning," he begins. " A year ago the Mayor of Yalta together with some of his colleagues on the Council were invited to a conference in London. None of them had been to England before, so naturally the invitation was accepted without delay. Why they went, what they discussed,what positive results they achieved and what the total cost was, we have never been able to ascertain. Such is the secrecy of our councillors, God bless them!

One rumour was that it was an official conference to negotiate a 'twinned city' status between Yalta and a seaside town in England, but as we know only too well no evidence to support this theory has come to light in any Council minutes.

However one interesting detail of their trip did emerge. Apparently it is not always foggy in England and one day the councillors were invited to take the train from London to a seaside watering place in the South East of the country.

It was a fine summer's day and they were taken for a walk along the beach. There they saw an amazing sight. You know before lunch we men were gazing somewhat pensively at the sea and wishing that we could go for a swim, rather than just splashing about and frightening you ladies. Well these English, as we know, are an inventive race. What they have done is to invent a sort of shed on wheels, which is placed on the beach facing the sea. Omnibuses convey the bathers from a convenient part of the town to the beach.There men and women dress themselves in specially made swimming costumes in these bathing machines, as they are called. Before your imagination carries you away, I should point out that this is Victorian England and to observe the proprieties there are separate bathing machines for men and women.

These sheds are then towed into the water by horses. When a suitable depth is reached the front door is opened and hey presto, the occupants descend a set of steps directly into the water. The bathers are hidden from the public and can enjoy undisturbed the therapeutic qualities of sea water bathing.

When the bather has finished his or her bath, the process is reversed and eventually the shed is drawn back onto the beach and the occupant disgorged onto the sand. Whole scientific volumes apparently have been written by eminent specialists in the field on the advantages of immersion in sea water. That's my story and I am quite certain that no one will beat it for interest."

"That is all very well,"complains Ivan. "All you have to do now is to persuade your Council colleagues to invest in some of these bathing machines here in Yalta and we can all go swimming together. We will see you in the water next summer, young water nymphs!"

"We are such stuff as dreams are made on." I laugh gently at his presumption. However, Prospero's pronouncement, "And our little life is rounded with a sleep" seems to have had more effect. The game is concluded and I am awarded the prize for my risqué exposé of Belle Epoque Paris, a bunch of grapes left over from our picnic.

One by one we fall silent. I shut my eyes and enjoy the feeling of sun and fresh air on my body. For a few moments I am living outside of time in a suspended hypnotic present in which there is no future. "Yesterday was history, tomorrow is a mystery, but today is a gift, un petit cadeau", as the French saying goes. Here we are today, nubile young girls with legs bare to the knee in the company of young men. I had spent too much time with older men and had forgotten that young people can have innocent fun together. Perhaps a little less than innocent, I thought, given the turn our conversation had taken.

It must have been the heat, the wine I had consumed over lunch and the sensuous arrangement of my bare legs and arms exposed to the view of the opposite sex that made me think sensually of another Impressionist picture which I had viewed with Dmitry. I can still feel my embarrassment when we suddenly turned a corner in the Tretyakov gallery and came across Edouard Manet's 'Le Déjeuner sur l'Herbe', on loan from Paris. That enormous canvas depicting two fully dressed men seated with a nude female casually partaking of a picnic and another scantily dressed girl bathing in the river in the background. I remember the little details of the picture that Manet had painted, the basket of fruit and a round loaf of bread on the grass. I turn over on my front and catch sight of the remains of our picnic. Here by chance is a similar wickerwork basket in which the boys had carried the fruit for our lunch, together with the remains of the loaf that we had eaten with our chicken.

I imagine myself as one of the women in the picture, being gazed at naked by these men. I feel myself blushing and arrange the folds of my dress more modestly around my legs. For goodness sake, this is Crimea, not decadent Belle Epoque France, I say to myself. But then I think of my similar state of undress as I sometimes posed for

Dmitry in my room in the *Slavyansky Bazar* and my blushes deepen. No one will notice, I reassure myself. The rest of our party are still dozing.

I turn again onto my back. I feel the bag which I had put under my head as a cushion and the hardness of the packet containing my tickets. How frugal is fortune in dealing out its share of happiness. Within twenty four hours I will be catching the ferry back to Odessa, where a train will transport me to Moscow. Dmitry will be waiting for me there. Who knows what will happen thereafter.

***

Later in the day, as the sun begins to set, we pack up our picnic things. But there is one problem to be overcome before we can leave. We ladies had forgotten to bring towels with us, as we had not envisaged that there would be such a light hearted moment when we stripped off shoes and stockings. We tell our male companions to go off and play on the rocks, while out of their gaze we try discreetly to brush the sand off our legs and put on our stockings and shoes. Our menfolk are relieved that the picnic which they had so laboriously carried on the journey here had now been eaten and their packs are somewhat lighter. We all decide to walk home, rather than take carriages, and once again we indulge in the pleasant, carefree conversation that had been the hallmark of the whole day.

My companions tell me that when I leave Yalta tomorrow they have decided to come and see me off. I have so enjoyed myself in their company that the thought of not being left to embark by myself is welcome. So is the thought that I can now persuade Anton that he need not accompany me to the port. I know that he would have done this, but I have planned to have one final tête à tête with him before parting. A crowded quayside would not be the place for this.

***

My last day in Yalta is spent packing my voluminous valise, taking Tuzik for a farewell walk around the Botanical Gardens and saying goodbye to Arseniy, Mariushka and the servants at Autka. When eventually I go up to Anton's study, the place where we have spent so much time together over the past few days, I find him looking pale and haggard. He says that he had slept badly but manages a weak joke about losing his nurse just as he is dying. He has booked a table for an early dinner at our restaurant on the Promenade. In preparation for this farewell dinner he has dressed most fastidiously, gold cufflinks, yellow shoes, a velvet jacket and a coat all in my honour.

At the restaurant we sit down facing each other. I can see that he is upset. He stretches out and takes my hand in his across the table, looking at me in silence.

"Anton, you know that I don't want to go. I would love to stay here, but you know as well as I do that's impossible. And please, I don't want you to come to see me off on the ferry. There's been enough silly tittle tattle in the town about our relationship and you know how crowded the pier gets with all those sightseers and passengers. In any case matters are beyond our control. My reputation will be enhanced or vilified when our story is published in December."

Anton looks at me intently. "Anna, you must have seen how much I have enjoyed your company these past few days. I cannot bear to think of a vulnerable young girl like you being hurt in any way. You must let me know if things turn out badly for you in Moscow.

Remember that here in Yalta you have good friends. We will all do anything for you if you need us. Come back any time you like and help me with my *Three Sisters*. I will tell my muse to move over and make room for you." Anton pauses for a moment. He refills our glasses with the special vintage he has chosen for our farewell dinner.

"It's uncanny how your real life, Anya, mirrors what I write. Take my new play *Three Sisters*. You've told me about your attempts to leave a boring provincial town and, lo and behold, I have three sisters in the same situation. You left your beloved St. Petersburg and yearn to return there. They left Moscow for the boredom of provincial Russia and like you they crave something more, a return to a life more suited to their cultivated tastes and sensibilities.

"I beg you, please keep a confidence and don't breathe a word of what I'm going to tell you now. I confess that at the moment I have no idea how to get my three sisters out of their predicament. You will find a way of getting to Moscow long before they do. When you do, come down to Yalta again, tell me how you managed it and we'll write a realistic Final Act together. But don't delay too long. Our cherry orchard is waiting for us. I go to bed with my compresses and hot water bottle here in Yalta and dream of us together on the exotic French riviera."

"I'm not as confident as you are that I'll be moving to Moscow," I reply. " But I promise that I'll write and tell you how I manage it if I do succeed. And whatever happens, I promise to come back to see you and my friends again."

I feel close to tears. Our conversation has become too emotional. We turn to practical issues. I promise to visit Masha and Olga Knipper on my return to Moscow. Chekhov jokes, calling himself a lousy letter writer even though he has made a bit of a reputation for putting pen to paper. He gives me a couple of wrapped presents for them as well as the letters he has found so difficult to write.

"And you must arrange to meet Nemirovich Danchenko as soon as you can. Tell him that if I am not subjected to any more interruptions, Act I of *Three Sisters* will be in his hands in a few weeks. The plot is there, the sisters are still waiting for a chance to get to Moscow, even if one of them has gone lame. And as I told you I have no idea about a proper ending. But I know you've promised not to tell him that."

I look at Anton quizzically. "Gone lame?" I ask.

"Not literally, you little goose, it's writers' jargon for a slight and hopefully shortlived lack of inspiration. It's just that I'm having trouble writing her into a credible relationship with her older sisters. A slight creative set back, one might say, but not a serious one for old Anton. I'll sort it out when I've finished gardening."

Seeing my dissapproving look he hurriedly tells me that he is only joking. Arseniy is the only one who will be working in the garden now. The days are getting too cold.

He starts to polish his monocle, a sure sign, as I have learnt, that there is something else on his mind. If he starts by calling me just Anna, it will be something factual, tickets for the journey home, dining car reservations, a cab to the station. If it is Anya, it will be some proposition or suggestion that he is going to present me with, something that will require a yes or no from me. And if, heaven forbid, it is Anushka then I have a good idea about the sort of proposal that he might be about to make. I hold my breath.

After a minute he continues. "Anya, here's an idea. If I remember rightly, you were talking about having an excuse to stay in Moscow after you've finished typing our little story. What would you say if I asked you to carry on doing the same for the play? If I send you the manuscript, would you be able to type each act as I send it to you? I've already written to the Secretary at the Art Theatre and asked her to find you space in her office and a typewriter for you.

What Anton had hinted at over our dinner with the Headmistress had been such an enticing prospect that I had deliberately tried to put it out of my mind. Now I have the opportunity to reply.

I tell him that he is the doctor, he is to get his third sister sound of limb and send me his completed manuscript, act by act. I can think of nothing more wonderful than being thus employed.

I cannot restrain myself. I kiss his hand which still holds mine and squeeze it tight. This is my promise. I do not need words to tell him that I will not let him down.

I am so sad for him. He seems so vulnerable with his pale face and hacking cough. And he is so sweet to have dressed up specially for our last dinner together. To lighten the mood I tell him that my new friends have arranged to see me off later in the evening. Relating the events of the previous day and our innocent escapades on the beach makes him laugh and helps to ease the awkwardness which threatened to attend our farewell dinner.

I call to mind something that had been troubling me as my relationship with Anton had developed. Astrov in *Uncle Vanya* makes a speech to the effect that a woman can only be a friend to a man through three stages, acquaintanceship, mistress and then friend.

"Anton, are we parting friends? I've been your acquaintance and I believe your friend, but the stage in between is missing." He catches my reference at once.

"Oh, that's only Astrov speaking. You don't want to take to heart what that old buffer says," he replies. "Given a different set of circumstances, Anushka, I would have loved to have known you not only as an acquaintance and friend, but of course, as Astrov put it, as that certain person in the intervening stage.

Maybe you would have reciprocated, I don't know. Anyway it's all too late now. But as to your question, of course we're friends and we will go on being so. God knows, I have few enough friends left around me now."

How ever am I to respond to such a declaration? I have no ready words to express the complexity of my feelings, simply a slight tightening of our hands across the table compensating for the insufficiency of the spoken word.

I catch sight of my friends peering in through the restaurant window and pointing at their watches. It is time to say good bye. We leave the restaurant. A long kiss, an even longer embrace, both longer than etiquette requires. Will we meet again, Yalta or Nice or Moscow, who knows? Chekhov wraps his muffler around his throat to protect himself from the autumnal chill. Poor man, it does him little good. In the silence of the night I can hear his rasping cough as he disappears into the darkness.

{21}

The journey back to Moscow is fortunately uneventful. The steamer departs punctually and I have plenty of time for the connection with the mail train in Odessa and then the long, long train journey northwards. As soon as we leave the coast and climb into the hills the temperature drops markedly. My lightweight summer coat is inadequate to keep me warm, so I drape myself in a travelling rug provided by the carriage attendant who stokes the stove throughout the journey and serves me with endless cups of tea from the samovar.

I know that I should be reflecting on my future back in Shchyolkovo. But to tell the truth it is more appealing to ignore those more important questions and occupy myself with the number of practical considerations which have to be faced. And when I have done with those, to daydream about my new life as Anton's amanuensis.

Of course my thoughts turn to Dmitry. I know that he will be at the station to meet me. But has he remembered to reclaim my fur coat from the *Slavyansky Bazar* where we left my winter clothes? It all seems such an age ago.

It is twilight and looking out of the window I can just discern the first snow flakes dusting the fields and trees. This is only southern Russian. The guard who passes through the carriage to check our tickets announces to the carriage as a whole that far more snow is forecast before we reach Moscow,.

I return to my thoughts. I imagine my meetings with Masha and Olga Knipper. What will they think of me? I have a neglected husband far away and a lover around the corner in Moscow. What exactly does that make me? That apart, I must appear to them as a very ordinary woman with no particular literary skills. One who has inveigled her way into their Anton's affections, but with what ulterior aim?

Can there be a degree of altruism in her motives or is it purely self interest that drives her on, they may well ask.

Once again I find my fingers checking that I still have the letters and parcels safe in my bag. The manuscript is there, proof that I have something of importance to prove my worth to any doubters.

***

Dmitry, my love, I murmur to myself as the train rumbles ever northwards. The *Slavyansky Bazar* beckons once again, though how seductive this exhausted peasant girl, wrapped in Ukrainian rugs with coal dust and smuts on her face, will be to her lover I cannot tell!

In all these imaginings I give no thought to my return to the family home in Shchyolkovo. I have written to Viktor giving him a date for my arrival. Being a stickler for punctuality he will expect me home on the day and at the time I have given him. Of course I have no idea how he will react to the fact that I had expressly contradicted his orders. The fact that I have to tell him that I need to return immediately to Moscow to write what is in essence an account of my adultery is of some concern!

***

And so through long hours of contemplation and intermittent slumber the journey passes without incident. The second morning I am roused by the guard, who comes through the carriage announcing that we will shortly be due in Moscow. He apologizes for our being some four hours late. Heavy snow falling practically all the way has delayed our arrival. I think of Dmitry pacing up and down in the First Class waiting room at the Kursky Station, clutching all my furs to him and questioning every station official for news of the Sevastopol Mail Express.

But before our arrival I have to resolve an awkward situation in which I unintentionally find myself. I have made the acquaintance of an elderly Muscovite lady in my compartment. She passes the hours of the journey by telling me about her son, whom she has not seen for a year. He is to meet her at the Kursky Station and she is so looking forward to seeing him again.

When she learns that I am married she assumes that I will be met by my husband. I cannot tell her that I am being met by my lover. I envisage all too clearly the scene in the compartment when Dmitry and I are reunited after such a long absence. Perhaps the old lady will simply assume this is the first time in our married life that we have been set apart. That we have missed each other so much that any excessive and public display of emotion can be countenanced and forgiven.

In the event I do not have long to wait. The train draws into the terminus. The windows of our carriage, obscured with snow and ice, make it difficult to discern the platform. Momentarily I catch a glimpse of Dmitry looking into each carriage as it passes him by. He suddenly sees me and the next moment he is on the train whilst it is still in motion. We embrace as best we can. My coat, muff, shawl that he is carrying in addition to his own thick coat limit us to a brief and clumsy embrace. My companion smiles at my evident pleasure in being reunited with the man she presumes to be my husband.

" Anushka, you look wonderful. Is this peasant girl fashion the new Ukrainian style for the winter?" Dmitry jokes as I drop my rugs and put on the furs he has remembered to bring. A porter arrives to take my luggage. I keep hold of my travelling bag.

"Leave that as well" says Dmitry.

"No, I can't," I reply. "There's something very valuable in it, I'll explain later." My old lady waves us good bye thinking, I hope, how nice it is to see a husband and wife so in love.

We walk carefully arm in arm along the icy platform towards the exit. Passing the locomotive, shrouded in snow, Dmitry calls to the engine driver and stoker standing on the footplate. He has roubles in his hand. "Thank you for safely returning my precious lady to me. It must have been hard for you with all this snow," he shouts up to the footplate.

"Thank you kindly, your Excellency." The driver's words are half lost in a hiss of steam as he tucks the notes into his oil stained pocket. "....nothing compared with the blizzards we get later in the winter.... And I see that your lady is pleased to see you again, if you will excuse my saying so." He winks at me and smiles. How does he know that I've been met by someone other than my husband? The sense of complicity adds to my growing impatience. As we drive through the streets towards the *Bazar* I become ever more aware of the insistent cravings of my body. As always I am hungry and thirsty. That is nothing new and can be easily rectified. But I am in desperate need of an ample supply of hot water to wash away the dirt of the journey. I can only recall the very limited facilities in the bedroom. And to put it as delicately as I can my body craves something more intimate than the kisses Dmitry and I have exchanged at the station. As we check in to the *Bazar* the manager himself greets us at the reception desk.

"Anna Ivanovna, what a delight to see you safely returned to us from your travels. I trust you had a pleasant journey." I see him looking at my begrimed features with concern.

"Perhaps Madame would like to avail herself of our newly installed bathing facilities. Since you've been away we have installed a 'salle de bain' next to your room, with as its

‘ pièce de résistance’ a beautiful Parisian hip bath, I am reliably told the very latest model from France. If Madame would care to avail herself of this facility, I will send Yermolay up with the coals to heat the water for your bath while we prepare your lunch.

Dmitry loses no time in approving of this proposition. I know perfectly well that it is the thought that he may be privy to my reclining demurely in a beautifully decorated Parisian hip bath that accounts for the haste of his response. While we eat and celebrate my safe return, my bath, situated in a small ante room adjacent to our bedroom, is being filled by the conscientious Yermolay. With a discreet knock on the door he informs me that the water has reached the correct temperature and everything is ready for Madame’s bathing.

Clean and sweetly smelling once again I am carried back to a comfortable bed, one that is not jolting and rattling. It is only some hours later that we are able to discuss how best to spend our two short days together.

***

Dmitry has promised to accompany me on my visits, particularly the difficult one to the publisher’s office which, as Anton informs me, is situated in a far from salubrious area of the city.

The afternoon melts into evening. We relate our separate accounts of the events of the past two weeks. Dmitry’s account is very short, I being the one with all the news. I tell him that Anton’s and my collaboration on the story has gone extremely well. I have the precious completed manuscript in my bag. And most wonderful of all I now have the perfect excuse to spend more time in Moscow. Viktor, objecting as much as he likes, cannot object

November 30th 1899.

Our first visit today is to The Art Theatre, where we meet Nemirovich Danchenko. I introduce myself and Dmitry.

"Please call me Vladimir Ivanovich", he replies. " I have unfortunately a very difficult and rather lengthy family name. I have heard so much about you from Anton's letters. I can see, young lady, that our mutual friend in the south has not lost his ability to surround himself with beautiful women. It is a pleasure to welcome you to MKhAT."

I pass on Anton's kind regards and his report that *Three Sisters* is progressing well. I hesitate about adding Chekhov's request to be left in peace, deciding that it would be more diplomatic not to do so.

I enlighten him on our successful collaboration on *The Lady with a Little Dog* and tell him that Anton Pavlovich has asked me to type the manuscript here at the theatre, something which I hope will not prove a problem. As a sweetener I mention that he has entrusted me with the typing of the *Three Sisters* manuscript, which I will produce again in typed format as soon as Anton sends me each completed act. This evidently impresses Vladimir Ivanovich. He ironically comments that this will be a great step forward, since neither he nor any of his actors are able to read a word of Anton's scrawled handwriting, a fact which makes rehearsing somewhat difficult.

The typewriter that Anton Pavlovich had asked for proves to be a very old one with an antiquated key board. Dmitry has a solution to that problem. We go back to his bank where he asks his secretary to buy the most up to date

Underwood and have it delivered the same day to the MKhAT offices.

Dmitry warns me that Viktor Aleksandrovich Goltsev, the editor of *Russian Thought,* has the reputation of being a womanizer and that I am to be on my guard when I meet him. He tells me that Goltsev has just fathered an illegitimate child by his secretary and boasts to all and sundry that he is proud that at his advanced age he is still able to perform such a service, should one wish to call it that. Dmitry has quite made up his mind and instead of letting me go by myself he insists on accompanying me to the premises, which are situated in an outlying district of the city.

As our carriage enters the suburbs, the stone and brick built buildings of the city centre are replaced with the original wooden structures which had escaped the fire of 1812. The publishing house of *Russian Thought* is housed in a decrepit wooden office in an unpaved, unnamed road which has not been cleared of snow. It strikes me that Viktor Aleksandrovich for one reason or another seeks anonymity.

Goltsev receives us coldly. He knows who I am and the reason why I have come to see him. He is plainly upset that I have brought someone to accompany me. After examining me intently over his glasses he asks Dmitry to leave us so that he and I can discuss Chekhov's affairs alone. He suggests that Dmitry return later in the day if he really thinks it necessary to provide an escort for me to return to my hotel.

This unsubtle ploy to get rid of him annoys Dmitry. He does not take kindly to being told what to do by an ink stained tradesmen with a lecherous demeanour, as he is later to describe Goltsev. Nor has he any intention of leaving me unchaperoned on his premises.

I undo my bag and with a flourish produce Anton's manuscript, holding it close to my body. I tell him that I will give him the complete typed version within a week. I can see the disappointment in his eyes when he realizes that the finished version of *The Lady with a Little Dog* is in my possession and that the deadline that he himself had imposed on Chekhov will be met.

Dmitry now finds himself on familiar territory. He says that he has read the contract that has been negotiated for the delivery of the text. He points out that an advance of 10,000 roubles is to paid into a designated bank.

But of course it is too naïve to believe that Goltsev would be prepared to part with any money at this stage. In his disappointment he snaps.

"You may of course have the completed manuscript with you now, but you are taking it away to be typed. Consequently I will not have the printed text till next week. And that means that I will effect no payment until I have the story, in whatever format, back here again and securely in my hands." He does not detain us any further and smarting from his highhanded manner we leave his office.

{22}

December 4th 1899.

A Sunday in Moscow and we are free to amuse ourselves as we wish. I intimate that I would like to do some sightseeing in a city with which I am still so unfamiliar. I tell Dmitry that I would like to visit the Kremlin, not having been there properly since a school trip to Moscow, when we schoolgirls were more interested in shopping in the Upper Rows on Red Square than taking in the sights.

In the evening we have dinner together in the Natzional hotel looking over Red Square. Despite the difficulty I foresee in broaching the subject to Viktor of my imminent return to Moscow after having just arrived back home, our mood is a happy one.

However there is an unpleasant thought lurking at the back of my mind which vexes me and which I cannnot dismiss. It is already the first day of December and I have only a week to complete the typing of the manuscript and return it to Goltsev. I will have to spend some of this week in Shchyolkovo and this will give me even less time to finish my assignment. But I convince myself that there will be no need to spend long with Viktor before coming back to Moscow. Just time to have a conversation with my husband, change my clothes, leave Tuzik in Dunyasha's care and catch the next available train back to Moscow.

Or so I had believed in my innocence. But upon a more careful consideration of the facts I came unwillingly to the conclusion that Viktor was not likely to accept a glib explanation of my conduct, which amounted, as he would no doubt impress on me, to no less than a contradiction of his orders. It would certainly not be a joyful meeting with a husband who had missed me in my absence and was delighted to see me back home safe and sound!

December 5th 1899.

Today Dmitry returns to his bank and I make my way by myself to the Kursky Station to catch the train home. Is Shchyolkovo really my home, I ask myself? In my head I rehearse what I am going to say to Viktor. Curiously enough I now feel at ease. The days of living on my own have given me the confidence I previously lacked. Back in my prison with its grey walls I wait till Viktor returns from his office. We meet in icy silence at dinner.

As I take my seat at the table I notice that he has already drained the larger part of a carafe of red wine. Unusual for him, I remark to myself with some consternation, as Viktor always drinks in moderation. Once our meal has been served and we are on our own this ominous silence is broken.

"Anna, perhaps you would be kind enough to explain your decision to gainsay my orders and travel to Yalta to live openly, I need put no finer point on it, with this man Anton Chekhov. Your behaviour, your impudence I might call it, has been reprehensible in the extreme. You have the nerve to send me a letter from Moscow, letting me know quite casually that you are going to Yalta. And then when you are down there, you follow this up with a further letter in which you simply tell me the date of your return. This is totally out of order and I await an explanation."

"Firstly, I did not live with Anton Pavlovich," I reply heatedly. "I stayed at the same pension as on my first visit to Yalta. Secondly I went at the express invitation of a man who has the reputation of being one of Russia's greatest writers. Can you imagine anyone in their right mind refusing such an invitation? Thirdly, I have to tell you that the visit was extremely successful. We now have the finished manuscript of the story that we collaborated on…."

I break off there, as it is obvious that none of this is of any interest to my husband. As far as he is concerned I have disobeyed his orders and made a number of decisions on my own initiative. I am to be punished for these transgressions, for which he will not forgive me lightly. And worse is still to come. I have yet to tell him that I am planning to return to Moscow tomorrow.

When he hears that I am intending to spend a week in Moscow typing this confounded manuscript, he loses control of himself. He seizes the carafe and pours himself another glass of wine. Wiping his lips with a knapkin already stained with spilled wine, he informs me that people at his office have been enquiring about my extended absence from Shchyolkovo. They ask if I was ill, or was I perhaps visiting relatives in Moscow. He tells me that he has had to make up explanations of my conduct which do not fully satisfy the curiosity of his colleagues.

I have the feeling that since my successful evening at the Gaslighting Ball I may have changed somewhat in the estimation of his cronies. They might well now be envisaging some lurid adventure that I have embarked upon. Fully justified,they would think, married as she is to a man such as her husband. Had I not come back to the frozen north with colour in my cheeks? She must have returned to Yalta again on the orders of her doctor, leaving her husband to fend once more for himself. Such are my musings as Viktor continues his tirade against my conduct. I interrupt him, telling him that I have no time to lose. I have to go back to Moscow immediately.

"What are you going to do for funds?" asks Viktor. Someone has to pay your bills even if you are staying with friends"

"No, Viktor, I am staying at the *Slavyansky Bazar* and working at the Moscow Art Theatre during the day. I have enough money, thank you, to afford this. If you wish to check up on my whereabouts, then you are of course at liberty to do so. But I beg you not to disturb me, I have a great deal of work to do."

Poor Viktor, he looks so bemused when I tell him my plans. Names such as Anton Pavlovich Chekhov, MKhAT, Slavyansky Bazar which I mention quite casualy seem to overwhelm him. Here is his little wife, who should be staying at home and running the household expressly for him, now dashing off to Moscow whenever she likes and mixing in exalted circles with people who are household names throughout Russia.This is totally beyond his comprehension.

We finish the meal as we had started it, in silence. After dinner I go to my room and pack some new clothes for my return to Moscow. I check on the parcel containing the manuscript. On reflection it seems so strange that Viktor has shown no interest in what our story is about. Nor has he made any further insinuations about my relationship with Anton Pavlovich. He has not seen me roused to anger before and perhaps for the first time in our marriage he can now see that I am a changed woman, one who is determined to do what she wishes. At any rate he makes no further objection to my leaving the next day.

But still I am not at ease. It all seems suspiciously easy. There must be a major confrontation which he is planning to spring on me, but I have no time to speculate on what this might be. For the moment I have enough with which to occupy myself. I need to plan for my return to Moscow. As I am begining to find out, it is not the easiest thing in the world to organize a change of lifestyle, exchanging my role of provincial housewife for that of copy typist by day and mistress by night.

***

Today Viktor has thankfully left for the office before I come downstairs. He has not made any arrangements for me to get to the station or to buy a ticket to Moscow. But by now this sort of thing is not a problem. I say goodbye to Dunyasha and ask her to look after Tuzik for a few days. It is not difficult to persuade Afanasy to prepare the carriage and take me to the station.

In Moscow I once again book into the *Slavyansky Bazar* and the following morning take a cab the short distance to the offices of MKhAT. There is my shining new Underwood in the corner of the Secretary's office. I pull out the manuscript, arrange my chair and begin slowly and cautiously to type. "*People said that there was a new arrival on the promenade…*"

I stop in consternation as I read again what I have typed. The printed words stare out from the page, daring me to continue. As far as my marriage is concerned, what I am doing is in fact signing my own death warrant. *The Lady with a Little Dog* is a good story, I know that, perfectly well, and it is to appear in print in a respected literary journal within the month. How could Viktor fail to read it, or if he does not, then have it mischievously brought to his attention by a colleague?

The themes of adultery and loveless marriages will appeal to many readers and there will certainly be speculation as to the identity of the lady in the story. Had not Anton foreseen that upon the publication of our story a number of his Antonovkas would be seen walking the Promenade in Yalta with newly acquired little dogs, each claiming to be the lady in question?

But the die had been cast. I had persuaded Anton to write the story as it happened, with no more than a simple change of names. I realize now that I have subconsciously challenged my husband to take the next step and like a prisoner awaiting the verdict of the court I am ready to accept what fate decrees. I type on.

December 10th 1899.

These days in Moscow are happy ones. The typing continues to go well, albeit slowly. I have counted the pages to be typed. There are only eighteen and each day I manage about four. I am easily up to schedule by the time in the evening when Dmitry comes to pick me up.

Uncle Vanya continues to be an enormous success. Members of the Tsar's family come to see the play as do famous literary figures. Only Tolstoy disapproves, noting just one word 'outraged' in his diary. He is invited to meet the cast backstage and adds a further comment to the effect that Astrov and Vanya, middle aged men lusting after a married woman, should marry peasant girls and leave the Professor's wife alone.

I wonder what on earth his comments would be if he were to read our story and realize that it could be taken as a defence of adultery and of course as a rebuttal of his views on society as expressed in *Anna Karenina*. '*Vengeance is mine, I will repay,*' he had written ominously in the frontispiece of his novel on the subject of those in society who break its conventions.

December 16th 1899.

Today I finish typing the manuscript and Dmitry once again accompanies me to the offices of Viktor Goltsev. I hand over the eighteen pages of a short story that I know is going to change my life. Goltsev has no excuse now for not agreeing to the transfer of the promised amount into an account at Dmitry's bank. He says he will send an acknowledgement of receipt of the printed text to Anton. Finally he confirms that the story will appear in the December edition of *Russian Thought.*

Goltsev, lascivious to the last, makes one final attempt to lure me back alone to his office. He points out that there is a printing convention of which I should have been aware. Whoever types the written text is expected to proof read the galley proofs. I am therefore required to return to his office in a week's time to undertake this laborious work. He has, however, not counted on Dmitry.

"That would be quite impossible, Viktor Aleksandrovich. I quite simply forbid Anna Ivanovna to travel through this rather undesirable part of Moscow on her own. You will send the proofs to the *Slavyansky Bazar,* where she will be able to correct any printing errors in the comfort and security of her own hotel room. It will only add one day to the whole operation. We will send back the corrected text by messenger as soon as she has finished. Goltsev is about to object, but seeing the determined look on Dmitry's face he mutters.

"Well, all I can say is that this is highly irregular. We simply do not do things this way in the printing business. Proofreading is a skill. It is not simply a matter of reading the text and adding one's own corrections.You will need a copy of our standard proofreading symbols. Heaven help you if our printers cannot understand your corrections. There will naturally be an additional cost should this occur."

He understands that there is nothing to be gained by arguing any further. Continuing to mutter dire threats he bids us goodbye. One concession that I have managed to extract from him is a promise that he will return my original type written text to me. It is after all my first tentative effort with a typing machine and I know that I will value it for the rest of my life, a sentimental souvenir of my affection for Anton Pavlovich and a memory of our days together in Yalta.

This evening Dmitry and I have a leisurely dinner, over which we compose a letter to Anton. I inform him that his debutant typist has completed her assignment and the typed text is with Goltsev. He will be relieved to hear that I have not succumbed to the latter's charms! Dmitry's part of the letter confirms that the sum of 10,000 roubles will be paid into the Chekhov designated account at his bank as an advance on publication of *The Lady with a Little Dog.*

Dmitry did not know till then that I am to receive payment for typing the manuscript. He immediately foresees a problem. He reminds me that under our Russian law women are not allowed to have their own bank accounts. Anything they earn is automatically deemed to belong to their husband. Any payments to me would therefore be credited to Viktor's estate. Dmitry explains that the only way to avoid this would be for Anton to pay the amount that I am due into his, Dmitry's, own bank account. I would then have access through him to any money that I needed to withdraw. Dmitry adds this suggestion to our joint letter.

{23}

December 18th 1899.

Much as I would have liked to linger in Moscow I know that I have to return to Shchyolkovo as soon as possible. The sword of Damocles is poised above my head, hanging by its proverbial thread. It could so easily be cut. Anton had left the ending of our affair unresolved in his story, but I know that from now on fact and fiction are heading on divergent courses. I sense that the main characters are poised to write themselves a final chapter and that the impasse in our story will at last be resolved.

On my return to Shchyolkovo I find a very different atmosphere in our house. The servants seem unhappy. Dunyasha unpacks my clothes and explains that her master is in a dreadful mood.

As usual it is only at dinner that we meet. The meal served and grace said, we are alone in the dining room. I can see that he is angry. He sits opposite me, this man whom I hate. Ignoring the food in front of him, he puts down his knife and fork in a slow, deliberate manner. There is a silence that seems to continue for minutes, broken only by the drumming of his fingers on the table, a mannerism that I detest. I break the silence. If this going to be a battle, then I will attack first.

"Viktor, please do not do that, it drives me mad. What is the matter with you? The servants are upset over how you treat them. I cannot stand being in the same house with you any longer, I need to get away, somewhere, anywhere, just so that I can be alone."

"Please be quiet, Anna Sergeevna. Your wishes are of no concern to me. I expect an explanation from you regarding your behaviour over the past few weeks.

First of all, you might like to know that in your absence I wrote to your aunt in Moscow. She knew nothing about your supposed visits to her, visits that you lied to me about when you said that you were lodging with her in Moscow. She has not seen you since the night you spent with her before your first trip to Yalta. I suppose you will now tell me that you stayed with one of your Lycée friends, all of whom appear to have husbands conveniently transferred to Moscow from St. Petersburg. I am waiting for your reply. Please do me the courtesy of not lying any further."

I take a deep breath. "Viktor, I will tell you what I've been doing. I appreciate that you deserve an explanation." I push my plate away. Food is the last thing I want now. "Listen to me, Viktor. This may not come as a complete surprise but I need to tell you that I am in love with a man I met in Yalta. He is a banker, a little older than me and married. He is also in love with me. If we were free to marry we would have done so by now. When I'm in Moscow I stay at the *Slavyansky Baza*r and he visits me there on occasion.

I have also developed a close relationship with Anton Chekhov, though this is of a purely platonic nature. But of course I know you won't believe that. You think he is a womaniser and pursues any young lady who crosses his path. But you must believe me that in my case this is not true. All we have been doing is quite innocently working together on a story that he is writing."

Viktor is silent for a moment. The drumming has ceased and I wait for his reply.

"I knew some time ago that there was probably another man involved in your life. You are young and pretty and it is natural that you are attractive to other men. That I can understand. But as for a working relationship with Chekhov, I just cannot see what you could offer him, apart from your body. As for the sexual favours you have been so generous to bestow, despite your protestations to the contrary, as far as I can see you have been bedded," he pauses to find the right words, "by a banker and plucked by a playwright."

"Oh Viktor," I laugh, though I am furious now. "I take objection to that slur on my character. But really, your use of alliterations, accidental as they may be, must be the first original thing you have ever said in all our married life."

I despise him now and want to shock him further. "Why leave it there, I can probably find you some more of your clever alliterations if I try. What about fornicate with a financier, deflowered by a dramatist, raped by a writer?" It is the first time I have ever spoken so coarsely in the presence of my husband.

Viktor gasps, rises from the table, his face crimson with emotion. He comes towards to me and strikes me fully across the face. The ruby stone on his signet ring scrapes my cheek, cutting into my flesh and drawing blood. I reel backwards, clutching my face and trying to shield my body from any further blows.

"You little whore, you little whore," he repeats. "Get out of my sight. Your presence here defiles my house. You are no longer welcome here. My house is for respectable people, not for a woman like you. Go to your room and wait for me there. I may as well take my turn in using your body, other men seem to enjoy it enough. Go upstairs and do not attempt to bar me entry. "

"How can you talk about respectability? What makes you think your idea of respectability covers men who hit their womenfolk and then threaten to rape them?" I shout at him as I stagger out of the room before any more harm can come to me.

In my bedroom I bathe my swollen, bleeding face in cold water, undress and lie on the bed. From there I can see my bedroom door. To my consternation I see that in my absence in Moscow the lock for some reason has been removed and only the door handle remains. There is no way I can prevent him from entering.

I pray that he will not come to me, yet am certain that I will, at some later hour, hear his footsteps along the corridor. I remember how once before jealousy had turned him into an animal determined to satisfy its animal lust. Then I had only flirted with a handful of men. This time, as far as he is concerned, my behaviour is far worse. I am no more than the courtesan of bankers and writers. If he cannot equal them intellectually and socially, he can at least show his contempt for both them and for me by forcing me to succumb to his sexual advances.

And so it proves. Viktor comes to my room after midnight. In his obscene mind he must have chosen this late hour both to punish me further by this delay and to heighten for himself the sexual anticipation of my punishment. He tears my nightdress from me, pinions my arms behind my head and despite all my efforts forces himself into me. My body is seared with pain. I am sobbing. I no longer recognize my husband as he takes his pleasure. This must be how the women whom he calls whores submit themselves. No loving words, no caresses, purely the obligation to endure the sexual perversions of their clients.

Not a word passes between us whilst this nightmare is played out. I can see that Viktor regards the pain and my stifled sobs that he is inflicting on me as rightful punishment for my misconduct . He must judge that it is safer for him to abuse parts of my body that will not show in public rather than to continue hitting me across the face. Eventually he leaves my bedroom. He does not look at me, averting his eyes as he pulls on his clothes.

"Oh Dmitry, help me, help me." I sob, as left alone at last, tears flow down my face. This is impossible. What will he do when he discovers that the details of our adultery are printed in thousands of copies of *Russian Thought?* All the bravado that I had shown in Yalta when I told Anton to go ahead and write the story, simply disguising names and locations, now seems misplaced, a stupid, empty gesture of defiance. The reality is that I will soon have to confront an incensed husband bent on revenge.

I wash myself as best I can. Does a pained and abused wife really have to suffer like this? No, one thing is certain. I know that I will never spend another night in this house alone with Viktor. I will come back only if I am accompanied by Dmitry. But first I have to escape from this wretched prison and return to Moscow, knowing that this will not be possible without a further confrontation with Viktor.

However in this I am mistaken. Thank goodness there is no need for another meeting. When I come down to breakfast I find a letter waiting for me by my place. It is typical of Viktor to avoid another scene. Perhaps he felt embarrassed as to where his temper had led him. Certainly there will be no feeling of remorse on his part, just a total conviction that I am the guilty party and that he has chastised me as I deserve. His letter gives a detailed account of how he envisages the situation between us.

To My Wife Anna Ivanovna.

I have taken the unusual step of writing to you to express my thoughts subsequent to the scenes that took place last night. I feel this is a more effective way to communicate with you, rather than risking another conversation such as the one that took place last evening, the nature of which I do not wish to experience again within the hallowed portals of my house.

First of all I apologize for my actions in striking you and for the abusive language that I used. But I must ask you to appreciate the extreme provocation that your behaviour over the past weeks has caused me and which led to my actions. I am quite certain that the vast majority of men, faced with such an admission from their wives, would have reacted in a similar fashion.

Secondly, on your part I demand a full written apology from you for your outrageous behaviour. You will also promise to give up seeing your lover, or your lovers, with immediate effect, nor will you have any communication with him or them now or at any time in the future.

I cannot deny you access to our house or to your belongings, but I believe it would be better if we were to live apart until I call for you. To this effect I have sent a telegram to your aunt in Moscow telling her to expect you today. Under NO circumstances will you stay at the Slavyansky Bazar hotel ever again.

When you return we will be able to discuss our future together more rationally. I am finding it more and more difficult to explain to my colleagues your absences from home. As you will appreciate, my elevated position in Government circles is of prime importance to me. Anything that might jeopardize this would be anathema to me.

Therefore I am willing to give you one last chance to make amends for your indiscretions, which I believe charitably may have been forced on you in your innocence by predatory men. Let there be no cause for rumour in official circles, no innuendo amongst my Government colleagues regarding your behaviour. You are my legal wife and are to be seen in public supporting me socially and professionally in the enhancement of my career. Anything less than this will unfortunately compel me to reconsider our matrimonial status.

I wish to receive your written compliance with these demands before you leave for Moscow.

Your suffering and aggrieved husband,

Viktor Aleksandrovich.

I have no appetite for breakfast. I simply ask Dunyasha to pour me a cup of tea from the samovar. I sit down by the stove in the drawing room and reflect on my response to Viktor's letter. I cannot accede to his demands. I will defy my husband one more time and not go to visit my aunt, who by now must be suspicious about my conduct in Moscow on my previous visits and will interrogate me till she finds out the truth. I need peace and privacy and as ever *the Slavyansky Bazar* calls to me and offers me sanctuary.

In all my misery there is one slender ray of hope, one that flickers briefly but is extinguished almost immediately. Viktor said, if I can remember correctly in the heat of our exchanges, that he has cancelled his subscription to *Russian Thought.* He may, therefore, not read the incriminating story himself. However, I then reason, if he does find out it will be through a third party, which will be worse still. I have no escape. How he will react should he be identified as the cuckolded husband I can imagine only too clearly. I put pen to paper.

To My Husband, Viktor Aleksandrovich.

I accept neither your apology nor your explanation of the events of last night. A wife must be able to legally defend herself and her body. Consequently your actions in my eyes constitute nothing less than rape. I am not spending my days in Moscow at my aunt's, whose opinion of me will have been tarnished through your correspondence with her. I shall stay as usual at the Slavyansky Bazar and will be in touch with Dmitry Serov. I need his advice on several matters.

When I return to Shchyolkovo it will be with him. You will need to arrange somewhere for us to meet, as I will not set foot in our house again unless I am protected from you. I will be busy working at MKhAT during the daytime and will be at the hotel in the evening. I am in no hurry to return, so I suggest that at least an absence of two weeks would be advantageous for both of us. I await your response in writing to my hotel, Slavyansky Bazar, Nikolskaya Street, Moscow. I am, sir, your suffering and abused wife,

Anna Sergeyevna

I fold the letter, seal it in an envelope for security and place it prominently on the table in front of Viktor's place setting. From now on my husband will be taking his meals by himself. Let him have something to read while he eats his solitary dinner!

There is nothing else left that needs doing other than to say farewell to my beloved Dunyasha. This time I wear a veil to hide my disfigured face. I leave the house and head for the station on foot. I know that Viktor will have forbidden Afanasy to take me in the carriage and I do not want to get him into trouble if he goes against my husband's orders. I must look like a very old fashioned woman as I totter along the uneven pavements. The veil marks me out as an elderly lady and my progress is slow and painful.

{24}

December 20th 1899.

Moscow. I write to Dmitry. " I'm here, my loveliest of men! Come to me after work." And almost before I have time to tidy my bedroom and my hair I hear the familiar footsteps on the stairs, the creak in the floorboards outside my room and the polite knock before he comes bursting in. As we kiss he catches sight of my face.

"Darling, you look terrible. Whatever's happened to your face? Have you had an accident?"

I start crying. Between sobs I tell Dmitry about the scene at dinner, when I revealed to Viktor the truth about our relationship, about his violent reaction and the nightmare I was subjected to when he came to my bedroom.

Dmitry holds my bruised face gently in his hands and kisses my burning cheek. He tells me that if Viktor thinks that he can get away with this sort of behaviour unpunished, he has made a grave mistake. They have a number of lawyers at the bank, one of whom is an expert on matrimonial matters and will advise on the best course of action.

"Dmitry, I'm frightened to go home by myself. Can you come with me when I have to go back. I need you to protect me. There are only the servants in the house and they are too much in awe, too frightened of Viktor to come to my assistance if he goes beserk again."

Dmitry is still incensed. "I'm not going to let you out of my sight again so long as you have any business with that pitiful creature of a husband. I ought to catch the next train to Shchyolkovo and challenge him to a duel."

"But darling," I interrupt his worthy but unrealistic plans for vengeance. " Don't forget that the worst is yet to come. *Russian Thought* is due out this week and I'm quite certain that sooner rather than later Viktor is going to find out about his cuckolded status. In that event he's bound to order me back home. Can you help me when the time comes?

"Anya, of course I can." He takes my face and kisses away my tears. We go down to dinner in the hotel restaurant as we have done so many times before. The familiarity of the surroundings calm me. I feel safe and secure, removed at a distance from the obscene events that are still so fresh in my mind.

December 21st 1899.

Today Dmitry arranges a meeting with a lawyer whom he has instructed to take on our case, should Viktor file for divorce. The meeting is in Dmitry's office, though this time the atmosphere is rather more serious and professional. Dmitry's lawyer, Konstantin Semyonovich, whom I had quite unreasonably expected to be old and rather dry, proves to be surprisingly young and sympathetic.

He listens to my account of our relationship, quietly making notes as I speak. I tell him that I am the guilty party, having committed adultery. I tell him that as far as I know my husband is not guilty of the same offence. However he has subjected me to an intolerable life, finally assaulting me and subjecting me to his animal passions. No further testament than this is necessary as I lift my veil to reveal my disfigured face.

Our young lawyer is visibly moved, but cannot add much more than consolation.

"However much I sympathize with you, my dear Anna Ivanovna, I must point out that in a court of law you would be found totally guilty. Many wives of professional spouses lead a dreadful life similar to yours. Even in this day and age married women are expected to satisfy the carnal desires of their husbands without let or hindrance. A jury, though maybe sympathizing with you over this attack, will still find you guilty. Evidence of sexual excess, assault on wives and a breakdown in normal married life, and I have personally been involved in all such cases, none of these condones adultery on the part of a wive. That, unfortunately, is the verdict that a court will come to."

Dmitry and I knew that this would be the likely outcome. We had spent hours analyzing the situation. Accordingly we had planned a more psychological approach, a more sophisticated and subtle playing of our cards, based on our awareness of Viktor's weaknesses.

I start to put forward the plan which we had formulated the night before. I would tell my husband that I would not initially contest a divorce and would be happy to settle out of court. There was little else that I could do. After all if forced to, the staff of *the Slavyansky Bazar* would testify under oath that Dmitry and I on many occasions had been sharing the same bedroom. There was no point denying any of this.

But I needed something from Viktor, a quid pro quo, if I were to refrain from challenging the divorce. In return for not having all the details of my adulterous behaviour made public and for not describing in detail his attack on me, I would require him to provide me with a small apartment in Moscow. That was all. I did not need money for every day expenses. I had my own small income now from Anton Pavlovich and Dmitry would always provide for any additional expenses.

That in a nutshell was our strategy. We had banked all our cards on one gamble, namely Viktor's fear that he would be seen as a cuckolded husband, weak and indecisive and unable to control his wayward wife. Concerned about one thing only, his position and career in the Governmental hierarchy, he would be desperate to keep the details of his wife's infidelity away from the general public. In return for my silence he would agree to my side of the bargain. A nice little apartment near Dmitry's house in Moscow would not seem an outrageous request. Such was my plan, call it rather my fantasy.

Should he hesitate or refuse, I would have no hesitation in twisting the knife. "Remember Viktor Aleksandrovich", I would remind him of his superior's words. 'A man who cannot govern his wife cannot expect to continue for very long to govern his country. 'Haven't I heard this sentiment before somewhere?" I will taunt him. " Either grant me my request or face the consequences of a long drawn out divorce trial and the publicity which will inevitably attend it."

Is this not a thinly veiled threat of blackmail, I ask myself as I finish speaking? No, I justify myself, perhaps just a little enticement, an inducement, an incentive, at worst an ultimatum to trigger a required response.

There is a silence in the room as I sit back in my chair. Konstantin is deep in thought,evidently a little confused, since in his short career I imagine he has not met many lady clients who have formulated their own defence in advance of his counsel. Nor one who is as determined to fight her corner as strongly as I am.

He was of course looking at my proposal from a purely legal position. Lawyers hate gambling and risk taking of any sort, and what I had proposed was exactly that.

"Anna Ivanovna, I can see that you are a determined and lucid young lady.Therefore my advice to you is to return to Shchyolkovo at a suitable moment. Taking Dmitry with you would certainly be a good idea. Arrange a meeting with your husband and tell him you would like a divorce. Even if by this time he has not learnt about the full details of your actions in Yalta and afterwards in Moscow, it might be better if you were to grasp the nettle and give him your story to read rather than for him to find out through a colleague's probably mischievous revelation. You can then in a calm and reasoned manner put forward to him your strategy as you have outlined it to me.

Should he prove unreasonable, then of course come back to me and I will represent you in court. But remember what I told you. Once a divorce case like this goes to court, you will not win. The law here in Russia is unfortunately stacked against women in matrimonial cases like these. But then of course your husband will also lose. As you say, his continued position in Government service and ultimately his career might well be in jeopardy. I think you have a good chance of coming to a mutually satisfactory conclusion. I wish you luck."

***

December 22nd 1899.

Today at breakfast a messenger arrives at the hotel. He leaves a packet addressed to me at the reception desk. This proves to be the galley proof which Goltsev had promised to send me for correction. I retire to my bedroom and begin reading the printed version of our story. It does not take me long to realize how laborious a task proofreading is. I am terrified that if I make a mistake that lecherous Goltsev will have an excuse to drag me back to his printing works to rectify my errors. I start to skim the text, but realize after a few lines that it would be far better if Dmitry and I were to collaborate together on this task.

He arrives to take me out to dinner. He's hungry. There is something on the menu at the *Stary Posad* restaurant just a short distance down Nikolskaya Street which has taken his fancy. I tell him that unfortunately there has been a slight change of plans. Poor man, he must have envisaged a much pleasanter way of spending the evening with me, but he acquiesces with my propositon. We have a frugal dinner brought up to my room and we spend the rest of the evening scrutinizing the text for any errors. Goltsev's type setter has done a really professional job since we discover few mistakes in the text. Von Diederitz was misspelt, as might be expected, and Tuzik suffered the same fate, being referred to as Muzik, which makes us laugh.

December 23rd 1899.

After breakfast I dispatch the corrected galley proof to Goltsev's printing works, requesting from him receipt of delivery. Later this afternoon I receive the curtest of notes in return, thanking me for the return of the proof and the news that the publication date for *Russian Thought* is now set for seven days time.

I put on my furs and walk out into the streets of the city. It has stopped snowing at last and the crisp, fresh air clears my head. I fall to planning the last few days of my life, when to all and sundry I am still known as Anna Ivanovna von Melk, a respectable married woman from a provincial backwater.

When I return from my walk I learn that a letter from Anton Pavlovich is waiting for me. I retire upstairs to my sanctuary and break the seal.

My dear Anna Sergeyevna,
It was with the greatest of pleasure that I took receipt of your letter and I thank you for all your news from Moscow. It was a shame that you were not able to meet my sister Masha and my beloved and greatly missed Olga. Please give them my kisses when you do see them next. I am relieved that you have escaped the snares of that philandering editor

of mine. You must be one of a small number of beautiful young ladies that have managed to do so, but no doubt your Dmitry had a great deal to do with that! However, as far as his professional work is concerned, he is a good man and I am delighted to know that our story will be out before the end of the year.

Please excuse a writer's inability to convey the truth about himself without exaggeration, but after you left me, as I told you, bereft and ill, I have missed your company so much. Here is some news from Autka, which I hope you will enjoy reading.

I have taken time off from 'Three Sisters' to work in the garden. We have planted a lemon tree and some more olive trees and camellias, though Arseniy has his doubts as to whether the latter will survive the winter. A stray puppy has come into the garden. I found her sleeping under one of the new olive trees, not an ideal place in this cold weather. I have christened her Kashtanka and made her a bed in our potting shed. Because of the cold I have taken to wearing a hat in bed and sleep under two eiderdowns. Life is made more uncomfortable by the fact that the Dutch stoves, you remember them smoking badly when you were here, are no better and our expert architect who installed them is at a loss to know how to make them draw properly.

I have pleurisy and have to wear a compress over my left collar bone. I do little walking and my only exercise is catching mice which have taken over most of the ground floor. I take them next door to the Tatar cemetery, where I let them loose. I should really paint their tails to identify them, as I am certain most of them creep back again. It is probably the crumbs in the kitchen that attract them. Mariushka, who by the way sends her love, is getting ever more blind and cannot see what she is dropping on the floor. She does not even see the cockroaches. I tell her to put one that she has not crushed by walking on it in the kitchen under her pillow at nights and she will dream of the man she is to marry. I dare not repeat to you the reply I received to that suggestion!

I have few visitors. One exception was a visit from Isaac Levitan. I remember your telling me that you and Dmitry had admired his landscapes in the Tretyakov Gallery. He is probably even more ill than I am, but bless him, he managed to find some cardboard in the scullery and painted a beautiful 'Haystacks in the Moonlight' to decorate that awful fireplace in the drawing room.

Tell our friend ND that Act One of my Three Sisters is nearly complete. The one sister who had gone lame, you remember my joking about her when you were here, well, she has recovered from her lameness and now caught up with her two older sisters.

If you are still in agreement with my proposal I will send my manuscript of Act One and even possibly Act Two to you early in the New Year.

I know that by then our little story will be out in print and life could be difficult for you. So, please let me know how your husband reacts when he identifies our characters, as he is sure to do, and remember that there is always a place waiting for you here, should you need shelter. Or better still, just come and nurse a sick old man, who goes to bed with his hat on!

All our servants send you their kindest best wishes for the New Year and of course the new century. Arseniy misses you dreadfully and wants you back here, as do all your young friends. Even the drinkers at Vernet's Bar make enquiries as to when you will be returning. So you are missed here in Yalta. Come and see us all as soon as you can. I would value your presence here so much.
Your affectionate story teller,
Anton

I finish reading with difficulty, the last lines being smudged with my tears. I continue lying on my bed for a long time. There are so many good people in my life who want to see me and look after me. My New Year resolution is clear. I will start the new century by finding a new life for myself, a life without Viktor.

For the first time I am impatient for the fatal edition of *Russian Thought* to be published. This reminds me that I need to order a copy. A short distance away on Nikolskaya Street, which is a wonderful street and seems to have everything I need, I find a bookshop. I tell the shopkeeper that I'm interested in purchasing the winter edition of *Russian Thought*. Would he be kind enough to leave a note at the *Slavyansky Bazar* the moment it appears?

"We've put in a large order to the printers," he replies. "It's rumoured that there is going to be a new short story by Anton Chekhov in this edition. So we anticipate a heightened demand from the reading public. Do not worry yourself, young lady, I will put a copy aside for you."

I smile to myself as I leave the shop. The man, with whom I have placed my order, has no idea that he has been talking to the heroine of this same story. How would he have behaved towards me had he known?

This evening Dmitry comes to me at my hotel. He seems in a serious mood, the reason for which become obvious after our first embraces.

"Listen Anna, we need to talk properly about your future plans. First of all, the more I think about it the more certain I am that it is not a case of if but when your husband is going to find out about our infidelity. If you get your way and avoid a divorce, it is not sufficient to tell your husband something as vague as wanting an apartment in Moscow. We need specific details to present him with.

I have a number of colleagues in the bank who deal with the provision of funds for clients wishing to buy or rent property in Moscow. They recommend the new houses and apartments which are being built or restored in the Stary Arbat region of Moscow. It's within reach of my bank, of MKhAT and of course of our *Slavyansky Bazar*. And there are a number of parks nearby for your Tuzik. I think you would like the Arbat. It's popular with the intelligentsia and some actors, poets and writers have taken up residence there.

Without being able to pry closely into your husband's financial situation, I have a rough idea of the salary of a senior ministry official in local government. You tell me that your house in Shchyolkovo has belonged to his family for some generations and as far as you know attracts few aaexpenses. He also, as far as we know, avoids another considerable expense, which many civil servants in his position do incur, that of maintaining a mistress. Since I do not perceive your husband being favoured with either the pleasures or expenses of a mistress, I feel confident that on his salary your husband could afford either to lease a modest property in the Arbat or to approach a bank, preferably not mine of course, in order to obtain sufficient capital to purchase one.

Should you feel like doing so, I suggest that over the next two or three days you have a look at the area and see what you think of it. If anything takes your interest, I can arrange for my office to let us know of any properties that are for sale or for rent."

30th December 1899

The last day but one of the 19th century and probably with the publication of *Russian Thought* the last day of my anonymity. I wake determined to visit Stary Arbat as Dmitry had suggested. I think it expedient to ask for a sleigh to be brought to the hotel, rather than offering Muscovites the unusual sight of a woman standing on the pavement trying to attract the attention of passing cabbies. Within a couple of minutes the doorman finds a driver who is quite happy to be engaged for the morning. He is a young man dressed in a new fur coat and wearing on his head an expensive red fox shuba. Though the temperature is well below freezing he has made no effort to turn the earflaps down, a sign of bravado amongst the young men of the city. He sees me looking at his furs.

"Don't be mistaken, Madame, these are my own. My uncle, he lives in Siberia and every year he comes up to Moscow, brings us something that he's shot. But of course being a Siberiak he swears it's never cold enough here in Moscow to need furs. Where to, my lady? I am at your service for an hour, two hours, the whole day, whatever your command."

"To the Arbat, Carpenter's Lane just off the highway!" I shout back to him as he mounts his seat. I feel my mood lighten and I know that today I am going to enjoy myself.

Snow had fallen during the night and a fresh covering lies over the streets and roofs of houses. The sun is shining, the bells of the Zaikonospassky Monastery begin to ring as we set off down Nikolskaya Street. Moscow looks beautiful again in its fresh panoply of snow. I snuggle down in the straw and blankets of the sledge, wrap my furs tightly around me and fall to reflecting.

Could this really be the city of my new life as a single woman? Could Shchyolkovo with all its attendant miseries be forsaken for the riches of these surroundings? I look out at the shops, the cafés and the people passing by in the street. How would I settle in to Moscow in my new role? What would people think of me? That man, well dressed, carrying a briefcase and hurrying to work, how would he regard me, should he know that I was an adulterous female? He might have a mistress and sympathize, or perhaps he is happily married and would therefore regard me as a threat to the fidelity of his marriage?

And that middle aged women in a passing sleigh who glances at me and has time even in this moment of passing to assess the quality of my clothes. A young woman with clothes as fashionable and expensive as those, she would think. They would be bought for her by a rich husband or more likely by a doting admirer. She would undoubtedly consider me to be a risk to her husband's constancy, would turn away from me if we met socially and find occasion to denigrate my character when speaking to her friends.

And those young people laughing as they come out of a café. They will still be young in the first decades of the new century. Would their views and opinions on marriage change as the years went by? Would they be as sympathetic and understanding to my altered status as are my new acquaintances in Yalta? I have no way of knowing, only time will tell.

We draw up at our destination in a flurry of snow. Red fox hat raised from his head, my driver enquires as to how long I will need in Carpenter's Lane. I explain that I wish to look at several houses that are being converted into apartments, and if time allows at a new purpose built block.

In the old days it was traditional for cabbies to stand by a brazier in the street to keep warm until their hire returned. But now, perhaps at long last, the perception of a new relationship between the social classes is beginning to appear. Both my driver and I are young and despite the difference in our social status we have established something of a rapport between us. But even so I am surprised when my cabbie offers to escort me to the houses which I have singled out for inspection. He hands over his horse and sledge to an old peasant in a ragged coat and worn out felt boots, who has come up to take the reins for a kopeck or two, and skillfully hands me out of the sledge.

My driver, whose name I discover is Osip, proves to be invaluable. It would have been impossible for me on my own to approach these rough and ready workmen and ask for permission to enter the half completed buildings. Osip, however, orders planks to be brought to provide a means of avoiding the melted snow and mud that cover the ground floor. Taking me by the arm he guides me into each of the buildings. No doubt he enjoys cutting such a superior figure in the presence of these humble workmen, who doff their hats and bow to me as we enter.

I am enchanted by what I see. I can envisage how these apartments will look once they are finished. I can imagine a life of my own here with my own belongings and furniture. Across the lane is the main highway through the Arbat with its shops, cafes and restaurants. I can even see the statue of Pushkin with his wife that Dmitry had told me about. I do not need to see more. I ask Osip to bring up the sledge and we return to the *Slavyansky Bazar*.

I cannot wait for Dmitry to finish work and join me for our evening together, so impatient am I to tell him about my adventures of the day. When we are at last together he teases me about my young cabbie. He congratulates me on the speed with which I have located a suitable apartment. He promises to look into the financial side of the business, this being one area where a woman is not to get involved, he insists. All we need is an approximate figure to give to Viktor when we meet face to face. This he can do quite easily when he knows the exact address. "Carpenter's Lane, off the Arbat, house 5, apartment 1, on the ground floor with access to a little garden at the rear," I burst out, sobbing with excitement.

{25}

December 31st 1899.

I sleep badly. My mind is too active, too full of the events of the past day, to allow me to find sleeep. I spend my waking hours engaged in a fruitless attempt to visualise my encounter with Viktor and to anticipate the arguments he may put forward to challenge our stratagem.

I wake late, feverish and feeling unhappy and apprehensive. This is the last day of December and *Russian Thought* is scheduled to appear before the end of the month. I call for breakfast to be brought to my room and scarcely have I time to straighten the bedclothes and tidy the room a little before a maid brings in my tray. On it is a note from reception. I tear it open in haste, consuming the short message in an instant. A copy of the December issue of the periodical is waiting for me at the bookshop on Nikolskaya Street.

I do not tarry in taking my breakfast. I have lost my appetite and drink no more than a little tea to moisten the dryness of my throat. I hurry downstairs, flinging on my coat as I go. The bookshop has just opened, I am the first customer, and on the counter lies a package wrapped in brown paper. I hand over the few roubles for a purchase that in all probability is the price that seals my future life. I hurry back to my room. In my hands lies the new edition of *Russian Thought* with its familiar heraldic crest on its front page. My hands are trembling hands as I turn to page one, the table of contents:

Anton Pavlovich Chekhov, a new short story: The Lady with a Little Dog.

It has been given pride of place in the new edition. I turn to page two and begin to read:
"People said that there was a new arrival on the Promenade, a lady with a little dog. Dmitry Dmitrych Gurov, who had already spent…"

I read the first page straight through without stopping. By now the words are so familiar to me, that I could recite them by heart, but somehow its printed format gives it an importance which I had not anticipated. Here in print at last is our story. It is no longer a manuscript or galley proof for the eyes of a select few. It will be read across the length and breadth of Russia by some tens of thousands of readers.

It is evening before I hear Dmitry's footsteps on the stairs. After the familiar tap tap at the door I rise to meet him, as always throwing myself into his arms.

"Dmitry Dmitrych Gurov, guess what I have here." I joke, holding the magazine behind my back.

"Anna Sergeyevna von Diederitz," he replies, guessing in an instant the reason for this appellation. "I presume we have been introduced, otherwise my conduct could be construed as lascivious." I feel his arm reaching behind my back, holding my body in a rough embrace. After a short tussle he manages to extract the magazine from my grasp.

"A bottle of champagne to celebrate. Then a second bottle for when we see the New Year in. I've told my wife that I will be dining at my club and then watching the firework display on Red Square. I also warned her that if I am in no fit state to find my way home, I might stay the night at the club or if that is full with fellow celebrants, then here at the *Slavyansky Bazar*.

So Anushka, we have the unexpected pleasure of a whole evening and night together. What shall we do? If you don't have a better suggestion, I propose we get to know each other properly by reading what Chekhov has written about us, then have dinner, go out and mix with the crowds watching the fireworks and then celebrate our new fictional relationship and the new century back here in the *Bazar*. Does that meet with your approval?"

As we lie side by side, engrossed in reading, I can see that Dmitry shares the same emotions that I had felt on opening the first page. We are no longer anonymous lovers with a secret life unknown to all. We are flesh and blood, two real, living characters waiting to be discovered through the fiction of a writer's imagination.

We finish reading the final pages over dinner. The night is still young. After spending so long indoors we are in need of fresh air and exercise. We walk the short distance down Nikolskaya Street to Red Square, greeted as we turn onto the square by the smell of bonfires and braziers. Wild boars are being roasted on gigantic spits, peasants gleaming with sweat as they turn the handles, muscles bulging and faces red from their exertions. A cheer goes up as the first boar is taken off its spit and is carved up for the hungry crowd. A beer stall nearby adds to the entertainment.

After the fireworks we wander back to the hotel, arm in arm like any couple out in Moscow to celebrate the New Year. We have our champagne waiting for us and we retire to bed as the chimes of the Kremlin churches usher in the New Year and the new century.

We raise our glasses and drink its health. The twentieth century, nineteen hundred, it sounds so strange to say the words out loud as we consign the eighteen hundreds to oblivion. What will people in a hundred years be doing as they speak of the new millenium and the year 2000? Whatever they may be doing, I know that they could not be happier than we are at this very moment, the start of our own new century together.

January 1st 1900.

My first entry in my diary for the New Year. The day is ours to enjoy as we wish. Dmitry has only to be home for his family celebrations in the evening. I know exactly how I would like to spend the day. Return with Dmitry to the Arbat and show him the apartment I had looked around on my first visit. I need a second opinion in case my excitement has carried me away and swayed my judgement. My young sledge driver Osip appears as if by magic. I introduce him to Dmitry and ask him to take us to the Arbat. I joke with him about his furs and he tells Dmitry, tongue in cheek, that he had to carry me around the building site in order to keep my boots and clothes from the mud. I protest at his account but my words fall on deaf ears.

"If that is true, my young friend," laughs Dmitry, slapping Osip on the back in a man to man gesture, "then you have proved more gallant with my lady friend than I have been myself. The closest I managed to achieve the likes of such gallantry was to help her across potholes many miles away in Crimea."

That midwinter day the thermometer above the doorway of the *Slavyansky Bazar* rises no higher than minus 28 degrees. We sit together in the bottom of the sledge, pile straw over the seats and wrap our coats firmly around us. Osip, declining to undo his earflaps and boasting to the effect that it is still balmy weather compared with his native Siberia, cracks his whip and we fly through the snowy streets.

Apartment 1, house 5 in Carpenter's Lane immediately meets with Dmitry's approval and so does my decision to take a renovated apartment in an old mansion rather than to wait for the completion of a new purpose built one in the same street. He says that they have more character. After all these mansions belonged to the aristocracy before hard times forced the owners to sell up and move to the suburbs. It is the new middle classes who can afford these apartments now, people like your husband in Government employ.

I am impatient to know whether Dmitry has been able to obtain any information on the cost of such an apartment.

"Well, it's certainly a prestigious district that you've chosen," he answers wryly. I ask him in the most sensual of tones whether he would envisage leaving his visiting card at such a prestigious address with the hope that he might be invited to meet the owner.

"That delightful prospect is rather premature, is it not," he replies. " We still have to persuade your husband that it is in his best interests to acquiesce to your conditions. Look at his prospects. He's relatively young, he already occupies a high position in the Ministry and can expect promotion in the near future, that is if he keeps clear of scandal. Yes, by my reckoning, on his salary he can afford it, so long as he avoids the additional expense of keeping a mistress. And I think that we have already discounted that likelihood. Goodness knows, these mistresses are expensive enough, aren't they?" Dmitry jokes, looking at me lasciviously.

" You are quite right. A mistress is not a very likely possibility," I reassure him, laughing at the thought of Viktor in the arms of such a woman.

But enough of Viktor. The day is still young, the sun is shining and the whole of Moscow seems to be out on the streets. Street entertainers are plying their trade, gypsy fortune tellers telling the gullible their life history, acrobats on stilts towering above the mob, bear handlers with their dancing animals, booths with food and drink for the hungry masses. Bonfires have been lit on the thick ice of the

Moscow River and the smell of spit roasted wild boar wafts through the air.

"Let's get away from the crowds," says Dmitry. "I know how democratic you are, how you can talk and mix with everyone, from junior Government employees to handsome sledge drivers, but I know a place that is more exclusive and one that you will love. I presume you can skate."

"Oh, Dmitry, how can you ask that? You should know that Petersburg girls are born with skates on their feet. I used to skate to school along the Fontanka canal and we were only dragged off the Neva when the Peter and Paul fortress cannon was fired and the ice broke up. So in answer to your question, yes I do know how to skate and probably better than you can. So where do you have in mind to take me?"

My question is not answered. Dmitry may be a little put out by my assertion that I could be the more accomplished skater. I resolve to abstain from further questions as he is in a teasing mood and has no intention of giving me an answer. Instead he seeks out Osip amongst the waiting drivers and whispers something to him, words which thanks to the raucous music from a nearby hurdy gurdy I do not catch. In a few minutes we leave the busy Moscow River embankment and turn into a small park. We drive past little wooden dachas, each with intricately carved eaves and verandahs, through fir trees and birches laden with the fresh coating of snow.

In the distance I can hear the sound of voices and the shouts of sledge drivers jostling for position in the narrow lane leading to a small lake. Beyond lies the Novodevichy monastery with its churches and golden domes. It is a magical scene.

Skaters of all ages and abilities are out on the ice; young boys at speed, young girls timidly negotiating a safe path through other skaters, middle aged couples skating elegantly arm in arm, an elderly gentleman cautiously carving a remote path for himself around the edge of the lake. Everyone is on the ice and I cannot wait to join them.

"Dmitry, be an angel, find me a pair of skates. These boots I'm wearing will fit skates, I've used them before."

"Your word, my command, Anna Sergeyevna." We have by this time got used to addressing each other both by our real names and by Chekhov's noms de plume. The latter we use when the situation demands a more intimate relationship, a secret and usually erotically charged code shared between us.

Such is the case here. While some demure ladies take themselves off to a little hut by the side of the lake to have their skates put on in privacy, others not wishing to waste time and not overly concerned about the decorum of the situation, are quite happy to be seated on a bench and to have their skates put on in public view. I join their number. Putting on skates is a difficult operation at the best of times and I am glad to have Dmitry help me. He relishes the situation where he is at perfect liberty to raise my skirts above my boots and place the skates on my feet!

"Dmitry Dmitrich," I tease him. "You have brought me here with one purpose, one that is totally unconnected with skating. You need to feed your craving for little feet, ladies' boots and ankles. Be honest, declare to me that was your intention all along, was it not?"

"That is totally unfair," he insists, defending himself against my accusation. " I asked you if you liked skating long before I had any idea of having to help you like this." He is struggling with the straps of my skates, an exertion that has left him red in the face.

"There you are, Anna, now show me how you skate," he calls out, having tightened the last strap, but his words are lost in the chill air as I fly across the ice.

I so well remember every detail of that afternoon and how there on the ice we tasted of the poetry and intoxication of a Russian winter. How on one occasion I dropped my muff on the ice, bending down to pick it up and sweeping the hoar frost off the fur with my bare hand before I put my gloves back on, by mistake placing the right hand where the left belonged. I remember how I chased Dmitry around the lake, realizing to my delight that I was indeed a far better skater than he. I teased him into playing tag with me and then catching him so easily, avoiding his attempts to do the same. A kiss was my reward for each time I trapped him and he could not escape

Later, to catch our breath, we sat on a rustic wooden bench by the lakeside and warmed ourselves with coffee laced with cognac. We sat in silence, ever closer together as the winter afternoon all too soon darkened and night began to fall. The temperature dropped and we hugged each other to keep warm. "I love you, I love you, I love you, Dmitry, whether you are Gurov or Serov," I whispered to him, my muted breath etched in the frozen air.

Reluctantly we took our skates off and sought out our faithful Osip, one of a crowd of sledge drivers warming themselves around a brazier. Within minutes we were back at the *Slavyansky Bazar*. Dmitry had to hurry home to fulfill his paternal duties. The pavement outside the hotel was crowded and we had to content ourselves with a chaste kiss. Never mind, the chasteness of the kiss was of the kind which lovers can indulge themselves in when they know that before long they will be together again.

{26}

The morning of the second of January finds me dressed and breakfasted by nine o'clock. In the solitude of my bedroom the previous evening I had made my New Year resolution. I am resolved to be a new woman to fit the new century. The first challenge facing me is my work. I have been asked to cover for one of the office staff at MKhAT who is taking an extended holiday over the New Year. I do not know what I can offer with my limited skills, but nevertheless I have been invited to fill her place.

The weather has turned a great deal milder and since the distance is not a great one, I decide to dispense with the services of Osip and his sledge, and now being an independent woman to make my own way to the offices of the Moscow Art Theatre. But this is not as easy as I had presumed it to be.

The thaw has caused a number of pavements to be closed. As I look up at the roofs of the tall buildings on Nikolskaya Street I can see the extent of the danger. Sharp, sword like icicles, caused by holes in the guttering or obstructions in the gutters themselves during the winter, are beginning to melt and crash to the ground. Pedestrians are in danger of being struck by these lethal shards of ice and for their safety the authorities have cordoned off the affected areas. I am obliged to reach my destination by a circuitous route, eventually reaching MKhAT to quite some degree exhausted by my journey.

I am delighted to learn that Masha has arrived in Moscow and as promised has delivered the manuscript of Anton's first two acts of *Three Sisters,* which now lies beside my new typing machine. I recognize the atrocious handwriting on the frontispiece and my heart sinks as I realize how diffficult the transcription is likely to be. And to make matters worse I am delayed in making a start by the arrival of the morning post, which brings a letter from Viktor. I can see no reason for him to write to me unless he is aware of the publication of my story. With dread I break the family seal on the envelope to unfold its contents and learn my fate.

To my wife Anna Ivanovna von Melk,

It has unfortunately been brought to my attention that a certain scandalous Russian literary magazine has had the audacity to publish a short story by Anton Chekhov which, despite its fictional setting,can be no more than a scurrilous retelling of the sordid affair that you have admitted to conducting last year in Yalta.

I have now no alternative than to recall you immediately from Moscow, where you are no doubt cohabiting with this renegade, to explain your conduct pertinent to this affair. Respecting your wishes not to return to our house, I have booked a room in the Grand Hotel in Shchyolkovo for a meeting with you at 2 p.m. the day after tomorrow. Present will be my lawyer who is fully cognizant of all the facts pertaining to this affair. Of course you are at liberty to bring with you any such person whom you feel may be able to help you with an explanation of your conduct in this despicable matter.

I am unfortunately unable to delay the timing of this meeting due to extreme pressure of work, the reasons for which I will explain to you at our meeting. I therefore await immediate confirmation by telegraphic communication of your return to Shchyolkovo.

I remain your husband, whom I hasten to remind you in our marriage vows, you have promised to obey,

Viktor Aleksandrovich.

I read through the letter once more and return it to its envelope. So this is it. The one thread holding my personal sword of Damocles hanging above my head has finally been cut. But strangely enough I feel no more than relief that at last matters are out in the open. I collect my thoughts. I have no alternative other than to acquiesce to my husband's demands and to delay my work on *Three Sisters* for a few days.

I curse Viktor once again under my breath for disrupting my life. The sooner I am free of this man the better. Leave me alone to get on with my own life, I repeat for the hundredth time. Give me the chance to live my life with the freedom that is given to a man and not be fettered as a woman to a jealous and bigoted husband.

In the afternoon I call at Dmitry's office where I leave a message for him to come to dinner. Over our evening meal I reveal the contents of Viktor's letter. I beg him, notwithstanding the short notice, to accompany me to my appointment in Shchyolkovo.

Of course, he reassures me, he will be able to arrange an absence from work for the day. There will be sufficient time to attend the meeting and catch the evening train back to Moscow. To justify his absence he is minded to pay a short visit to his bank's Shchyolkovo branch to introduce himself to the local staff.

Dmitry and I rehearse what we have decided we must use as my bargaining position in this face to face confrontation. I am concerned by Viktor's mention of the urgency of the timing for this meeting. He has cited pressure of work as the reason. He always keeps on telling me that he is kept busy in his office due to his important position, but it seems unusual for him to give me so little notice. I have a lurking, nagging premonition that there may be more than just wounded pride in his insisting on such a hurried schedule for this rendez-vous.

***

For our confrontation I choose to dress soberly in a black dress with a matching jacket edged in black velvet. I wish to give the impression to both my husband and his attorney that I am a mature, respectable woman accompanied by a highly regarded member of a leading Moscow bank. I decide to continue wearing a light veil, since to my continued embarrassment the scars on my face have not yet fully healed.

We catch an early morning train to Shchyolkovo. This gives us time to have lunch in a discreet restaurant that I know, well away from the Grand Hotel and any possibility of an untoward, premature meeting with Viktor and his attorney.

As we emerge from the railway station we realize how cold Shchyolkovo is compared with Moscow. There is a great deal more snow on the streets and pavements, which have not been properly swept, and an icy wind blows off the Klyazma river. The city looks grim and wretched, reflecting our sombre mood. A miasma hangs over the central square where the streets lights have been installed. A ghastly sulphuric smell of rotten eggs pervades the air.

I put this down to the town's renowned malfunctioning sewage facility and think no more of it. After the euphoria of our recent days in Moscow I feel this wretched town now reflects the reality of our situation and the paucity of our case. In a chastened mood we make our way to the Grand Hotel as the bells of the cathedral of the Holy Trinity strike two.

I hardly recognize Viktor when we meet in the foyer. He has changed both physically and more subtly in the way he holds himself. There is something in his bearing that is different from the last time we met. He looks older, yet somehow more substantial, more self confident and assured of himself.

He makes no effort to receive Dmitry politely. He ignores his proffered hand, confining himself to a curt bow to satisfy the minimum requirements of convention. Viktor makes one paltry gesture in my direction to acknowledge my presence, otherwise ignoring me until we are seated in the formal surroundings of the Grand Hotel's best suite of rooms. As for his attorney, I take an instant dislike to him, as I knew I would. He is elderly, dry as the law he practises every day, advising his male clients on how to win their cases in the divorce court. Viktor stands and turns to me.

"Anna Ivanovna, if you have no objection I will open the proceedings, since I am certain that what I have to say will affect the rest of our discussions." He speaks in that cold voice which I have so long associated with being chastised for some minor infringement, some slight misdemeanour that I have committed. He leans forward, tetchily waving away a servant who appears with glasses and a carafe of water. He is impatient to start.

"Firstly I do not wish to discuss at this initial stage the consequences so unfortunately pertaining to the publication of this unfortunate story and which have necessitated our being brought together. If you and your friend here," he pauses to identify Dmitry with a dismissive glance, " are both willing to be identified as the protagonists in this sordid story we can deal with that situation at a later stage."

He pulls himself up to his full height. " Secondly I need to inform you of a major development in my ministerial career. As you will no doubt be aware I have played a major part in the successful project of bringing gas lighting into the city. My success has not gone unnoticed in higher places. In recognition of this achievement I have been promoted to the rank of Collegiate Assessor in the town of Irkutsk with responsibility for administering the new oil and gas fields which are being developed in Siberia. Naturally I have had no hesitation in accepting this position and I will shortly be starting my new employment in Irkutsk. You will now appreciate the need for my arranging this meeting at such short notice.

I will now explain to you, Anna Ivanovna, how this affects you as my wife. I have decided, after lengthy reflection, that if you will accompany me to Irkutsk and consider a new start to our married life together, then I will forgive you your recent unfortunate indiscretions. I truly believe that you have been led astray through the pernicious vices of your male admirers."

He returns to his seat, his arms folded. Dmitry cannot remain passive in the face of such provocation. I lay a restraining arm on his as he begins to rise from his chair.

"If I might be allowed to speak without any further interruption, I would be most grateful," Viktor dryly continues. "As you may know, Irkutsk has been described by someone from your beloved St. Petersburg as being the Paris of Siberia. If I might be allowed to digress for a moment, I will remind you that several of the Decembrist wives, including of course Princess Maria Volkonsky, the wife of Prince Sergey Volkonsky, whom you will remember as one of the leaders of the Decembrist uprising, chose to accompany their husbands to Siberia to start a new life there.

I have digressed briefly in the belief that given some effort, some good will on your part, you would be able to adapt quite satisfactorily to the move. And just as these wives made a new life there with their husbands, you yourself would be able to do likewise."

I cannot restrain myself any further. I rise to my feet, and in what Dmitry later described as a theatrical gesture which I must have learned at MKhAT, I throw back my veil to expose my face. There is a moment's shocked silence as the full effect of my wound becomes apparent to both my husband and his lawyer.

"Viktor Aleksandrovich, I stand before you as the physically abused wife of a man who, if I understand correctly, is suggesting that there would be some sort of a truce if I were to give up everything here in Moscow and accompany you to some God-forsaken place in Siberia. You must have taken complete leave of your senses if you think I would entertain for a moment such a ridiculous proposal.

You mention the Decembrist wives, but you conveniently forget that they were in love with their husbands and had certainly not been attacked and raped by them. I am not in love with you. I tell you again, in case you did not catch my meaning the first time, that I will neither now nor at any time in the future give any credence to your patronizing proposal, which can only come from a man totally divorced from the realities of modern life. I have my own life and work in Moscow and am far too busy to….."

I am interrupted by a rustling of papers and a dry cough from the direction of Viktor's attorney. I realize that I am in danger of going too far. I sit down and pull my veil once more across my face.

Viktor takes the floor and asks with mock irony in his voice, "In that case, since you have made your feelings abundantly clear and have rejected my very generous offer, perhaps you would be kind enough to tell me what you propose to do with your young life, which, despite what you have told me, you seem to be in imminent danger of destroying."

Dmitry, who has been silent up till now, rises to answer. "Viktor Aleksandrovich, may I be allowed to explain the situation as Anna and I see it. She is obviously a little distraught at the moment." For my part I am not so distraught as to miss the sharp intake of breath from Viktor when Dmitry simply refers to me by my first name.

"Anna and I have discussed the situation and our views are as one. Please let me continue, this time without interruption on your part. We consider your past and present behaviour towards Anna to be unforgiveable. No man should be allowed to behave in such a tyrannical manner towards his wife. And to judge from your attitude to her today you are still intent on doing so.

You must have realized how unhappy she has been over the past years, yet you have done very little to alleviate her unhappiness. When she returns from her trip to Yalta, you have an argument and you lose your temper, striking her across the face in the presence of a servant. We have all seen only too clearly the scars that you have inflicted on your wife's face and, sir, to any civilized man's way of thinking, your behaviour can only be thought of as beneath contempt."

Viktor flushes with displeasure, half rises from his chair, but Dmitry has the floor and continues.

"In the light of what I know about your conjugal life I would suggest that a divorce is the only solution to the debacle of this marriage. As you will be well aware, and have doubtless been advised by your attorney here, there are two ways to proceed in initiating a divorce. One is a contested divorce where the petitioner seeking a divorce is challenged by the respondent to prove his or her case. This, where adultery is alleged, would require witnesses to be subpoenaed to appear in court to provide the necessary evidence in order to prove the culpability of the indicted party.

As you will realize this course of action will always attract a great deal of unwelcome publicity, both for the petitioner and the respondent and is therefore something to be avoided if at all possible. In this case Anna would contest the charge of adultery and the evidence to prove this allegation would be for you to produce. I imagine that this is a course that no sensible man with a public position such as yours to uphold would wish to pursue. In addition Anna would bring a charge of cruelty against you and she would be able to provide witnesses within her household to corroborate her accusation.

The second option for you to consider is an uncontested divorce. Anna has been living away from her home here in Shchyolkovo for some considerable time. During this time she will admit to carrying on an adulterous relationship. You would then be free, with a minimum of publicity, to file for divorce. The issue would be resolved in a manner that would be acceptable to both parties.

However there would be a requirement from Anna, who no longer would be able to remain in her marital home here in Shchyolkovo, for you to provide her with suitable accommodation in Moscow. This could either be in the form of a rented apartment for as long as she requires it, or in one that is bought by you and given over to her, again for as long as she requires it. That, to put it in simple terms, is the price she would accept from you for her silence. You, sir, are in no position to confound my argument. We would ask you to accept our terms."

My husband, who at this point had started drumming the table with his knuckles, a sure sign that he had lost his temper, breaks in. Rising to his feet to emphasize what he is about to say, he replies with tightened lips.

"With due respect, Dmitry Dmitrych, I must stop you there. I am not confounded by your argument, as you call it. I utterly reject these extortionant demands, which you have just had the audacity to present to me. And let me tell you why. I will repeat myself one more time." He pauses for a moment, shuffling the papers he holds in his hand. His evident self confident manner lends credence to my premonition that my husband holds in his hand some trump card, as yet unknown to us, but which he is now about to play.

He continues. "As my wife may have told you, I am a person with a respected position in local Government, a position which I will do everything in my power to protect and enhance. I am a career civil servant and am ambitious to exercise my talents, as far as I can do so, in the service of my country.

If I had decided to stay here in this small town I would not have faced the thought of divorce proceedings with equanimity. However, since I will be some 20,000 versts away in what amounts basically to a foreign country, I do not care a damn as to what happens here in Shchyolkovo in the way of sordid divorce proceedings, be they contested or uncontested.

What also needs to be made clear to you both is that ultimately Anna Ivanovna will be found guilty of adultery and this will provide grounds for divorce. Nor do I care a damn what happens to her if she decides to reside in Moscow. She has made her bed and must accept that she has to lie on it, sharing it of course with whomsoever of her admirers she may favour at the time."

Viktor sinks back into his chair. He stares at me with a malicious smirk on his face, pleased with the crudeness of his brazen remark. What is so galling is the fact that he has so easily been able to trump what we had considered to be the one strong card in our otherwise weak hand.

I rise from my seat pulling my veil from my face and trying to keep my voice calm though my blood is boiling. I confront him.

"Viktor Aleksandrovich, if that is your decision, then so be it. I will contest the divorce as strenuously as I can. The costs, which will be considerable, will be for you to settle. As a married woman in Russia, you will be aware that I have no private income of my own and all my assets, pitiful as they are, are lodged in your bank account. I too, living in Moscow, will be well away from this wretched little town and I do not mind having my reputation besmirched here, if that is what public opinion decides.

And now, if you please, I would like to return as quickly as possible to Moscow. I have better things to do with my time than to remain here a minute longer than I need to. I have an appointment tomorrow morning with the Director of the Moscow Art Theatre, after which I will be transcribing from manuscript form the latest play by Anton Chekhov. But of course, Viktor Aleksandrovich, this means nothing to you. You are a philistine. Pack your warmest furs, go to Siberia and get frostbite! I will not be joining you, now or ever. And that is my final word.

{27}

With that final caustic, and I must admit in retrospect rather childish remark, I fling myself out of the room. Dmitry follows on my heels. We collect our coats from the cloakroom and start walking towards the station. It is now late afternoon and already darkness is falling. But surely, it comes to me, the gas lights in the central squares should have been lit by now.

However, to my astonishment, everywhere is in darkness. Pedestrians are stumbling along the icy pavements, running into each other and muttering curses about the lack of lights. What should have been my husband's crowning achievement before he left for Siberia, I reflect ironically, now looks somewhat tarnished.

It is too cold to talk. As we walk, holding each other's arm in case we slip and fall, I have time to reflect on the real impact of what transpired at our meeting. Why had Viktor accepted the post in Irkutsk? It seems a desperate step to take, all for the sake of some minor promotion. After all, as I know quite well from being married to a government official, a rise in the hierarchy of the civil service from his present rank of Titular Counsellor to that of Collegiate Assessor could hardly be worth such a transfer. Is his decision to move to Siberia really due to this slight promotion or, as a cynical thought comes to me, is it that his superiors have already been made aware of the content of our story and have suggested to him that his only move now is this drastic one?

And just as galling is the realization now that my dreams of an independent life in Moscow are as nought. Will I really have to spend more time in the *Slavyansky Bazar*, much as I have grown to love it. Once my work on *Three Sisters* is complete, I will have no proper employment and nowhere to live. The start of the twentieth century suddenly appears decidedly less conducive to the efforts of a soon-to-be-divorced woman, who has promised herself an independent life.

The temperature is dropping rapidly as night sets in. Pulling my fur stole tighter round my face I clutch Dmitry and let him direct me towards a small, discreet café, where I can sit out the hour before he returns from visiting his bank.

In saying goodbye to him at the entrance to the café I fail to notice a young gentleman who, arriving at the doorway at the same time as me, steps aside gallantly to let me enter first. I look up to thank him. Even in the dim light I cannot fail to recognize the features of my young dancing companion from the Ministry ball. Raising his hat he smiles at me.

"Sergey Ivanovich Platonov at your service, Madame von Melk, allow me to hold the door for you. I am quite certain that you will not remember me of course, but I am the young gentleman, whom you met at the Gaslights Ball last year and…."

He stops in mid sentence. " Anna Ivanovna, you look a little fatigued. Let me order you a coffee." We find a secluded corner table and divest ourselves of our coats. I leave my face concealed by my veil. He calls a waiter.

"It would appear that we both need something stronger than a simple black coffee. Coffee Royale laced with armagnac will do nicely."

The coffee arrives in tall glasses. I drink and feel better as the cognac begins to take effect. Rather too quickly, I think as I drain my glass. Sergey calls for a second glass.

"Sergey Ivanovich, I interpose." Please could I have mine this time without the cognac? You may remember, when we last met, your taking advantage of a young lady by plying her with champagne with its inevitable consequences. I would not wish to repeat my mistake again."

But there is a twinkle in my eye that I cannot disguise. He looks quizzically at me. It is not difficult to read his thoughts. He is asking himself if I am the same young woman who had played so blatantly with his emotions when we first met, or had I reverted to being the upright Minister's wife that I promised him I would be, if and when we were to meet again.

What I love about this young man is that he cannot conceal his emotions. I can read on his face so clearly that he has decided the safer path will be to accept that I am playing the latter part of virtuous Minister's wife. Our coffees arrive. Sergey looks at me as I put my lips to the glass.

"I promise you, no armagnac this time," he laughs. "Well, tell me what you've been up to in our lovely little town of Shchyolkovo since last we met. And after that I'll reveal to you the latest scandals in our local government offices, ones I am quite certain your husband would not wish to hear me telling you about.

Oh, and before we start, I ought to tell you that I now have a lady friend of my own age, so you do not have to be concerned that I may disgrace myself again in the company of a married woman."

We laugh at the shared memory. I feel that there could be no more pleasant way of spending an hour than in the company of this young man, whose innocent charm had so easily led me astray at our previous meeting.

Despite his attempts at humour Sergey looks distraught. His curly hair is all awry. There is a haunted look on his face. This is not the same young man, immaculate and self confident, whom I had last seen with his arm around my waist, bidding me goodnight after our final dance. The awful events of the past few hours begin to slip from my mind as I seek something lighthearted with which to continue the conversation.

"Tell me, Seryozha," I could not resist the intimacy of calling him by his diminutive. " What have you done to the street lights in this sordid, little town of ours? You told me that the street lighting had been a great achievement. Now the whole town is plunged into darkness. What exactly is going on? Am I mistaken in believing that the Council cannot afford to settle the Gas Board bill?"

"Believe me, Anna, it's not something to joke about. The Council is facing a catastrophe, which.... "
He stops in mid sentence as in the dim light he catches sight of the scar on my cheek. He pulls my veil to one side to see more clearly and traces the line with his hand.

"Anya, what have you done to your cheek? How did you get that mark on your face?"

"Sergey," I reply, replacing my veil. "I owe you an explanation. I'm sorry, but I think you'll be shocked at what I have to tell you. At the Ball, if I remember, we talked about my stay in Yalta, about my reading Madame Bovary, but I omitted telling you that I had entered into a relationship with a man, a certain Dmitry Serov, whom I met on holiday there.

Sergey was looking at me in amazement. "There's more to come," I continue. " Dmitry and I made the acquaintance of Anton Chekhov when we visited his new house at Autka. Some time later Chekhov wrote to me in Shchyolkovo, inviting me down to Yalta to help him write a short story called 'The Lady with a Little Dog,' based on my relationship with Dmitry. This I did, quite successfully I believe, and the story has been published in *Russian Thought,* should you wish to read it. The gentleman you may have caught sight of as we came into the restaurant is in fact the protagonist in our little story. Dmitry will be coming to collect me in an hour.

Oh, and one final detail to explain why I am in something of a flustered state today is that my husband recently discovered my infidelity and rewarded my behaviour by striking me, his reward for my telling him that we could no longer live together under the same roof.

Today Dmitry and I had a meeting with my Viktor. He boasted that he has been offered promotion, a post in Irkutsk and would be leaving Shchyolkovo in the next few days. During our very bad tempered meeting I had hoped to force him into accepting some sort of compromise, a financial inducement not to contest our divorce which now looks inevitable.

But of course, now that he's going to Siberia, he says that he is not worried about his standing in a small, provincial town like Shchyolkovo. He will be beyond the Urals and safely away from any kind of malicious gossip which might damage his career."

"Anna, I'm so sorry. Not of course because of you and your husband separating. That has to be the inevitable consequence of his conduct towards you."

He touches my face gently, tracing the line of the scar along my jaw. "But that monster of a man, excuse my language. He's been a nightmare to work with ever since our evening at the Ball. Maybe he's jealous that we spent so much time together, possibly that we were dancing a little too intimately, and for this he is seeking revenge through his behaviour towards me at work.

He drops thinly veiled hints all the time that I should be sent to Novosibirsk to a new department there dealing with gas exploration. But that's nothing compared with what happened today. You obviously haven't heard the news. There's been a malfunction in the city's new gas lighting. You must have smelt the gas around Central Square and seen that the street lights aren't working. There's been a major leak in the installation and for safety reasons we've had to cut off the gas supply to the town.

I've just come from the Ministry where everyone is blaming everyone else for the disaster. Our Engineering Department is being accused of technical miscalculations and your husband's office is openly being accused of mismanagement and even corruption. It just so happens that since I was involved in this scheme from the start, as was your husband, I find that I will be acting as one of the key witnesses in this fiasco."

Sergey stops talking, drains his glass of coffee and orders another. Despite the warm atmosphere in this little café and the effects of the coffee I still feel cold. I start to shiver.

"Let me warm your hands," he says,taking them, holding them flat on the table and stroking my fingers. I remember the last time we had made physical contact. Sergey was guiding me back to Viktor after our last dance at the Ball, his arm guiding me through the tightly packed tables. We were joking about his speech. Viktor may have seen this innocent little action and mistakenly taken it for an intimacy which had already been formed between us on the dance floor. We sit in silence for a moment deep in our separate thoughts.

"Anna," he continues. "I don't know whether you'll agree with this, but listen carefully. I can see a way of making life unpleasant for your husband. Hubris is his fatal flaw. Look at the man for a moment, this husband of yours. Analyse his recent behaviour, then tell me what you think the characteristics of hubris are?

I think for a moment. What is hubris, I ask myself ? It's not a difficult question to answer. "If you ask me, I would say Viktor's arrogance, the way he overestimates his competence, his overbearing pride and self confidence, his loss of contact with reality and most importantly his excess of ambition are signs of hubris. And he has well and truly demonstrated all this today."

"My goodness, Anna, I am impressed. You never told me you were so deep into psychoanalysis. Perhaps you've had time to fit in a visit to Vienna since I saw you last?"

"Oh yes, Sergey. Sigmund and I are on first name terms." He laughs. "But seriously Anna, I can corroborate what you've said about your husband's behaviour at home since he shows these same characteristics at work. I would love to see him suffer both for the way he has been treating you and for the way he's behaved to me from the moment I was assigned to his office. What I have to say is confidential.You must swear not to repeat a word of what I tell you to any one." He leans across the table so that our heads are close together. "Anna, I can see the way to bring about his nemesis, or to put it in cruder terms the way to exact our revenge on him."

I look at Sergey. "I'm sorry, I don't quite catch your meaning. Are you telling me that Viktor is vulnerable in any way?"

"Yes, he certainly is and I will tell you why. You told me that Dmitry Dmitrych is coming for you in a few minutes, so we don't have long. I'll try to explain as quickly as I can. As I said a minute ago, I find myself in the unwanted position of being a key witness in this gas lighting debacle.

The problem first came to light about a month ago. You remember that really cold spell of weather we had when the Klyasma froze over and the ferries stopped running. It was then that the gaslights began to perform erratically and I was instructed to join an investigation team into what had gone wrong. I'm sorry, I'm going to bore you now, but I need to explain things properly.

I was certain that we engineers had done a proper job in installing the system. We had branched off from the main gas feed line running to Moscow, as authorized, and laid connecting pipe work to the gas lights which had been installed in the central area of the town. I was involved at every stage of this operation and can vouch for the fact that the work was carried out properly. And to prove this, the gas lights worked perfectly up till a short time ago. Analyzing the breakdown more closely I came to the conclusion that something must have been wrong with the quality of the materials used.

One major cause of concern for me was that I found it difficult to accept the fact that the whole system had been successfully installed on budget. These large construction projects practically always overrun their estimates. Why was this one the exception? Remember the praise your husband received for delivering the project on time and within budget. Something wasn't right, the sums didn't add up correctly, and I sensed that there seemed to be a reluctance on the part of the Council to make public the full accounts.

Our Engineering Department needed this information in order to reorder materials for a future expansion of the project. But the Administration, headed by your husband's office, refused to give us access to the costing of these materials. I began to believe there had been some kind of cover up, something they didn't wish to disclose, call it collusion if you like. It was then that I think your husband sensed my suspicions and wanted to get rid of me. He began to criticize my work, suggested that I might prefer a transfer to a bigger department in Siberia. In short he made my life in his department untenable.

Sergey pauses for a moment. I begin to see the implications of what he is saying and urge him to go on.

"Now that we were experiencing difficulties with the whole gaslighting project I wasn't happy that the Engineering Department, and I in particular, had been cast as the guilty party. So I managed through a lady friend of mine, who works in the Accounts Department, to get access to the paperwork involved in the requisition of the materials for this project. One evening, staying late when everyone else had gone home, she was able to find in her office's filing system the relevant contracts for this gaslighting project. What I discovered, when she handed these documents to me, was amazing.

I realized that although the Purchasing Department had the specifications for the pipework and connecting joints supplied to them by us, they had failed to follow our advice. Instead of ordering from proven suppliers in Germany as we had stipulated, they had offered the contract instead to a cheaper company based in one of the Baltic provinces."

Sergey pauses to allow the effect of his words to sink in. " You remember my telling you at the Ball to mention the German produced joints and piping when your husband asked you for your comments on his speech? Well, they never came from Germany. I've copied out the invoices, with delivery times and prices, and can produce this when needed. But that in itself is not nearly enough evidence. I now need to prove that the new equipment was substandard.

In technical jargon I need to demonstrate that it was due to the inability of a compound, structure or facility to perform its intended function that the project failed and not its installation. Until we can examine the pipes and joints used it is only a matter of conjecture. Somehow I need to get my hands on some parts that I think have failed. It could be corrosion, breakage due to excessive brittleness in the pipes due to faulty manufacture, or whatever, but what I will stake my life on is that it was not due to faulty installation. And yet, that is precisely what your husband is suggesting.

What happened with the finances of the operation I do not know. All I do know is that your husband's office must have been some thousands of roubles better off by buying cheaper materials from the Baltic rather than expensive ones from Germany. What they did with the extra funds is not known, and I am not insinuating for a moment that your husband was involved in the financial aspects of this affair. I dislike the man intensely, but I do not perceive him as a dishonest man. All I can say is that he appears to have made a monumental error in authorizing the purchase of materials from an unproven source."

Sergey looks at me across the table to gauge the effect of his revelations.

"Sergey, if what you say is true and these allegations of yours are proven, it must mean that Viktor's career is in jeopardy. Likewise if they are not proven, then your own career will be in danger."

" Don't worry about me, Anna. I've always liked the idea of resettling in Siberia," he jokes. "As for your husband, the first thing that will happen is that his so called promotion, will be blocked. He will have to stay here in Shcholkyovo until all the investigations have taken place, and that could be years from now."

It takes me only a moment to realise the implication."That means that if Viktor has to stay here in Shchyolkovo, divorce proceedings in a small, provincial town like this one, will attract all the attention that he hoped to avoid by being so far away in Irkutsk. So my bargaining position of accepting an uncontested divorce might yet work. Viktor might still agree to an out of court settlement if it wasn't likely to harm his reputation. And of course you would presumably be rid of him as your Head of Department."

A group of students comes in and sits down at an adjoining table. They start talking loudly, so I have to lean forward again across our table to make myself heard. We must have looked like an amorous couple discussing some very intimate matter.

"Seryozha," I whisper. "You know what they say, revenge is a dish best taken cold. You and I, we've both suffered for months at the hands of this husband of mine. Do we now really have a chance to bring him down, to make him pay for what he's done to both of us? I have less to lose than you. There will have to be a divorce now and I will probably be left destitute. But that is nothing compared with what will happen to you. If you make these allegations publicly and you don't win your case, that surely will be the end of your career in local government.

"Anna, it's a gamble, but one that I have to take. I have no choice in the matter. To clear my name I will have to confront your husband and put the blame on him personally for this failure. I have the evidence of the invoices and requisitions, but as I said, if it comes to a full enquiry I will need more evidence. This is something I will need to work on now.

There will be an unholy row in our Ministry, with department set against department. I know that I will have the support of all the Engineering Department, which is going to be furious that its recommendations have been ignored and that it has been made the scapegoat for a catastrophe for which it is not responsible. There is bound to be a Board of Enquiry to listen to all the evidence and make a final impartial judgement as to the guilty party.

This Enquiry will be held in Moscow and I will almost certainly be called to attend a preliminary meeting to arrange the dates and to submit the names of our defence counsel. If this is the case I will let you know when I'm coming to Moscow. Perhaps we could meet somewhere in the evening. That would be one little pleasure to look forward to in all this sordid business."

"Seryozha, of course we can meet in Moscow. Tell me, can members of the public attend? If so, can you invite me? When will you know the dates?"

"Anna, please don't be so impatient. So many questions to which I don't have an answer. But I promise, I'll write and let you know all the details. And what a shame it is that your impatience, as I perceive it, is purely limited to the satisfaction of your curiosity. I was hoping you might really want to see me again and that you would be waiting for me impatiently."

"Oh, you men, you are all the same, you need to be flattered all the time. All right, I shall be waiting for you in Moscow, impatient in even parts to hear your news and to see you again. There now, does that satisfy you?"

"Yes, thank you, Anna Ivanovna." But Sergey's mind had returned to the matter in hand. " You must know that your husband is not the most popular figure in the Ministry. His so called colleagues will turn against him if they sense that they may be losing their case. And of course, the Mayor and Governor, who would be publicly lampooned for their failure to provide properly functioning amenities in their town, will wish to extricate themselves as fast as possible from this unpleasant mess by blaming someone else, a public scapegoat in effect. And we don't have to look far to guess who that person will be. None other than your husband, Viktor Aleksandrovich von Melk."

"Seryozha, you know how our simple folk refer to your gaslighting. They call your invention 'the devil's candle.' The gaslights here in Shchyolkovo are widely denounced by the peasants as the work of the devil. But, who knows, perhaps in the end the devil will be our salvation."

Sergey laughs " I've heard the peasants' saying 'Better to light a candle than to utter a curse,' but in the hallowed corridors of our Ministry I've never heard mention of 'the devil's candle'.But I like what they call our invention. Good luck to the devil if he can solve our problems...."

He stops in mid sentence as he catches sight of a figure approaching our table. It is a young girl who greets him with a kiss. She glances at me with a quizzical look. Sergey stands up. He asks the students at the next table if he can borrow one of their empty chairs. "Sonya, may I introduce you to the wife of my present Department Head, Madame von Melk. Anna Ivanovna, this is the young lady who has been helping me with the problems that I mentioned. As I told you, her work has been invaluable."

I feel a moment's stab of jealousy as I look at the girl. There is something intimate in her actions as she smooths his ruffled curls and straightens his cravat. With a woman's intuition I can see that she obviously thinks the world of this young, good looking man. But I remember my having told Sergey to leave married women alone and to find a girl of his own age. I cannot blame him. He has done just what I told him to do. Sonya, a very sensible choice and quite attractive as well.

At that moment the café door opens, admitting a blast of cold air. I see Dmitry looking around, expecting to see me sitting alone at a corner table. He looks exasperated and angry. Finally he catches sight of me.

"Anna, there you are. I'm sorry I'm late. It's these confounded streets. There's no lighting anywhere. I could hardly find my way back here and they haven't even cleared the snow from the pavements. And then there's that awful smell all over the place. If we hurry we can catch the evening train back to Moscow, otherwise if we miss it, it will be that awful hotel for me and you."

He looks at my companions enquiringly. I feel I should introduce him to them. As far as he can see we are three youngsters engaged in an interesting discussion, which he has interrupted. This is neither the time nor place to explain our relationship. I make hurried introductions and ask Dmitry to get my coat and hat from the rack in the corner of the restaurant.

As Dmitry goes off to fetch them I hurriedly give Sergey my address at the *Slavyansky Bazar* and make him promise to keep me informed of any developments in the case. Unfortunately Dmitry forgets to collect my fur wrap as we prepare to leave and cursing this oversight he returns to the coat rack.

As he comes back he sees that Sergey and I are still in conversation. Irritation is written on his face. We walk in silence, struggling through the dark streets to the station. The Moscow train is just about to leave and I hope that once we are on board we will be able to discuss our meeting with Viktor and his lawyer. But I have miscalculated. This is not to be the case.

"I suggest you tell me what you and your friends were so busy talking about while I was at the bank." It is not the usual calm Dmitry who is talking. One of his most admirable traits has always been that he has never shown any signs of jealousy in all the time I have known him.

But on this occasion he is not in his usual consoling mood. He has taken badly the defeat meted out by my husband. He also seems cross with me for being entertained by an attractive younger man. But I think that what upsets him most is the feeling of guilt. Guilt over the possibility of a divorce where he had raised my hopes to an impossibly high level, only to have them dashed so easily. Guilt that he was not able to provide for me financially on a permanent basis, something which I had no desire or need for him to do. I cannot convince him that I will never reduce myself to the position of a kept woman, but his feeling of guilt clings to him, however hard I argue. I do not tell him the substance of my conversation with Sergey. We continue our journey in silence.

{28}

The receptionist at the *Slavyansky Bazar* pulls out my room key from the row of little boxes behind her desk. With it there is an envelope addressed to me. The handwriting looks vaguely familiar.

"This is the last straw, Dmitry. I've had such a horrible day and now I've got a letter from Nemirovich Danchenko. He's going to tell me that I'm no longer needed at MKhAT. They'll say that as I couldn't start on time they've found someone else to do the transcription."

"Anna, for goodness sake, you haven't even read the damned thing yet," he replies irritably. Open it for God's sake." The letter is, as I had surmised, from our Director, but the contents are far from being what I had feared.

Come and see me tomorrow as soon as you can, we have some news here that you may find of interest. N.D.

Dmitry leaves me to return to his family. I am glad to be alone. For the first time in our relationship, given the mood he is in, I do not wish for Dmitry's continued company.

Rather, I need to be alone to go over in my mind what Sergey had told me about the gaslighting fiasco and its potential consequences. I remember his final words, "You realize this whole thing is about revenge." He had mentioned revenge, but revenge is not a concept I am familiar with. Never had I thought of it as a possible way of alleviating my sufferings. But now it seems more and more alluring.

A moment of ambivalence comes upon me. There is one of our proverbs that runs: "No revenge is more honourable than the one not taken." But this unease passes quickly and I put my qualms to one side. I feel this desire has been kindled in me so urgently because for so long I have been oppressed by a combination of fear, anger and worst of all by a feeling of impotence in the face of this perceived injustice. Another aphorism comes to mind. 'Hell hath no fury like a woman scorned.' This afternoon I have been scorned and humiliated. My conscience is clear. Let Viktor feel my fury. As far as I am concerned, Sergey is free to do what he likes and to use whatever means he has at his disposal. Revenge is a sweeter dish when eaten cold, I remind myself. Let Viktor wait.

***

As expected I sleep badly, spending the night tossing fitfully in bed. I dream that I am typing in front of an audience and constantly making horrendous mistakes. And Dmitry is sulking somewhere in the background, saying something I do not catch. I wake unrefreshed to discover that it is snowing heavily. Remembering my previous ill fated journey to MKhAT on foot, I decide prudently to take a cab. Even so I arrive late and dishevelled. My snow covered furs are taken away to be dried, a cup of coffee arrives and I sit down in front of my typing machine. I take Anton's scribbled manuscript from the safe. Here at last in my hands are Acts One and Two of *Three Sisters.* Yesterday's bad tempered outbursts, however acrimonious they may have seemed at the time, pale into insignificance. This is the work with which I have been entrusted. I turn to page one and start typing: *Three Sisters, A Drama in Four Acts….* As I do so the door opens and in strides Vladimir Ivanovich.

Seeing me at my desk he says. "Ah, Anna Ivanovna, my dear, you've made it in at last. I was worried you hadn't received my note. Put away Anton's latest masterpiece for a moment if you will and come and have a word with me."

I follow him along the dark, winding labyrinth of corridors to his office. Without further ado he motions me to a chair. "Please be seated, Anna Ivanovna. I've called you in because we need to have a little talk about what we can offer you here at MKhAT.

Firstly, we can't have you wasting precious time getting from your hotel to the theatre every day, particularly in this winter weather. What we can offer you instead of your hotel accommodation is the room in the annexe which Masha has just vacated. She has taken up a teaching post at a school here in Moscow which has its own accommodation, so she no longer needs a room here. It's not very large but it does have cooking facilities of its own, should you feel the need on occasion to cater for yourself.

Otherwise you would be most welcome to use the staff canteen. The food is not haute cuisine, but you might be interested in meeting some of our actors, who take their meals there. For their part, they would certainly be interested in talking to you about your *Three Sisters.* You know what our Thespians are like, they are all anxious to know what parts there are in the play for them. Just keep Konstantin Sergeevich quiet if he asks, he's convinced that the play is simply about three women, there being no proper role in it for him.

Oh, and by the way, you would have company. My wife and I have an apartment in the same annexe, and of course Olga Knipper has a room there for the occasions she is on stage and finds it inconvenient to return home late at night."

What I admire about our Director, or ND, as I had learned to call him, is his ingenuousness. Although his relationship with his leading actress is well known throughout the theatrical world, he must be clinging to the belief that I as an innocent newcomer know nothing of this menage à trois. I decide to be diplomatic and thank him innocently and profusely for his offer of the room. At a stroke one major obstacle, the expense of living in Moscow, has been removed.

But there is more good news to come. Vladimir Ivanovich tells me that a lady in the office, who is expecting a baby, has been taken into hospital with complications and will not be back at work for the foreseeable future. What he would like me to do when I've finished the transcription of *Three Sisters* is to take her place in the office.

"It's only fairly basic administrative work," he apologizes, " but it does require some typing skills which I believe you now have.

However there is another much more important reason why we would like to put you on the books of MKhAT. Let me explain. Quite simply, it's your relationship with Anton Pavlovich in Yalta which we would like to take advantage of. He is our priority. He has written to me yet again. Instead of telling me about the progress of his play, he moans that he has flu, he feels terrible but still has time to catch mice. And to make matters worse his new puppy Kashtanka has broken its leg. And believe it or not, Anton has stopped writing to nurse it. In addition, his housekeeper Mariushka is still feeding him on fish and soup, which he abhors. How he expects to finish Acts Three and Four of his *Three Sisters* neither he nor I know. What I do know is that our Moscow audiences are getting a little tired of *Uncle Vanya* and are clamouring for a new play.

Now let me spell out where you could be useful to us. By all accounts Anton would dearly love to have you back in Yalta, where he thinks you could nurse the old fellow, keep an eye on him, get him to eat properly and generally make certain that he does seriously commit pen to paper.

He sends his best wishes to you and remembers with affection the week you spent with him. To make you laugh, he asks me to let you know that there are already a number of young ladies parading along the sea front with little dogs, all claiming to be the eponymous lady in question. He's very gratified that the initial reception of your story has been so positive.

But none of that concerns us here at MkHAT. What I want to ask you is whether, when you've finished your transcribing here in the office, perhaps you could see your way to going down to Yalta. Anton in all honesty does need you and you are the one person who could keep him concentrating on what he needs to be doing. Quite simply, your mission would be to get that completed play to us as soon as you can. *Uncle Vanya* won't live for ever.

To my horror I believe he even mentioned to Masha that if he doesn't feel better he might take himself off to the French Riviera. He seems to be very fond of Nice. In that extreme case we might have to ask you to follow him there with a view to keeping an eye on him. But for the time being, you would be charged with doing whatever you can you to keep him writing in Yalta. That is our priority."

"Do whatever I can to keep him writing?" I raise a quizzical eyebrow." Fine, so long as I am not required to become another of his Antonovkas," I joke.

"Excellent, my dear," our Director replies. "I see you are a woman of the world, one who appreciates the delicacy of the situation. With your charm I'm sure you already have our dear Anton with his penchant for pretty women twisted round your little finger. Need I say more?

One blessing, I suppose, is that for the moment our Anton is not short of money. Unless that is he goes and buys more trees for that garden where he spends far too much of his time. He has promised to pay you handsomely for the hours you spent with him. And of course he will do the same for the time you spend on your transcription here at MKhAT. And as you probably know, he's been promised a sizeable advance on the completion of Acts One and

Two. So now, no further delay, I must let you get started on your transcription."

Seeing me to the door he hesitates. " Of course we can discuss the financial aspect of your work here in the theatre at a later date. But please let me know as soon as possible if and when you can get yourself down to Yalta. We need to write back to Anton with an answer. "

I go back to the office, but my head is too much in a whirl to be able to concentrate on any typing. I owe it to my colleagues in the office to tell them about my conversation with Vladimir Ivanovich. Hardly have I started when the door opens and Stanislavsky comes into the office.

"Konstantin Sergeevich, haven't we told you not to come in here when we're working? We don't come on stage to watch your rehearsals, do we?" Lydia Petrovna harangues him in mock seriousness. "I just wanted to congratulate Anna Ivanovna on her new appointment," he replies. " I've been having a talk with Vladimir Ivanovich and he's explained his proposals to me about how you can help us." He puts his arm rather too intimately round my shoulder and peers at the scrawl that constitutes Chekhov's first page of *Three Sisters*.

" Ah, I see you have Anton's manuscript on your desk. My God, how are you supposed to decipher that handwriting? Remind me to give you the name of my optician when you need spectacles. By the way, now that I have braved Lydia Petrovna's den, might I be bold enough to enquire about my role in this play? I imagine Anton Pavlovich told you all about it when you were closeted with him in Yalta"

I pretend to be serious. "Yes, Konstantin Sergeevich, I do know how he's written you into the play. He imagines you as an elderly, balding schoolmaster, totally in awe of his domineering wife, and one who pathetically tries to seduce one of the sisters. Unfortunately, not a pleasant character at all."

I look Konstantin in the eye and for a moment I am certain that he believes me. It takes a second or two for him to realize otherwise.

"You little minx, I can see why Anton has fallen in love with you. You are a beautiful young lady who has the priceless gift of being able to flirt with men at a level of intimacy which we poor creatures find difficult to resist."

I blush but manage some sort of lighthearted reply. Lydia Pavlovna has no desire to keep silent any longer. "Konstantin Sergeevich, flirting is something we young women practise in self defence. Otherwise how are we to deal with all this flattery, which does us no good if it is not a truthful reflection of a man's feelings?

And it's not only the fair sex that engages in flirting, Konstantin Sergeevich. You've only known Anna Ivanovna, as you should properly address her, for a few days and here you are, hanging around my office and carrying on with her in your outrageous theatrical manner. Go away and leave us in peace."

"Touché, Lydia Pavlovna, ma chérie," he lapses into French as she escorts him to the door and out he goes, as if off stage left, with a theatrical gesture with his arm to signify token defeat.

Now I am free at last to concentrate on the manuscript. But I have one more thing to do before I can start. Having related all of today's events to the office staff, I have for the moment forgotten that poor Dmitry still knows nothing of what transpired this morning. I quickly pen a note and have a messenger deliver it to the bank.

Dmitry, I have some wonderful news for you. Please come by the theatre after work, it doesn't matter how late you are, but come, my love. I shall be here working on the manuscript till late in the evening.

My imagination, as always, is running away with me. I can see him here later this evening in the intimacy of an empty office where I describe to him my new life; working at MKhAT on the transcription of *Three Sisters,* living in the theatre where he can visit me after work and at the weekends, another visit to Yalta in the offing, and so on. I finally open the manuscript, squint at Anton's appalling handwriting and begin to type:

> *CHARACTERS:*
> *Andrey Sergeevich Prozorov (also known as Andryusha, Andryushanchik)*
> *Natalya Ivanovna (also known as Natasha), his fiancée, later his wife….*

{29}

I am alone in the office.The realisation comes to me as I decipher his handwriting that I am privileged to be the sole person in the world privy to the text of Anton Chekhov's new play. It is late in the evening before I can drag myself away from my typing. But I am not the only person in the theatre. I can hear the sounds of a rehearsal on stage. Stanislavsky is shouting something and being shouted at in return. But I take no notice. Rather my ears are tuned to hearing a knock at the door which will herald Dmitry's arrival.

However he does not come. I am disappointed, but my role as a mistress should have prepared me for this kind of disappointment. I have become used to his absences, which he explains in the briefest of notes. Every time I receive a letter from him I am forcibly made aware how precarious our relationship really is.

I am lonely in the evenings, spending the long hours moving my few belongings into my new room in the annexe of MKhAT. Sometimes there is a late rehearsal taking place and I am invited to attend. But Konstantin Sergevich makes it embarrassingly obvious that he requires more from me than just my opinion on the quality of the rehearsal. When I do not succumb to his charms, he redoubles his efforts!

In all this time there is one thing missing. Dmitry continues to be conspicuously absent. Two weeks are gone since he might be supposed to visit me. I am not satisfied with any of the different conclusions that I can draw to explain his absence. He writes apologizing for meetings which he has to attend most evenings and complains that at weekends he is forced to spend time with his family. Can this really be the reason? Surely not. He may be busy, but hasn't he always in the past found time to visit me? My thoughts turn fanciful. Perhaps seeing me with younger friends has made him jealous and I have upset him in such a way that sensing I wish to lead my own life, rather than continuing purely as his mistress, his regard for me has cooled. My mind fluctuates between each of these explanations with one then another being held the most probable.

On the other hand there is one figure that will not go away; one young man who has sworn to fight gallantly for justice against the actions of my husband. My knight in shining armour! Every time I reflect on what Viktor is engaged on in that wretched Shchyolkovo, Sergey's image floats in front of me. I remember our last conversation and his promise to keep in touch. And as it happens the first letter to be sent to my new address at MKhAT is from him.

My dearest Anna Ivanovna,

I sincerely hope that you have satisfactorily settled into your new accommodation in the Moscow Art Theatre. I have been letting it be known to my friends that I have an acquaintance who works in this theatre and even has an address there, and they, like me, are heartedly impressed. They imagine your going to a different play every night and being on familiar terms with the great thespians of our time. I am quite convinced that this must be how it is!

Now to the point of my letter. I promised to contact you as soon as I had news to impart of any developments in our case. To this end I must inform you that I have been summonsed to attend a preliminary meeting in Moscow at which, when the Board of Enquiry convenes, I will be called to appear as a defence witness. Unfortunately I have also to inform you that your husband will be attending this meeting as counsel for the prosecution. As I intimated when we last talked, it has all the appearance of being a battle to the death between our Engineering Department and the local Shchyolkovo Government

Administration. Rather a case of David versus Goliath, I'm afraid, with the biblical outcome likely to be overturned.

This first meeting is purely to determine suitable dates for the holding of this Enquiry and to give the Moscow City Duma sufficient time to convene an independent and impartial panel, a jury in effect. I am in a far more confident mood now. I have provided copies of the invoices that Sonya found in her office files to my superiors in the Engineering Department. As far as I know, no one in your husband's office is aware of the discovery of these papers. I believe that they will prove to be a crucial piece of evidence for our defence. But I must remind you, please treat everything you read here as confidential.

I also have another piece of evidence, details of which I cannot as yet reveal to you. Suffice it to say that I have been extremely busy. Let your lovely feminine curiosity dwell on what this piece of news might be until such time as we meet again. I cross my fingers and hope that we shall see Viktor Aleksandrovich and his Department being held totally responsible for this debacle.

Looking ahead, what will happen to your husband, should we win our case, is open to conjecture. One thing is certain though, he will not be going to Irkutsk before this Tribunal reaches a verdict. No department in Siberia would be willing to accept a transfer of personnel from European Russia in such circumstances. So for the time being your husband stays in Shchyolkovo. Let us put his fate to one side for a moment and turn to a lighter matter.

Now this is where I put my head on the block, dear Anna. As you will be aware, I am very good at overstepping the norms of accepted etiquette regarding relations with married women! Please excuse me and of course you are at perfect liberty to regard my request as yet another faux pas by a young gentleman admirer.

Let me explain. After two days of this preliminary meeting I find that I will have a Saturday night free in Moscow before returning to Shchyolkovo on the Sunday.

I have been in correspondence with a close friend of mine at Moscow University who will be graduating that week end. I have been invited by him and his partner to join them at his Graduaton Ball. But of course, being outside Muscovite society I have no partner to invite to this function.

Then it came into my head that in fact I do know one beautiful young lady, who not only resides in Moscow but also dances like a dream. Anna, it would give me the greatest pleasure if you would consent to be my partner at the Graduation Ball on January 31st 1900 to be held at the University of Moscow.

You did ask me to keep you informed of any developments in this enquiry. I will of course honour this request, but to my mind it would be much more pleasurable if we could find a quiet corner during the evening in which to conduct such a tête à tête.

I await with trepidation your reply to this bold request of mine. I do so hope that we will have another opportunity to meet and enjoy each other's company.

Finally, Anna, I must admit that I am rather anxious not to encounter your husband during my stay in Moscow. I know that I will have to come face to face with him professionally at the enquiry, but perhaps you could book me into that hotel of yours, the 'Slavyansky Bazar'. That is one hotel I know for certain that Viktor Aleksandrovich will not be choosing!

So, please write to me at the address I gave you after our meeting in Shchyolkovo. And as always I am at your service to do whatever bidding you may require of me.

I remain your devoted young gentleman and, may God grant, your companion on the dance floor for next Saturday week.

Sergey Ivanovich Platonov

Sergey's letter requires an immediate answer. I recall with pleasure the flirtatious enjoyment of the Gaslights Ball when we first talked and danced and I can see no reason why I should not accept the invitation. I wait till the office staff have gone home and then settle down in front of my typing machine. I think it would impress him immensely if he were to receive a typed letter in response to his handwritten one. I therefore compose a very formal reply to his invitation.

Anna Ivanovna von Melk thanks Sergey Ivanovich Platonov for his kind invitation to partner him at the Graduation Ball of Moscow University to be held on Saturday 31st January 1900 and is delighted to accept his invitation.
P.S . I have booked you a room at the 'Slavyansky Bazar' for the two nights you will be in Moscow.
P. P.S. Please indicate what sort of dress would be suitable for such an occasion. I would certainly not wish to distract you again, should my choice prove inappropiate!

It takes me a considerable time to add this final postscript. I want to soften the formal acceptance of his invitation by ending on a more intimate note. By doing so I hope that my business like reply is not to be taken too seriously and that I am expecting our usual flirtatious relationship to continue as before. I close the letter with the MKhAT official seal and will post it to Sergey tomorrow morning.

It is only now, envisaging an evening with a man other than Dmitry, that I realize that Dmitry himself has not come into my thoughts. Busy at the weekend he might well be, but I had not even thought of this when I accepted Sergey's invitation. What is happening to me? What is happening to our relationship? Is he deliberately avoiding me or is he really too preoccupied with work and family commitments? I have a real need now to see him. If nothing else, I owe it to him to tell him about the Graduation Ball. There never has been, and there never will be, any secrets between us.

My second letter delivered to my MKhAT address is a great deal less welcome than the first. It comes from Viktor's lawyer stating simply that his client has asked him to initiate divorce proceedings. He requests the name of my lawyer. I reply with the relevant information and send a note to Dmitry. In it I ask him to come and see me as soon as possible and to alert our young lawyer Konstantin Semyonovich to the fact that Viktor's lawyer is in the process of writing to him.

The third letter to my new address a couple of days later is of course a reply from Sergey. He is delighted that Madame von Melk is able to accept his invitation. He will meet me at MKhAT on 31st January at 6.30 p.m. As regards my dress, I am to wear anything other than that dress, underlined! He confesses that it had been his undoing at the Gaslights Ball. I laugh at his frankness and in my mind select another altogether more modest outfit.

January 15th 1900.

My diary entry for today is longer than usual. Dmitry at last comes to see me in my new room at MKhAT. It seems so extraordinary that I have been installed there for some three weeks and as yet he has not been to visit me. It is evening time and both staff and actors have gone home, leaving me alone in the theatre.

When we meet after such a long absence we both feel awkward towards each other. A perfunctory kiss, no little jokes, and I know in my heart of hearts that our relationship has changed. To settle my nerves I show him my office, my typing machine. I chatter on about the manuscript and show him Anton's impossible handwriting. He expresses polite interest, but it is clear that we have something more important to discuss. The canteen is closed, so I suggest dinner in a local restaurant.

When we are settled at our table I tell him about Sergey's invitation to the Graduation Ball and how he has been so concerned not to intrude on any of the plans that Dmitry might have made for us that evening. I am surprised.that Dmitry seems so relieved to hear this news.

"Anna, my love, that will be a much more pleasant way for you to spend the evening. What I have seen of Sergey I am certain that he will be an excellent partner for you. Far better than your old Dmitry who doesn't dance very well and anyway has to spend the evening with his family."

He pauses for a moment. I have seen him serious before but not like this. " Listen Anna, you have every right to wonder why I've not been to see you since your return to Moscow. The reason is quite simple. Let me explain." He toys with the cutlery around his plate, searching for suitable words with which to continue.

" I noticed when we went to Shchyolkovo and I saw you in the café, you were so at ease with Sergey and that girl, I'm sorry I don't remember her name, anyway with people of your own age. I felt I was intruding on you all as an uninvited guest at your table. You must see how things have changed. I have become a friendly father figure to you, available with help and advice when needed but no longer the only man in your life. And why should I be? The last thing I want to do is to inhibit your making new friends. You and I have had a wonderful time together, one that I will always cherish and remember."

He pauses. I feel sick at the realisation of what he is going to say. " When we met for the first time back there in Yalta I was sure that I had never before set eyes on such a beautiful woman. And that beautiful woman came to me and held out her arms. Anushka, I will never stop loving you and I think that you will remember me with more than just affection. But time moves on, circumstances have changed and I must set you free."

"Dmitry, I don't understand what you're saying, it's not like that," I break in inarticulately through my tears. My sobs are to no avail as he continues. "Anya, let me finish. I can't offer you the sort of life that a single unattached man can offer you. I have a wife and family and I can't break free from them. Worse than that, I've just discovered that my wife has been querying a number of withdrawals that I've been making from our bank account.

You remember my telling you that I had assigned our personal accounts into her hands simply because I didn't want extra work with family business when I have so much to do at the bank. Some of the withdrawals I've been making have been to pay for your expenses here in Moscow, such as settling the account at the *Slavyansky Bazar* or for your new wardrobe. It's a little difficult to explain these withdrawals to my wife without involving an increasing amount of deception.

You know I would give you anything you wish for, but my inability to support you properly adds to the reason why we must part."

" No, Dmitry, what you're saying is ridiculous. I can stand on my own two feet now. I don't need any new clothes, I've given up the *Slavyansky Bazar,* and as you see I'm happily installed here in the annexe. And I have an income of my own. All I need is your love."

"I wish things were as simple as that, my precious. I assure you, Anna, you will always have my love. But our situation has changed. As I see it, a man's relationship with his mistress involves a simple equation; economic security for the woman and to put it bluntly sexual intimacy for the man. That is no longer the case with us. In the position I now find myself in I cannot offer you the former and heaven forbid, nor can I have you continuing to offer me the latter. You are young and beautiful and deserve something better than the company of an ageing man who tries to hang on to something he prizes and will not let go of, and worse still, cannot even pay for.

If we were to continue seeing each other it would not be fair on you. A young mistress is one thing, but to have you growing older and still remaining faithful to me is quite simply unrealistic and ridiculous. And whatever you may say, I am not going to stop you from pursuing a new life. So go to your ball, enjoy yourself with only the regret that you and I have never had the chance to dance together.

Anya, my darling, we both must be willing to free ourselves from the dream of living those idyllic, but hopeless lives together which we planned in our days of innocence. Instead we can have the real lives that are waiting for us. I need to bow out of your life, in sadness of course but also in gratitude for all the happiness you have given me, this selfish old man whom you see before you now. I can do no other."

By now I am crying, tears welling up in my eyes and running down my cheeks. "Dmitry, my darling Dmitry, I was wondering why you hadn't been to see me in Moscow. You could have slept the night here in MKhAT with no one knowing, we could have carried on seeing each other. And remember how we always assured each other that we would have a future together. After all, if all goes well, I will be a divorced woman in a few months' time. I can't understand what you're saying."

"No, Anna, nothing will make any difference. It's not possible to go on living a life of deception as we've been doing up to now. We don't know what settlement, if any, you'll receive from the divorce. It may all depend on what happens to your husband as to how generous he will be. Be free from me and go and find a nice young man like Sergey, who given a chance I know would marry you tomorrow. I just ask you to remember me from time to time."

I cannot argue any further. It seems impossible that our relationship is going to end like this in an anonymous restaurant, a couple deciding in cold blood their respective futures. We finish our meal and leave the restaurant in silence. Have we nothing left to say to each other? I cannot let him go like this, a brief kiss and then parting in different directions through the streets, turning round once perhaps to wave goodbye.

"Dmitry, come and spend one last night with me," I sob. He looks at me, as if pleading not to be given the temptation to change his mind. He hesitates. "No Anna, it would solve nothing. All it would do would be to prolong the agony. I promised to be home this evening, I need to hear my children's homework."

This banal reply extinguishes any hope I might have had of persuading him to stay. We agree to meet again when we need to discuss my divorce arrangements. But we both know in our hearts that this is the end of the affair.

I stand there on the pavement, watching him disappear into the snow.As he reaches the corner of the street I begin to raise my hand to wave a final goodbye, but Dmitry does not turn. He is gone. My tears melt the snowflakes falling on my cheeks. Chekhov's ambiguous ending to our story has finally been rewritten with a dénouement so savage in its suddenness that I am left with nothing more than a desperate emptiness reaching up within me.

{30}

From a wretched night of intermittent sleep I wake to the same consciousness of misery in which I had immersed myself the night before. My first thought is that I need to remain alone, in solitude and silence, to brood over the bitter emotions that flood my heart. I put away the clothes that I had selected for my day at the theatre and collapse back on to my bed. I want no companions, no sympathy, nothing more than to be face to face with myself. The future looms like a dark corridor, as Emma Bovary had discovered, and at the end of this corridor the door is bolted. To know that I have lost him is unbearable.

I spend the whole day imprisoned in my room, tears my only steady companion. Towards nightfall I eat a little supper and begin to think more rationally. The pain, I know, will not go away, but I have to survive somehow. I will not succumb to despair. What I have to do becomes perfectly clear.

The only way I can now survive the misery of the next few days, the next few weeks and months, is to throw myself into my work. I shall be like Sonia at the end of *Uncle Vanya.* Doctor Astrov, the man she loves, has gone away, telling her that he is busy and will probably not see her again for months on end.

"What can we do?" she asks her uncle. Vanya replies. " We must live our lives. We shall live through the long procession of days before us, and through the long evenings. We shall work for others without rest."

The days pass slowly. I try to extend the few minutes when I can forget Dmitry's final words by throwing myself into my work. I do not succeed, even though I rise early every morning, take a light breakfast in the staff canteen and am ready to start on Anton's manuscript as soon as the office staff arrive. I find it difficult to concentrate but I know that I have to finish both Acts One and Two in little more than a week. I have a feeling that my life will somehow be changing after that. I do not know how or why, but it is a woman's premonition and these premonitions are rarely wrong.

However this work which I have promised to throw myself into does not progress well. I notice to my horror that Anton has started putting in stage directions in the margin of his manuscript. I find it impossible to decipher his tiny scrawled instructions.The only recourse is to ask Stanislavsky to come in and help me. He needs no second bidding! He explains pompously that he will be able to guess, from a professional point of view of course, what Chekhov is trying to convey. This slows my progress and by the end of the first day I am totally frustrated. Konstantin Sergeyevich has brought me to the verge of tears. All I want from him is a quick explanation of the stage directions and notes in the margin, but instead of this he pontificates, with his arm too closely around my shoulder, on how impossible Chekhov is with his instructions to his actors. In the end I manage to get rid of him, as ever the actor unable to leave the stage without his usual theatrical flourish.

Friday 30th January.

I am in a total state of nerves. I presume that Sergey has booked into the *Slavyansky Bazar.* It is difficult for me to resist the temptation of going to see him at the hotel. But no doubt he will be dining with his colleagues and still occupied with the details of the forthcoming Enquiry. I know that I cannot intrude.

Saturday 31st January.

The morning dawns cold, with a violet sky that promises snow at any moment. It does not get light till mid morning and then it begins to snow. Soft fluffy snowflakes build up against the glass of my one small window, making my room even darker and more dismal than ever. The hours drag by so slowly, an age for each minute passed. I stretch out my preparations for the ball. Choice of a sensible ball gown, dressing slowly, attending to hair and selecting jewellery, but even then it is only four o'clock. I still have two and half hours to wait before Sergey is due.

I sit in front of my mirror in this lonely little room. For the first time in my life, despite my pledge not to let it happen, waves of self-pity wash over me. I address my image. Is my life to continue like this? There is no Dmitry to take me out of myself, to provide love, companionship and entertainment. A soon-to-be-divorced woman living on her own, growing older and losing her looks. What sort of prospect is that? The theatre had promised so much, but already I see that the work here is limited.

Once my usefulness as Chekhov's amanuensis is exhausted, there is little I can do. The thought of secretarial work, typing, menial office jobs and the like does not excite me. Watching rehearsals, talking to the actors, seeing productions, all so exciting if shared with Dmitry, now seem drab and uninteresting, if I am to be on my own.

"Anna Ivanovna, for goodness sake look at things sensibly," I sob, as I regard my wan reflection in the mirror on my dressing table. " To spend an evening with young people at a Ball will be a pleasant change. It won't be like the balls in Shchyolkovo. Forget Viktor's office colleagues, those dreadful elderly men grasping me round the waist, gazing down my décolletage and treading on my toes. It won't be like that this evening."

Such are my thoughts when suddenly I realize it is six thirty. I find myself nervous, almost wanting Sergey not to come after all. Time has somehow accelerated and I am unprepared for the knock at my door and the sound of Sergey shouting to his cabbie to wait outside for a few minutes. He comes bursting in, presenting me with a large bouquet of flowers and resounding kisses on both cheeks.

I am about to put my cloak around my shoulders when he insists on seeing where I live in this bohemian milieu, as he calls it. I have no option than to take him up to the annexe, arrange his flowers in a vase of water and show him my tiny room. He looks around, inspecting everything.

It must seem such a novelty to him. He knows me only as the wife of a successful civil servant with a large house and servants in Shchyolkovo. Here am I living on my own in Moscow, caring for myself and living a totally different life. He seems so young, so enthusiastic about everything. I gaze at him as he looks around my room, examining the few scant pictures and ornaments I have been able to bring with me from Shchyolkovo.

Here is a young man who has changed so dramatically from the first time I met him. Then, at the Ball he was a charming, attractive young man who knew exactly what he wanted on that occasion, namely an opportunity to dance and talk to a woman who had attracted his attention. In his approaching me, the wife of his Department Head, he had put himself in a potentially dangerous position and had been so thankful that I had not rebuffed him.

Now I see a man, who despite his youthful age, possesses a certain gravitas, a firmness of character which I had first noticed at our café meeting in Shchyolkovo. By a curious set of circumstances this man, whom I hardly know, and with whom I am becoming more and more fascinated, will in all likelihood be instrumental in deciding not only both our individual fates but also that of my husband. I think that I now owe it to him to tell him what has happened between Dmitry and me.

But Sergey is in a hurry and we have little time to talk as he helps me into my coat. However he wouldn't be Sergey without giving me a compliment, telling me once again how beautiful I look in my furs. Out on the street we find his cabbie waiting patiently for us.

Once we are seated and covered with our furs I cannot restrain myself any further. "Seryozha, I have to know. How did the meeting go? How was my husband? Have you got a date for the Tribunal? Oh, and what is this extra piece of evidence you promised me? You must tell me everything. And then I have something to tell you." I find myself clutching his arm as I ask all these questions.

He can see how agitated I am. "Anna, I think there's a word in Russian for a woman who asks too many questions? It's something like 'Pochemuchka'. I can remember my grandmother calling my little sister that, when she got too excited over her presents. You're just like her. Just calm down. I promise I'll tell you everything all in good time. Let's just enjoy ourselves. Now what is it you have to tell me that cannot wait a moment longer?"

Illogical as it is with the streets all but deserted at this time of the evening I need to whisper my response. I lean close to him and take a deep breath. "Sergey, Dmitry and I have decided to part. Our affair is over. We will always remain the best of friends but that is all. I'll tell you everything when we have a proper chance to talk, but please don't ask me about it now. I change the subject.

"Sergey, why are we going this way?" I ask. "Moscow University is quite near here. Isn't it on Mokhovaya Street opposite the Aleksandrovsky Gardens? Why are we going towards the Sparrow Hills?"

"Thank goodness, Anna, that's one of your easier questions," replies Sergey. "Moscow University is in the centre of town as you say. But the old buildings do not have a ball room. I don't think Empress Catherine expected her students to be dancing when she founded the university. So every year the authorities take over a ballroom in a small palace belonging to Count Sheremetyev or perhaps it's Count Menshikov, I don't know which, up on the Sparrow Hills. There they can hold the Graduation Ball in a more auspicious setting."

As we start to climb up hill and our progress slows I turn to him. "Sergey, as a mere female denied entry to Russian universities, perhaps you ought to warn me about this evening's entertainment. Have I not heard rumours that these balls are a bit wild? I would not wish to be shocked, being but a simple provincial maid," I tease him. Hardly that, I imagine Sergey thinking to himself. Simple provincial maids do not have husbands and lovers!

"Maybe the Summer Balls are a bit, what should I say, a bit bacchanalian," he replies. "But that's St. Petersburg for you. Hundreds of young people celebrating and walking till dawn through the streets, jumping in fountains and swimming in the Neva. But that's not going to happen tonight in staid old Moscow. It's simply too cold to venture out of doors.

We'll simply spend the evening with Nikolay and his partner. Celebrate and dance. Anya, can you imagine us dancing again without that husband of yours peering out at us from behind every pillar? Quadilles and cotillions and the usual polkas and waltzes. There is bound to be at least one mazurka." He pauses for a moment. Looking at me closely to judge my reaction he continues.

" Do you remember in Turgenev's *Fathers and Sons* Arkady reserves the mazurka for Madame Odintsova, a married woman with whom he is falling in love. With your permission I'll mark your card with the same reservation. After all Arkady and I share the same fate, two young men falling in love with married women, in my case with a certain Anna Ivanovna von Melk, formidable wife of my Department Head and with whom I am justly in awe."

"What total rubbish, Seryozha. I forbid you to say things that are patently untrue. If you had been so in awe of me, as you claim, you would never have had the nerve to engage me in conversation in the way you did."

"I know it was a risk worth taking, wasn't it?" He looks at me hoping for confirmation. Any response I might have made could only have jeopardized our fragile relationship. For a silent answer I put a finger to his lips. I am not to be drawn further on that subject.

Our sledge arrives at the entrance to the lodge. We stand for a moment on the escarpment of the Sparrow Hills looking down on a Moscow illuminated by a thousand lights. The last time I had stood here had been as a young girl on a school trip. How different, our teacher had explained then, from the time earlier in the century when Napoleon and his Grand Army had stood on this same spot gazing down on Moscow. All they saw then were lights, but those were the flames of houses and buildings that had been torched by a retreating population. Now the city looked magnificent again, rebuilt to its former glory.

Sergey pulls my coat more firmly round me. A cold wind is blowing at this height, the sky is leaden, presaging a heavy fall of snow.

We enter the ballroom, leave our furs at the cloakroom and look for our table. There we find Nikolay and his partner Larissa waiting for us with four glasses and a bottle of Crimean champagne. Introductions are made and Sergey proposes a toast to Nikolay and his successful graduation.

Kolya receives his diploma and afterwards we take to the dance floor. I had forgotten just how exciting it had been to dance with Seryozha. After all, we had only had three dances together and the atmosphere then had been poisoned by my husband's presence. Now we are free to enjoy each other.

Champagne is going to my head and I feel that dancing this evening is the ultimate aphrodisiac. Seryozha holds me in a waltz with an intimacy that would not be allowed anywhere but on a dance floor. And then I look across at him in a formation dance when he is dancing with another partner, catch his eye, smile and know that at the next set of steps he will be mine again, touching hands and arms in brief moments of regained intimacy.

I think for a moment of Dmitry. This dress I'm wearing is his gift and I remember his one regret that we would never dance together. I ask myself if I still love him as ardently as I did before. I don't know. The memory of the excitement of falling in love that afternoon at Autka is still so vivid in my memory. I look at Seryozha innocently chatting to Lara. Am I falling in love again? If he looks across at me and smiles, will I be as lost as I had been with Dmitry that afternoon at Chekhov's house? With Dmitry it was a 'coup de foudre', as the French put it so succinctly. It hasn't been a 'coup de foudre' with Sergey, how could it have been? But love, I tell myself, can grow more slowly and in different ways.

The announcement that dinner is served interrupts my thoughts. I suggest that the men sit together to discuss the technicalities of the tribunal. And it's a chance for me to get to know Lara. She is an intelligent serious girl, not beautiful but attractive in other ways. I think that Chekhov would have described her as Sonya describes herself in *Uncle Vanya*. 'When a woman isn't beautiful people always say: You have lovely eyes, you have lovely hair.' And that is the case with Lara. Her long dark hair is tied, like mine, in a chignon at the nape of her neck and her blue eyes sparkle behind her glasses. As we talk I find myself warming to her. I put her initial seriousness down to no more than a shyness in meeting someone who by all accounts had lived a rather more exciting and to put it bluntly a more promiscuous life than she had.

I find that she and I do in fact have a number of things in common. Like me she had graduated from her Lycée with a love of the Arts. Like me she had also found it difficult to settle down and find employment suitable to her talents. Skirting around the details of my involvement with Dmitry in Yalta I tell her how Anton Pavlovich had offered me the task of transcribing both my story and subsequently the manuscript for *Three Sisters.*

"Listen Anna," she says. " You really ought to come to the next seminar at the University. I'm auditing a course on "European dramatists of the second half of the 19 th century. We'll be discussing plays by writers like Turgenev, Ibsen, Shaw, Wilde and of course Chekhov."

"But Lara, how on earth could I do that? I thought women weren't allowed to enroll in our universities. How can you attend a course like this if you are not a male student?"

"I know women cannot officially enroll on degree courses, but there is a way of getting round this. There's nothing to stop us auditing courses if we get permission from the relevant professor. In my case Kolya made a few enquiries and found out the name of the professor giving these seminars. I went up to the university on my own and had the temerity to beard the great man, a Professor Nabutkin, in his office. He turned out to be a lamb, utterly charming.

"My dear young lady," he enthused. "You must come to my lectures. You would be a worthy addition to the class. Can you imagine how stupid it is, how frustrating, having a class of thirty students, all young men and not a woman to be seen amongst them?

How are we to discuss the European theatre and its plays when we have no women to represent the fair sex in our discussions?" And so he carried on for a full five minutes. By the time he stopped to draw breath I found myself enrolled on his next series of lectures as an auditing student.

Our first lecture is in the middle of February at the start of the second university semester. It would be wonderful if you could join me. I don't want to be the only woman in the class, and you with your contacts with Chekhov would be able to make such a contribution. What do you think? Why don't I go back next week and ask my dear professor if you can join me in auditing the course?

"Oh Lara, that would be wonderful. There's nothing I would love more. Together we could take on the bastions of male privilege. Fight our corner and wave a banner for the educational rights of women in Russia through the plays we read in class. Today a fight for education for women, tomorrow a fight for women's suffrage. All I ask is to have an equal opportunity to live my life with the freedom of a man," I finish far too dramatically.

" Anna, thank goodness I've at last found a kindred spirit. I don't know if you've read Aleksander Herzen's memoirs *My Past and Thoughts*. There's a wonderful passage in it. I've had a little too much champagne and excitement this evening to quote it accurately, but the gist of it goes something like this:

'What breadth, what beauty and power of human nature and development there must be in a woman to surmount all the palisades, all the fences within which she is held captive.'

She stops for a moment to take breath, such is her enthusiasm "That's us he's talking about," she continues. "Women held captive in a repressive, staunchly masculine society ruled by men and for men. I believe it was an English woman novelist who wrote: ' *The important work of moving the world forward does not wait to be done by perfect men.'* It is up to you and me to act.

And you'll never guess, the first play we'll be studying is *A Doll's House* which I've already read. The final scene ends with the heroine Nora slamming the door of the family home as she defies her husband and leaves him for good. Imagine the fun we could have discussing that with a class of young men. "

Our conversation is interrupted by our partners returning to our table. In response to their question as to what we have been talking about all this time, we reply that our lips are sealed. They do not know that unbeknownst to them their fate as Russian men in the first decades of the twentieth century hangs in the balance!

At midnight the ball concludes with the final waltz. Most of the graduates, including Kolya and Lara, then depart for Moscow. We say our goodbyes, with Lara promising to keep in touch regarding our planned assignation.

The few couples who have not returned to Moscow now form themselves into a sort of impromptu promenade through the quickly cleared ballroom. Rather than joining them, we find a quiet room furnished with leather chairs and a settee. Four gaslights cast their glow rather too brightly for the intimate nature of the conversation that we know will shortly ensue. At my suggestion Seryozha turns off three of the 'Devil's Candles', leaving just one alight to provide a more romantic ambience.

{31}

Stretching ourselves out comfortably on the settee, Seryozha begins his account of the past two days, which he reflects have been the worst he has ever experienced since joining the staff of the Shchyolkovo Municipal Government. Here in Moscow he has come face to face with Viktor, who to all and sundry disparagingly refers to him in public as a 'boy sent to do a man's work.' He also feels that the members of the Moscow City Duma, who have been called to this preliminary meeting, are not well disposed towards giving up their time over a dispute, which they consider should have been settled back in Shchyolkovo.

Worse still, he has the impression that most of them are also firmly of the belief that the failure is the fault of the Engineering Department and the Municipal Administration is not to blame. Seryozha's Department now has the herculean task of trying to overcome their initial hostility. In fact the chairman of the Tribunal, sensing the mood of the meeting, had made it clear to some of the more outspoken members of the Duma, that they had been elected to form an independent and impartial committee and were not in any way to prejudge the case.

The date of the hearing has been set for two month's time, the beginning of April, which will give both parties the necessary time to subpoena witnesses and prepare their respective prosecution and defence statements.

There is nothing left to do now, Sergey concludes, other than to wait patiently through these two months and pray that somehow or other there will be a favourable verdict when the Tribunal reconvenes.

Enough of this earnest conversation. Curled up alone together on the settee with a rug stretched over us for warmth I feel a mischievous urge to tease this dispirited young man. I tell him to turn low the single flickering gaslight and I begin my mischief.

"We've been together all evening," I say. "Look at the time, it's well past midnight and both of us have been on our best behaviour. Let's talk about the first time we met. You remember that first conversation we had when you so impudently introduced yourself at the ball in Shchyolkovo? We discussed all the things we had in common. I admit I was guilty then, a married woman flirting with a younger man. How disgraceful of me! But I can admit to you now that I had an ulterior motive. I wanted to carry on talking to you as an excuse for not going back into the ballroom and being sought out for further stumbles around the dance floor.

I remember telling you about all the things we had in common. But of course you will have forgotten. What a shame, there might have been a little reward for each one you could remember."

"That's easy, Anya. How could I forget anything told me by a woman with whom I have been in love from my first setting eyes on her?" He takes my fingers in his hand and folds each one over in turn as he enumerates his answers.

"Firstly we both come from St. Petersburg. Secondly we both have Ivan in our names. Thirdly we both love dancing. And fourthly, and I can't tell you how shocked I was with you of all people, the wife of a Government official, to be told that we had both read *Madame Bovary*.

And by the way, what do you mean by telling me to find a younger girlfriend? You should know that engineers have to be good at their maths. I have had time to do some calculations. I graduated from my Lycée when I was eighteen, the same age as you. I spent four years at university and the two years in Government service. I have now reached the great age of twenty four.

As for you, you told me you spent two years at home before meeting Viktor and that you were engaged for a year. That made you twenty one when you married. You then had two years in Shchyolkovo with your husband and another year, if I am to believe it, misbehaving yourself around Russia. That makes you twenty four, the same as me, if I'm not mistaken, and that's the fifth thing we have in common. Now I claim my reward." He takes me in his arms and I fulfil my promise, a lingering kiss for each of his answers.

Sergey, with the boldness that our new found intimacy allows him, asks the one question that must have been puzzling him all evening. He asks why Dmitry and I have parted.

My teasing mood is over, yet I find it difficult to find the words to explain. "You don't know him, Seryozha, but he is the most lovely, upright, altruistic man you can imagine. When we first became lovers in Yalta, and then later in Moscow, we had endless discussions about our future together. All the time we were certain that something could be worked out, that our lives would come together.

But in the end we realized that this was impossible. How could he spend time with me when he had a wife and family demanding ever more of his free time? How could he go on deceiving his wife without one day being found out? And how could I go on being his mistress. Mistresses by definition are supposed to be young and beautiful, not ageing and care worn as I would become.

So he told me quite simply that our affair had to end. We would just see each other when we needed to. There was nothing I could do. To be honest with you I tried to make him change his mind and let us continue our affair. But he was adamant that it had to be. I was to find a younger man.That's so simple, isn't it, when you are nursing a broken heart!

As I expected, I've had a letter from my husband's lawyer. Viktor has filed for divorce and instructed his lawyer to deal with the necessary procedure."

"But Anna, surely this means that you are free now, or at least will soon be. I'm just a simple engineer. I may be good with pieces of machinery but I'm hopeless in trying to express what I really feel. You must know by now that I love you. Our innocent little flirtations and all your teasing cannot hide the fact that I love you. Will you marry me?"

I loosen his embrace. " Oh Seryozha,that is so beautifully put. But I'm sorry, I can't say yes. Look at me. At the moment my life is a mess. I don't seem to be very good at relationships with men. My husband wants to get rid of me as soon as he can. Dmitry has just told me that our relationship must end. And now I need to be honest with you.You must understand, the last thing I want to do now is to rush into something, promise you something that I might later regret and drag you into this mess of mine.

Remember *Madame Bovary*. I could so easily have suggested that you come back to my room in MKhAT tonight, be tempted to play a substitute Emma Bovary to your Leon, my new young replacement for a lost lover. But, Seryozha, just give me time to sort my feelings out. Please be patient and wait a few more weeks. We can have dinner together some evenings, spend some time together, you can see the really nasty side of me, which I promise you I have, and then hopefully we will know for certain how things are between us.

"Anna, I apologise. Of course you're so much more mature and sensible than I am. I should have had the sense to realize that this was the worst possible moment for you to take any sort of decision. I shouldn't admit to this, but I had thoughts of inveigling you back to the *Slavyansky Bazar* tonight. But even I realized this wouldn't have been in good taste. Anna, you've seen enough of me to know that I'm an impetuous, impulsive sort of man and find it difficult to hide my feelings. I wear my heart on my sleeve and when I am with you, I lose all sense of propriety. I… "

I put my finger to his lips to stop him from continuing. "Seryozha, you mustn't feel guilty. Of course you had every right to tell me how you felt and I'm really flattered that you did. It is simply the wrong time for me to give you an answer."

" Anya, please don't get me wrong about Sonya. She and I are just good friends,that's all there is to it. I must admit that I really only used our friendship to obtain the documents I needed from her office."

" Seryozha, be quiet. You've told me already all I need to know about her. I'm not jealous of Sonya. She's got nothing to do with it. I can see perfectly well that she's in love with you and that you probably led her on. In your view the end no doubt justified the means. I don't want to hear any more about her."

We become aware of our surroundings. Time has moved on and students and their partners have long since made their way home. We decide reluctantly that it is time to do the same. Seryozha goes off to collect our coats from the cloakroom. He comes back with them in his arms. He looks worried.

"Anna, I've just spoken to the old lady in the cloakroom and she's told me there are no sledges back to Moscow till the morning. The weather's closed in. Look out of the window, it's snowing heavily. And she says there are no drivers willing to risk taking their horses down the road in the dark. It looks as if we'll have to spend the night here. We could stretch out here on the settee and keep warm under our furs. A certain impropriety of conduct may be levelled against us, should we be disturbed, but I don't think that we have an alternative. I'm so sorry!"

"It's not your fault, Seryozha. On reflection I think our Gustave Flaubert would have been delighted to write his heroine in to spending a night like this with one of her amours. So how can I complain? So long as I can have your shoulder as a pillow."

We make ourselves comfortable on the settee and Seryozha extinguishes the gaslight.

***

Indeed we are not disturbed. I wake as the pale gleam of dawn lights up the room. I open my eyes to see Seryozha gazing at me. I ask him whether he too has slept.

"Anya, my darling, how could I sleep when I had the chance to gaze at you so close to me? I've been watching you sleep through the night. You know that scene in *Uncle Vanya* where Astrov, who is hopelessly in love with Elena, imagines himself at night comforting her during a storm. He picks up a chair and caresses it. Well, I didn't go as far as that, but I did imagine sleeping with you in my arms and spending every night like this for the rest of my life."

"Seryozha, that's the most beautiful thing any man has ever said to me." Tears come welling up in my eyes. "This night has been a dream a 'midwinter's night dream' and I have loved every perfect minute of it. Thank you for making it so."

By this time the snow has stopped and within the hour we are back at MKhAT. Seryozha, in doubt as to when we'll meet again, asks if I'll come to Shchyolkovo to meet his parents. They simply know me as the wife of his Department Head and probably have an image of me as a stout, rather pompous middle aged lady. They only know about my husband from Seryozha's constant lament about his superior's behaviour in the office. The fact that he has a wife, with whom their son has fallen in love, will only make sense if I am to meet them in person.

I feel so sad. This innocent suggestion from Seryozha that I should meet his family, such a natural thing for him to allude to, makes me think of my relationship with Dmitry. How could I ever have met his wife and his children, when I was no more than his mistress? But now, as a soon-to-be-single woman again there is no reason not to accept his invitation. But first, as we have just agreed, we are to remain apart for a few weeks. After that, I assure him, I would love to meet his family. One more kiss on the doorstep of my annexe and then he climbs into his sledge and is gone in a swirl of snow.

After my few hours of sleep I feel exhausted and am not able to concentrate on anything for very long. I fill the day with household chores. From time to time I stop what I am doing to think about Seryozha. I look at the clock. By now I reckon that he will be back in Shchyolkovo, faced with the thought of a Monday morning ahead of him in the Ministry. He will be called to report on the proceedings of the Tribunal.

And then I find myself imagining the two of us in the most mundane of situations; my straightening his clothes, and smoothing down his ruffled hair, as Sonya had done in the café, making breakfast for him before going our separate ways to work.

Viktor comes unbidden and unwanted into my thoughts. I call to mind that adage that where there is marriage without love there will be love without marriage. I try to justify my behaviour, telling myself that for so long there has been no love in my marriage. And though I may try to deny it, I know that I am falling in love with Seryozha. In justification I ask myself why I should be concerned about what is happening. It's not as if I have any marriage left. I am a married woman in name only.

February 10 th 1900.

The midwinter weather continues to be atrocious. For the last three days it has been snowing ceaselessly and each day seems to be colder than the last. Today the temperature on the streets of Moscow stays at -22 degrees. The few occasions when I need to venture out from MKhAT are painful. The snow squeaks under my feet and when I breathe in too heavily my nose begins to freeze. But like Uncle Vanya's Sonya I immerse myself in my work and try to forget for a few hours each day the otherwise perpetual worry over the impending Board of Enquiry.

Today Lara pays me a visit whilst I am engaged in the triviality of office work. What a delightful surprise! She tells me that her Professor, as she calls him, would be delighted for me to attend his lectures. She has dropped a hint about my relationship with Anton Pavlovich and to my being the eponymous heroine in the *Lady with a Little Dog*. Apparently he could not hide his curiosity and wants me to tell him about the story and all I know of *Three Sisters*. There are apparently so many contradictory rumours circulating in Moscow about the play, from it being retitled "*Two Sisters*" to whether it will be finished before the playwright's demise. He will be delighted if I can provide any illumination on these innuendos.

The first session of the Winter semester is scheduled for tomorrow. Lara needs to know if I can take leave of absence from my duties at MKhAT? At that moment Stanislavsky walks into our office. He notices the presence of a new attractive girl, turns his attention to her straight away and asks if she has come for an audition.

"Konstantin Sergeyevich, you are impossible," I interrupt his advances. " Not every attractive young lady wants to act in the theatre under your direction. This is a friend of mine, Larissa….I'm sorry Lara, I don't remember your patronymic."

"Petrovna. Larissa Petrovna, but please, every one calls me Lara."

"Konstantin Sergeyevich, would you allow me to take a couple of hours off from my work tomorrow afternoon? I can make up the time later one evening. I swing my chair around to face him. I put on a stern face. You may be interested to know that Lara and I are working towards the total emancipation of Russian womenhood from male domination, a noble aim I'm sure you will agree. As a first step in our battle for this equality we have been given permission to audit a course at the University entitled 'European Playwrights of the second half of the 19th Century.'

You may have heard of Professor Nabutkin in the Faculty of Arts. He has kindly allowed us to attend his lectures. He feels that having women in his class, which is apparently composed of rather immature young men, those are his words not mine I hasten to add, could be beneficial to tomorrow's debate on Ibsen's *A Doll's House.*

Instead of simply answering yes or no as I expected him to do, Stanislavsky reflects for a moment. "Anna, you may take the whole afternoon off. Take notes on what you learn about *A Doll's House.* I believe it was produced in St. Petersburg back in the eighties, but to be honest that is all I know. Last year we put on *Hedda Gabler*, which was a great success for our new company, but to my shame I know little of Ibsen's other plays. Come back and tell me how you find the play. And of course, my dear Anna, you can select a suitable leading role for me, should we be tempted to produce it here one day. And try to find one a little more sympathetic, more romantic should I say, than the one you teased me with when last we discussed the subject of casting!"

After all this nonsense with Konstantin it is time to finish work for the day. " Lara, come and have a look at my little apartment next door. Better still, let me treat you to supper in the canteen. You may see some one really famous there, not just our Konstantin Sergeyevich, who never seems to go home to his wife. And of course there's bound to be Vladimir Ivanovich Nemirovich Danchenko making his presence felt. He doesn't go home to his wife either, being somewhat fonder of the company of his leading lady, for whom he has conveniently provided a room here. But, mind you, all this is only theatre tittle tattle."

Lara follows me up the stairs. "You mean to say that you know all these famous people, you just bump into them over dinner and chat to them?" she asks in amazement.

"Well, it's not quite like that. Probably my being a young woman here makes a difference. In my short time in the theatre I've discovered that actors have enormous egos, they all think we women will fall in love with them and swoon into their arms. So there are a lot of flirtatious conversations going on all the time, but they don't mean anything."

Over supper we discuss how we are going to transport ourselves to the University. I tell Lara that I know a cab driver at the *Slavyansky Bazar*, so we arrange to meet there tomorrow. "Lecture Theatre Number 104, Faculty of Arts Building, 11 a.m." Lara repeats the setting for our clandestine assignation as she leaves my room.

February 11th 1900.

I wake later than usual to discover a wet, bad tempered day. A thaw blows melting snow on to us as Lara and I meet as planned at the entrance to the hotel. I ask the receptionist if Osip is available. A minute later my dashing driver comes round with his cab. I introduce him to Lara who seems slightly uncomfortable to be addressed rather familiarly as 'another beautiful Muscovite lady.'

"Take you back to to Carpenter's Lane?" he asks. "Not this time." I reply. " Can you take us to the Moscow University building on Mokhovaya Street?"

"And what do you intend doing there," he wants to know. "It's only for men. You'll not be allowed in."

Stretching the truth a little we tell him that we are enrolled on an undergraduate course. I can see that Osip is impressed, but of course he will not admit to it.

"When I marry, my wife will be in the kitchen looking after me and our children, not dashing off to the university. Anyway, I'm off back to Siberia next year. Making exception of course to you, my fine ladies, I find Muscovite girls a bit too dainty for my taste. No university nearer than a thousand versts from Shelkovka, that's my home town. So I've no need to worry that my wife will be filling her head with some clever stuff out of books. And I must say, when a man puts his arm round a Siberian girl there's a bit of flesh there to squeeze. Unlike these Moscow girls, a snow flake knocks them over."

Having discussed the advantages of Siberian life and women for some time with our driver, we realize that we have reached the university. I pay off Osip, who insists that he'll wait for us.

"No, Osip, you don't need to, but thank you all the same. If you get a return fare into Moscow, then take it. Don't wait for us, we'll probably walk back into town, if the weather clears. If we don't, we'll see you here after our lecture, bringing out a cab full of young men with us!"

"To be serious for a moment, Anna." Lara has had her fill of badinage, particularly if it emanates from cab drivers.

"Remember what we're doing here. Are you really ready to storm the bastions of male privilege here at Moscow University?"

No, is my simple answer. The University buildings, built in the eighteenth century in a severe classical style look forbidding. But I have made a pact with Lara to engage in what now seems a ridiculous adventure, a schoolgirlish dare as it were, and there is no going back.

Indeed I do feel like a young schoolgirl entering her Lycée on the first day of term. But there is a major difference. At the Lycée there were hundreds of girls and lady teachers, whereas here, as Lara had warned me, we find a very maculine environment.

Feeling nervous and awkwardly out of place we make our way along the endless corridors of the Faculty of Arts. We receive curious glances from students, who must wonder what we are doing by entering their preserve. Our first challenge in our fight for emancipation is truly mundane. We are in need of a ladies' cloakroom, where we can take off our furs and straighten our hair.

We do not have the courage to approach a member of this all male world. At last we hear the sound of female voices in an office, where to our relief we are invited to leave our coats and avail ourselves of the sole cloakroom in the university reserved for ladies. Russia has a long way to go, we mutter to each other as, unable to find a looking glass anywhere, we appraise each other's appearance.

Finally we find our appointed lecture theatre, pluck up courage to open the door and walk in. The events of the next few minutes are pure vaudeville. Professor Nabutkin had unfortunately forgotten to inform his students that we would be attending his course, so our entry is understandably unexpected.

When our bemused male students have sufficiently recovered from the shock of seeing two young ladies entering their lecture theatre, they politely stand up and continue standing till we take our seats inconspicuously in one of the back rows. Just as they are beginning to sit down again, the door opens and Professor Nabutkin enters. With a formal swish of his gown he advances towards the rostrum. His entrance necessitates his students to stand up once again. The excited hubbub takes some time to be quelled.

"Gentlemen, gentlemen, please settle down and be seated," he jokes. "You are not usually in such high spirits before one of my lectures..." He stops as he catches sight of Lara and me at the back of the hall.

"My dear students, you must forgive me for forgetting to mention at our last meeting that today we woud be graced by the presence of two new students who will be attending our current seminars. As you will see, we are most fortunate to welcome here today two young ladies, and their attendance here marks, may I say, something of a landmark in the history of our esteemed Faculty.

In our study of literature we need always to evaluate the role of women in the various genres that we discuss. However, I for one, have always felt a certain lack in our discussions in as much as we have conducted our examination of these literary texts purely from the male perspective.

I am therefore delighted to welcome our two new students. I am certain that their contribution to today's discussion of *A Doll's House* by Henrik Ibsen will be most welcome, a contribution that will, I hope, be both controversial and thought provoking.

I suggest that for the sake of a lively discussion we consider the sacrificial role of women as portrayed by the female characters in the play. For example, does Nora's understanding of the meaning of freedom which evolves over the course of the play have any relevance to the position of women in present day Russia?

I am certain that our two new students will have plenty to say on that matter. And what they say may well contradict some of the views which a number of our young men here may hold. I look forward to what will undoubtedly be a lively debate."

An hour later Lara and I make our way out of the lecture theatre, our heads filled with the heady realization that we have at last been able to represent and defend our own sex in open argument.

We find Osip waiting patiently for us. He seems quite disappointed that he is not called upon to defend us from the unwanted attentions of so many young men flocking out of the university at lunch time. Lara and I settle down under the rugs of the sledge. Just time enough to evaluate the proceedings of the last hour. What a splendid start, we both agree, to our campaign to storm the bastions of higher education. We will meet during the week and share our thoughts on *A Doll's House* and prepare ourselves for our next assault on male bigotry!

February 13th 1900.

This evening Lara and I meet in the MKhAT canteen for dinner. We have both reread *A Doll's House.* I find it so relevant to my own situation. As a married woman who has left her husband I can so easily identify with Nora Hemmer who at the end of the play takes the same decision as I have done. We have both been belittled by our husbands, my being perceived as nothing more than a useful appendage to a man's career and Nora being treated as nothing more than a plaything, a doll in a doll's house.

If this is the conventional way for men to regard their wives, then heaven help our young male students if they show any sympathy for the male characters in Ibsen's play when next we meet. We will tear them to shreds, should they have the nerve to voice support for the attitude of Torvold towards his beautiful caged bird of a wife.

{32}

February 15 th 1900.

By two o'clock on the morning of my name day Seryozha and I are lovers. Though I hardly think that Saint Anna would have approved of our celebrating her Saint's day in such a manner. A consummation of sorts it was, though by no stretch of the imaginatiom could it be called a very satisfactory conclusion to the climax of our ever closer relationship.

For the past two weeks Seryozha and I have not met. He has been working in Shchyolkovo and I have been occupied with my work at the theatre. We are holding to our decision to meet only occasionally, though of course we have exchanged letters.

In his latest one he asks if we could attend a performance of *Uncle Vanya.* This is not a problem. One advantage of my working here is that it is ridiculously easy for me to obtain tickets for a performance, even at the last minute. I ask Konstantin if I could possibly have two tickets for Saturday's performance. I know quite well that he has a soft spot for me and knowing that I to some extent have Chekhov's ear he probably wants to be seen acting in a positive manner. He might even believe, quite erroneously of course, that I have some influence with Chekhov over deciding who is to be given specific parts in *Three Sisters.*

He has confided to me when he sees me in the office that he would like to play the part of Vershinin. " I like the idea of playing the part of a Lieutenant Colonel in an Artillery Battalion," he says, twirling an imaginary moustache, "and of course seducing one of the three sisters."

" I'll pass your wishes on to Anton Pavlovich when I see him, just tell me which one takes your fancy." I reply with a straight face. I cannot believe that he takes me seriously, but he continues.

"Perhaps at my age I have more in common with the eldest. She will do nicely, thank you. And in return, I will reserve for you two seats in the Royal Box for Saturday. We have no bookings for those seats for the evening performance. So you and your partner, whichever lucky man you are favouring at this moment, my dear Anna Ivanovna, can be my guests. Enjoy the experience of being royalty for the night. I will produce a memorable performance for you, gazing up at the Royal Box and wondering who that beautiful young lady is!" He leaves, as usual exit left theatrically!

I write to Sergey telling him that I have tickets for Uncle Vanya and will meet him at the theatre. Only later do I realise that we have not arranged where he is to spend the night.

***

This evening I feel in a lighthearted mood. It is Saturday night and there will be no early start for work tomorrow morning. And most importantly it will be my name day.

Seryozha's train from Shchyolkovo is delayed and he arrives at MKhAT just in time for us to take our seats in the Royal Box. The curtain goes up, revealing the familiar stage setting. Olga Knipper enters stage left and takes her seat on the swing. Playing the part of Elena she swings her legs, her dress revealing the contours of her body. She looks sensuous and beautiful. "That is how I was in the garden at Autka," I whisper to Seryozha, explaining how Chekhov had posed us for his troublesome first scene.

In the Royal Box we can talk without being overheard. "And Dmitry playing the part of Astrov, and Chekhov was Vanya, both of them in love with Elena." I chatter on, carried away by the memories of that enchanted afternoon. I must say Stanislavsky, despite my reservations about his behaviour off stage, plays the role of Astrov superbly and the cast receives a standing ovation when the curtain falls.

The end of an evening at the theatre always leaves me with a feeling of anticlimax unless there is something pleasurable to follow. The night is still young and my high spirits have not deserted me. I know that if I say good bye to Seryozha in the usual way and send him back to Shcholkovo on the last train, it will for both of us be a dismal ending to a happy evening. And in any event he has left his coat in the annexe and will have to collect it from my room before he leaves. A perfect excuse to delay his departure if he so wishes.

As the audience makes its way out onto the street, we are left alone in the theatre. I have to make a decision. I tell him to go back to the bar and ask for a bottle of champagne. The barman is a friend of mine and I know he will put it on my account. After all, tomorrow is my name day, and I do not see why we should wait till midnight to celebrate.

Seryozha returns in triumph, clutching not one bottle but two, informing me that guests in the Royal Box are generously provided with as much champagne as they like. We take a bottle each as we make our way up the narrow stairs to my room. There, sitting facing each other across the kitchen table, we drink to my name day. There is an awkwardness between us, an uncertainty as to how the evening will progress. We sit in silence, both parties silently wanting the other to take the initiative.

I know perfectly well that Seryozha would love to be invited to stay the night here with me. But his shyness does not allow him to suggest this. And although I have practically compromised myself by inviting him up to my room, I cannot brazenly go further and offer myself to him. But we cannot continue sitting opposite each other like this.

Suddenly the perfect way out of our dilemma comes to me. Seryozha, despite his protestations to the contrary, has always enjoyed my teasing him. Despite being aware all too well of the possible consequences I make the opening bid.

"Here we are in the theatre, Seryozha, so here's a theatrical question for you. If you reply correctly you will receive a reward. If you do not answer correctly, you will have to pay a forfeit. Pay attention, I need to know where these lines come from."

In my haste I grasp at the first suitable speech I can think of. It has to be something to do with the theme of seduction. The lines between Rosalind and Orlando in Shakespeare's *As You Like It* come into my head. Undoing the top button of my blouse as provocatively as I can, I begin.

"*Come woo me, woo me, for now I am in a holiday humour, and like enough to consent.*"

Seryozha laughs. He can see that my being in holiday humour means that, whatever his answers are, he is likely to receive a pleasant reward from a woman in such a mood. He tries to put his arms round me but I resist. "Just answer the question, Sergey Ivanovich, the rules haven't changed."

"Anna, that's hardly fair. You know I'm not a great expert on the theatre. Alright, let me think for a moment. After all your talk about our dear Anton Pavlovich, I know you wouldn't have chosen him. And anyway the language you use, he searches for the right word, is in the wrong register. So we can ignore him. What about some of the 19 th century European playwrights that you and Lara are so keen on. But there again, the language is wrong. No one talks about wooing any more, and the idea of a holiday humour must be centuries old.

I don't know much about early Russian literature, but it cannot be Fonvizin or Ostrovsky, their characters would never consent to anything unseemly on stage. That leaves us with the greatest playwright of all. So long as I don't have to name the play, I would suggest that the answer to your question is William Shakespeare."

"Seryozha, you've so excelled yourself," I reply. "You're quite right, it is Shakespeare and the play is *'As you like it.'*, one of his comedies about mistaken identity." I tease him further. " Would you like me to tell you the story?"

However, Seryozha seems keener on learning more about his reward than my expanding on the plot of the play. I turn off the gas light and light some candles which dimly illuminate my little room. The similarities with my seduction in Yalta are now all too clear. The darkened room lit by candlelight, my would be lover about to undo my clothing button by button. One difference this time, I think, it is I who will be in control of the seduction.

In this, however, I am mistaken. Seryozha leans down, lifts my skirt up a fraction. Not needing to venture out of doors to reach the theatre from my annexe, I am wearing a simple pair of silk slippers. He reaches for one of them.

"You said you needed to be wooed," he says. "This is what they do in Paris. It's all the rage now, drinking champagne out of ladies' slippers."

He fills my slipper and we toast my coming name day in this novel manner. I tell him with a theatrical gesture across my brow to simulate the maiden's final surrender, that I have been wooed enough. I am waiting to find out what I have consented to. I feel his hand under my dress reaching for my other slipper. Oh no, I think, men and their fixations for little feet. Dmitry on our first walk to Autka, all those times afterwards when we were making love, and of course putting on my skates at the rink. Now I have apparently found another would be lover with the same proclivities.

"Prithee, Sire," I tease him, deliberately continuing in Shakespearian vein. "Unhand me this moment, you are unconscionably forward with your behaviour. How could you use a poor maiden so?"

"In truth, young maiden, I was not cognizant of your preserved maidenhood, else would I not have acted so boldly." Seryozha is more than equal to my repartee.

Unlike the bedroom in Yalta, warmed still at night by the heat of the southern sun, my bedroom in the annexe is cold.

"Seryozha, I do forgive you for your youthful exuberance, but I would wish to divest myself of my apparel in a warmer chamber. Pray wait for me here and modestly attired I will return to you ere long."

A few minutes later we go to see whether my narrow bed is big enough to embrace both of us.

***

I wake for a moment in the night. A strange way to celebrate my name day, I think, lying in bed in the arms of my new lover and celebrating with champagne. This is how emancipated women in the twentieth century behave, I reassure myself.

When we wake properly later in the morning, Seryozha is so concerned. Taking my face gently in his hands he says, "I can't believe what happened, Anushka? I'm so sorry, it wasn't very good and…"

"My darling Seryozha, it was fine, I knew it would be." I say, touching his lips with my finger to stop his words. We lie together, half awake.

I remember how after intimacy I used to tell Dmitry that I was hungry, something so mundane that it would always make him laugh and lead him to teasing me. The memory of those post coital meals in the restaurant of the *Slavyansky Bazar* sharpens my hunger. But I know that there is nothing in the larder of my miniscule kitchen that would make a breakfast. Will the MKhAT canteen still be open this late in the morning and can I order my usual eggs with ham and a slice of rye bread and coffee?

But if by chance it is open, how can I order for two? There is a wide spread rumour at MKhAT that when Olga Knipper stays the night in the annexe, our Director orders two breakfasts to be served on one plate. I am a very big man with a very big appetite, he explains his request to the kitchen staff.

However I cannot send Seryozha down to the kitchen, where he is a complete stranger, with a note from Anna Ivanovna asking for two breakfasts. It will have to me. I quickly dress. There is a rehearsal scheduled for later in the morning and the canteen is open. One or two actors and stagehands are eating breakfast.

To my good fortune my favourite cook is on duty. Quite shamelessly I wink at her and ask if I can have two portions of my usual breakfast. I am exceedingly hungry, I tell her. That will not be a problem, she replies, and in no time I am handed a tray piled full with eggs, ham, bread and coffee. It is only on my way back up the stairs that I notice that I have been given two sets of cutlery, two plates and two cups. My reputation has either been enhanced or destroyed. "This young lady with an enormous appetite. Don't we know other members of MKhAT with the same appetite for breakfast?" I can imagine her regaling her colleagues in the kitchen.

I find Seryozha risen, not yet dressed but diligently addressing the business of lighting the stove. I have time whilst he is doing this to reflect on the events of the night. My mood darkens. I am full of remorse. I remember how Dmitry had been so kind and considerate when we first made love. The experienced man of the world constantly reassuring an innocent girl that she was beautiful and sensuous. What had I done to help Seryozha? I had complained about the cold, the bedsprings, the noises in the corridor. My inconsiderate actions, I now see so clearly, had done nothing to help a young lover.

The Sunday chimes of Moscow's churches begin ringing out again and the snow piles up against the window pane, obscuring what little light there is. I reach for the gas light. Its warm glow and the welcoming crackle of the stove suddenly transform the previous bleakness of my annexe room. We eat our breakfast slowly and in silence, each busy with our own thoughts. How can I make amends for my mistakes of the night, I wonder?

I remember how Dmitry had loved watching me undress. I stand up facing Seryozha and slip out of my blouse. In my hurry to go down to get our breakfast I had not bothered to get properly dressed. Seryozha gazes at me. " I hope you will do more than just look at me, take me to bed," I whisper. He picks me up in his arms and carries me across the room. With the heat from the stove we no longer need to burrow under a mound of blankets. "Anya, Anya, my love, my darling," he keeps on repeating my name as we make love.

Afterwards when the world comes back into our consciousness and we again become aware of the church bells, now ringing out for Mass on this my name day, it is as if Saint Anna has answered an unspoken prayer.

The stove has cooled a little. We pull the blankets over us. The short mid winter light has already faded from my window and there is no incentive to go outside. It is far too comfortable lying in bed to consider getting up. I want to prolong the moment, so we talk of this and that, inconsequential questions and answers. Our love making had meant so much to Seryozha, a young man, uncertain of his masculinity. Yet I know how vulnerable he really is beneath the shield of self-confidence and professional competence that he always shows. I need to be gentle with him.

Seryozha asks again how I am feeling. Dmitry would never have asked that question, considering it in bad taste to ask a woman so pointedly about such a private matter. He waits for my reply. I would be embarrassed if I told him the truth. I can only answer with another tease.

"You want an answer on the basis of one night?" I ask him in feigned amazement. "Seryozha, have you never heard of a lady by the name of the Countess Praskovya Bruce?"

He looks at me, not knowing what is to come. "No, I haven't, and if this is another of your questions that requires an answer I have no desire to participate. You've already exhausted me with your rewards!", he jokes. Anyway, what do you mean on the basis of one night?"

"I'm going to recount a little anecdote, which will explain your quandary." I reply. "I promise you, no questions and no rewards. This is a history lesson, the like of which you are not likely to have been taught at school."

Well, this Countess I mentioned, married to Count Jacob Bruce, governor of St. Petersburg, was lady in waiting to Empress Catherine when she arrived in Russia in 1744. She was best known in history as 'l'éprouveuse' to the sovereign, the role she played in Catherine's love life.

According to legend, her position was to 'test' the prospective lovers' sexual performance before they were elevated to Catherine's bedchamber. Each potential lover was subjected to a number of tests before her approval was given. It was a role she carried out dutifully and presumably enjoyably until, to her considerable misfortune, she was found in bed with one of Catherine's own favourites, whom she ironically had passed as 'satisfactory'! Whereupon both she and the lover, whose name by the way was Ivan Rimsky Korsakov, were banished from court. I just thought it might be useful for me to do the same. You see, subject you to a little test before committing myself to a longer relationship."

In our short relationship Seryozha has learned to know when I'm teasing. He is silent for a moment thinking over the implications of my story.

"That's fine," he jokes. "Just let me know when our next history lesson is scheduled.

His mood changes. He is serious again. "Anna, you told me that in Yalta ladies who fancied a dalliance with Anton Pavlovich were called Antonovkas. And you said that because of your platonic relationship with him you would like to be called his Platonovka. I can believe all that. But darling, you could do better than just being a Platonovka. Simply take the 'k' out of the word, marry me and become a Platonova. It's so simple. Please say 'yes', just say 'yes', he pleads.

Even before we became lovers I knew that Sergey would propose again at the first suitable occasion. When he did I was prepared, though it was not a difficult answer that I had to make. "Darling, of course I will. I love you and the answer is yes. I promise, I'll marry you. But there is just one difficulty. At the moment I'm a married woman with a husband whom I need to divorce. Just be patient and give me time to be free myself from Viktor."

Later we dress in silence, tiptoe along the creaking corridors and let ourselves out into the cold evening air. Without having to ask each other what we want to do, we find ourselves walking in the direction of our usual restaurant. It is snowing again. Great puffy snowflakes land on our faces. We play the children's game of trying to catch them as they settle on our skin and kiss them away before they melt. I take Seryozha in my arms and kiss him. We are in a world of our own, oblivious to the gaze of passers by and deaf to the evening peals of church bells. What more could I have needed than a marriage proposal to bless my name day?

{34}

Sunday April 1st 1900.

Winter, which this year has overstayed its welcome, lingering on till late March, has finally loosened its icy grip on the city. Spring comes in a flash, the pavements reappear again after six long months under snow and ice and yesterday I even saw Council workmen planting out the flower beds in our local park.

Nearly two months have passed since Sergey and I became betrothed and the entries in my diary are brief for these weeks. My daily routine follows an orderly pattern. Lara and I attend lectures at the University and gradually find ourselves accepted by our male colleagues. A group of six of the bolder ones go as far as inviting us for a coffee after the seminar, when we feel rather conspicuous, being the only females in the Student Cafeteria. Rather sweetly and solicitously they take upon themselves the role of chaperones. I believe for their part they appreciate hearing our views on the various themes presented in the plays we study. Lara and I will never be 'feministkas' as the more stridently outspoken members of our sex are called, but here in the company of a half dozen relatively free thinking young men we are given the opportunity to express our views on a range of subjects concerning women.

I notice to my amusement that, when we subsequently discuss these issues in class, our young men are often the first to support the women's side of the argument; sympathy for Nora rather than for Torvold in *A Doll's House,* for example.

Lara and I play them along mercilessly. I honestly think that these young men are, for the first time in their lives, being exposed to views on a range of subjects, intelligently and forcefully expressed by members of the opposite sex. If this is the case, Lara and I are slowly doing our bit in the struggle for the emancipation of our sex.

I have had little news from my beloved Sergey. He stays in Shcholkovo, keeping as far away from Viktor as possible. He is so busy with his fellow engineers preparing for the Tribunal, that he has not been to able to come to Moscow to see me. But he does have time to write love letters to me, which I keep in a bundle under my pillow and read and reread at bedtime.

As regards news of Anton Pavlovich, there has been a long silence from Crimea. He cannot therefore be ready for my visit and no one is able to explain his long delay in finishing *Three Sisters.* It sounds ominously as if his geese have all gone lame at the same time. But doubtless I will receive a letter from him one day and I will be summoned post haste to do his bidding.

I enjoy my work at MKhAT, but I feel that I am just impatiently biding my time till I find myself working with Anton again, a mindless way to fill in the days before the Tribunal hearing, which has now been set for Monday April 15th.

I see Dmitry from time to time. We have lunch together on those occasions when we are both free. He is as lovely as ever, dependable and considerate. We still love each other and as usual he assures me that there is nothing that he would not do for me. But I know that I have moved through the three stages of Dr Astrov's clinical analysis of relationships between man and woman; from the status of being very briefly an agreeable acquaintance, to that of mistress for a much longer time and finally to that of a friend.

Sunday 14th April 1900.

At last, on the very eve of the Tribunal I receive a letter from my playwright. As I suspected, he obviously expects me to be free to join him at a moment's notice.

Autka, 10 th April 1900

My dearest Anna,

First of all I must start with belated apologies for the long silence since my last letter. A reason, but in no way a half decent excuse for this silence, is that I have not been well and to add to that I am thoroughly depressed. I know you will understand and forgive me and am sure that with your lovely nature I will not find myself berated by you for the pathetic content expressed in this letter.

So I beg you, can you come down as soon as possible? I need your company and your help as never before. I am suffering down here, bouts of flu, a diet of fish and soup from Mariushka, too many visitors and constant pressure from Messrs Stanislavsky and Nemirovich Danchenko to finish my 'Sisters' Act Four. Even Olga wants me back in Moscow with the completed manuscript before the winter.

I tell them that all these midwives surrounding me aren't making the birth any easier, that they are raping creativity. Some wag in Moscow is going around calling my play 'Two Sisters' as I had inadvertently confided that my goose had gone lame again and that one sister was giving me trouble. And they forget that we have promised a typed copy of the text, which no doubt will take you a few days.

So Anna, please book yourself onto the next train to Odessa. I will pay all your expenses of course. Wrap up well, it's still surprisingly cold down here. Last winter was cruel and with the colder weather one of my tame cranes flew away and the other one, I'm sorry to say now blind in one eye, just hops dejectedly after Arseniy. My dear young lady, we all need cheering up, which your presence here, I have no doubt, will effect.

I wait with impatience to hear from my dearest typist, nurse, confidante and companion,

As ever, your suffering playwright,

Antosha

P.S. Don't forget our little trip to Nice. You will need a passport to leave our dear country!

P. P.S. We have now fixed the stoves, no more coughing and freezing!

For the moment I cannot concentrate on any suitable reply. I have promised him that I will fulfil his wishes the moment I am free, as I have told him so often. But please be patient, dear Anton, my thoughts can only be on the events of tomorrow. A reply will have to wait.

Seryozha writes to me informing me that the public has been permitted access to the Tribunal, which will be held in an ante chamber of the Moscow City Duma. There is a gallery from which members of the public are able to look down on the proceedings taking place in the improvised court room below. He doubts that there will be much interest amongst the Moscovite populace in the internal wrangling of a provincial municipality such as Shchyolkovo and he is certain that I will be able to find a seat there.

I have told Konstantin that I will have to be absent for the day and will make up the lost hours of my employment during the week. I do not reveal to anyone at MKhAT the reason for my absence. If we lose our case, as I feel certain we will, the repercussions will be too dire to envisage and I would not want the inevitable commiserations from these kind people.

The only person whom I have told is of course Dmitry. I don't feel that on my own I could brave the complications of getting myself to an unknown destination in a strange city, being stopped at the door by some official and explaining why I wish to attend the hearing. Dmitry has arranged to take another day off from his bank. Thank goodness for his kindness and understanding.

Monday April 15th 1900.

The day breaks warm and sunny, a typical spring day with Moscow looking at its best, though I have no inclination to admire the city or delight in the weather. Does a condemned man lift his eyes to the heavens as he is being led to the scaffold? Despite Seryozha's reassurances that all will go well, I am not convinced. Viktor has the support of his entire Department and from bitter personal experience I know how effective he is in winning his arguments.

Dmitry and I take a cab to the Duma buildings. On arrival he explains to the door keeper why we wish to attend the hearing and are directed up some narrow stairs to the gallery.

The small windows block out the sun light and the chamber below has the appearance of a stage set on which a play is to be enacted. I know the two protagonists and their respective roles, but I am not privy to their lines, and have no way of knowing how the play will finish. We are the patient audience waiting for the curtain to rise and the actors to make their appearance.

In the half light I discern a long table, presumably for the chairman and committee members of the Duma, and a couple of separate tables for the Clerks and other officials. The rest of the chamber is divided into two halves, which I imagine will be for the prosecution and defence counsels as well as for any witnesses who may be called.

We have arrived in good time and find seats in the front row of the balcony, from which we have an uninterrupted view. I say a quick prayer. Please, Lord, I whisper to myself, as I look down as the players in this drama begin to drift in to the court room, please take pity on Seryozha and guide him. Let him not be intimidated by my husband or the Committee. Dmitry smiles, seeing my lips moving and guesses the substance of my prayer. He takes my hand in reassurance.

As I reread my diary I realize how inadequate is my portrayal of the events that took place today. The emotions engendered by trying to follow the arguments and counter arguments put forward by Prosecution and Defence witnesses, combined with my limited knowledge of the technicalities of the case, mean that I have written only a very inadequate account of these events.

There is an unexplained delay before the start of the proceedings, which causes us a nervous wait until finally the Chairman calls for order. He then briefly outlines to the Board, consisting of some dozen elderly gentlemen, the case which has been brought for resolution by the Shchyolkovo Municipal Government.

Some of these members taking their seats with the utmost difficulty could, I think, be of such a venerable age that they might well have signed the original Moscow gas lighting contracts awarded, as we are told in the Chairman's preamble, to English and Dutch entrepreneurs in 1865. I cannot see Seryozha's youthfulness being anything but a disadvantage and Viktor's remarks about his being 'a boy sent to do a man's work' ring unwelcomely in my ears.

Counsel for the prosecution rises and in a few succinct words outlines its case, stating simply that the gaslights had failed a few months after their installation. Viktor is called to explain why this has happened. He looks so confident, smiling obsequiously at the Committee. Ominously, he seems to be personally acquainted with most of them. He lays the blame squarely on the Engineering Department of the City Council and produces two witnesses who testify to the effect that they smelled gas escaping in the vicinity of Central Square, the location of the gaslights.

His argument is that there can only be one explanation, namely the failure on the part of the engineers to supervise the correct implementation of this project.

He turns to the Committee and apologizes for wasting their time. As far as he is concerned, the case is closed. There is no need at this juncture to produce any more witnesses. He thanks the Board for its comprehension and he sits down with that hateful, complacent look which I know so well.

There is a brief break in proceedings whilst some of the members talk amongst themselves or retire from the chamber for one reason or another. I have a dread feeling that a verdict has already been reached and that this aged jury has come to a decision of guilt against the engineers without even listening to their defence. Dmitry tries to reassure me, but I can sense the nervousness in his voice and see that he too is worried.

After what seems an eternity the members reconvene and Sergey is called to the bar. By this time he has arranged on a separate table a number of bulky items concealed in oilcloth wrapping.

After a brief introduction from the Chairman Sergey begins his defence. "Gentlemen, if we may start at the beginning. For the installation of street gaslighting in our city the Engineering Department of the Shchyolkovo City Council, which I am here today to represent, decided as you would expect to use tried and tested practices as our guideline. Accordingly we took note of the terms of the January 29th 1865 street lighting contract which was awarded to English and Dutch concessionaires by your own Moscow City Duma.

By the way, I believe that I have the honour of addressing some of you gentlemen, who although probably not involved in that particular contract have certainly been instrumental in drawing up the January 29 th 1895 contract which prolonged the privileges accorded to foreign concessionaires for a further period of ten years.

Judging by what I have seen in my short visit to Moscow, I must congratulate you on your achievements in providing such excellent street lighting in your city. I only wish that we could have done the same in our home town. However, I will now endeavour to show you why this unfortunately has not been the case in Shchyolkovo."

He pauses for a moment. Despite the tenseness of the situation I find that I am smiling. I remember Seryozha telling me that he had learnt sycophancy at an early age in Government service. He sees that his last comments have been favourably received. He is in no hurry to proceed, taking a sip of water from the carafe on his table and calmly and deliberately searching out my husband on the prosecution bench. I recognize that indefinable aura of self-confidence that I saw in Seryozha as he told me in the restaurant how he planned to destroy my husband. Our revenge will come, he had reassured me. We have waited long enough.

"Our first step was to order cast iron pipes and joints from the Procurement Department of our City Council and stressed that these were to be obtained from the same reputable supplier in Germany that the City Duma had used in Moscow. As in your original Moscow contract and following standard engineering practice we also stipulated a system of socketed pipes and joints. The connections in the pipework were to be sealed with a mixture of hemp and paste and the joints finished with a covering of lead. Narrower gauge pipe used to connect the 3 ½ inch pipeline to the lights themselves were to have threaded connections, again sealed with a mixture of hemp and paste. I am certain you will agree that both these methods of installation are the preferred practice in our northern regions of Russia which have to bear such inclement fluctuations in temperature.

I do not need to remind you that historically cast iron production has had its inherent problems. To some extent, even in this day and age, it constitutes something of a hit and miss operation. It is still difficult to control impurities such as carbon and sulphur from entering the manufacturing process. Should this happen, then there is a serious risk that the cast iron produced will be too brittle and cracks will eventually appear. These cracks can be internal, external or in extreme cases circumferential. That is why it is imperative that only materials produced by a reputable supplier should be used.

From a close examination of the materials which were purchased by the Shchyolkovo City Council it has became apparent that they were bought from an unreliable source and were of inferior quality. It would also appear that the casting temperature of the cast iron had been too low. This resulted in cracks appearing in the piping which were not initially discernible by visual inspection.

We, the Engineering Department, carried out the installation in good faith last summer. Piping was laid successfully and joints were made by filling the gap between the socket of one pipe and the body of the next pipe with a mixture of hemp and paste and sealed with a covering of lead, as I mentioned earlier.

Shortly after the start of winter the alternate freezing and thawing of the soil evidently led to a flexing of the piping which caused it to fracture in a number of places. I should hasten to add that on close examination no fault whatsoever was found in the actual jointing process which we had carried out.

That, gentlemen, is the reason why our installation in Shchyolkovo failed. To repeat one more time if I may.

Despite our proviso that only a reputable company in Germany should be selected for the provision of our supplies, the paperwork that I have here shows that our advice was ignored and that the contract for some reason or other was awarded to an unknown and unverifiable Baltic supplier.

I will pause here to give you time to examine the purchase documents and invoices payable to a Latvian company and which were signed personally by Viktor Aleksandrovich von Melk, acting in the capacity of the Head of the Shchyolkovo City Council Procurement Department. They are on the table for your inspection.

Sergey pauses here to give time for the Board to take in the significance of his remarks. There is a hushed silence as all eyes turn towards Viktor.

At the mention of his name my husband bounds to his feet. Losing his self control he waves his fist at Sergey, shouting that these papers prove nothing and that they must have been stolen from his office. The Chairman asks him tersely to sit down and reminds him of the proprieties of the Tribunal. The members of the Board pass the relevant documents from hand to hand for inspection.

Sergey sits quietly, there is no need for him to add anything. The evidence is there for all to see. The Chairman eventually manages to call the court to order and the hubbub of excited voices subsides. He asks whether the Defence has finished its statement. Perhaps Mr Platonov would be kind enough now to explain how he has obtained these documents.

"Your Excellency, I must admit that I am guilty of a certain deceit in this respect," replies Sergey. "However, I deem that in this case my actions were necessary to bring matters fully into the open. I am quite happy that the ends I used fully justify the slight subterfuge which I employed to obtain these documents. I will explain my actions.

I asked a certain Sonya Smirnova, employed in the Procurement Office of the Shchyolkovo City Council and with whom I am slightly acquainted, to locate these documents in the relevant files in her office, a request with which she duly complied. I hold myself totally responsible for this action and no blame whatsoever should be attached to this young lady.

Initially I would have preferred to have had copies made of these documents and their authenticity signed by a Council lawyer, but I am afraid that after much consideration I felt that producing the authentic documentation itself, taken from the files in the Procurement Office, would be more effective. Mea culpa!

Putting this documentation to one side for a moment, I now present you with something of far greater significance, namely the exhibits that you see on the table beside you. I ask you now, if you would be so kind, to leave your seats and closely examine these exhibits."

There is silence, save for the shuffling of feet, as the members of the Board rise and approach the table. There is a palpable sense of unease emanating from the Prosecution bench, but for the moment there is nothing that they can do except to accept the Chairman's order. The exhibits are passed around the Board from hand to hand.

When this has been done, Sergey continues. "Gentlemen, you have seen with your own eyes and held in your own hands the evidence on which we base our case. You will see that on the exhibits marked 'Baltic pipes and joints' there is cracking and pitting around the seals and casing, whereas on the exhibits marked 'German pipes and joints' these are still in pristine condition."

Whilst this examination was taking place the Prosecution team, led by my husband, had entered into a heated debate amongst themselves. They had not expected to be asked to give a reply to this charge and are obviously uncertain about how to continue.

The Chairman is impatient for a response. "Viktor Aleksandrovich, if you please, be kind enough to inform the Board how you wish to proceed. Perhaps you would like to adjourn for a few minutes to discuss the implications of what has just been revealed in what I must say has been an exemplary manner by this young gentleman? Or would you prefer to accept that the Defence evidence is conclusive and that you would wish to withdraw your allegations?"

After a hasty consultation the Prosecution asks for an adjournment. A break for luncheon is announced. When proceedings resume in the afternoon Viktor immediately returns to the attack. Firstly he demands that Sergey be impeached for stealing official documents to which he has no entitlement. Secondly he demands that he produce evidence that the exhibits of alleged poor quality pipes and joints, which have been shown to the Board, are in fact those that were used in the gaslight installation in question. The Prosecution argument is that he could have found them anywhere and could have used them fraudently to make his case.

The Chairman appears annoyed with Viktor's demands. He dismisses the first demand by saying that although Seryozha had acted incorrectly in obtaining these documents by deceit, the severity of the allegations against the Engineering Department are such that his conduct can on this occasion be excused. He is to be reprimanded for his indiscretion, but no further action will be taken against him in this matter.

Some of the elderly gentlemen of the Board appear to be smiling benevolently. Perhaps they see themselves in the role of an indulgent father gently berating a young son for a minor misdeed, others seeing him as a young David battling gamely against the might of Goliath. Once again I feel that the sympathies of the Board are slightly shifting in our favour.

The second charge, however, could potentially be more serious. Sergey explains to the Board that he was convinced that, unless he obtained specimens of the faulty material from the stockyard, his case would fail. To this end he has subpoenaed the Supervisor of the Shcholkovo Storage Depot where the equipment had been stored, as well as the nightwatchman who had witnessed the events of that night's successful raid.

The supervisor is called to give evidence. He swears on oath that the equipment exhibited here in court is from the failed installation. The nightwatchman in his turn appears terrified that he will receive a reprimand for letting this young man into his compound in the middle of the night. Sergey again states that he assumes total responsibility for his actions.

All that the nightwatchman is asked to do is to confirm that he observed the defendant and an unknown female in the vicinity of the stockyard on that particular night. The poor man makes a pitiful spectacle, twisting his beard in agitation and bowing ever lower and lower. It is a painful scene to watch and I am relieved when he is ushered from the hall.

On disclosing that he had taken an unnamed female acquaintance to assist him in carrying away the necessary exhibits and that together they had posed as a courting couple to gain entry to the stock yard, Seryozha is rewarded again with an indulgent smile from the Board. I presume, rightly as I find out when I question him later, that this unnamed female acquaintance is none other than his Sonya, an eager accomplice in this intrigue from the beginning.

Viktor Aleksandrovich is apoplectic with rage. He repeats in vain that the invoices have been fabricated, that the engineers have deliberately produced as evidence one faulty length of pipe and a couple of joints that could have come from any source and that therefore our testimony is worthless. The Chairman reminds him impatiently that two witnesses have confirmed under oath that this is not the case.

The final scene is played out late in the afternoon when the Board rules in favour of the Engineering Department. One proviso is made, namely that before a definitive judgement can be made there will have to be metallurgical tests carried out in a laboratory. But we are led to believe that this will just be a formality.

As for where the blame is to be apportioned, the Chairman makes it abundantly clear in his summing up that Viktor Aleksandrovich and his Department are to be found to be ultimately responsible. My husband leaves the tribunal ashen faced. His professional future, he knows, lies in the balance.

That evening the three of us celebrate over dinner. Dmitry excuses himself shortly afterwards, saying diplomatically that he needs to be at home to say goodnight to the children. Though discreet as ever, he can sense that Seryozha and I need to be together to talk over the events of the day.

Our waiter clears the table of the remains of our dinner and brings another bottle of wine. We are both intoxicated, heady with the euphoria of victory. "A toast to the Devil's Candle," I propose, raising my glass.

Serozha joins me in our toast, but I can see that he has something more serious on his mind. " Anna, we need to look further ahead. Consider what will happen in the next few weeks. First of all I can assure you that there is now not the slightest possibility of Viktor being rewarded with a move to Irkutsk. No one there would want to employ him, given his proven record of incompetence.

Looking further ahead, your divorce taking place in Shchyolkovo can only be to our advantage. Your Viktor will not want any adverse publicity to further damage his career and I can see no reason why he should not accede to your terms for maintenance. Dream on, Anna, you may be moving to Carpenter's Lane a little sooner than you expected."

Tuesday May 30th 1900.

Much has happened during the past six weeks, so much in fact that only now am I in a position to record these events.

First of all, Sergey has been given promotion and transferred from Shchyolkovo to the Moscow City Duma. He must have made a great impression on those elderly members of the Board as he is now part of a team of experts working on a feasibility project to build a gas pipeline from Siberia across the Urals and into European Russia. I imagine that will keep him nicely occupied for a year or two!

His transfer was immediate, as he and my husband met by accident the day after the Tribunal in a corridor of the City Duma and a very unpleasant incident was narrowly averted.

This incident must have hastened the decision to separate these two warring factions by some several hundred versts. Sergey has also been granted a month's leave of absence as an award for his achievement at the Tribunal. Viktor, on the other hand, has been moved to another Department where, Seryozha tells me with evident satisfaction, his performance can be more closely monitored. From now on he will be kept well away from the work of rebuilding the town's gaslighting installation!

As for my divorce, proceedings progressed rapidly when it became clear to Viktor that his whole career was likely to be examined in detail, unless he agreed to an uncontested settlement out of court, exactly as we had urged him to accept from the start. For my part there was no reason for me to pursue my allegations of physical violence and mental cruelty against him, whilst likewise he did not continue his allegations of my adultery. Thank goodness we did not have to meet face to face in court, our respective lawyers simply requesting from us both written statements to the effect that we had come to a mutually satisfactory agreement regarding the final settlement. The divorce will be granted without too much of a delay and I will soon find myself at last a free woman.

However the price for my silence had been wildly optimistic. Although poor Viktor is now being paid a reduced salary, there is still family money available for him to make me a reasonable offer, 'to see me off', as he so politely described it.

Seryozha, working in Moscow on a higher salary but without a permanent abode, has dropped several hints that I should take a lease on one of the apartments on Carpenters' Lane. I can see his ulterior motive rather too clearly! Anton has at last received an advance on *Three Sisters* and has paid me handsomely for my work in Yalta. This I can add to my rather pitiful salary from MKhAT. We have done our calculations and think that together with Sergey's income and Viktor's contribution we can afford the necessary monthly payments.

However his latest suggestion that we should share the apartment, essentially living together as an unmarried couple in this day and age, filled me initially with shock. When we discussed it seriously Seryozha teased me.

"You tell me that you are an emancipated woman of the twentieth century, a feministka no less. What could be a better way of demonstrating this than your cohabiting with a young gentleman? And I may point out," he continued his argument, "From a purely economic point of view it is a fact universally acknowledged that two can live together as cheaply as one."

I mulled over his suggestion, not wishing for decency's sake too appear too eager to accept. I had to admit that my tiny annexe room did have its limitations and the thought of setting up home in a new apartment was appealing. In Moscow I am unknown, with no social status to protect. I tell myself that as we would be renting the only finished apartment in the converted mansion there would be no neighbours to observe us. I think of Seryozha going off to work unobserved in the early hours of the morning, with my following shortly afterwards. My fate, I laugh to myself, having another lover leaving clandestinely from my bedroom at break of day. The prospect appeals to me and it does not take me long to be persuaded.

I have received another letter from Anton. He tells me proudly that he has been making better progress with Act Four of his *Sisters,* though the whole play needs to be 'tinkered' with, as he expresses it. The warm summer weather has made him feel better and I am not needed till later in the year, when all Four Acts will be ready for my attention.

I reply to Anton Pavlovich, telling him that I will come down to Yalta as soon as he calls me. May I bring Sergey with me? He is in urgent need of rest and recuperation after all he has been through. Do emancipated women have a honeymoon before their marriage? I know Anton well enough to know that he would have no objection. A chuckle from him and a hint that this situation might well be the plot for another seaside short story!

July 10th 1900.

We have sent for Dunyasha as both Sergey and I are working long hours and need help with household matters. I am to meet her at the Yaroslavsky Station, a station which has a host of bitter sweet memories for me. So many times in the past had I said goodbye to Dmitry on this same platform. As I wait for Dunyasha's train I wander to the end of the platform and find the little shed, where they keep bags of salt to melt the snow on the frozen platforms.

I remember the little scene Dmitry and I used to play out. As the train came in, a final farewell kiss behind this shed, hidden away from the prying eyes of fellow passengers. We would cling to each other till the second bell rang. Then I would scamper aboard, breathless and laughing. People in my compartment would smile, hoping perhaps that they too might be infected with a little of my happiness.

But the Shchyolkovo train arrives and I spot Dunyasha as she descends onto the platform. A burly porter is helping her with her luggage. She needs this help as she is clutching Tuzik tightly in her arms. I kiss her and my precious dog. I am so happy. My two faithful friends have arrived to join me in Moscow. I arrange for her luggage to be sent on to our apartment. "What address?" asks the station master. "Carpenters' Lane, off the Arbat," I reply. How wonderful it sounds as I say the words aloud, watching him write them down.

We take a cab from outside the station. Dunyasha looks around her in amazement as she sees the broad streets, the churches and stately buildings. Her clothing, obviously the best that she can afford, marks her out as a lady's maid from a provincial backwater. I make a mental note to take her shopping to improve her wardrobe. Perhaps not

DeMoncy's in my reduced financial state, but we can still have fun exploring the local boutiques together.

***

Dunysha has already made herself invaluable, unpacking all my clothes and placing them in one of the few pieces of furniture we have in our new home, a magnificent wardrobe for which Seryozha's parents no longer have room in their new apartment..

I am eager for news of Viktor. I call to mind that new word in psychiatry which has come to us from Vienna. *Schadenfreude,* a feeling of enjoyment that comes from seeing, or in my case, hearing about the troubles of other people. It is an ignoble sentiment but it would be untrue if I did not admit to it.

Dunyasha tells me that until she left the house Viktor had been making life increasingly unbearable for her. She is relieved to escape his clutches. He knows that she was my confidante during the time of our quarrels, was witness to his attack on me and that she would defend her mistress if called as a witness in divorce proceedings. It is not in Viktor's nature to forget or forgive.

Out of spite, she tells me, he had not allowed Tuzik into the house, but made him live in a wooden shed in the garden even in the coldest weather. Every evening Dunyasha would smuggle him shivering into the kitchen the moment Viktor had gone to bed. She would rise early to prepare breakfast and put him back in his shed.

I bless her for her attention to my beloved Tuzik. I ask her about the cockroaches. Had there been any success as regards the little creatures?, I ask jokingly. She catches the allusion.

"No", she says wistfully. "That awful fisherman's son tried to force himself on to me once when his father was in the kitchen with Pelageya. He expected me to kiss him, but he was horrible. He smelt of fish and his hands were always cold and clammy. And the cockroaches were useless. They just gave me bad dreams about being chased by a bear."

Just so Freudian, I think. "Well," I commiserate."You won't find any coackroaches in our new apartment, so you'll have to make do with the king of diamonds instead." For compensation I tell Dunyasha that there will be lots of suitable young men here in Moscow, far more appealing than smelly fishmerchants' sons back in Shchyolkovo.

July 20th 1900.

Anton has written again telling me that he is ready for me, so can I come as soon as possible? Of course I can, and I mail my reply in the morning's post. I spend most of the morning packing my clothes for Yalta. It is a strange feeling to look out the same outfits that I have worn before. I would love to go shopping but I have no generous Dmitry to accompany me now. Anyway, I tell myself, there is nothing suitable for the Yalta climate here in the Moscow shops where the fashions are all for the coming autumn and winter.

As I pack my clothes I continue to daydream about Yalta. Doubtless I will be recognized by the Vernet set and I wonder what they will make of my being with Seryozha. Our appearance will be bound to set tongues wagging. "A new man each time she comes to visit us, but this one for a change does seem to be about her own age," I can imagine the drinkers' conversation as we pass by arm in arm.

It's a hot, torid mid summer's day and after a morning indoors I need to get out into the fresh air. I tell Dunyasha that I will do the shopping as I have one or two errands to make. I leave our apartment and turn right onto the Arbat. The last time I walked down the street had been in mid winter. Now it has a much more pleasant appeal. Shops are open, cafés have put their tables and chairs out on the pavement and people are sitting out of doors enjoying the sunshine. At first appearance it could almost be the Promenade in Yalta!

But then I realize that the Generals with their fat wives are missing and that there is a bustle about the place that had been missing on the Promenade. There, the leisured classes on holiday, had promenaded in order to be seen, whereas here on the Arbat business is the order of the day. Carriages go by, shouts and laughter ring out. A group of young men carrying books and files dashes past me, intent on catching one of these new horse drawn trams that have just appeared on the major roads of the city.

But then something catches my eye which takes me immediately back to the Promenade. In the distance I notice a bar where a number of elderly men are drinking at tables on the pavement. Just like Vernet's I think, especially when they raise their hats to me as I pass by.

Tuzik must have remembered the attraction of table legs from his experience in Yalta and is eager to acquaint himself with the smells of his new world. "Come away,Tuzik," I call him gently to heel, but not before one of the gentlemen addresses me.

"Good afternoon, young lady, can we offer you a seat, order you a coffee and a bowl of water for your dog? It's unconscionably hot for the time of year, is it not."

I graciously decline his offer. "Thank you gentlemen, another time perhaps. But I would be very grateful if I might solicit your help in finding a bookshop. I've been told that there is one here on the Arbat."

"Quite right, my dear. Just carry on down the road, my lady, but be wary of old Semyon Semyonovich in there, he just cannot resist pretty girls," one of the drinkers replies. I can hear them chuckling as they bid me goodbye.

I complete my shopping for our supper and then enter the bookshop. There is no problem with the proprietor, from whom I buy the Autumn edition *of Russian Thought* and order some of the plays on my University booklist. After a successful first semester Lara and I have been able to enroll for another literature course taken by the same Professor Nabutkin and covering the same period, namely the second half of the 19 th century. After the furore that Lara and I caused in class over our impassionated attack on male prejudice in *A Doll's House* Professor Nabutkin has provocatively suggested that we start the new term with *Hedda Gabler*. Lara and I are already sharpening our knives!

I then take Tuzik for a walk around a park which I have discovered nearby. I let him off the lead so that he can chase around and acquaint himself with new Muscovite smells. Whilst he scuffles around in the leaves that are already falling from the silver birches, I find a bench to sit on and open my diary. There is just one more entry that needs to be written. After that I think my story will be complete.

I can remember telling Dmitry just after we met for the first time, that I had started to keep a diary to reveal something of my life in Yalta. He had asked me if it was not too arduous a task to set down the events of each day. No, I had replied, it was amusing to try to reveal my secretmost thoughts on paper. As Montaigne wrote in his Essays, I told him, we must do so in order to explore our own nature. And over the period that I have kept a diary and used it as a basis for these memoirs I realize how much I have indeed explored my nature. It is in truth revealing and amusing to record the changing facets of my character.

Naïve, self indulgent, sensuous, temptress, lover and mistress, amanuensis, teasing, vengeful, feminist, the list goes on in no apparent order.

I have frequently not been a good person, I admit, but I hope that the circumstances that I have described in my writing will go a little way to mitigate the harshest of criticism. I open my diary and put pen to paper, but almost immediately halt my writing. I have been much given these last days to introspection and this is an ideal moment to collect my thoughts. I start to take stock of my life.

Here I am at last living with a man whom I am shortly going to marry. I have employment with MKhAT and am looking forward to the long delayed journey to Yalta with Seryozha for our preemptive honeymoon. And I cannot wait to work with Anton Pavlovich again and to meet my new friends in Yalta. And who knows, maybe at some future time I will be applying for a passport and a chance to meet Anton again, this time on the exotic Côte d'Azur.

My thoughts return to the present. We have just moved into our own apartment just off the prestigious Arbat, which we can now afford to turn into our first home. Seryozha has gained promotion and consequently been awarded a rise in salary. I know that Lara and I are kindred souls. We meet once a week to discuss our university assignments and assure ourselves that we will fight our corner for women's rights. First of all Moscow University, then the rest of Russia! And thanks to Seryozha and the 'Devil's Candle' revenge has been a sweet dish eaten cold.

Which brings me to Viktor. I think of him from time to time. I have no sympathy for him even though I am living in an apartment which he partly finances. Men like that have no place in my vision of a new Russian society. When I look closely in the mirror I can still see the vague outline on my cheek of the parting present he gave me. I had dared to oppose his views of a woman's position in his life and I had won. I cannot say that I am sorry for his predicament.

I think back to the scene in Anton Pavlovich's study when he dictated those last words of my story and I copied them down. "..*and it seemed, given a little more time, a solution would be found and then a new and beautiful life would begin.*"

How prophetic had been those words and how little at the time had I believed them. I think of Dmitry and our wonderful but ultimately doomed adulterous relationship. How self sacrificing he had been to end it. And then of Seryozha coming home this evening to our new home. I realize then how lucky I am. This new and beautiful life is no longer a dream, it is a reality.

An old man, whom I had noticed shuffling slowly through the park with the aid of a stick, approaches me. I look up as his shadow momentarily blocks the sunlight from my face.

"Do please excuse me, young lady, I believe your little dog is a Pomeranian. What a fine fellow. May I be allowed to give him a little titbit?"

"Of course you may, he doesn't bite." I answer without thinking. And then the full impact of those fateful words, which must have seemed so innocent to this stranger, but meant so much to me, comes home to me with a stab to my heart and I stifle a sob.

" I am so sorry, my dear, I should never have bothered you. Please accept my apologies, I should not have approached you. How inconsiderate of me." The old man is embarrassed, turns and doffing his hat painfully heads towards the park gate. I want to call out to him that it is not his fault, that it is just the effect that a poignant memory has had on a silly young woman. But it is too late, he is out of earshot and does not look back.

I collect myself and dry my eyes. The Dmitry and I who met in Yalta belong to another age. It is time to return to the present. Seryozha will be home shortly and I want to be there to meet him. I too head for the park gate and turn onto the Arbat.

During my first stay in Yalta I would have gone out of my way to avoid passing Vernet's bar. Now it does not even occur to me that I might need to make a detour to avoid the bar where today some similar gentlemen had engaged me in pleasantries. I am recognized, of course. The spokesman of this little group, the one who had warned me about the shopkeeper, raises his hat. "How was old Semyon Semyonovich, has he proposed to you?" The banter is innocent and well intentioned.

"No, I'm disappointed to say that he hasn't," I joke. "But excuse me, I must get home. I have my husband's supper here. Our maid will be waiting for me, she'll think that I've got lost."

"Oh, it is always the way, is it not? The really pretty ones get snapped up before they are old enough to appreciate that the best wines are the matured ones. Never mind, my lady, we were only joking. But if you are living in this locality we are bound to see you again.You will observe, no doubt, that we tend to gather here every afternoon. Before you go, perhaps you would be kind enough to tell us your name."

"You do not need to know my name, gentlemen," I pause for a moment. "Just call me 'The Lady with a Little Dog.' And with a twirl of my parasol I turn on my heel and Tuzik and I head towards our new home. Chekhov's opening paragraph,which of course I know by heart, comes to mind. Misquoting slightly I recite to myself, *"People said that there was a new arrival on the Arbat: a lady with a little dog..."*

EPILOGUE

Moscow. March 22nd 1954.

As I read the last page, still fully dressed and wrapped in my blanket for warmth, I realized that I must have been reading for most of the night. The rattle of the first trams of the day passing on the street below coincided with a knocking on my front door which opens directly onto the communal stairwell. It was still dark, several hours still needed before that ghastly late winter lightening of the frozen Moscow night would filter into the apartment. This time I recognized the knock. I knew who it would be and my heart sank.

Cursing this further intrusion into my privacy I opened my door to find Vasilissa Mironovna, our kommunalka concierge, standing there, armed with bucket and mop. As soon as she saw me she started her usual diatribe.

"I need to remind you, Anna Pavlovna, that on the twentieth of March you failed to fulfill your citizen's duty to clean the staircase and empty the rubbish bins in our kommunalka, as clearly designated on your duty roster. Any further failure to do so will automatically be reported to the Comrades Court."

Here she paused for breath before continuing. "I need to inform you as well of the fact that on the twentieth of March you were heard entertaining a male visitor in your apartment until 11.30 p.m.

According to Comrade Witness, room 102 on the floor below you, this visitor of yours was undoubtedly drunk, as hehe was careless enough to trip over an empty vodka bottle. The comrade in question did not appreciate being woken up. As you are no doubt aware she is employed in a manual capacity at her place of work and such work requires her to retire to bed at an early hour. Unlike some of us who are fortunate to have office jobs, of course," she added maliciously.

"However, she has decided on this occasion not to bring charges against you, but wishes to inform you that as a single woman your behaviour can only be regarded as a promiscuous sexual relationship and cannot be further tolerated."

I bit my tongue. It would have been so easy to remind her that empty vodka bottles had no place on the communal stairwell and that she had failed in her duty to have the light bulbs replaced when needed, thus making it difficult to avoid such obstacles in the dark. But it was wiser, I had learnt from experience, not to antagonize this fearsome harridan.

She put down the kommunalka bucket and mop on my doorstep. Her tone became more inquisitive and confidential. "Tell me, Anna Pavlovna, is it true that you received a letter from the Soviet Writer's Union earlier this week?"

"No," I lied to her face, cutting her short. "It was a mistake. The letter was addressed to my grandmother who as you no doubt will be fully aware died recently. I sent it straight back to the Chairman of the Writers' Union. Excuse me, Vasilissa Mironova, I must get dressed, I'm due at work in an hour, even if my employment is only in an office."

Clearly disappointed by her failure as unofficial spymaster to obtain any further information to report back to the Kommunalka Residents Association and thence to the Police Department of the Moscow City Council she disappeared down the stairs, which I had been reminded so forcibly I would be cleaning that evening.

Back at my place of work I had plenty of time to reflect on what I had read during those long hours of darkness.

The old Soviet adage of the State pretending to pay us and we, the long suffering workers pretending to work, held good in the Moscow City Archives Department. I made myself a cup of insipid Cuban coffee and gave myself up to the luxury of my private thoughts, an activity which as yet one did not need to account for to the State.

First of all, I decided that I would not hand over these memoirs to the Moscow Branch of the Soviet Writers' Union. Although Comrade Stalin had referred to writers as 'the engineers of the human soul' at the First Congress of the Union of Soviet Writers in 1934 I did not think that twenty years later my grandmother's tale of the tyranny of marriage, love both licit and illicit and concern with the self at the expense of the State would rank as a good example of Socialist Realism.

On the other hand her successful attempt to breach the all male enclave of Moscow University in 1900 and her untiring efforts thereafter to gain recognition for women in different academic fields, her outstanding biography of Anton Pavlovich and her critical essays on Pushkin, Turgenev and of course Chekhov himself had led quite rightly to her admission to the Soviet Writers' Union with its perks and privileges. Perhaps in a more enlightened age in years to come the 'subjectivism' of her story would not bar publication.

Draining my cup of coffee and yet unwilling to return to the duties of Assistant City Archivist, I turned my thoughts to the Committee's offer to lease me grandmother's dacha in Peredelkino. It came to me that this would be a way to escape my existence in the dreaded kommunalka, at least for the summer months. I could live simply in the countryside and commute to work on the elektrichka, the journey, as I had been informed, taking no more than some twenty minutes. I could easily sublet my room for those months, bid a so painful goodbye to Vasilissa Mironovna and return to the city when the first snows came.

But to be a resident of Peredelkino, living amongst those famous writers, extolling the virtues of optimism in the eventual goal of Communism through their differing genres of Socialist Realism, I realized wryly that I would have to become a better Soviet citizen. My current behaviour deserved a slap on the wrist. I must not forget my duty roster with bucket and mop, I must attend more regularly the evenings at the Library devoted to 'agitprop' and above all persuade my purely platonic male friend to leave my room before eleven o'clock and to avoid the empty vodka bottles on his way down the stairs! So be it, if that was the price to be paid for residence in Peredelkino.

My library had been granted the unwanted and unsought honour of finding a replacement for my grandmother, who before her illness had been asked to make a speech at the fiftieth anniversary of Chekhov's death on 15th July 1904. Little progress had been made in finding such a replacement and I had been nursing the farfetched idea, that perhaps in Yalta itself there might still be someone, perhaps even a former 'Antonovka', who had known Anton Pavlovich at a personal level and would be able to make a worthwhile contribution to this anniversary.

To this end I had hoped that my name might be put forward as someone suitable to undertake such an investigation. In Soviet society wise individuals do not propose themselves for any course of action, it being more expedient to wait for an invitation, which in this case did not come.

However, what I could do by myself was to visit Peredelkino and make arrangements to move into grandmother's dacha in the summer. I took the elektrichka and walked the short distance from the station to the Writers' Colony. I knew that I would have to go through the correct channels, introduce myself to the necessary authorities and sign endless documents before being given any keys. But at least it was pleasant to be out in the countryside after the gloom of Moscow.

I had chosen a Sunday to visit and by chance I came across the Chairman of the Peredelkino Committee, one Vladimir Kuznetsov, who was doing nothing more official than chopping firewood in the garden of his very palatial dacha. Leaning across the fence I introduced myself as the granddaughter of Anna Ivanovna Platonova, and of course that was all that was needed as an introduction.

He put down his axe, wiped his brow and invited me into the house. It was warm and cosy with the stove in the kitchen drawing well and we sat informally at the table.

"Well, I must say that this a very pleasant surprise for me, my dear young lady. A chance to meet the granddaughter of one of the icons of our Soviet literary scene here in my own house."

He looked at his gnarled hands which he was warming against the stove. " And a perfect excuse to give up log cutting for the day," he added.

"But before I go any further I must express my commiserations on the death of your grandmother. She was a wonderful woman and gifted biographer, who despite her obvious liberal views never fell foul of the authorities, even though she repeatedly expressed views that were not strictly in line with the tenets of Socialist Realism. But Anna Ivanovna, please treat these remarks of mine with the greatest confidentiality and do not repeat them to anyone, inside or outside our literary milieu. It is so easy to have them misinterpreted."

Our conversation then turned to the present state of Soviet literature. Vladimir Antonovich, as he asked me to address him rather than as Comrade Chairman, said that he was cautiously optimistic. He cited the publishing of a number of poems by Boris Pasternak, the new novel 'The Thaw' by Ilya Ehrenburg and the rehabilitation of writers like Marina Tsvetaeva and Isaac Babel, both of whom had previously been denounced as 'unpersons'. And Ehrenburg, he continued, had publicly praised Western writers, particularly Hemingway and Steinbeck, calling attention to the fact that Chekhov, Tolstoy and Gorky had written without having their subject matter prescribed for them.

Books cannot be written to order or planned, Ehrenburg had argued, taking up a position on the side of creative freedom. All this, in the current year of 1954, seemed to offer an element of hope for those writers who did not wish to describe the achievements of cheerful Soviet heroes and heroines engaged in excessive agricultural or industrial production.

Up to now there had been too much of this kind of literature. What the reading public really wanted was a more mature, a more adult exposé of the inner lives, the private emotions and passions of the fictional characters in the books they were reading. All this pointed towards the possibility of a 'thaw', a period of relative liberalism at last taking place in our literature. Vladimir Antonovich paused for a moment. He again felt it necessary to remind me to treat his remarks with the greatest confidentiality.

Since Anton Chekhov had been mentioned in our conversation I took out of my bag my grandmother's manuscript, which I had been rereading on the train journey to Peredelkino, and passed it to him. Vladimir Antonovich was intrigued as he quickly skimmed though the first chapter.

"What I think you'll find fascinating," I dared to interrupt his reading, " is the fact that Chekhov wrote his *Lady with a Little Dog* based entirely on the account given to him by my grandmother. In the story he deliberately goes no further than to leave his heroine and Dmitry, her lover, meeting occasionally in a Moscow hotel and bewailing their fate. A very Chekhovian ending, of course. But grandmother's memoirs carry on further from that point in their relationship, as you will see. And for me that makes the following years of her life, which she describes, so fascinating.

Unfortunately these memoirs, as you would expect, are a very personal and intimate account of her life. Our literary masters will no doubt label this preoccupation with self as pure 'subjectivism' and the rather too explicit account of sexual relationships in the story as unacceptable 'naturalism.'

" Let me worry about that, my dear," Vladimir Antonovich breaks in. "I told you that I had detected a new, more liberal attitude to literature now amongst our literary masters, as you call them. What you have given me is fascinating. Well, well, to think that your grandmother was the catalyst for Chekhov's *Lady with a Little Dog.* That is something that is bound to excite the entire literary world both here in Russia and in fact wherever our dear Anton Pavlovich is read and cherished.

I have an idea about how we can present these memoirs at the Fiftieth Anniversary Celebrations. I will need a week to read them thoroughly and if I think them suitable I will present my ideas to our Committee. So long as we can win over some of the more stalwart and old fashioned of our members to a realization that our contemporary literature can embrace more than just the strictures of Socialist Realism, then I think we may have a chance of success.

It is not often that I have the opportunity to converse with such a beautiful young lady, and you have led me quite astray," he chuckled, rising from his chair to end our discussions. "I have been rather too indiscreet in our conversation, my dear, so I will say no more, except to promise that you will be hearing from me within the week."

I returned to Moscow on the elektrichka, confident that Chairman Kuznetsov would be as good as his word. I had a woman's intuition that he had enjoyed our meeting. My ability to endear myself to older men, no doubt a talent bestowed to me by my grandmother, had fortunately not disappeared.

***

A week later a letter arrived in which I learnt to my astonishment that I had been invited to read extracts of my grandmother's memoirs at the anniversary celebration, the Committee considering me as the suitable and logical replacement for my grandmother.

The ceremony took place on the afternoon of 15 th July in front of Chekhov's flower-strewn grave in the Novodevichy cemetery. I had not visited the monastery for many years, and I had even to consult a metro map to check that Sportivnaya station was the nearest one for the cemetery.

As I approached the venue I caught sight of the stark white walls and golden domes of the Cathedral of Our Lady of Smolensk. It was a beautiful sight. Its magnificent bell tower rose into the sky complementing the deep red of the Gate Church of the Intercession. As I made my way towards the fortress-like walls of the Monastery a small lake came into sight.

On a summer's afternoon there was just a handful of people sitting on the grass at the edge of the water, but I remember hearing that in winter it was a popular place to skate. I recalled that in grandmother's memoirs Dmitry had taken her skating. He had mentioned the lake being near the monastery and I could visualize them now in this idyllic setting. And it was no wonder that in *Anna Karenina* Tolstoy had Levin meeting his future wife Kitty skating on this same lake. But there was no time to indulge in literary recollections and I could afford to tarry no longer. Another more pressing engagement awaited me.

Despite the very limited publicity that had preceded the event, I was amazed at how many people had come to pay their respects to our most famous dramatist. At that stage I did not understand the reason why so many had turned out, but it was to become apparent as the afternoon progressed.

It was a typical midsummer day, hot and humid, and those of the audience who had not had the foresight to bring parasols and find a place around the grave itself had found shade under the trees a short distance away.

The ceremony began with a number of eminent Soviet scholars rising one by one to give the standard eulogies which the occasion demanded. They were received with a certain lack of interest and enthusiasm as none of them contained any new interpretation of Chekhov's work, just the rather tired pronouncements on his legacy, delivered without a spark of originality by a series of elderly Soviet academicians.

Finally it was my turn to address an audience which looked as if it had decided that it had heard enough of speech making and was preparing to leave. Perhaps the fact that I was a woman and relatively young, in marked contrast to all the previous speakers, aroused their curiosity and induced them to stay at least for a minute or two to see if I had anything of interest to say.

Comrade Chairman of the Moscow Branch of the Soviet Writers' Union, somewhat wearily I thought, mounted the podium for what he evidently hoped would be the last time. Up to now the afternoon had not been a great success. After wiping his brow he began his introduction.

"Dear Comrades, it is my pleasure to introduce Comrade Archivist Anna Pavlovna Platonova, who has graciously agreed to speak at short notice on behalf of her recently deceased grandmother Anna Ivanovna Platonova. Comrade Platonova as you all will be aware recently passed away after a long and fruitful literary career and will be sadly missed."

There was a subdued round of applause as I took the microphone. Many of the audience must have been wondering what on earth I was doing on the podium, given my lack of literary credentials.

I began nervously. "Dear Comrades, all of us have come here today to pay homage to the memory of Anton Pavlovich Chekhov. This afternoon we have been reminded by some of our leading academicians of the continued importance of his work and its place in our Soviet society. However, what I would like to do is to turn the clock back some fifty years and tell you about the events which led my grandmother to meet and work with Anton Pavlovich when she was recuperating in Yalta after an illness. The year is 1898.

I felt that as I began to speak there was now a more attentive and sympathetic audience. I told them how, after my grandmother's death, I had found some memoirs of hers, which had hitherto lain undiscovered. I held up the two battered volumes and explained that one contained her memoirs and the second her first transcription of a certain short story for which she had been the catalyst.

I asked the audience to understand that these memoirs were not intended to be anything other than jottings from a diary, and should not be taken as a literary work of quality. As for the transcribed short story, I assured them that they would be able to identify the story as soon as I began to read.

There came a murmur from the audience, a murmur swelling as one by one the opening lines were recognized: *"People said that there was a new arrival on the Promenade, a lady with a little dog. Dmitry Dmitrych Gurov, who had already spent…"*

As I continued I began to realize with a certain thrill that I was holding their attention, something that did not happen often in the life of a humble library archivist. I stopped reading from the text and turned instead to her memoirs describing the affair that grandmother had entered into with this Dmitry Dmitrych and how their romance had been the inspiration for Chekhov's story.

I read a little from the pages that her lover had written to grandmother, describing how he had first met this beautiful young lady on the Promenade. Then the scene when young Sergey had the temerity to approach the wife of his Ministry Head of Department and ask her for a dance. And finally how my grandmother had become involved in working with Anton Pavlovich. This I stressed was a platonic relationship and she certainly was not to be included in his list of Antonovkas, a humorous aside which drew the first laugh of the afternoon.

Concluding my talk, which I felt had gone on far too long, I hinted that what I had revealed to the audience in my resumé concealed a hidden twist or two in my grandmother's life which I said I would not reveal. Nor would I elaborate on the title of her memoirs '*The Devil's Candle.*' Everything would become clear, I told my audience, should these memoirs ever be published, which I fervently hoped would eventually be the case. I could not resist looking over my shoulder at the Committee as I did so.

Vladimir Antonovich, representing the Peredelkino Branch of the Writers' Union, came onto the stage to present me with a bouquet of flowers and to thank me for my talk, which he assured me had been of the greatest interest to everyone present.

Thereupon he declared the afternoon's events to be concluded. But his final words were drowned out by voices raised in protest. My account of a young woman travelling alone to Yalta at the end of the nineteenth century had not satisfied the majority of the audience. They now wanted to have the opportunity to read her complete memoirs, to find out what had really happened to her after Chekhov's ambiguous ending to his story.

What they were asking for in essence was a chance to read a literature which dealt with the preoccupation of self, a study of an individual with a rich interior life, such as had been portrayed in my grandmother's memoirs and was so far removed from the current banal accounts of Soviet heroes and heroines.

A group of the most vociferous spectators had forced its way to the front of the crowd to harangue the Writers' Union delegates. Some of them were holding up school exercise books which they waved angrily at those on the podium. A rather formidable, middle aged woman, who seemed to have appointed herself as spokeswoman for the group, introduced herself.

"Comrade academicians, I am a teacher of literature at Spets Skola No 21 on Kropotkinskaya Street. What we have heard from the last speaker is something totally removed from the humdrum Soviet fiction that we are forced to read nowadays and even worse to teach our children."

There was a barely suppressed murmur from the audience, but the speaker continued undeterred. "These memoirs are taken from real life, characters who, even in the briefest of insights that we have been given this afternoon, are far more interesting than anything we are forced to read nowadays. I am sure that I speak for all of the audience here, when I say that we as women want to know what happens to our heroine Anna Ivanovna. And the older men here can identify, perhaps too easily I might add, with this Dmitry Dmitrych Don Juan of a hero, whilst the younger men can see themselves as Sergey Platonov, whose audacity in introducing himself at the ball must give him a major part later in the story.

After all, was it not our own Anton Pavlovich who wrote that if a gun is referred to in Act One it must be fired before the end of the play? But I digress. I believe that I have adequately reflected the views of my colleagues, which to summarize are a demand for greater freedom in literature to be made available to our reading public."

Undeterred by gestures from the Chairman to halt her tirade she paused to take breath.

"However, it is not often that we have the attention of so many of the Moscow Writers' Union Committee gathered in one place and I would be grateful if I could add one further comment.

Comrades, I know that it is some years since you were pupils in school, but I am sure you will recognize these same exercise books with lined, blank pages, in which you wrote your first tentative works of literature. And are you aware why I and my colleagues had to bring these exercise books here today? We arrived at nine this morning, to sit here and read some of the works of Chekhov which for one reason or another have not been reprinted in our adult life.

Each one of us has copied out in long hand our favourite stories. Otherwise we would be in danger of losing a vital part of our literary heritage. What a way to have to preserve this priceless heritage, writing out word by word our country's forsaken masterpieces. This situation is an absolute disgrace, and all of you sitting up there so importantly on your podium should be ashamed of being part of this literary cabal."

Undeterred she carried on. "We demand a more liberal interpretation of what can and cannot be published. We have had enough of arbitrary censorship. It is ridiculous that the last speaker, the granddaughter of Anna Ivanovna

Platonova, is holding there in her hands the transcript of a story, written over fifty years ago and which has not been reprinted for decades.

Who made the decision that, since the subject matter of this story deals with adult themes, it is deemed too 'naturalistic' for our Soviet readers? We demand the reprinting of all Chekhov's work without exception, and immediately the printing of these memoirs."

Comrade Chairman, who at this stage was still wiping his brow, struggled unwillingly to his feet. His perfunctory reply that he would report the sentiments of the audience to higher authority did little to satisfy the most vociferous, who continued to vent their anger. At a signal from the Chairman the meeting was quickly brought under control by a number of plain clothes police, whose unwelcome presence in the crowd I had earlier observed.

We were then informed that there would be a reception afterwards for members of the Writer's Union and for those who had spoken at the ceremony. To my surprise I found that I had been included amongst the guests. Vladimir Antonovich led me through the gatehouse of the Church of the Transfiguration into the monastery itself. I felt painfully ill at ease in the company of so many talented writers and critics, none of whom showed the slightest intention of engaging me in conversation. I had invaded their all male preserve and I sensed in their attitude towards me their feeling of jealousy, expressed quite openly, that an unqualified woman had managed to engage with an audience in a way that they had been unable to do.

Refreshments were served, an abundance of vodka of course to satisfy the wishes of the predominantly male presence. With glass in hand and with nothing better to do, I fell to examining the room where the reception was taking place. From my knowledge of Russian history I remembered how Tsarina Irina Godunova, the wife of Tsar

Feodor the First and sister of Boris Godunov, had been forced to take the veil in this monastery. She had lived the rest of her life in these very rooms. I shuddered as I looked at the small, iron barred windows and low vaulted ceiling that still now gave the place the feel of a prison cell.

I felt very vulnerable, alone in this all male enclave. Even my kind Vladimir Antonovich had temporarily deserted me. I could see him in the corner of the room deep in conversation with a number of Committee members. They seemed to have come to some sort of agreement as Vladimir Antonovich hurried back to me.

It is strange how sometimes a few minutes can decide the course of one's future life. And so it was for me on this occasion in the Irina Godunova chambers in the Novdevichy Monastery on the sunny evening of 15 th July 1954. Vladimir Antonovich raised his glass.

" I would like to propose a toast to celebrate the success of your appearance on stage, Anna Pavlovna Platonova. It is no exaggeration to say that your speech and the reaction to it has contributed a great deal towards making our Committee aware of what our public really wants in literature.

I have been asked by members of the Moscow Branch of the Soviet Writers' Union to inform you of a decision that we have just taken, which may be of interest to you. You may not be aware that Chekhov's precious house in Yalta has gradually fallen into disrepair over the years of economic hardship which our country has been experiencing under Comrade Stalin. Initial plans to turn it into a museum have repeatedly been put on hold. However, to coincide with this Fiftieth Anniversary celebration, we have been assured that there are now funds available to initiate a number of repairs and to turn the study and living room into a modest museum.

We have for some time been looking for a suitable candidate to take on the position of Museum Curator, so far without success. However with your experience in the Archives Department of Moscow City Library and with your grandmother's connections in Yalta we feel that you would be the obvious choice for this position, and we would therefore like to offer it to you. Being a State employee, it would be simple for you to transfer to Yalta and keep your salary at the same level as it is now. And as a sweetener, we would be able to provide you with a room in the house, where you could lodge free of charge.

Obviously we do not know whether you would want to leave Moscow and move such a distance away, or maybe you have family ties here that would make it difficult for you to do so. But we would be grateful if you could let us know as soon as possible whether you would wish to accept our offer."

I looked at Vladimir Antonovich and could not hold back my tears. I do not cry easily and if I do, then it has to be in private. But this afternoon was an exception and the sudden realisation that my life could be about to be turned upside down was enough to bring the tears.

Disgusted looks were directed at us by the assembled literati but it was in vain that I dabbed at my eyes. There was no way that I could restrain myself. To give up my tedious job in the Archives and my pathetic room in that horrible kommunalka, to move to Yalta and oversee the project to restore the White Dacha, to be back two generations later in the very place where my grandmother had experienced so much in her young life, could not but bring tears to my eyes.

Obviously embarrassed by this scene being played out in public,Vladimir Antonovich took me to one side, asking me whether my emotional response denoted a yes or a no?"

"Yes, yes," I gasped. " Of course, all I need is for you to give me two weeks, till the end of July, to clear my desk at the Library, give up the tenancy of my room, pack my things and I'll be ready to move to Yalta as soon as you wish me to. Then I hesitated for a moment. One of those wild thoughts of mine had come fluttering into my head.

"No, if you could let me start at the end of August, that would be better. I can't explain to you why, but I would need that extra time to do something that I know you would laugh at if I were to tell you."

What I hoped was going to delay my departure by a month was the thought that I might be able to buy a puppy in Peredelkino. On my first visit I had passed the time of day with an old man, obviously the caretaker of a large dacha, where in a lean-to kennel attached to the side wall of his modest cottage I had seen a bitch suckling a litter of puppies. The old man had said that they would be ready to leave their mother in a couple of weeks, but at that time this remark had meant nothing to me. Now I would return to Peredelkino and take possession of one of them.

Just as grandmother had told me so often as a child, my thoughts had raced ahead of me. In my imagination I had become the proud owner of a little dog and taken up my duties as curator of the Chekhov House Museum in Yalta. I could see myself strolling along the Promenade. The sun would be shining, the band playing and as I passed Vernet's Bar, the drinkers not knowing my identity would refer to me simply as " the lady with a little dog!"

THE END